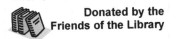

HEART
OF THE
SUN
WARRIOR

ALSO BY SUE LYNN TAN

DAUGHTER OF THE
MOON GODDESS

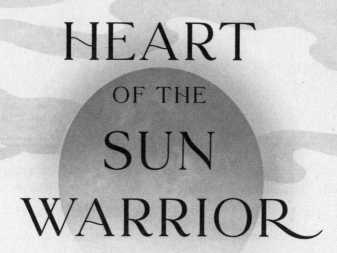

HEART
OF THE
SUN
WARRIOR

BOOK TWO OF THE
CELESTIAL KINGDOM DUOLOGY

SUE LYNN TAN

HARPER Voyager

An Imprint of HarperCollins Publishers

HEART OF THE SUN WARRIOR. Copyright © 2022 by Sue Lynn Tan. All rights reserved. Printed in the United States of America. No part of this book may be used or reproduced in any manner whatsoever without written permission except in the case of brief quotations embodied in critical articles and reviews. For information, address HarperCollins Publishers, 195 Broadway, New York, NY 10007.

HarperCollins books may be purchased for educational, business, or sales promotional use. For information, please email the Special Markets Department at SPsales@harpercollins.com.

Harper Voyager and design are trademarks of HarperCollins Publishers LLC.

FIRST EDITION

Designed by Alison Bloomer
Map illustration by Virginia Norey
Frontispiece © Xinling yi fang/Shutterstock
Cherry blossom illustration © baoyan/Shutterstock
Decorative frame illustration © Riverway/Shutterstock
Cloud illustration © Peratek/Shutterstock

Library of Congress Cataloging-in-Publication Data has been applied for.

ISBN 978-0-06-303136-4
ISBN 978-0-06-327524-9 (international edition)

22 23 24 25 26 LSC 10 9 8 7 6 5 4 3 2 1

To those who hold unspoken dreams in their hearts

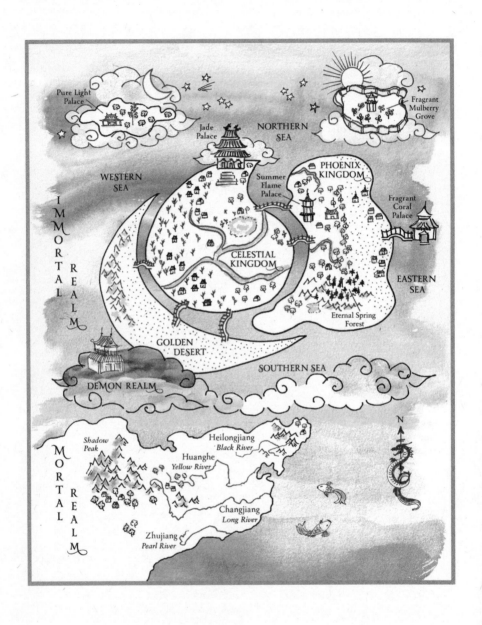

HEART
OF THE
SUN
WARRIOR

PART
I

1

NIGHT CLOAKED THE SKY IN darkness, draping shadows across the earth. While this was the time of rest for the mortals, on the moon, our toils were just beginning. Winter white flames curled from the splint of wood in my hand. Crouching down, I brushed away a stray leaf from the lantern, wrought of translucent stone and twisted strands of silver. As I lowered the splint to the wick, it caught fire with a hiss. I rose, shaking the soil from my robe. Rows of unlit orbs stretched before me as pale as the osmanthus which flowered above—moon lanterns, one thousand in all, that would cast their glow upon the realm below. Through wind and rain, their light would not falter, until they were extinguished at the first breath of dawn.

Each time I lit the lanterns, my mother urged me to be diligent, to perform the task by hand. But I had not her patience. I had grown unused to such quiet work, to peace and calm. Reaching inward, I grasped my energy, the shining magic that flowed from my lifeforce. Flames rippled from my palm, streaking across the lanterns, leaving half ablaze in their wake. My Talent lay in Air, but Fire was useful at times as these. The ground now glittered like stardust, and in the world below, the mortals would be lifting their heads to the curved wedge of light in the sky, its face partially hidden.

Few wrote poems about the half-moon or immortalized it in paintings—devoid of the elegant arch of a crescent or the perfect wholeness of the orb. Clinging to both light and dark, and lost somewhere in between. It resonated with me, a child of mortal and immortal heritage, in the shade of my luminous parents.

Sometimes I would find myself slipping into the past, threaded with a sliver of regret—wondering what if I had remained in the Celestial Kingdom, reaping glory across the years, each accomplishment strung to my name until it shone like a strand of pearls. A legend in my own right, revered as the heroes like my father, Houyi, or beloved and worshipped like my mother, the Moon Goddess.

The mortals honored her during the annual Mid-Autumn Festival, a celebration of reunion, though this was the day my mother had ascended to the skies. Some prayed to her for good fortune, others for love. Little did they know my mother's powers were limited, perhaps untrained or a remnant of her humanity— shed when she had consumed the Elixir of Immortality, the one gifted to my father for slaying the sunbirds. When she had flown to the heavens, my parents were parted as irrevocably as though death's blade had severed them, and indeed it had, for my father's body now lay entombed in a grave. A sharpness pierced my chest. I had never known my father, cherishing him as an abstract figure in my mind while my mother had mourned him every day of her immortal existence. Perhaps this was why the tedium of her task did not trouble her; relief to a mind splintered with regret, easing a heart clenched with grief.

No, I did not need renown and reverence, just as my parents had not asked for them. Fame was often accompanied by suffering, the thrill of glory came entwined with terror, and blood was not so easily washed from one's conscience. I had not joined the Celestial Army to chase dreams as fleeting as the dazzle of fireworks, leaving a darkness twice as deep in their wake. I would temper this restlessness, untangle such desires. To be home again with my mother and Ping'er, to have love in my life . . . these were the things that made me whole. It was what I had dreamed of, what I had fought for, what I had earned.

To many, this place might be humble compared to the opulence of the Jade Palace. Yet there was no place more wondrous to me—the ground shimmering as starlit waves, the osmanthus blossoms hanging from branches like clumps of white snow. Sometimes I woke in my bed of cinnamon wood, taut with uncertainty whether this was just a dream. But the sweetness curling in the air and the soft light of the lanterns were gentle yet unassailable assurances that I was *here*, in my home, and no one would tear me from it again.

As a breeze wound through the air, something clinked above. The laurel, its clusters of seeds aglitter as ice. In my childhood, I had longed to string them into a bracelet for my mother but could never pull the seeds free. From habit, I wrapped my fingers around one, translucent and cool. I tugged hard, but while the branch dipped and swayed, it held fast as before.

The air shifted with the presence of another immortal, though the wards remained undisturbed. I reached instinctively for the bow slung across my back. After this peaceful year at home, my lifeforce had recovered much quicker than anticipated. I no longer strained to draw the Jade Dragon Bow; I no longer feared an intruder's trespass. But almost at once, I lowered the weapon. This aura was one I knew as well as my own—shining, summer bright.

"A warm greeting, Xingyin." Liwei's voice rang out, tinged with laughter. "Or are you keen for another challenge with the bow?"

I turned to find him leaning against a tree, arms folded across his chest. My pulse quickened though I kept my tone steady. "You might recall, I won our last challenge. And since then, I've had a lot more practice compared to Your Highness, spending all your time at court."

An intended gibe for he had not visited in weeks. Yet I had no right to expect more. While we had grown closer of late, no promises had been exchanged—we were at once more than friends and less than what we had been. The seeds of doubt once sprouted were much harder to uproot.

The corners of his lips curved into a smile. "Our tally remains even. I might win."

"You are welcome to try," I said, lifting my chin.

He laughed, shaking his head. "I prefer to keep my pride intact."

He strode toward me, stopping when the hem of his lapis-blue robe brushed mine in a soft rustle. A gray length of silk encircled his waist, from which hung an oblong jade tablet and a crystal sphere, agleam with the silver of my energy. The Sky Drop Tassel, its twin swinging from my sash.

I fought the urge to step back, as much as I did the pull forward. "I did not sense your arrival. Did you adjust the wards?" A simple matter for Liwei to circumvent the enchantments that guarded my home, for he had helped me to craft them. While they were not as powerful as those of the Celestial Kingdom, a warning thrummed through me whenever the boundaries were crossed. I was not concerned about those familiar to us; it was the strangers I was wary of.

He nodded. "If they are disturbed, I will sense it, too. An inadvertent outcome is they now recognize my presence."

"Does it matter when you are so rarely here?" The words fell out before I could stop them.

His smile widened. "Did you miss me?"

"No." *Yes*, but I would not give him the satisfaction. And I would never admit it—not even if someone pressed a knife to my neck—that since his absence, a hollow ache had gaped within me, that only now began to subside.

"Should I leave?" he offered.

How tempting to turn my back on him, but it would be like kicking myself in the shin. "Why did you not come sooner?" I asked instead, which was what I truly wanted to know.

His expression turned grave. "An urgent matter arose at court; the appointment of a new general to share command over the army with General Jianyun. My father's relationship with him has grown tense of late."

Guilt burrowed in my chest. Did Their Celestial Majesties bear a grudge against General Jianyun for defending me a year ago, the day I won my mother's freedom? They rewarded those who served them well, but insults were repaid in full.

"Who is this new general?" I asked.

"Minister Wu," he said grimly.

A shudder coursed through me at the recollection of the courtier who had argued so vehemently against mercy for us. If he had his way, the emperor would have clapped my mother into chains and sentenced me to death that day. Had I offended the minister without knowing it? Or did he really believe us a threat to the emperor, to whom he was undoubtedly loyal? Whatever it was, my stomach churned at the thought of him wielding such influence over the Celestial Army.

"I did not realize the minister harbored these aspirations," I remarked. "Is he qualified for the position?"

"Few would refuse so illustrious an appointment whether they are capable or not," Liwei said. "I stayed to lend General Jianyun my support in hopes of changing my father's mind, but he is adamant. While Minister Wu is a loyal subject of my father's, I have always felt uneasy around him, even before he spoke against you."

"Unclouded by emotion, instinct can be a powerful guide." As I spoke, my insides knotted at the memory of Wenzhi's betrayal. Who was I to preach such things when I had stifled my own instincts, seeing only what I wanted to believe?

Something pulsed through my mind like a soundless drumbeat; someone had come through the wards. I probed the stillness, sensing the unfamiliar flickers of energy. Immortal auras, several of them, yet none familiar to me. As I stiffened, Liwei's eyes narrowed. He had sensed it, too, these strangers who had come to my home.

Since the moon was no longer a place of exile, many immortals visited us. An unfortunate outcome of the emperor's pardon was having to suffer their curious stares and callous remarks like I was some object to be paraded for their amusement.

How did it feel to be struck by Sky-fire? a Celestial courtier had asked breathlessly.

A miracle that you survived. A face alight with anticipation.

While another had wondered in a too-loud voice, *What of the scars? Do they still hurt? I hear those will never heal.*

Feigned concern. Gloating commiseration. False sympathy. As hollow as those puppets wielded by street performers in the mortal world. If I had detected a fragment of genuine care, I would not have resented them so. But all that spurred their interest was greed, for a scrap of gossip to share. How my fingers had itched to draw my bow, summoning a bolt of lightning to send them fleeing from our hall. I would not have released it but the mere threat would have sufficed. Only my mother's glare and the manners she had instilled in me since I was young kept me fixed to my chair.

Yet better by far their idle curiosity than those with malice in their hearts.

A crash rang out, something shattering against stone. Lifting my skirt, I sprinted toward the Pure Light Palace. Each time my feet hit the ground, kicking up clumps of powdery earth, the Jade Dragon Bow thumped against my back. Liwei's footsteps were never far behind as he ran after me.

Shining walls rose ahead, then the mother-of-pearl columns. I stumbled to a halt by the entrance, examining the porcelain fragments strewn on the floor, drenched in a pool of pale-gold liquid. A sweet and mellow fragrance wafted in the air, soothing and languorous. Wine, though we kept no stores of it here.

Liwei and I stalked through the doors, along the corridor that led to the Silver Harmony Hall where visitors were received. Jade lamps cast their soft glow upon the strangers, seated in wooden chairs around my mother. As I entered, their heads swung my way as they rose to their feet.

The jade tassels on my mother's vermilion sash clinked as she came toward us. "Liwei, we have not seen you for a while," she said warmly, dropping his title as he had long urged her to.

"Forgive me for my lengthy absence." He bent his head in courtesy.

As I greeted our guests, I studied them in turn. Their auras were not strong, which meant any trouble could be easily subdued, nor were there any ominous flashes of metal or subtle thrums of magic held at the ready—only discernible if one was searching for them. A frail immortal stood beside my mother. His eyes were the shade of a sparrow's coat and his hair and beard gleamed silver. A bamboo flute with a green tassel hung from his waist. Beside him were two women in lilac robes with turquoise pins in their hair. The hands they lifted in greeting were smooth and unblemished, that had never wielded a weapon or done a day's work. I breathed easier until I caught sight of the last guest. The hard planes of his features seemed like they were chiseled from wood, while his neck was corded with muscle. Beneath his fine brocade robe, his shoulders were thrown wide, yet his fingers twitched restlessly.

A prickle of warning slid over my skin as I smiled to conceal my concern. "Mother, who are our guests?"

"Meina and Meining are sisters from the Golden Desert. They wish to stay for a few weeks to observe the stars." She gestured to the elderly immortal beside her. "Master Gang, a skilled musician, has come to seek inspiration for his latest composition. And this is . . ." She paused, her forehead creasing as she stared at the younger man. "I am afraid we were interrupted before I could learn your name."

He bowed to us, holding out his clasped hands. "I'm honored to be in your company. My name is Haoran, and I'm a wine-maker from the Phoenix Kingdom. My patron, Queen Fengjin, requested a new wine for which I require the finest osmanthus. It is said the most beautiful ones bloom in your forest, and I humbly ask your permission to harvest some of the flowers. I would be eternally grateful for your boundless generosity, that is famed throughout the realm."

I recoiled inwardly from the obsequious flattery in his words, the way his eyes darted around the room. Something about him set me on edge like a tune played in the wrong rhythm—and it was not just that he was from the Phoenix Kingdom, the closest ally of the Celestial Kingdom and the home of Liwei's former betrothed. A refusal hovered on the tip of my tongue, an urge rising to send him away. Not just Haoran; all of them. We were safe here, our peace hard-won.

As though sensing my unease, Haoran turned to my mother.

"It would be no more than a few days. I brought a humble gift, several jars of my finest wine, one of which was unfortunately dropped outside," he said with artful cunning.

"Master Haoran, you are most courteous but there is no need for any gift," my mother replied graciously. "We welcome all of you. I hope you will excuse us for the simple way we live; we do not entertain in a grand manner."

Master Haoran inclined his head again. "I am grateful."

The others bowed in acknowledgment before they followed my mother from the room, leaving just Liwei and me in the hall. As I sank onto a chair, pressing a fist to my lips, Liwei took the seat beside me.

"What do you think of Master Haoran?" I asked.

"I would like to try his wines."

I was in no mood to jest. "Perhaps I'm searching for trouble where there is none. Perhaps I'm used to it."

Liwei leaned toward me, his face grave. "Trust your instincts; I do. Keep watch over them. If anything happens, send word to me at once."

As his eyes dropped to the Sky Drop Tassel by my waist, his expression tightened. Memories crowded me—of a dark cave, a taunting laugh, the tip of Liwei's sword pressed to my flesh . . . and how close we had come to losing each other.

I stared through the doorway until the footsteps receded to silence. For the first time ever, strangers would reside beneath the roof of my home. I forced from my mind the recollection of the last time I had felt this way here—a child hiding from the Celestial Empress, pressed against the stone wall, half frozen with fear.

2

M Y FINGERS STILLED ABOVE MY qin as I stared out the window. Master Haoran was heading toward the forest as he had done every evening for the past week, a bamboo basket strapped onto his back. His whistling pierced the air, its pitch scraping my nerves. Silver scissors glinted in the evening light as he twirled them deftly. Would his fingers be equally nimble when wielding a weapon?

"This song you are playing is one even *I* can attempt." My mother's voice from behind interrupted my thoughts.

I smiled faintly, pushing the qin aside. My mother had neither skill nor interest in music, which was why it had been Ping'er who instructed me.

She sat down, clasping her hands on the table. "You don't seem fond of our guests."

"Just one in particular." I tilted my head toward the window.

"Why don't you like Master Haoran? He is well-mannered and considerate."

I had no real cause to dislike him. It was just a feeling, like the shift in the air from an immortal's aura, the prickling sensation of being watched. And, as Liwei had said, I should trust my instincts . . . or at least not silence them in favor of what I wished were true.

I did not want to be right; I did not want any danger to come to our home.

"He is guarded. Tense, as though he is hiding something," I explained haltingly. "Whenever I ask him a question, he deflects it, moving the discussion from himself." Evasion was something I was attuned to, having spent years concealing my identity.

"Maybe he is unused to company. Some people feel uncomfortable talking about themselves; some prefer to listen." My mother added, "Master Haoran is afraid of you. Do you realize how you look at him? Eyes pinched, lips curled." She touched my hand gently. "Xingyin, I know you've been hurt. If you suspect everyone, you might eventually be proven right—but you will end up disappointed nonetheless. Sometimes, by treating others with mistrust, you invite it upon yourself. By refusing to see the good in them, you might lose something precious that you never allowed yourself to find."

Her words rang true. These days I caught myself finding a sneer in a smile, menace in a frown. Searching for enemies in every shadow.

She rose, smoothing out the folds of her robe. As her palms grazed the cloth, the tips of the embroidered silver lotuses glinted brighter. Was it a trick of the light? I did not think it was her power; it had never manifested in any other way.

"I came to tell you Shuxiao is here."

My spirits lifted. Apart from Liwei, she was my most frequent visitor, and always welcome. "Where is she?"

"In the dining hall, plaguing Ping'er for food."

I headed there at once. The floor was paved with gray stone tiles, covered with a silk carpet in shades of violet. A round table with curved legs rested in the center of the room, surrounded by barrel-shaped stools. The rosewood was inlaid with iridescent mother-of-pearl, forming scenes of flowers and birds. Eight could fit comfortably around the table, and in my childhood I never imagined the day would come when it would be too small.

A warm, savory aroma wafted from the food already laid out: a thick soup brimming with chunks of meat and sliced lotus root, whole eggs stewed in herbs, tender pea shoots, fish fried to a golden crisp, and bowls of steamed rice. Simpler fare than in the Celestial Kingdom, yet rich with flavor. Master Gang took the stool beside my mother, while the sisters from the Golden Desert sat on her other side. Master Haoran was absent, as he had been for the past week—though his jars of wine were on the table, our cups already filled. It was an excellent brew tinged with the sweetness of plum. Though I still doubted his tale, his skill as a winemaker had not been exaggerated. The last few nights I had emptied my cup without hesitation, falling into a deep and untroubled sleep, although I awoke in the mornings with an ache that pounded at my skull.

I filled two bowls with lotus-root soup, then made my way to Shuxiao. Though she smiled, it did not reach her eyes. "What is troubling you?" I wasted no time in pleasantries, sliding one of the bowls toward her.

"Things have been tense in the Jade Palace," she admitted. "The new general keeps a tight rein on us."

"General Wu?" The minister's recently acquired title was stiff on my tongue.

She nodded. "With General Jianyun sidelined, General Wu is now the real power behind the army. He is rigid and harsh. Rules are enforced to the strictest letter, with punishments meted out for the slightest offense. It's considered a lapse of our duties to converse with another, even during mealtimes. Now we just sit there in silence, not daring to look at each other, like we're children again with the fiercest tutor in the realm."

An army divided is easier to control. An unwelcome thought.

Was the Celestial Emperor wary of the soldiers uniting against his will again? The soldiers had not realized their support of me could be seen as a challenge to the emperor—they were ignorant of what I had done to earn his wrath. My true defiance of the emperor that day, my calculated misinterpretation of his command to bring him the pearls, was something only the two of us knew. And likely, the newly elevated general, his most trusted advisor.

"Is that the worst of it? Quiet mealtimes?" I spoke lightly, trying to brighten her mood despite my own reservations.

She wrinkled her nose. "It's hard to keep track of the rules when new ones are added each day. Soon, it will be an infraction to leave the palace without permission. I won't be able to visit then."

The thought unsettled me. How things had changed since I left the Celestial Kingdom. How I would have chafed beneath these restrictions. The worst punishment I could recall was a stern rebuke from General Jianyun or Wen—I recoiled, casting aside the unwelcome memory. "What happens if you ignore the rules?" I asked.

"Kneeling. Confinement. Lashings." Her voice cracked over the last word.

My fingers clenched around the bowl. "You must be careful."

"Oh, I am. I've never been so circumspect before," she said with feeling. "But they seem to be keeping a close eye on me, particularly after General Wu's elevation."

"Why?" When she did not reply, I probed, "Is it because of our friendship?"

She looked down, stirring the soup with her spoon. "It is others, seeing threat where there is none. It changes nothing; I will not pander to them."

Remorse gripped me. This was what I had dreaded all this

time, that she might come to harm for simply being my friend. "If things are that bad, if they're looking to punish you, why stay?"

"I can't leave yet. While I serve the emperor, my family is safe. We have no powerful friends who would speak for us should trouble arise again. My younger brother hopes to join the army when he comes of age, and if I resign, he will lose the chance." Her gaze turned distant. "Sometimes, steering clear of trouble doesn't keep you safe. Pebbles by the side of a path still get trodden by careless feet, and idle words carry too much weight when whispered into the wrong ears."

"There is room for you and your family here," I offered at once. "The eyes of the Celestial Kingdom are far away."

But they are still fixed here, a voice inside me cautioned.

"I wish I could," she said wistfully. "But my family will be reluctant to move. These roots we have set down are not so easily wrenched free."

A familiar longing swept over me. During my years away from home, I had often felt adrift—a weed, sprouted in strange and hostile soil. I glanced around the hall, taking in the familiar furniture, the worn carpet, the stool I had sat on as a child. Countless memories thronged this place, each precious and irreplaceable. Yet what mattered most were the people within these walls. Family, whether through blood or bond, who gave a place its heart. And that was more important than any tile or brick, whether of gold, silver, or jade.

The lilting strains of a flute drifted into the air. Master Gang was playing, the tassel on his instrument swinging with each breath he took. The chatter in the room quietened as the others turned toward him. He played exceptionally well, his notes soaring pure and true.

When the last note faded, my mother said, "Thank you, Master Gang. Your music is a gift."

"You are too kind, Goddess of the Moon."

"Do you play often for your family?" she asked.

"My wife. She was fond of music." He smiled as he turned to me. "I hear your daughter is a skilled musician. When might we have the pleasure of listening to a song? I would be glad to share some of my compositions with you."

"Thank you, Master Gang, but I would be hard pressed to follow your performance." I did not decline out of modesty, but because I preferred to play for the audience of my choosing.

As an awkward silence descended, Shuxiao asked, "Master Gang, have you found much inspiration for your music here?"

He nodded enthusiastically. "Ah, Lieutenant, this place is wondrous indeed: the wind rustling the leaves, the rain beating on the roof, even the soft fold of soil beneath my feet. I am inclined to stay a while longer, if my hostess permits."

"Stay as long as you wish," my mother replied with faultless courtesy, though I caught the hitch in her tone. Perhaps she, too, missed the solitude of our home.

After the meal, I accompanied Shuxiao outside. The veil of night had cloaked the sky, though the lanterns had yet to be lit.

As she stepped upon her cloud, I touched her arm. "Be on your guard. Don't do anything you should not."

"As you so often did?" Her laugh rang hollow as she shook her head. "I've reformed my ways. I'm now a paragon of obedience."

I passed her a silk-wrapped parcel. "Osmanthus flowers for Minyi." When I had studied with Liwei, she prepared our meals and had become a friend.

Shuxiao tucked it under her arm. "Your trees will be bare soon with every winemaker and cook knocking on your doors. How do they even know of the flowers?"

I did not reply, raising my hand in farewell as her cloud sped away. She would be safe, I assured myself, as I strode to my room. Shuxiao was astute, she had many friends in the palace, and Liwei would watch out for her. Though as I lay in bed, her question lingered in my mind, my last thought before I drifted off to sleep: How *had* Master Haoran heard of our osmanthus? Most of our guests did not trouble themselves to walk through the forest, and I had not offered to show it to them.

THUD. THUD. THUD.

A silvery rustle followed like the tinkling of a wind chime. Rhythmic but muffled, as though it came from far away.

My eyes flew open, blinking in the dark. From the deep quiet it was either late at night or far too early in the morning. Had I imagined those sounds? Perhaps I should have drunk some of Master Haoran's wine, my slumber might have been as restful as the nights before.

Thud. Thud. Thud.

I jerked upright in bed, straining my ears to listen. This was *real*, like something solid being struck. And what was that rustling that trailed after like a persistent echo? Tossing aside the covers, I strode to the open window, inhaling the cool air laced with a delicate sweetness. The sky was dark, the ground infused with moonlight. In the distance, the laurel towered, its branches swaying as though assaulted by the wind—yet the osmanthus trees remained still.

Fear slithered through me, cold and hard. My fingers shook as I pulled a robe over my inner garments, knotting it around my waist. I slipped on my shoes, grabbed my bow, and climbed out through the window. My gaze was pinned on the quivering laurel, my feet flying over the ground—stumbling, almost falling over. Once, twice, thrice, those strange knocks sounded again, sending the tree into agonized spasms. Just before the clearing I halted, my grip tightening around my bow.

A man stood beside the laurel, with his back to me. The aura that rippled from him was thick and opaque, like congealed grease. There was an odd familiarity about it, my senses prickling in warning. A glint snared my attention, moonlight catching the silver curve of an axe blade, a green tassel swinging from its bamboo handle. It swept down, striking the laurel, the metal splintering the bark. Something dark trickled from the woodcutter's palm onto the tree—was it blood? Had he wounded himself? But then the tree shuddered violently, pale leaves rustling as a seed fell to the ground, glittering as a fallen star.

I drew a blazing arrow and stepped out from the shadows, my heart pounding to a frantic beat. As the man swung around, a sharp breath slid between my teeth as I swiftly trained the arrow at his head.

Master Gang.

Gone was his meek demeanor and stooping posture—his brown eyes gleamed like those of a predatory hawk. An adept disguise, I thought wrathfully, as he had also masked his powerful aura. I should have known better than to be tricked by this simple enchantment, the same one Liwei and I had used to slip out of the Jade Palace undetected. If I had sensed this before, I would have drawn a sword on him instead of offering tea. My suspicions of Master Haoran had blinded me to the true menace among us. I cursed myself for letting Master Gang's frailty lull me into thinking he was no threat when I should have learned by now, things were not always as they seemed.

"Are you here to exchange compositions?" he taunted, making a mockery of his earlier offer.

"I have no interest in the music you play," I replied, my gaze fixed on his axe. Small, round holes were carved along the slender handle—it was his flute, I realized with a start. My insides churned to think he had brought this weapon into our home, my fingers itching to release the arrow, but I wanted answers first. "Don't move, don't reach for your magic. Tell me who you are, and why you came here."

"Why should I?" His eyes crinkled in seeming amusement, even as they lingered on my arrow. "You have no right to ask me anything. What I'm after does not belong to *you*." One of his hands unclenched briefly, revealing thick scars winding across his palm, dark ridges of raised skin glossy with blood.

A moment's distraction. My head snapped back to him, too late—he was already springing toward me, his axe swung high. I spun aside, releasing my arrow as he dipped back, the shaft whizzing harmlessly over him. As his axe flashed before me again, I darted away, twisting out of reach as his blade sliced a stray lock of my hair, scattering it like shorn grass. A second later and I might have been cleaved apart.

A shiver shot down my spine, the bowstring biting into my fingers as I drew another arrow, releasing it at once. Lightning hissed, scorching a path through the air as it plunged toward him. Something shimmered across his body—a shield—just as my arrow struck. Veins of white light crackled across the barrier. As it fractured, his energy surged forth to seal the crevices. Drawing back his arm, he hurled his axe at me, spinning through the air in a silvery blur. I dropped to the ground, pressing my cheek and palms into the powdery earth. The axe whistled over my body, slamming into the trunk of an osmanthus tree, petals scattering down like rain. As I rolled away and sprang to my feet, his weapon twitched before jerking free and plunging back into Master Gang's grasp. Light sparked ominously from his hand as another arrow formed between my fingertips, already soaring toward him—even as he swerved deftly, the bolt vanishing into the night.

"How many times can you do this?" His tone was pleasant, almost conversational.

"As many as it takes to kill you."

Sweat beaded my skin as I grasped my energy. He swung at me again, but this time, I held my ground. Magic surged from my palms in glittering coils of air, binding him fast. With a flick of my hand, he was flung against the ground, the back of his head striking a rock. A groan spilled from his throat as his eyelids fluttered shut, his axe falling from his grip. I approached cautiously with an arrow drawn, my nerves jangling. He seemed too strong to be felled so easily, and I had been taken in by his pretense before—

A gasp broke the silence. "Master Gang! Are you hurt?" Ping'er cried from behind me, rushing to where he lay.

"Ping'er, get back!"

I leapt out to block her path—too slow—as Master Gang's eyes flicked open. He sprang up, seizing her arm. As his axe flew back into his grasp, he wedged its monstrous blade against her neck.

"What are you doing?" As Ping'er struggled against him, he tightened his grip, the edge slicing her skin. She froze at once, her chest heaving.

"Let her go." I drew a deep breath, quashing the urge toward recklessness.

"Drop your bow and step back," he warned me. "Let me leave, and no one will be harmed."

"What will stop you from killing us then?" I demanded.

"I give you my word." He spoke as if it were worth anything, as though he had not come to our home clad in deceit.

As I hesitated, his weapon dug into Ping'er's flesh, a dark trickle of blood streaking across her pale robes. A strangled sound slid from her throat, though she remained deathly still.

"Hurt her again and you'll regret it tenfold," I said in my most menacing voice. "I need no weapon to make you pay."

His teeth gleamed as his lips parted. "Of course. I would not dare take on so renowned a warrior." A hint of derision glazed his tone.

I stifled my anger, letting my bow fall to the ground. At once, he shoved Ping'er at me and dashed away. As I caught her, a cloud swept down, bearing him into the skies.

I would have given chase but Ping'er gasped, clutching at her neck. Her palm came away wet with blood as she dropped to the ground. My stomach lurched as I crouched down beside her, folding her icy hands between mine. I released my energy to heal her wound, the torn flesh closing into a thin white line. Clumsily done, but there was no one around who might do better.

Ping'er groaned as she rubbed her temples. "Xingyin, what happened? Why . . . why did Master Gang do that?"

I frowned. "I don't know. He is a liar and a thief."

As she pushed herself up, something fell from the folds of her yellow robe—an oblong pearl hanging from a thin gold chain. It shone with inner fire, almost like that of the dragons' pearls, but without a trace of their immense power. Had she always worn this? Had it been concealed beneath her garments all this time?

"Ping'er, what is this?" I brushed a finger along the pearl's lustrous surface, warm to the touch.

Her face clouded over. "This formed the day I left my home. For Southern Sea immortals, only the tears sprung from our deepest emotion transform into pearls."

"Do you miss your family?" A thoughtless question, a foolish one. Of course she did, though Ping'er had never returned there, not once in all these decades.

A brightness surged in her eyes, which she blinked away. I turned aside, giving her time to herself. Something glittered among the blades of grass—a laurel seed. I picked it up, rolling it between my fingers, its cool, hard surface familiar to me, yet it was the first time I held it untethered from its branch. A pulse of energy grazed my skin. Why had Master Gang wanted this? Why had he gone to such lengths? My gaze darted to the laurel, its trunk riddled with deep grooves as though it had been clawed by some beast, and smeared with a dark liquid. Was it his blood? Had he hurt himself while chopping the tree?

A woody fragrance suffused the air, a lustrous golden sap seeping from the crevices to spill over the bark. The edges of the splintered wood lengthened, braiding together till they merged seamlessly once more. My gaze drifted upward to the laurel seeds that glistened like silvered frost, peeking between the leaves. I had always thought them beautiful. Precious and rare. Yet a coldness shrouded me as I wondered what secrets they concealed within their shimmering depths.

3

IN THE LATE AFTERNOON LIGHT, the laurel gleamed like a pillar of ice. I ran my fingers down the bark, as smooth as marble—as though it had never been ravaged by the axe, as though I had imagined it all.

"Is this where you spend all your time?" Liwei asked as he approached.

I grimaced. "It was where I spent last night. Unplanned." Without delay, I told of Master Gang's attack.

His face darkened. "Did he hurt you?"

I shook my head, holding the seed out to him—smaller than my thumbnail, something opaque swirling within like a wisp of cloud. "This fell from the laurel. There is some magic here that I cannot identify."

He lifted it up, examining it intently. "Cold. Its energy is strong but unfamiliar. Let's test it."

As he raised his other palm, the seed floated into the air. Crimson flames engulfed it with a crackle, leaping high then dying out abruptly, leaving the seed charred like a fragment of coal. Relief swept through me that this was no great treasure after all, no mysterious power. Certainly not worth the efforts Master Gang had taken.

"Xingyin, look."

The urgency in Liwei's tone startled me. The seed was shining once more like it had shed its outer skin, just a trace dimmer than before. For it to have survived Liwei's fire intact meant its power was strong.

My magic flowed in a shimmering stream, binding the seed in layers of air, clenching harder until thin fractures webbed the surface. I tensed, channeling more of my energy, intent on crushing it to prove it was of no consequence—but a brightness flared from the seed's depths, sealing the cracks.

Liwei's eyes narrowed as he raised a hand to the tree, more flames erupting in thick waves to consume it. As they swept over the silvery leaves and bark, I recoiled, biting back my instinctive protest—I had loved the laurel since my childhood, playing in its shade, entranced by its beauty. As Liwei's fingers closed into a fist, the fire surged hotter, the bark darkening in patches . . . yet the flames shuddered and stilled before going out in a hiss of smoke. The gleaming sap spilled forth once again, sliding down the bark in rivulets. A luminous radiance suffused the laurel, the scorch marks fading, leaving the wood unblemished.

"Regeneration. Except I have never encountered anything as powerful," Liwei remarked, staring at the tree.

I recalled the ease with which my magic had flowed, a far cry from when I had sacrificed my lifeforce to free the dragons. I had recovered here quicker than anyone believed possible. And now I knew why.

"It healed me too. When I first returned I could barely manage the wards, and now . . . I am almost as strong as before." Tangled with my relief was a sinking dread.

"I am glad for it." Liwei tilted his head to me, "But why do you look so worried?"

"What else can this be used to do? What does Master Gang

want with it? Who is he? For he is no harmless musician or petty thief."

"We will find out," he assured me. "Have you managed to pluck more of the seeds?"

"No. Weapons didn't work, whether swords or daggers. None of them made a scratch, the marks vanishing as soon as they appeared—just as with your fire. I do not know how Master Gang did it."

"Maybe his axe was enchanted? Do you recall anything else from last night?" Liwei asked.

I paused, sifting through the blur of my thoughts. "He was strong and quick, surprisingly so. His weapon was able to carve the laurel's bark, unlike ours, but I sensed no magic around it."

Something caught my eye then, a cloud descending from the skies, toward the guest wing. Who had summoned it? Trailing the cloud's path, we made our way swiftly to Master Haoran's courtyard. Magnolia trees shaded the grounds, their roots rippling over the grass, their branches weaving above a round stone table.

As I rapped upon the latticed door, a muffled oath filtered through, followed by the urgent tread of feet. Liwei shoved the doors apart, the panels flying open. It was dark inside, cloth draped over the windows. Light poured in through the entrance that we stalked through. A heady sweetness clung to the air from the crushed blooms piled into silk bags—some tied shut and others left gaping wide, petals strewn across the floor.

Master Haoran leapt up from where he had been huddled, stacking jars of wine sealed with red fabric into a wooden box. He blinked, a hand thrown up to shield his face from the glare. "Be careful, the light will harm the petals!"

With a surge of my power, the coverings were ripped from

the windows, the sunlight streaming in. "Stop the pretense. You're not here for flowers."

"What do you mean?" He stared at me blankly. "Why are you here?"

"We might ask you the same question," Liwei replied coldly. "Why are you leaving so soon, without bidding your hostess farewell?"

"A pressing matter has arisen. Family affairs." His words fell out awkwardly, strung in haste.

Caught unaware, Master Haoran was as bad a liar as I had been, before my own tongue was gilded with deceit. My mind worked quickly, fragments falling into place: his arrival with Master Gang, his eagerness to ply us with wine, his haste to leave. "Why did you come here? Why did you lie to us?" I demanded.

Master Haoran stiffened, then bolted toward the door. Fiery coils erupted from Liwei's hand, winding around him like a snake.

"Stop! Spare me! I'll tell you all I know." He struggled amid the writhing flames. Yet no stench of burning flesh tainted the air; the fire did not sear but merely held him in place.

I spoke more gently. "The truth is the best chance for you to leave here unharmed." However, if he *had* schemed to hurt us, he would find little mercy.

He nodded jerkily. "Queen Fengjin is not my patron. My wines are the best in the kingdom, but those arrogant palace stewards refuse to give me a chance. Her Majesty enjoys osmanthus wines and I . . . I wanted to win her favor. Master Gang visited my shop and told me of the osmanthus trees on the moon, each flower in perfect bloom. In return, all he wanted was a small favor. It seemed harmless enough, and it was customary to bring one's hostess a gift."

"The wine." I chided myself for drinking it. Master Gang

must have added something to it, to put us all to sleep. If I had drunk it last night, I would have slumbered through, ignorant of all that had transpired.

As I glanced at Master Haoran, his skin a sickly pallor, my anger at him dissipated. He had been used as a mask—his petty lies distracting me, allowing the true villain to roam unhindered. By fixing on a single sapling, I had lost sight of the forest.

"What else did he tell you?" Liwei pressed.

"Only that he needed to retrieve something which belonged to him. I didn't think there was any ill intent."

Master Gang had said as much when I confronted him. I had thought it bluster, a lie to excuse his actions.

"Who is he?" I probed.

"He didn't say and I dared not ask." Master Haoran gnawed his lower lip. "The first time we met, he wore a jade ornament carved with the sun. I haven't seen it since."

The symbol of the Celestial Kingdom. Liwei inhaled slowly as my chest squeezed tight.

"I know nothing else. I swear." Master Haoran's voice trembled.

"Let him go. He was tricked too," I said to Liwei.

As his binds vanished, Master Haoran slumped to the ground, shaking, yet his gaze lingered on the silk bundles scattered around the room.

"Take the osmanthus. You are free to go," I told him.

"Thank you." He bowed to us, then snatched up as many bags as he could cram into his arms. Without a backward glance he fled the room, the wind outside rustling as his cloud shot into the skies.

Silence stretched taut between us. "Many people wear such an ornament," Liwei said. "Even if he was from the Celestial Kingdom, it does not mean he is here upon my father's command. My father has no need for such devious measures. The moon falls under Celestial rule. If he wished, he could have commanded your mother to accept Master Gang's presence."

Not if he wanted his interest to remain a secret. But I nodded, eager to grasp at this sliver of comfort. I had no urge to confront the Celestial Emperor again.

"We must find out more," I said. "Would Teacher Daoming know anything about the laurel seed?"

Teacher Daoming was one of the few I trusted in the Jade Palace, who had looked out for me, though it had not felt that way in the beginning when I struggled with my lessons. Only later did I realize she was helping me overcome the barriers of my power, and only after I yielded her my respect did I earn hers.

"I will ask her," Liwei assured me.

As he tucked the laurel seed into the inner pocket of his sleeve, the embroidered cranes spread their wings as though poised for flight. His robe was of the finest blue brocade, fastened around his waist with a silver brocade sash. My gaze drifted up the smooth column of his neck to his black hair gathered into a top-knot encircled by a crown of sapphire and gold.

How magnificent he looked. How regal and formal. An irrational desire swelled in me to have dressed with more care, to have coiled my hair in a different style instead of tying it partway down my back. Here, there was little need for finery.

"Are you attending a banquet later?" I asked, despite knowing how he disliked such events.

He shook his head. "Why do you ask?"

"Because you look . . . because you are dressed like that," I finished clumsily.

A corner of his mouth curved up. "Does it please you?"

I met his gaze. "It suits you." It was not flattery; he looked just as the Celestial Crown Prince should, yet the disparity in our positions had never seemed more stark.

His power flickered forth, his crown morphing into a simple circlet of silver, the cranes on his robe stilling before they vanished. "You were never much good at disguising your thoughts."

"Not to you," I admitted. "And you did not need to do that." Yet I could not deny feeling more at ease with him.

"I wanted to." Liwei paused, brushing a stray strand of hair from his forehead. "Xingyin, I would like to show you something."

The intensity in his voice struck me. "Now?"

He glanced at the darkening skies. "There is no better time. I will bring you back before dawn."

His fingers clasped mine as he drew me from the room. Outside, a cloud was already waiting. The wind glided over my face as we soared higher, until my home was no more than a pale orb in the distance. Once before we had flown like this, our hearts entwined before the storms that swept us apart.

As our cloud halted, I looked up, all thought driven from my mind. Stars glittered before us, spanning the breadth of the sky, as dazzling as moonlit frost.

"Liwei, where are we?" My breath misted the cool air.

"The Silver River."

"Are those the stars that parted the Weaving Goddess from her mortal husband?" It was a renowned legend of the Mortal Realm.

He nodded. "Such a union goes against the laws of our realm. It was said the goddess fled to the world below, until she was ordered to return to the skies. Her husband braved great peril to follow her and after much suffering, they were finally allowed to reunite for a single day each year. The seventh day of the seventh lunar month, that the mortals celebrate as the Qixi Festival."

In the past, I had been entranced by the romance and ethereal beauty of this myth. But after having suffered heartache of my own, my pity was roused. I could not help thinking of my parents and the similarities in their tale. Perhaps all such unions were doomed to tragedy, for what future could a mortal and immortal have when death divided them?

"Why do you look so sad, Xingyin?" Liwei leaned closer until his head grazed mine. "It's just a story."

Yet the mortals believed my father's tale a myth, as they did that of my mother's ascension to immortality. Perhaps the legends that touched us deepest were those spun from a wisp of truth.

"Is it true?" I wished it was not, that no one had to suffer so—their hearts locked in yearning, forever enmeshed in despair.

He was quiet for a moment. "Perhaps, a long time ago? This place is deserted now; there is no one here, but us."

"Can any love be worth such misery? One night for a year of pain."

His hand clasped mine, his grip firm and strong. "It depends."

"On what?"

"On the night," he said softly. "On what they were waiting for."

Our shoulders brushed as we stood side by side, staring into the sea of infinite light. Silk rustled as he reached into his sleeve and drew out a hairpin, lacquered in all the hues of heaven, studded with clear stones. The one he had crafted for me, the one I had returned to him after his betrothal to another. My gaze lifted to his dark eyes, a warmth blooming through my body.

"When I gave you this before, I pretended it was a gift in exchange for yours. I was a coward for not saying what was in my heart then. When we parted the first time, I regretted that so much was left unsaid between us and I feared never to have the chance again." His voice shook with emotion. "If you would have me, I would pledge myself to you—for now, forever."

Hope blazed through me, only shadowed by the remembrance of how we had trodden this path before and the hurt that trailed in our wake. Our families. His kingdom. My cautious heart. Such were the seemingly insurmountable obstacles that lay between us. There would be no exchange of betrothal gifts between our families, no joyous coming together of two households. The last time I had seen the Celestial Emperor, he tried to kill me. The scars across my chest itched at the remembrance of the writhing agony, clinging to my flesh like a web of pain. More than that, how could I leave my mother alone, once more, mired in grief for my father's death?

In the silence, Liwei stiffened, drawing away. "I thought you wanted this too. Perhaps I was mistaken."

He sounded formal, withdrawn—and I hated it. I clasped his hand, threading my fingers through his. "I do. I just need time. Your parents detest me, I can't leave my mother yet. And—"

My words faded, leaving unspoken a new fear which had sprouted in that very moment. For if I married Liwei, I would have to live forever in the Jade Palace shrouded in silk, shackled in gold, and bound by ceremony. While Liwei was not his father, nor was I his mother—we would be fettered by the same gilded tethers. I was not one to be caged. This year of freedom had awakened me to the possibilities of a life away from the confines of the Celestial Kingdom. It might seem a fantasy to many, marrying the prince of the realm and living in a palace among the clouds. Yet with a mother-in-law who despised me and a father-in-law who had tried to end my life, it was more a nightmare than a dream.

Liwei smiled as he slid the pin through my hair until it was nestled tight. "I will wait. It is enough for me that you feel the same way, but I will tell my parents of my intentions."

"You will?" My words rang with disbelief.

"The last thing I want is another unexpected betrothal."

The thought needled me, followed by a stab of anxiety. "What will they do?"

"My mother will rage. My father . . . I am beyond the age he can discipline me as he used to. I will be a disappointment to him as I have been most of my life. I never did learn my lessons to his satisfaction."

I was glad he had not, even as my insides clenched at his words. I had felt the force of the emperor's displeasure; I had seen how he struck Liwei down without hesitation. At that moment, I loathed the Celestial Empress a little less, relieved that Liwei had one parent who cared for him, who had tried to help him in her own way.

"It does not matter, as long as we are together," he said.

As he drew me to him, his eyes darkened with an intent that stirred my blood. No, I would not let doubt taint this moment; such joy was both precious and scarce. I leaned against him, inhaling his clean scent. It had been a long time since he held me so. As his other hand slid around the curve of my waist, fire surged through my veins, a sudden hunger consuming me as my arms wound around his neck to pull him closer. His lips found mine—firm and tender, soft yet relentless. How I had missed this sweetness, this tantalizing sensation of our bodies pressed together. His hold around me tightened as we fell, as one, onto the billowing folds of the cloud, its coolness a balm to my heated skin.

Closing my eyes, I drifted away upon a tide of dreams, glittering as brightly as this river of stars.

4

A RINGING THROUGH MY MIND YANKED me from the embrace of slumber. Someone had come through the wards. My eyes flew open as I probed the intruder's energy. Familiar to me, yet fury flared hot and bright.

Wenzhi.

I would not see him; I would ignore him as I had done all the times before. He came more often now, disrupting the wards with careless abandon when he could have unraveled them with ease— just as he had done with those of the Celestial Kingdom. Perhaps it amused him to have them clang through my mind like a gong newly struck. Perhaps it saved him the trouble of rousing me himself. He never ventured to my chamber; maybe he did not know where it was, though I preferred to think he did not dare to. After the initial disturbance, silence would ensue. Yet his presence on the balcony of my home irked me relentlessly like dust in my eyes. Wenzhi was ever patient, only leaving with the approach of dawn.

From the beginning, I resisted the urge to chase him from our grounds. Ignoring him would be the best recourse, denting his iron pride. And I did not like the bitterness and rage his presence roused in me, the memories that seared. Those were sleepless nights as I tossed until the silken coverlet was twisted around my body, my only solace imagining his own futile wait.

The lilting strains of a zither drifted into my room. Beautiful and haunting, yet played so softly I would not have noticed had I not been awake. Each drawn-out note melded into the next, reverberating with restrained passion. The melody stirred an ache within me, an image sliding into my mind of the last time I had heard it—of Wenzhi plucking the strings of his qin just before I had drugged him to make my escape. Rage seared me. How dare he come here? How dare he play this *now*?

Scrambling off the bed, I pulled on a robe, fastening it with a length of silk tied into a clumsy knot. Snatching my bow from the table, I slung it onto my back, tucking a couple of daggers through my sash for good measure. I moved swiftly but quietly, to avoid awakening anyone—making my way along the corridor, up the flight of stairs. At the top, I pushed the doors apart, stepping onto the balcony.

Wenzhi sat cross-legged on the ground with his red-lacquered qin laid across his lap, his black robes pooling over the stone floor. His long hair was partly drawn into a jade ring, the rest spilling down his back. I could not see his face, bent down, as his hands slid across the instrument's strings deftly. His fingers stilled—halting the music—as his gaze swept up to mine. My insides twisted at the sight of his eyes, their silvery hue a jolting reminder of his betrayal.

I struck first, channeling coils of air that spiraled toward him. As he leapt to his feet, his body swerved gracefully in evasion. Without a pause, I lunged at him, a dagger in my hand—but he caught my wrist in midair, in an iron grip. I snatched the second dagger from my sash and slammed its tip against his chest just as a shield glimmered over him. It sparked against the blade, a shock coursing through my arm. As my fingers jerked apart, the dagger fell, striking the floor with a clatter. We stood there, locked in place, unsated rage swelling in my chest until I could barely breathe.

"This is a better reception than I anticipated." He grinned unrepentantly. "If you really wanted to kill me, you would have used your bow."

"A dagger would hurt more." Gritting my teeth, I drove my knee into his gut. As he flinched, I wrenched free of his hold—stepping back, out of reach. At once I cast a shield over myself, gleaming as it settled over me.

He tilted his head to one side. "Did you like my playing?"

"As little as I did the last time." My fingers curled by my side. "Leave. Don't come back."

"After all these months of hiding away, of avoiding me, did you come here just to tell me that?"

"I was not hiding; I have no wish to ever see you again."

His expression was inscrutable. "You seem angrier than the last time we met here."

"What do you mean? Was it not a dream?" I demanded.

He paused. "Yes and no."

"An infuriating answer," I said scornfully. "What despicable magic did you use?"

"I would not do such a thing to you," he said tightly. "I did not toy with your mind, just your surroundings."

I did not want to ponder his words nor the meaning in them. "A needless effort."

"I disagree." He spoke with an infuriating assurance. "You would not have come otherwise."

My eyes narrowed as I recalled the silver pin, lying in the drawer I had tossed it into. "Why the pin?"

A small smile formed upon his lips. "I thought you might appreciate the memento. You almost ripped my throat out with it."

"It was a shame I missed."

"You did not miss. I stopped you."

"How brave you were, restraining a helpless captive," I taunted.

"You are anything but helpless." His smile widened. "Call it self-preservation on my part. I liked my throat where it was, intact."

As he moved toward me, I unslung my bow. "Another step, and you'll get that arrow you so richly deserve. Why are you here? You must know I want nothing to do with you."

He tensed, almost imperceptibly. "To offer my congratulations. When is the wedding?"

"There is no wedding," I replied unthinkingly, regretting the words once they were out.

Light flared in his eyes, startlingly bright. "Did he not propose or have you not accepted? According to the rumors, few could conceive of you refusing, though nothing would delight me more."

"I did not refuse." My tone was sharp, my nerves taut. He had a way of stirring me that I did not like. "I *will* accept, once we resolve certain matters."

"Like how you might stop Their Celestial Majesties from trying to murder you, their intended daughter-in-law? Ask yourself, does the present empress appear content with her lot? Or whether you could really be happy, locked in the gilded cage of the Jade Palace for the rest of your days?"

"Fine words from the one who locked me up before." I infused each word with scorn, concealing how close he had struck to the mark.

A dull flush crept up his neck. "Xingyin, don't marry him."

"How *dare* you," I seethed. "You are nothing to me, less than nothing after what you did."

"Could you forgive me?" A strain in his voice, which was usually so steady. "If only we could start over—"

"There is no starting over, it *is* over, Wenzhi." Something pulsed through me as I spoke his name. A vestige of the past, something I must learn to quench. "I *am* happy. You thought you knew me but you did not. You only saw in me what you wanted, a tool you could mold to your liking."

"As you did in me," he countered. "Did you ever see the real person behind the Celestial Captain? Did you ever try? Or was I just a stand-in for—"

"Enough." I raised my voice, careless in my fury. "We were both mistaken in each other, and regardless, 'we' are at an end."

He shook his head. "We had a bad start, you and me. Both of us were liars and frauds, hiding who we really were."

"Bad start?" I repeated disdainfully. "Don't play word games with me. Don't try to diminish what you did. And don't you dare compare us. I did it because I had to, not because I wanted to."

"As did I."

"You did it for yourself. Your ambition. To take a crown."

His jaw clenched. "I'm not one for futile tolerance, to meekly accept my lot. I seek my own opportunities, make my own luck. Why should I let myself and those under my protection suffer when my brother was the heir? Why shouldn't I reach for more?"

His words mirrored uncomfortably what I had felt before; the ambition burning in me when I had fled to the Celestial Kingdom. Could I truly fault Wenzhi for this? Perhaps I had not suffered as he had—who knows what I might have been driven to do, to keep myself and my loved ones safe. Who knows what darkness might have bloomed in my heart, the honor I might have discarded to survive.

No, I told myself. I had been tempted, I had faced unspeakable danger and yet, I had not lost myself. I was *not* like him.

"This is not about ambition. I fought for what I wanted, but never intended to hurt anyone. While you—" I could not finish the sentence, choked by the memory of his betrayal.

"I never wanted to hurt you." His eyes pierced mine, pale ash in the moonlight. "I was mistaken in thinking there was nothing more important than the crown. I know now, there is nothing more important to me than you."

He spoke with such sincerity, as though he had not lied to me and taken me captive, stolen the dragon pearls, and along with them, my hope of freeing my mother. Not to mention his vicious plan of destroying the Celestial Army. He had let Liwei and me go, but that did not erase what he had done. I could never forget how he had clasped my hands in his and promised me his heart—and how much I had desired it then, ignorant of the treachery that lay within.

I dug my nails into the flesh of my palm. "I do not care. I want nothing from you." If I was vicious, he had made me so. His was no minor offense that could be swept aside; my nature was neither so magnanimous nor forgiving.

"Then why are you here? Why are you talking to me?" He was relentless. Yet there was a shift in that he did not push forward, merely standing his ground.

"Anger. Curiosity," I flung back. "Why do you come here? Not just tonight, all the nights before."

"Need you ask? For a chance to see you." A harsh breath slid from him. "I regret what I did to you."

"Easily said when you have accomplished everything you set out to. You are your father's heir; the kingdom will be yours."

His gaze pinned mine. "Ask me to relinquish it. Tell me what you want."

"Would you truly give up your position?" My voice rang with disbelief.

He did not flinch. "Is that what it will take for you to give me another chance?"

"More word games, Wenzhi? Must you always play to win?"

"You play the same way."

"You are wrong," I told him. "There are some games I will not play. Sometimes those who think they have won are the greatest losers."

"I just want to understand the stakes," he countered.

"It's finished. We both lost."

He regarded me in silence for a moment. "I did not think you would run. I never took you for a coward."

The silken bite in his tone stung. It was what he wanted, to goad me into retaliation, into saying something I should not, but I reined in my emotions. "I am not a coward, just not a fool."

He sighed. "I don't want to fight with you, Xingyin. I wronged you. I wish to make amends if you will let me. If there is anything you desire, you have but to ask."

He was so proud, I never thought to hear such an admission from him. Even knowing all I did, my pulse quickened, a familiar ache rising within. If only I could erase the foolish, sentimental part of me that still cared, that should have died the moment I learned his true nature.

But could we truly hate those we had loved before? I was learning that such a transformation was not as seamless as I had hoped. Wenzhi was right; I had wanted to hurt him, to chase him from my home, to cut him from my life . . . yet I did not really want his death. Not then, and not now. However, forgiveness was a different matter. I was still furious; I could never trust him again. Any tenderness I had felt, any hope for a future was irrevocably destroyed. Yet I could not deny that his offer tempted me, for I was not one to toss away an opportunity. If danger lay ahead, I would do all I could to arm myself against it.

I walked to the balustrade and rested my elbows against the cool stone, staring at the luminous earth that stretched beneath us like the starlit sea. "I am only speaking to you now because you let Liwei and me go, because your plan failed. If you had truly cost me my freedom and that of my mother, I would shoot you now without hesitation."

"Would you really?" His voice lifted with challenge.

Anger seared me as I spun to leave, but he moved in front of me.

"Wait. I'm sorry." He stretched his arms wide. "You may aim at your leisure."

I glared at him, my fingers tightening around my bow. "That I don't, for now, does not mean we're friends or even less than enemies. Nor do I despise you any less."

"Not friends. Less than enemies?" A mocking lilt to his tone. "You are generous indeed."

"More than you deserve. But know this: I will *never* forget your treachery. I will never forgive you. This is as far as things will ever go between us."

He inclined his head. "I understand, though I will endeavor to change your mind."

The wind surged then, tossing my unbound hair, our robes fluttering wildly. He shrugged off his outer robe and offered it to me. I did not accept, staring at it like it was a venomous snake.

"I need information," I said instead. "What recent news have you heard of the Celestial Court?" As the heir to the Demon Realm, his reach went far; they would be certain to keep close watch over their greatest rival and foe.

He sighed as he pulled his robe back over himself. "There

was another reason I came tonight. Why I was more . . . insistent. Beware the newly elevated Celestial general. According to my sources, he has a keen interest in you."

"General Wu? Beyond the fact he wanted the emperor to sentence me to death?" My gut clenched. Wenzhi was not one to issue such warnings lightly. Moreover, I had been unsettled ever since learning of Shuxiao's troubles. "Why do you believe this?"

"He keeps a careful eye on those close to you, on your home. He studies books of this place. He has turned the emperor's attention here."

A coldness spread from the pit of my stomach. Part of me wanted to confide in him, just as I used to. Though I bore the scars of his deceit, he might know something of use. Slowly at first, I told him of the laurel, my words flowing easier toward the end.

"Was the intruder trying to destroy the tree or harvest its seeds?" he asked.

The first possibility had not occurred to me, but I recalled Master Gang's deliberate pause after each strike. This had been no frenzied attack intent on destruction. "He wanted the seeds. Fortunately, it seemed a laborious task, taking several blows to dislodge one. There was blood, his blood, staining his hands and the tree."

"Why don't you show me the laurel?" When I did not reply, he added, "I just want to help you. I swear this on my life."

"You have sworn many things to me before."

"I am not who I was then."

I did not believe him, already probing his face and tone for trickery. I did not think he had changed; he would say anything to obtain what he wanted. However, I wanted the assessment of his keen mind. Something gnawed at me, that it would be a betrayal of sorts to allow him into my home—both of Liwei and myself. But I was on the alert; I would not be caught unaware. And if he betrayed me again, he would pay in full this time.

ALL WAS SILENT, EXCEPT for the careful tread of our feet. I was relieved for the lateness of the hour, that everyone was asleep, that I did not need to explain his presence to my mother or Ping'er. Wenzhi stared at everything intently—whether a silk-paneled lamp, the painted screens, or a carved wooden table. Outside, he paused, gazing at the silver roof, the glowing earth, the forest of moon-white osmanthus.

"I have wondered about your home," he said quietly. "It is beautiful."

I nodded curtly in reply, unwilling to engage in conversation with him.

As we walked through the trees, the light from the lanterns threw our shadows across the ground. Neither of us spoke again until we arrived at the laurel, its seeds glistening like fallen stars caught in the web of branches. Wenzhi pressed his palm against the smooth bark before yanking hard at a seed. It did not break away, though the leaves trembled and the branch dipped from his force.

"The energy in this tree is strange. Cold, as most things are here, but also discordant—as though there are two sides to the whole," he observed.

"What does that mean? What can it do?"

"I'm not sure." He frowned. "Upon your return here, did you notice anything different?"

I hesitated before saying, "My lifeforce recovered quicker than anticipated. I thought it some mysterious power only obvious to me now that mine had been unsealed."

His hand swept toward the laurel. "Except it came from this."

Regeneration, Liwei had said. Why would the emperor crave such power? The Jade Palace thronged with healers. I stole an assessing glance at Wenzhi, trying to discern if the light in his eyes was concern or avarice—

"Xingyin, do you suspect me still?" His mouth twisted into a wry smile. "I have no wish to be your enemy again."

"What of next time?" I asked. "What if our desires were to collide once more? Undoubtedly your self-interest would reign."

"It will not," he said flatly.

"How can you be certain?"

"Because I will not allow it. To set myself against you, would be akin to going against myself." He paused. "When I hurt you . . . it hurt me too."

I stared at his unyielding face, taken aback by the implacable way he spoke. No words rose to mind, neither protest nor insult.

"Despite what you think, I'm not bloodthirsty by nature. Nor do I crave power for its sake alone. Now I hope to convince my father that peace is the best recourse. The price of war is far too high, even for the victor."

In our battles together, Wenzhi had never taken undue pleasure in a conquest or relished an enemy's defeat. His decisions were calculated to reduce bloodshed, even when he served in the army of his enemy. And I believed that at least for now, he wanted to help, that he did not mean me harm.

His head jerked up, his eyelids lowering. I stilled, sensing the approach of an immortal's aura, though there had been no warning from the wards.

Liwei was here.

A knot formed in my chest. I had no desire to repeat their last encounter when swords were drawn. While I had my years of comradeship with Wenzhi to balance against his offenses, Liwei would view him—rightfully so—as a traitor and a threat.

Wenzhi inclined his head. "I have no wish to cause trouble." Before I could respond, a shimmer glided over him, shrouding him from sight. A moment later, a light breeze wound through the trees as Wenzhi's aura vanished. He had left as suddenly as he had appeared.

My tension eased, even as guilt followed swiftly on its heels. Liwei emerged from the trees, coming toward me. A gray robe was thrown over his white inner garments, knotted loosely at the waist. He must have left in haste.

"I sensed someone coming through the wards. At this hour, I wanted to make sure it was nothing untoward." He smiled. "Was it another uninvited 'guest'?"

It was the first time Wenzhi had visited since the wards were altered. My head poised to nod, a ready lie springing to my tongue—how easily they came to me now. Yet I could not deceive him so lightly.

"It was Wenzhi." I braced for disapproval.

A brief pause. "Has he come before?"

His face was calm despite the tautness in his tone. I almost longed for his anger instead. Something to rouse my own emotions from this sinking sensation of having disappointed him.

"He has," I admitted. "I refused to see him."

His expression was stony. "Why this time?"

I fell silent, reluctant to tell him of the music. Of the things Wenzhi and I had spoken on the balcony.

"Did you ask him to come?" he pressed.

"No."

"You did not turn him away either."

Liwei thrust a hand through his hair, the dark strands gleaming against his white robe. How this reminded me of the time he had rushed to my room from his bed, in the Courtyard of Eternal Tranquility. When he had kissed me with such hunger and tenderness, awakening the passion that burned in me still. Yet tonight, his expression was far from that of a lover's.

"I thought you despised him, that you never wanted to see him again. And now I find you taking a midnight stroll together—"

"It's not like that," I said tightly, fighting back the sting of shame. "He wanted to see the laurel. I thought he could help."

"You told him? You trust him? After everything he did?" His shock rang clear.

I lifted my chin. "I don't trust him, but he might be able to aid us. He wants to make amends." How feeble this sounded when spoken aloud; lies told to children to secure their trust.

"All he is doing is playing a different game because the rules have changed, and he still wants to win," Liwei argued.

"He is not a friend, but he might be an ally. Isolated as we are, I am in no position to turn any away," I said steadily.

"You have me by your side." Liwei clasped my hand. "I trust you; it's him I don't trust. Promise me you will be careful."

"I will," I said gravely.

"Perhaps I should adjust the wards again, to bar *certain* unwanted intruders." His voice lightened; gone was the last trace of anger.

I laughed, relieved that the worst had passed. "Perhaps *all* outsiders should be barred from entry."

"I hope to not be an outsider for much longer." His knuckles brushed my cheek, feather-light, gliding down my neck. "Next week is my father's birthday celebration. Would you accompany me?"

I swallowed hard, biting back my instinctive protest. It felt more like an invitation to an execution than a banquet.

He drew away to stare into my face. "This is a chance to

mend bridges and heal old wounds. For them to know you as I do."

"I will go," I said, even as my insides curled. I could not insult his parents with my refusal; I could not make Liwei choose between us. By accepting him, I accepted them, and somehow we would have to learn to exist together, no matter our past offenses.

I just hoped *they* understood that too.

Perhaps at the banquet I might be able to soften the Celestial Emperor's suspicions, to show him I was no threat—it was easier to malign those unseen and unheard. And if not, I might learn something more of his intentions. Too many things were happening at once: the shift of power in the Celestial Army. The theft of the laurel seeds. The emperor's interest in my home. The pieces were set on the board, and I only wished I knew what game was being played.

One thing was for certain; I was done being a pawn, and if I moved, it would be of my own volition.

5

THE EVENING WAS CLEAR AND calm; not a single cloud would have dared to mar the Celestial Emperor's celebration. Liwei and I landed by a mirrored lake, embraced by lilac-gray mountains and graceful cypresses. Gold-tipped lotuses bloomed upon the waters, illuminated by hundreds of floating candles, their light spilling across the waves like ribbons of flame. A crowd of immortals had already gathered within a large pavilion, its roof of malachite tiles gleaming beneath the starlit sky. Stone peonies encircled the base of each gilded column, so intricately carved and painted, they seemed to spring from the ground. Glowing lanterns were strung up between the trees from which clusters of bells cascaded, tinkling with the breeze.

My spirits lightened at the sight of the gaiety, having dreaded another stiff banquet in the Hall of Eastern Light, a place that brought back too many troubling recollections.

"What is this place?" I asked.

"Luminous Pearl Lake. When the moon is full, as it will be tonight, its reflection upon the waters is exquisite," Liwei said.

I straightened the sash around my waist that held together my azure silk robe. As my fingers brushed the embroidered magnolias, they swayed like a breeze had swept through, raining silken petals that morphed from white to rose. It was beautiful, yet for this evening's company I would have preferred my bow slung across my back.

When we entered the pavilion, the conversation dwindled to a hush. Guests turned to us before stepping aside, clearing a path to Their Celestial Majesties. They appeared as twin pillars of flame, seated upon carnelian thrones, draped in vermilion robes sewn with dragons and phoenixes encircled by rolling clouds.

Sweat broke out over my palms. I wanted to leave but forced myself onward. Before the thrones, I clasped my hands and lowered myself to the floor. As I bowed my head, the silver pins in my hair pinched where they pulled tight. Ping'er's deft fingers had twisted my hair into intricate coils that lent me the illusion of belonging amid this dazzling crowd, at least for the night.

"Your Celestial Majesties, I wish you a joyous celebration." My greeting paled in light of the other extravagant compliments offered, but anything more elaborate would have stuck in my throat.

A long silence followed before I lifted my head to the emperor. Strands of pearls clicked above those stony eyes, glinting with the embers of a simmering wrath. My skin prickled with an echo of the torment the emperor had inflicted upon me, his Sky-fire stabbing like a thousand tiny blades.

"Rise. You are welcome." The emperor's tone was gracious, his expression morphed into a mask of calm. Had I imagined that flash of rage? He acted as though we were meeting for the first time, as though I had never defied him and he had not tried to kill me for it. Perhaps it was better this way . . . if only I could believe it was true.

The empress did not hide her emotions so well. She uttered no words of greeting, her lips mashed into a scarlet bud. The gold headdress on her hair was exquisitely crafted into peonies, studded with pink tourmalines that darkened to the shade of congealed blood as though reflecting her thoughts.

A smile hid my turmoil, the dread entwined with hostility I had always felt around Their Celestial Majesties. They would never be as family to me, yet for Liwei, I did not want us to be enemies. I was glad when another came forward to claim their attention, relieved to leave so cold a reception. I had expected no less, and how I wished the evening had already ended. Would this be my life if I married Liwei—this endless churn of unease, of hollow words and false praise? How would I bear it?

Someone called my name, rousing me from my daze. It was General Jianyun, and for the first time tonight my smile was un-feigned.

I cupped my hands and bent from my waist in greeting. "Have you been well, General Jianyun?"

"Well enough. I trust His Highness has informed you of the recent events? The coils are tightening, though around what I do not know."

There were lines on his face that had not been there before, etched with new cares. "Perhaps the emperor will see reason," I said, trying to ease his worries.

"While I have angered His Celestial Majesty on occasion, I have only ever acted in his best interests and those of our king-dom. Which is more than I can say for others."

General Jianyun was typically discreet; he must be under great strain indeed to make such revelations. As his gaze shifted behind me, his mouth drew taut. From the corner of my eye, I caught a glimpse of gray brocade, gold embroidery winking from the hem and sleeves. And those gloves—only one person in the Celestial Court wore them.

"General Wu." General Jianyun's head dipped in a curt nod.

This close, his aura swept across my senses—opaque, dense, and oddly reminiscent. Hardly surprising after our encounters at the Celestial Court, my insides knotting at the recollection of the vile things he had said of my mother and me. He was already turning my way, his lips peeling back into a grin, the jade ornaments clinking by his waist. Something else was nestled among them: a bamboo flute dangling from his sash, its tassel a bright green.

My gaze darted to his eyes. How could I have overlooked their sharp glint, even shaded by white brows and masked by a lined face? Anger pulsed at my forehead, a redness descending over my vision as I reached out to grab his glove. He jerked back as I wrenched it free, revealing dark scars streaked across his palm, the same ones on Master Gang as he had hacked away at the laurel.

"You!" At the thought of him sitting beside my mother, speaking and laughing with her—bile rose in my throat.

"Xingyin, what do you mean?" Liwei's tone was guarded. A reminder that I had few allies here, and none the emperor might listen to.

Whispers slithered all around. I steeled myself for condemnation, for the guests to rush to the general's defense. None did. While some glared at me, just as many scornful glances lingered upon General Wu as though savoring his humiliation. Some raised their sleeves, exchanging malicious whispers. I had always felt an outsider at the Celestial Court, but was not the general one of their own? Why did they not accord him the same deference as General Jianyun?

The glove was snatched from my grasp. General Wu tugged it back down over his hand, his fingers shaking a little. "Your manners leave much to be desired."

"Courtesy is reserved for those who deserve it. Not for liars and thieves." I spoke as steadily as I could.

"Xingyin, have you mistaken the general for someone else?" General Jianyun asked.

"There is no mistake." I turned to Liwei. "Those scars on his hand are the same as Master Gang's. Don't you recognize his flute?" It was the first time I had seen it on him. Perhaps it was not something he wore with his ceremonial court attire.

Liwei frowned as he stared at General Wu, as though searching for the resemblance between this haughty courtier and the frail visitor to the moon.

"He masked himself, his hair and face." A simple disguise, yet cunning, as a more elaborate enchantment might have been detected.

General Wu faced Liwei as he asked in ringing tones, "Your Highness, do you wish for your father's festivities to be disrupted by these groundless accusations?"

He was a master at deception, his expression conveying nothing but righteous outrage. I struggled to contain my anger, tempering my words. "I know what I saw. I know what you did."

Liwei's fingers tightened around mine in a reassuring grip. "General Wu, if you tricked your way into the Moon Goddess's domain, it would be a violation of hospitality. A dishonest and underhanded act." He spoke in his cold, imperial voice—edged with a calculated detachment. This was one of those court games where he had to appear impartial to sway opinion.

General Wu spread his hands wide. "I am your father's loyal servant who obeys his every command. If my actions have caused offense, Your Highness should address your concerns to him."

A veiled threat that he had the emperor's support. And he must be high in favor, to show such little respect to Liwei.

"Be certain that I will," Liwei replied tersely.

General Wu bent in a shallow bow. "If you would excuse me, Your Highness. I must attend to your father." Without waiting for a dismissal, he strode away.

"Wugang has grown bold," General Jianyun remarked with distaste. "Few would dare gainsay him now when he, alone, has the emperor's ear."

"Wugang?" I repeated uncertainly.

"General Wu," General Jianyun explained. "Wugang is his rightful name. How I first knew him, though he prefers not to be called so."

General Wu. Master Gang. He had not lied; both names were his. The devious courtier turned ambitious general. The woodcutter and the thief.

"Why do you think Wugang came to my home?" It gave me a petty satisfaction to use the name he disdained, and a part of me wondered whether the noble general felt the same way.

"It must have been at the emperor's command. He does nothing without His Celestial Majesty's permission." General Jianyun added, "The emperor would send no other there, for Wugang is most familiar with the moon, given his past."

I stared at him. "What do you mean?"

"It was long before your mother ascended to the skies. Wugang was a mortal then."

"A mortal? I did not hear of this." Liwei echoed my surprise.

"As Wugang is the current favorite, His Celestial Majesty prefers that such humble origins be forgotten. Wugang is ever obedient, discarding part of his name to disassociate himself from his past."

"The mortals would be glad of it," I said with feeling, smothering my ire at how immortals often disdained those in the world below. In truth, the mortals could teach us far more in resilience and strength of will, as they bore the trials that came their way.

General Jianyun smiled faintly. "I would agree."

"How did Wugang come to our realm?" Liwei asked.

The corners of General Jianyun's eyes creased like he was reaching deep into his thoughts. "Wugang was a common man with an uncommon grudge. His wife had an affair with an immortal, the son of a Celestial courtier. When Wugang discovered her infidelity, he did not confront the perpetrators—instead, he set off to Kunlun Mountain."

I quashed a flash of pity for the hurt he must have felt. "Did he venture there to seek recompense? Was that how he became immortal?" Kunlun Mountain possessed a powerful mystical energy, and was the only place in the Mortal Realm where immortals were permitted to dwell.

General Jianyun shook his head. "The only way a mortal can become immortal is through His Celestial Majesty's elixir. Wugang's plans were far more nefarious. In Kunlun, he befriended an immortal and learned our secrets: that we were not invulnerable, that we could be killed by the weapons and magic of our realm. After that, he stole the immortal's axe, using it to slay his wife and her lover."

My skin crawled. How cold and ruthless he was, how terrifyingly patient. *My wife. She was fond of music,* he had said, speaking of her in the past. I had thought nothing of it then because of his unwavering calm—when in truth, he had murdered her with his own hands.

"He should have been sentenced according to mortal law," General Jianyun continued. "Except the victim's father, the Celestial courtier, beseeched the emperor for vengeance, citing the shame of an immortal killed by a weak mortal. Persuaded by his pleas, the emperor summoned Wugang to the Jade Palace and sentenced him to chop down the everlasting laurel, using the very axe he had taken."

A lump formed in the pit of my stomach. "The laurel on the moon?"

"It was different then, its leaves as green as jade. There were no seeds, not as there are now. Yet it was no ordinary tree, possessing the power to heal itself. And Wugang soon discovered that this undertaking was a futile, never-ending torment."

An impossible task. "How did Wugang earn the elixir?"

"He was given an Immortal Peach at first, not to prolong his life but to extend his suffering. The Elixir of Immortality was promised, if he succeeded. A disingenuous offer, for how could a mortal perform such a deed? For over a hundred years, Wugang toiled, without a moment's respite. 'Wugang the Woodcutter,' the court mocked him, as they lauded the emperor's cunning. Some arranged viewing parties where they would laugh as he strained over his labor. I attended one and wished I had not. There is no pleasure in taunting one brought low, who cannot fight back."

Little wonder that the Celestials treated Wugang with a mixture of loathing and fear, and their malice must have been worse before he rose to power. "Did the emperor take pity on him and rescind the punishment?"

General Jianyun's expression was grave. "Perhaps it was inevitable after the years of hacking at the laurel that a bond was formed between the tree and its tormentor. Wugang discovered that his blood could halt the laurel's healing—at least temporarily. He requested the emperor's presence to witness the fulfillment of his task, despite knowing failure would earn him a death sentence. The court followed eagerly, many certain it was an empty boast. How frail Wugang looked, worn to a shadow of the strapping mortal who had arrived, his hands ravaged by welts and wounds."

"Is that why he wears those gloves? To hide the scars?" I asked.

General Jianyun nodded. "Wugang is proud, though he conceals it. He would loathe such a visible reminder of his humiliation." His tone grew heavy. "I recalled his face as he slashed his hand: blank with despair, devoid of hope—like he did not care whether he lived or died. Blood spurted out, splattering the laurel's bark, sinking into the soil around its roots. In the next moment, he swung his axe into the tree. Again and again, without pause, as though his labors had granted him an inhuman strength. Until, at last, the laurel came crashing down, the sound so loud the mortals must have heard it."

I frowned. "But the laurel still stands; it was not destroyed."

"His Celestial Majesty's command was that Wugang had to *chop down* the laurel, not to destroy it—if such a thing can be done at all. It only took a few moments for the laurel to regenerate, new shoots sprouting from its withered stump, springing up until the tree was full-grown once more. Except its leaves were no longer green but silver-white, its bark so pale, like it was encrusted in frost. As though in its throes of death, the laurel had shed spring for winter."

My mind spun. This must be why Wugang had such an avid interest in the moon, a personal one—studying its aura, discovering my presence. Why he had not troubled himself with me until he learned my identity. "The laurel's power must be immense to regenerate so quickly, to restore my lifeforce too."

General Jianyun's expression was somber. "We thought it could only heal itself. We did not realize it could heal another."

"What does the emperor want with it?" I asked.

The corners of the general's mouth dipped. "I have lost His Majesty's trust. He no longer confides in me."

Something else picked at me. "Wugang's blood was on the laurel the night I caught him. While there were grooves in the bark, the tree was otherwise unharmed. I can't imagine how he could have brought it down before."

The general's lips pursed. "Since that day, the energy in the tree has changed. While the laurel's power has strengthened, its bond with Wugang might have weakened. Maybe he can no longer harm it as before."

"Only enough to harvest its seeds." An unwelcome thought. "Why would His Celestial Majesty send Wugang? The emperor could have seized our home if he wished."

"Because His Celestial Majesty's position is no longer unassailable. Too many eyes are upon him, and voices that were long silent have been roused to question." General Jianyun paused, rubbing his chin contemplatively. "The gods among us bear an additional burden—the desire to be worshipped, whether through fear or love. While they might believe themselves above such things, they dread its loss. Other immortals, such as us, have fewer concerns. We care less how our actions appear to the world, and whether we will be maligned or adulated."

"Too jarring a move might also alert our enemies," Liwei observed. "If they descend upon the moon, it might cause an unwanted tussle. My father's hands are tied for now, unless he has just cause."

I would not give it to him. While the laurel's power seemed benign, to heal instead of harm—I did not trust the emperor's intentions.

A clang reverberated through the air, a gong struck by a mallet. Everyone turned toward the thrones where the empress had risen, raising her jade cup high. "A toast to His Celestial Majesty, the Emperor of the Immortal Heavens. To ten thousand years more of his glorious reign. Tonight, the moon shines brightly in his honor."

With a sweep of the empress's hand, the malachite roof disintegrated into shards—scattering into the night like emerald fireflies. Yet where the moon should have glowed in its full glory was a void of darkness.

As I searched the sky frantically, gasps erupted from the guests, their upturned faces taut with shock and foreboding. Whispers swirled through the air like a pestilent wind.

"Where is the moon? It should have risen long before."

"An eclipse, on His Celestial Majesty's birthday? An ill omen indeed!"

"What does Chang'e intend with this insult?"

At the last, ice seeped into my bones. My mother . . . what had happened to her? Never had she abandoned her task of illuminating the moon—not through heartbreak, grief, or loss. I spun to the entrance but my feet would not move, as though they were embedded in stone.

"Daughter of the Moon Goddess, what do you and your mother mean by this?" The empress's fingers were clenched around her cup.

"I must go to my mother. She might be in danger!" Again, I tried to move, struggling against her enchantment. I gathered my energy to break it but caught Liwei's eye, that slight shake of his head in warning. To use my magic here would be in blatant defiance of Their Celestial Majesties' command. I had to tread carefully, at least for now.

General Wu stepped forward, his features arranged into a veneer of solemnity. "Chang'e is daring indeed to bring about such an ominous omen, this terrible insult to our beloved emperor. Unsurprising, as we are all aware of the Moon Goddess's grudge against Their Celestial Majesties."

How dare he malign my mother who had treated him so graciously? I swallowed a furious retort, casting my eyes down in a guise of humility—though inside, I burned. It was safer if Their Celestial Majesties thought us meek and afraid, rather than vengeful and proud.

"My mother bears Your Celestial Majesties no ill will," I protested.

"What of you?" General Wu interjected.

"I . . . I do not wish Your Celestial Majesties ill." The barest crack in my tone, yet all in this discerning court heard what remained unspoken: that I did not wish Their Celestial Majesties well either.

Liwei clasped his hands together and bowed. "Honorable Father, Mother. Xingyin and her mother are no threat to you. Allow us to find the Moon Goddess, to ensure her safety and request an explanation."

The emperor's expression hardened, his knuckles white over the carnelian armrest. "Liwei, do you not care for your own family and the insult paid to us today?"

That tone, curling with menace, was the one that echoed in my worst nightmares, the moment before he had struck me down.

"Honorable Father, they mean you no harm. Those of the moon only wish to protect their home." Liwei spoke calmly, and I was glad for his steadiness in times as these, when my emotions crested and broke.

"Enough, Liwei," the empress said sternly, despite her pallor. As she threw her hand out, the air between us gleamed with magic, the enchantment on my feet loosening. "She can go. *You* must stay for your father's celebration."

"You say they mean no harm, Your Highness," General Wu said silkily to Liwei. "How do you know what thoughts lurk in their minds? Or perhaps you do not care, your loyalties clouded by your feelings—"

"Remember your place, General," the empress snarled. "Do not reach above yourself. My son is not to blame."

"Of course." He bowed, even as an insidious smile stretched over his lips. "His Highness must have been deceived."

How strange to see them at odds when they had united against me in such accord before. Yet the empress was vigilant against those who threatened her son, even past allies. My throat closed tight at the skillful picture General Wu was painting: my mother and I, treacherous and false, while Liwei was a fool whose opinion was to be disregarded.

I raised my voice to be heard. "This is an innocent mistake, Your Celestial Majesty—"

The emperor's hand shot up, silencing me. His lips were ringed with white, his eyes bulging. "Liwei, where do your loyalties lie? With your family and kingdom, or this deceitful girl? I warned her once, there would be no mercy if Chang'e, or she, ever shirked their duties."

"Imperial Husband, Liwei does not mean that," the empress began, but when the emperor swung to her, she shrank back against her throne.

I tried again, desperate to leave. "Your Celestial Majesty. Let me find my mother to explain. Liwei is loyal to you—"

"His loyalties lie with *you*." The emperor's voice broke like thunder. "Liwei, you have been secure in your position for too long. Denounce her now, and prove your loyalty to your family."

Silence followed, unsullied by breath or whisper. It was as though a spell had been cast over the gathering, transforming everyone to stone. Could any father be so unfeeling toward their child? It was not a command—not yet—but a threat, a line drawn clear in the ground.

I touched Liwei's arm gently, my turn to caution him against rashness. "Stay here; I will go." I did not want to fracture his bond with his family, even as dread sank over me that it might be too late.

His hand covered mine, squeezing once before letting go. Sweeping his silver-and-white robes aside, he sank to his knees, folding over to press his palms and brow to the floor.

"Honorable Father, I am your loyal son and subject, but I will not denounce her. She has done no wrong to you or our kingdom." He rose to his feet, taking my hand—his skin no longer warm but like it had been pressed in the snow.

General Wu's eyes shone with a keen light, while a muffled cry slipped from the empress, her pale knuckles pressed against blood-red lips. Liwei's expression was bleak as we turned away, leaving behind the magnificent splendor of the Celestial Court.

Joy and sorrow twined like fire and ice in my chest—a crushing weight, a soaring lightness. While I had wanted Liwei unfettered by his obligations, I would never have asked this of him; his family and heritage were an intrinsic part of who he was. And though fear shadowed me at how the night's events had unraveled, for the moment, I indulged my wild dream of us living as freely as two cranes soaring into the boundless sky.

6

MY MOTHER WAS NOT HOME. I stared at the smooth covers of her bed, my slender hope that she had overslept shriveled away.

"Could she be in the forest?" Liwei wondered.

"She's not there; I searched for her aura as we flew over it." I turned to Ping'er. "What did Mother say when she left?"

"She asked me to summon a cloud for her. I had done it before and taught her how to ride it." Her face was ashen as she clasped her hands together. "Is the emperor angry? Surely it can't be that great an offense, forgetting to light the moon once in all these years?"

"I will light the lanterns in her stead," Liwei offered, evading her question.

"What use is that now?" Despair welled up as I recalled the empress's outrage, the guests decrying the "ill omen," and General Wu's spiteful accusations, all fanning the emperor's temper into a raging blaze.

"Better late to a task than to leave it undone," he said, striding toward the door.

I flushed at my thoughtless words. "Liwei, thank you," I called out to him.

He stopped by the entrance, a ghost of a smile on his lips.

"Xingyin, I have said before, there is no need for thanks between you and me." Without another word he left, his back straight, his shoulders pulled more taut than usual.

I searched my mother's room, as neat as always, the wooden shelves uncluttered except for a few plants and ornaments. A book lay on the table beside her bed, with an archer and the ten suns painted on its cover. The story of my father's legend, of how he had slain the sunbirds. A folded piece of paper lay beside it. I picked it up, startled to see the characters in unfamiliar strokes—who would have written to my mother? A violation to read something addressed to another, but perhaps this was a clue to her disappearance. Smoothing out the paper, my eyes darted across the characters:

Tonight, you will find what you seek in the
realm of mortals.

My chest clenched with foreboding. Racing to my room, I grabbed my bow, heading outside to summon a cloud. Careless, to not think of this before. Since regaining her freedom, there was one place my mother returned to whenever she could get away. Even though it was frowned upon, even though she risked punishment by entering the Mortal Realm without permission.

At the point where the two rivers merged, near where the Black Dragon had been imprisoned, rose a hill covered with white flowers like snow half-thawed in spring. A marble grave lay upon it, curved like a crescent, the characters of my father's name gleaming in gold. Ash crumbled from the glowing tips of incense sticks recently pressed into the brazier, their heady scent coiling in the air, thick with hope and grief. Offerings of apples, leafy mandarins, and sponge cakes were piled beside it, along with a slender sprig of osmanthus, its pale petals already rimmed with brown. My mother had been here, except where was she now?

With magic forbidden in the Mortal Realm, I ran down the hill, calling for her—along the river that smelled of earth and rot, before plunging into the forest where shadows darker than night crawled. Was I mistaken? Was she not here? It was then I sensed it, her aura fluttering like the wings of a frantic moth. Sprinting toward it, I almost crumpled with relief to find her wandering the outskirts of the forest, her steps stumbling and uncertain, her gaze hollow.

"Mother!" I embraced her, flinching from the chill that glazed her skin. "What happened? The lanterns were not lit tonight."

Her lips parted to whisper, "I received a note. It told me to come here."

"I read it," I admitted. "Who was it from?"

"There was no name. It was left on my table."

"A trick. Why else would someone leave a note this way, to deliver it in such a furtive manner?" If only I had sensed the intruder coming through the wards, but my attention had been diverted at the emperor's banquet.

"It was no trick. I saw your father. His hair was gray, he looked different . . . but I would recognize him anywhere." She lifted her eyes to me, huge and dark. "Why would he run from me? Why would he hide?"

Something prickled along my spine. "It's not possible. Father is dead."

"I know what I saw."

The tremor in her voice gave me pause. I stroked her back, trying to soothe away her anxiety, a reversal of the times she had comforted me before. I did not mention the emperor's wrath or the accusations flung our way. The damage was done, and what mattered most was that she was unharmed.

"I will help you find him," I told her.

Together, we combed the forest, the riverbank and hill—but there was no sign of life beyond the wild creatures who fled at our approach. When the golden shafts of dawn speared the night, I summoned a cloud to bring her home.

"I won't leave. It *was* him." Her words fell out in a cry.

"Mother, you must return," I said.

"Your father—"

"I will continue the search," I assured her. "You should leave. Rest. The Celestial Emperor might summon you at any moment."

She paled at the mention of the emperor, climbing upon the cloud without further protest. "What should I say?"

I thought quickly. "Tell him you overslept. Don't mention anything about coming to the Mortal Realm. His Celestial Majesty would not look kindly upon it. It is better he believes us incompetent than a challenge to his authority."

She nodded as her cloud ascended, borne upon a gentle breeze—though her eyes remained fixed below until she vanished into the heavens.

Guilt pierced me for sending her away, yet I could move quicker alone. More than that, I wanted her back in the safety of our home, fearing this had been a ruse to distract her into forgetting her duties, to incite the emperor's wrath . . . though I did not know why.

I scoured the forest again, alert for any trace of immortal energy or danger, following the path along the river until it wound toward a village. Only then did I turn around, making my way back to the hill. Beneath the lightening sky, before my father's grave, I knelt upon the stone. The faded paintings upon the marble were the mortals' renditions of my father's heroics: aiming an arrow at the ten crimson suns in the sky, riding at the head of a great army, battling a monstrous bird. A heaviness stole over me as I sank back onto my heels, tucking my hands into my lap.

"Father, I wish I knew you." I was unsure why I plucked these words from my heart and spoke them aloud. Perhaps it was the break of dawn, the moment despair is edged with hope. Or perhaps my guard was lowered, comforted by my father's presence even though it was just his bones that remained.

A twig snapped. I leapt to my feet, dragging the bow off my back, suppressing the urge to draw an arrow. Its magic might attract unwanted attention, and besides, there was little that could hurt me here.

A mortal stood at the bottom of the hill, long past the prime of life. His hair was the soft shade of ash, bound with a long strip of cloth. His skin was weathered and lined, bitterness reeking in the curl of his lip. Yet his shoulders were broad beneath his black robe, and he carried himself like a cypress. His steps toward me were measured, with a seasoned warrior's grace. As his eyes fell upon my bow, they widened visibly.

"Who are you?" Few came here these days. Perhaps when my father's deeds were fresh in their minds, the mortals had come in droves, bringing offerings of flowers and food. It was how the Black Dragon had learned of this place. However, mortal memories were short-lived. I did not doubt they still told the tales of Houyi in the teahouses, a fine legend to stir the crowds—but who would make the lonely trek here to honor a hero long fallen?

The man did not answer, his gaze startlingly bright as he stared at me. His chest heaved, his throat worked, though I could not tell whether he was trying to speak or stifle his words.

"Daughter, you are full grown," he said at last, his voice breaking with emotion.

I froze, forcing back that cresting lightness within. It could not be true. Oh, I wanted to believe him, I had dreamed of such a moment so many times before, until the Black Dragon's news had crushed my hopes. But I had learned deceptions could be uttered with a straight face, a warm smile might conceal malice, and that the most dangerous lies were those we most desperately wanted to be true.

"My father is dead," I told him flatly, quelling the pang in my heart.

He flinched like I had struck him. "He might as well be." The man swung around, his robe flaring as he strode away.

I stared at the bow slung over his shoulder, intricately carved from silver, the points of its limbs curved like fangs. Something pulsed through me, reminiscent of the first time I had seen the Jade Dragon Bow—though there was no pull this time, just the thrum of power.

This was no mortal weapon.

"Wait!" I cried out. "Your bow. Where did you get it from?"

He halted but did not turn. "It was given to me."

"By whom?" I found myself bracing for his answer.

"You know him as the Celestial Emperor," he said slowly. "Though it was poor recompense for everything else he took."

It was as though the breath was knocked from me, the strength sapped from my limbs. I sank down, shaking, though I was not cold—battling the reckless hope surging within when all I wanted was to unleash it, to write my future anew. One with my family whole, with both my mother and father.

"Impossible," I whispered.

His eyes creased with sorrow. "Daughter, you are mortal-born, yet immortality flows in your veins. Your home should be here, yet you live on the moon. You, more than anyone, should have learned that nothing is impossible."

I forced my mind to clear, to piece together the fragments of my thoughts. He was an archer. A mortal in the early winter of his life. He carried the silver bow from the legends—the one painted on my mother's book, upon this very grave. He knew who I was. And as I stared at his features, at the cleft in his chin . . . I knew him too.

This was no trick. More than anything I had reasoned, this was knowledge that sprang from within. There were so many things I wanted to say, countless more I had whispered in the solitude of my mind, and yet nothing emerged except this one, halting word from my throat.

"Father."

I bowed, fighting back the emotions that flooded me, the hot tears surging into my eyes. He was almost a stranger; he had never been a parent to me, as I had never been his daughter. We lacked the memories, the *living*, that gave such a bond its strength. And yet, deep down, there was this undeniable link between us—forged through flesh and blood and something more profound, impossible to decipher.

A brightness glazed his own eyes, a smile breaking out, softening the harsh angles of his face.

"My name is Xingyin. Mother named me for the stars." A strange thing for a daughter to tell her father, but perhaps he did not know and was unsure how to ask.

"A good name," he said hoarsely. "You're taller than your mother, though you have her look about you."

His words were tender, yet a jarring reminder that while we had been ignorant of his existence, he had been aware of us all along. "Mother grieves for you; she thinks you're dead. You must have seen her here. Why didn't you speak to her?" I could not suppress the accusation in my tone for the misery he might have spared her.

"I could not."

Was it regret that flashed across his face? Yearning, sorrow, or anger? I thought of how she had taken the elixir from him— the one he had earned, the one he had forsaken for her.

"Do you blame her? Me, for endangering her life?" A tentative question that I both longed and dreaded to learn the answer to.

He released a drawn breath. "I will admit, I was furious at first. When I saw her flying to the skies, I wondered, had it been her scheme all along to become immortal? A goddess? Only later did I realize my own mistakes: letting my fears silence hers, ignoring the doctors who said what I did not want to hear, which terrified me more than any battle I had fought. That's what comes of being revered—you start to believe you're infallible, that you can bend fate to your will. But there are some things in the world no power can alter."

He fell silent before adding, "I would have given the elixir to your mother had she asked it of me. I should have done so before."

"Why did you let everyone believe you had died?" I probed.

"In my last battle, I was struck down and lost consciousness. When I recovered, I found myself abandoned in a strange land. It took months before I made my way back, a shock to find news of my death abounded. However, there was also freedom in this, a chance to live for myself again without being commanded or begged to go where danger lurked." His gaze dropped to the ground. "I also hoped your mother might hear of my death. For even if she no longer loved me, she might come to pay her respects—out of obligation, if nothing else, so I might see her again."

A shadow fell over his face. "I waited. Eagerly at first, my mind turning over all we would say. I need not have bothered. The years crept up on me before I knew it. My hope grew tarnished with dread, then shame—that she would see me this way while she remained untouched by age. And when I finally saw her, it was too late." The tips of his fingers brushed his cheek, tracing the lines on them.

A tightness gripped my chest. Despite their parting, my parents loved each other still. "Don't blame her, Father. She could not come before."

"Why not?" He hurled the question as though it had haunted him all this time.

"She was punished by the Celestial Emperor for taking the elixir. She could not leave the moon until a year ago."

His fingers curled into a fist. "I should not be surprised. It was the Celestial Emperor who deceived me, sending me from my home with false promises and lies. Not this place, but my real home, in the Eastern Sea."

"*You* were immortal?" The moment the words came out, I flushed from their thoughtless cruelty.

"Long ago, before this mortal life."

"Father, what happened to you? Why did Mother not tell me?"

"She didn't know. Nor did I, then. When immortals are reborn in the world below, they lose their powers and memories— only regained once they are restored to the heavens." He unslung his bow as he lowered himself to the ground beside me.

"Was it common for immortals to be sent to the Mortal Realm?" I asked.

"It was most rare. While it can help strengthen an immortal's powers, few are willing to undergo the trials of a mortal life. It is only done in the gravest of circumstances with the Celestial Emperor's consent, for the elixir is needed to restore them to the heavens."

I glanced at the Jade Dragon Bow in my hands, recalling the recognition that had lit his face, the inexplicable bond that had always existed between me and this weapon. "Were you in the Eastern Sea with the dragons?"

His expression turned distant. "Some called me their ruler. A hollow title, as I never commanded them for my own ends."

My father was the fabled warrior who had saved the dragons, binding their essence to the pearls. How strange this cycle of fate that had led me down the same path, but to free the dragons instead. Was this why the bow had cleaved to me? As I ran a hand across its limb, light rippled through the jade. It pulsed in my grip, for the first time pulling away with a sudden eagerness, dispelling the last flicker of doubt from my mind.

I held it out to him, the jade bow lying across my upturned palms. "Father, is this yours?" Regret coiled in my stomach; I did not realize how attached I had grown to it.

A brief hesitation, before he pushed it away. The bow stilled, its light fading. "It is yours now. I have grown accustomed to mine; we have been through much together."

Relief—selfish and shallow—trickled through me as I lowered my hands. "Father, how did you end up in the Mortal Realm?"

A dangerous gleam sparked in his eyes. "The Celestial Emperor had long coveted the dragons' might. Maybe he was unaware of the constraints on their power, that they would die if he turned them into instruments of war. Maybe he didn't care. He was wary of me, though I gave him no cause, for I had no ambitions to rule as he did."

Dread traced its spidery touch along my skin. Another entanglement between Liwei's family and mine. Would we ever be free of them?

My father rubbed his fingertips against his brow. "The emperor summoned me. He brought forth the most respected elders in the kingdom, who swore the Mortal Realm faced a grave threat and that only I could save them."

"The sunbirds," I said slowly. "They were the cherished kin of the Celestial Empress. I thought the emperor allowed them to roam free to avoid angering her, but what if this was his ploy to trap and weaken you? To seize the might of the dragons?"

He nodded. "Such schemes would fit his nature, both cunning and grasping."

"Why did you believe him, knowing what you did?" I asked.

"Fool that I was, I did not ask too many questions—my pride stroked at so noble a cause. I believed those respectable Celestials who told me that to protect the mortals, I had to become one of them. Perhaps the emperor tricked them too—there is no better liar than those convinced they speak the truth. The emperor vowed he would protect me, that he would grant me the elixir once I fulfilled this quest. A sacred and unbreakable oath, sworn upon his honor and the lives of his descendants."

He drew a heavy breath before continuing, "And so, I accepted. I returned the pearls to the dragons—the last thing I did before drinking the tea of oblivion, which erased my memories before I was cast down to the Mortal Realm."

"How do you remember this if you drank the tea of oblivion?" I asked.

"A drop of elixir remained in the bottle. After your mother left, I swallowed it—though sometimes I wished I had not. It's no blessing to have such memories restored. Rage and grief are pitiless beasts that devour the heart and mind."

Something jarred me. "The dragons' ruler has been gone for centuries, while the sunbirds were shot down just a few decades ago."

"That was the depth of the emperor's deception," he seethed. "I was sent down far too early, living one mortal life after the other. Until finally, the foretold calamity arose, the ten sunbirds taking to the skies. An immortal appeared, gifting me this bow and a jade pendant to protect me from the sunbirds' flame. Even emperors must keep their word, especially those sworn upon the lives of their kin. Moreover, the dragons were no longer a threat to him, nor was I."

My fingers brushed the pendant around my neck, pulling it out. It was cracked, its power gone, though I wore it out of sentimentality. He stared at it, his throat working with sudden emotion.

"I gave that to your mother. I told her it would keep her safe, but I was wrong. No amulet could have protected her from the danger which threatened her," he said in a low voice. "The rest you've heard in the tales. I shot the sunbirds; I fulfilled the quest, believing myself a hero when I was the Celestial Emperor's dupe."

His face flushed with anger. Yet if he had not been tricked, he would never have met my mother. It was hard for me to mourn that which had given me life.

"I do not regret it," he said firmly.

"Because of Mother?"

"Because of you both. When the emperor bestowed the elixir upon me, I thought it a magnanimous gift, ignorant of the true reason behind it. Even if I had, it would have changed nothing."

"Except it was Mother who drank the elixir." Had the emperor's anger at this turn of events been a pretense to satisfy the court? Perhaps it was also to instill fear in those who thought of disobeying him. It struck me then, my father had been better protected as a mortal from the Celestial Empress's wrath, for immortals could not strike them without just cause.

"I should not have come," he said. "I stayed away for a while because to see your mother gave me as much pain as it did joy."

Tendrils of unease unfurled within me. "Why did you come today?"

"I received a note. I was curious, even as I sensed something amiss. Your mother seemed different today. Restless, like she was searching for something. Caught off guard, I was careless. She saw me before I hid."

Who had sent the note? Who had plotted for my mother to forget her duty? Wugang's gloating face swam across my mind, his readiness in accusing my mother of treachery at the banquet. Moreover, he knew our home, where to plant the letter—he could easily have instructed one of his servants. And he was familiar with this realm, having been mortal himself. Was this an elaborate scheme to give the emperor an excuse to fault us? My throat went dry at the thought.

"Daughter, it was selfish of me, but I wanted to speak to you just once. I didn't know if I would get another chance. Don't tell your mother. I do not wish to cause her more grief, to have her mourn me again."

A fit of coughing came over him, his body heaving as he pressed a piece of cloth to his mouth. When he dropped it down, it was soaked with a dark liquid. Blood. My insides wrenched tight.

"Father, are you ill?" When he did not reply, I imagined the numerous ailments that could end a mortal's life. Taking his hand, I channeled my magic sparingly to avoid detection. While I was no healer, I possessed some minor skills. I searched his body, seeking the cause of his discomfort. Yet I could find no bone to heal, no wound to staunch. Those sicknesses bred within the body, those ingrained in the flesh, I could not heal—for immortals did not suffer them. And even if I could, I could not protect my father from the greatest threat to his life, I could not return what time had stolen . . . unless I restored the immortality he had lost.

"Will the emperor give you the elixir again?" I asked urgently.

"He has fulfilled his obligation to me, he will never relinquish it again."

Despair swelled through me, heavy and bleak. "What can I do, Father?"

His smile struck the years away; I saw the man my mother had loved, with gentle humor and warmth in his eyes. Then the shadows descended once more, cloaking him in gray. "This is enough, more than I had hoped for—to see you this once, to hear you acknowledge me. Don't endanger yourself. There is nothing you can do, for the doctors say I have just a little time left."

I lifted my chin, studying the paintings of his accomplishments upon the marble grave. A miracle, and yet almost a curse, that I had found my father only to learn he was dying. Joy, tainted with the promise of sorrow. No, not a curse, I corrected myself—an opportunity. It was not too late, not while he lived. We had a chance to be a family again, to mend that which had been broken. A prize beyond my wildest dreams, though I did not delude myself into thinking it would be easily won.

"I am your daughter," I told him. "And I will bring you home."

7

F ROM THE MORTAL REALM, THE moon shone like a silver
disc against the black of night. My mother had completed
her task, though it would do little to assuage the Celestial
Emperor's wrath—a stark reminder of its absence yesterday. My
spirits sank at the thought of my mother and Liwei cast in his
disfavor; it would have mattered less had he been infuriated with
me alone. I had confronted his wrath before and survived—
though barely.

I could not let that daunt me now. My father was ill. Dying.
I had to help him, and who knew more about the mortals than
the Keeper of their Fates? He had been a teacher to Liwei and
me before, if only I had been a more attentive student. I could
have sought him in the Jade Palace, except there were too many
prying eyes and loose tongues. Fortunately, I was familiar with
his routine and how he descended to the world below each night.

I searched the sky eagerly but there was no sign of him.
Flicking the long blue panels of my robe aside, I sank upon the
cloud. A wide belt was fastened around my waist from which
hung my pouch and tassel. The sleeves tapered at my wrists,
bound by silk cord, enchanted to hold fast or unwind upon my
command. While less flattering than the gown I had worn to the
emperor's banquet, this attire was far better suited to my current

needs. Ping'er had helped me craft this garment with deliberate sighs and shakes of her head. I had returned home only briefly to change—keen to avoid my mother and Liwei, and the probing questions they might ask.

The air stirred, a cloud soaring ahead. A white-haired immortal clutching a jade staff stood upon it, with a younger woman beside him, her black hair coiled into a neat bun. I frowned, wishing the Keeper were alone. Stealthily, I tailed them through the skies, landing at the outskirts of a mortal town ringed by a gray stone wall. All was quiet at this late hour, dinners long eaten and beds filled with dreamers.

Leaping to the ground, I followed them at a discreet distance. When they stopped abruptly, I drew back into a cluster of bamboo, their stalks silvered by the moonlight.

"Who are you? Immortals are forbidden from coming here without good cause." The Keeper of Mortal Fates' tone rang with reprimand.

I stepped out, cupping my hands before me and bowing from my waist. "Honored Teacher." While he had not taught me for a long time, this bond linked us forever.

"Xingyin?" He spoke slowly, fragmenting my name. "Why are you here? Where is His Highness? Many are concerned for him."

I recalled the dense silence when Liwei had knelt before the thrones. "Perhaps they should have spoken up when it mattered."

"That is unfair. Only a year has passed since you left the Celestial Kingdom, surely you have not forgotten how things are there." His tone was stern, as though he were instructing me once more. "Who can challenge His Celestial Majesty without fear of repercussion? Would it have changed anything if another spoke up, or merely stirred the emperor's wrath? Do not scorn those who bide their time, awaiting the right opportunity to act.

Not all battles are won at the point of a sword, nor are they decided at the first strike."

I dropped my head. "Forgive me. I spoke rashly."

The Keeper sighed. "Please inform His Highness that while
the predators are circling, there are many who would support
him upon his return. Bear in mind, His Highness is most vulnerable when absent."

My teeth caught my lip as a selfish dread consumed me. I
would have been glad to see the last of the Celestial Court. Happiness seemed an elusive prospect, trapped beneath the censorious
judgment of Their Celestial Majesties, bound to a duty that did
not call to me. I had no loyalty to the Celestial Kingdom. What
did I care for the power that came alongside royalty, the chance to
leave your mark on the realm, to mold it to your beliefs? I would
choose a flowering forest or a tranquil shore over all the banquets
in heaven.

Yet Liwei's heritage was an integral part of him, interwoven
with his identity, honor, and pride. The emperor and empress
were his family, the only one he had. I could not ask him to give
them up, not even at the price of my happiness.

"I will tell him." I glanced at the woman, hoping she would
leave so I could speak freely. As the Keeper turned toward the
mortal town, I discarded caution. "Honored Keeper, I have a
private matter I wish to seek your advice on."

His gnarled fingers stroked his beard. "I trust Leiying, my
apprentice, in all matters."

Did he desire a witness to our meeting? I dared not imagine
what the emperor might do should he discover my father was
alive. I had to tread cautiously.

"Is the elixir the only way for a mortal to become immortal?" I kept my tone light as though this were idle curiosity.

"Yes."

My heart sank though I expected no less; it was as General Jianyun had said. "How might one obtain the elixir?" The question came out too quickly, my urgency unmistakable.

His gaze shuttered. "Why do you ask?"

How easy it would be to use Liwei's name to gain the Keeper's compliance. He had been his student far longer, their bond went deep—yet I could not choke the lie out. I could not risk harming Liwei's reputation further, inflaming his father's suspicions should the Keeper report our conversation.

"I can't say," I admitted. "Though it is important to me."

"Such information cannot be freely shared."

I clasped my hands, resisting the urge to plead. What did pride matter when weighed against my father's life? Though from the set of the Keeper's face, it would be futile. Before I could speak, the woman shook her head, flicking her eyes toward the bamboo grove in an unmistakable invitation. Hope flared. As the Keeper's apprentice, she might have the information I sought and be more willing to share it. There would be a price, undoubtedly— but less onerous than others had demanded of me before.

I bowed to the Keeper again, concealing my eagerness. "Honored Teacher, thank you for your guidance."

"Xingyin, these are strange and uncertain times," he said gravely. "Be careful. Watch over His Highness."

"Always," I replied.

The Keeper left then, striding toward the town with his apprentice following behind. I slipped between the bamboo trees and sank upon the ground. The stillness was broken by the occasional rustle of leaves, the scurry of small creatures. I drew a long breath, my head spinning from the scents of this world— the fragrance of rainfall laced with the decay of wilted leaves, the gritty undertones of salt and earth.

Hours slipped by, still there was no sign of the Keeper's apprentice. Just when I rose to leave, thinking I had been mistaken—the air shifted, a pair of immortal auras drawing closer. A man walked beside Leiying, of a similar height, though with a more slender build. His face was striking with its high cheekbones, full lips, and sweeping brows, and his assured smile showed he was well aware of his charm.

"I apologize for the wait. My brother, Tao, takes too long to ready himself." Leiying's tone was at once resigned and exasperated.

He ignored her, his gaze moving from the top of my head to my toes, then to the bow I carried across my back. "You'll do," he said drily.

"I'm not sure *you* will." I raked him with an appraising look of my own, taking in his teal brocade robe and gold sash, which were as ornate as any royal's.

He grinned as he slanted his head back. "My sister told me that you seek the Elixir of Immortality? If so, we can aid each other."

"What do you mean?" I asked carefully.

Leiying's tongue clicked impatiently against the roof of her mouth. "We want the elixir too."

My eyes narrowed. Was this a trap, to rid themselves of a rival? "How many are there?"

"One for each of us," Leiying replied. "I do not know when His Celestial Majesty will create another, for their crafting is a strain on his power."

"Why do you want the elixir?" I asked.

"Someone we care for needs it," Tao said.

"Who?"

Brother and sister exchanged a cautious look. "You came seeking help. We offer it. We've already told you what we can."

Tao added pointedly, "Just as we're not asking why *you* seek this. It is safer this way, the less either of us divulges of our plans."

He spoke the truth, for I had no wish to reveal my own intentions. And I was reluctant to antagonize my newfound allies even as I wondered what they concealed. "What is your plan?"

"We steal the elixir."

A shiver coursed through me to hear the words spoken so baldly. My heart raced with the possibilities, even as my mind urged me to refuse. "Where is the elixir kept?" I found myself asking.

"In the Imperial Treasury," Tao replied.

I recoiled. "You want the three of us to break into the Imperial Treasury? That is madness." In all my years in the Jade Palace, I had never ventured there. While I had been curious about the place, I had not wished to invite scrutiny through an unplanned visit—and what I most desired then did not lie within its walls.

"Two of us; you and me," Tao clarified, undaunted. "I won't jeopardize my sister's safety."

"This will never work."

"How else do you propose we obtain the elixir? Do you think the emperor will give it to you?" Leiying countered.

"I've scouted the Jade Palace for years, waiting for the right chance. I've been close enough to the elixir to inhale its fragrance," Tao assured me. "I can get us in and out of the treasury undetected."

"How?" I pressed. "If this is going to work, I must know everything."

"I have a key."

"Where did you get it from? Will it work?" Perhaps I hoped he would give me a reason to refuse, something to bolster my wavering will.

"The same way I got anything I'm not supposed to." He ran

his fingers across his fine garments. "You've got a suspicious mind. Rest assured, the key will work. I've used it before."

I ignored his gibe. "Why do you need me?"

"To dispatch a small nuisance guarding the elixir. It would be nothing to a competent fighter such as yourself." He lifted his hands, smooth and fine-boned. "My skills lie in procurement, not combat."

I bit the inside of my cheek, my father's image flashing through my mind—not the powerful warrior from the tales, but worn in both body and spirit. There was not much time left, for what if he died?

"I've heard that an immortal's memories are restored upon their return to the heavens. What of a mortal's memories?" I asked the Keeper's apprentice.

"Death erases all mortal memories," Leiying said gravely. "Once gone, those can never be regained."

A cold knot of dread formed in my chest. My father had not known my mother as an immortal. If I did not save him in his mortal lifetime, he would forget my mother and their love. He would not know me. He would be a stranger to us.

Temptation warred with caution. "If we are caught, it's not me alone who will pay the price," I said, thinking of my mother and Liwei.

"We won't be. I know the palace like the back of my hand, and I have no desire to rot in a Celestial prison for eternity. They do not look kindly upon thieves." Tao grimaced. "Disguise yourself and conceal your face, as an added precaution. Guard my back, and I'll do the rest. The time has never been better. With the recent changes in the army leadership, the palace defenses have been weakened. Fewer guards are on duty; the wards are not as strong as they once were."

General Wu was undoubtedly a poor replacement for General

Jianyun. "Have you told anyone else of your plan?" I asked, wary of discovery.

Tao cocked his head at me. "You're the first person we've approached. We asked you because you want it as much as we do, and you're competent with that bow, by blood if nothing else."

I stared at the pair, sensing nothing but an urgency that matched my own. And if we were caught, all of us would suffer the consequences. The thought of stealing from the Celestial Emperor flooded me with trepidation. Yet beneath, coursed a more profound terror, that I might lose my father just when I had found him.

"Very well," I agreed.

"Tomorrow night. We'll meet within the grove of camphor trees, just south of the Imperial Treasury." Tao exchanged a guarded look with his sister. "One more thing. You can't tell anyone else about our plan, especially Prince Liwei."

"Why not?"

Tao's eyes flashed. "What if His Highness tried to stop you? What if he spoke to the Keeper of Mortal Fates about my sister? If you can't promise us your discretion, we'll take our chances elsewhere."

My gut twisted as I nodded tersely. I did not want to lie to Liwei, even as I struggled with how to tell him the truth. Yet this was my best hope to help my father, and I would not fail him.

My worries consumed me throughout the journey back. As I stepped off the cloud, I found Liwei leaning against one of the mother-of-pearl columns that flanked the entrance. Waiting for me, undoubtedly.

His eyes slid over my garments, my fingers itching to smooth my robe, crumpled from those hours spent hunched in wait. A far cry from the embroidered silk dresses I had worn in the Jade Palace.

"I like what you're wearing," he said quietly. "It suits you."

Warmth flared in me at his words. I tapped the silk cord around my wrist, which sprang free, writhing in the air. "It's useful too. They have been enchanted to tie themselves."

He caught my wrist, catching the end of the cord to wind it back into place. "This is too delicate; you might need something stronger," he observed, running a finger across it. The threads glowed with his magic, hardening to gleaming strips of chestnut-brown, which crisscrossed over my wrists. From the pulse of energy thrumming against my skin, this was no ordinary material; more pliant than leather and yet sturdier.

"Thank you." I held them up to examine them. "What is it?"

"This can withstand even the sharpest blades, though not for long." As his gaze searched my face, I tensed. "Where have you been? I haven't seen you all day," he asked.

"The Mortal Realm. I was at my father's grave." My deceit lay in concealment.

His eyes darkened with understanding. "I know how much you grieve for him."

I hesitated, before asking, "Liwei, what have you heard of the Elixir of Immortality?" I did not want to steal from his father. If there was another way, I would seek it—but if not, I would not falter.

"Its creation is something only my father is privy to. He guards it well, for such a thing might change the fate of the world below." He paused. "Why do you ask?"

A longing swept through me to confide in him, but I had given my word to Tao. Yet I would tell him what I could, for I wanted no other lies between us.

"My father is alive. I met him in the Mortal Realm," I said haltingly. Even now it seemed a dream, though all my hopes were entwined with fear.

Liwei stared at me, wide-eyed. "The Black Dragon said he had died. Why do you think he's your father?"

"He's of the right age. He carries a bow of our realm. He knew my past and my mother's."

"Many a fortune hunter will claim anything for the chance to win an immortal's aid," he cautioned.

"I know my father here." I pressed my fingertips to my chest.

Liwei clasped my hands in his. "You want to believe him, Xingyin—but this could be mere coincidence or contrivance. Many mortals are familiar with your parents' tale, countless more are of the right age. Perhaps he obtained that weapon from Kunlun Mountain. At least *consider* the possibility that this mortal is not who he claims to be."

His reasoning was sound, though his doubt stung. Yes, I wanted this to be true, yet I was not oblivious to the facts. Once before, I had allowed this to happen. But while my trust was bruised, I believed the part inside me that sensed the truth—my father was alive.

"He *is* my father. The Jade Dragon Bow—"

"Are you asking about the elixir for him?" Liwei's grip tightened. "It's too dangerous. We must find out more about this mortal; this is not something to rush into."

My father's cough rang through my mind, his crimson blood staining the cloth. Time was something I did not have. "He is ill. He needs the elixir."

"My father will not yield it, neither to you nor me," Liwei said heavily. "We have few allies left in the Jade Palace, and we cannot act rashly. Don't risk yourself until you know for sure."

My lips formed a smile as I nodded in seeming assent, despising myself for the trickery. Liwei did not believe the mortal was my father—I could not blame him for the dragon had told us he was dead, and it was impossible to explain the certainty of a feeling only I sensed. I could not ask more from Liwei, nor could I add to his concerns or pit him further against his family. And the greatest reason I held my tongue—one I shied from myself—was the worry that he would object to my plan, that he would try to dissuade me . . . and that I would proceed regardless.

He was right; the emperor would never *give* me the elixir, which was why I would take it from him. And if I failed, it was safer for my loved ones if they did not know, for I was certain the Celestial Emperor had his ways of extracting the truth.

"Have you decided what you will do?" I asked him, shifting the conversation to safer ground. "I met the Keeper by chance in the Mortal Realm. He said there are many at court who would support you, should you return."

"I have no plans to return. Not yet."

I breathed easier, though there was little joy in that which caused him pain. "I know your family is precious to you; I never wanted to make you choose." I paused, asking, "Do you regret it?"

"No. This time there is no threat to the kingdom, no pressing alliance to secure. This time . . . you will not be rid of me so easily." His eyes darkened. "Though I wish I had not parted with my parents on such terms, to have disappointed them."

Your father disappointed you, I wanted to tell him. Liwei need not have been forced into a choice where all would undoubtedly lose.

"I meant what I said to you those years before, in the market." There was a wistful note in his voice.

The stalls in the clearing. The woody fragrance of tea winding through the air. A white shell nestled in my palm. His words drifted back to me as though it were yesterday: *We could travel the realm, stopping where we choose and leaving when we grow restless.*

"It would be a good life." I repeated what I had said then.

"As long as we're together." His dark gaze held mine, my heart quickening. "Though I fear for myself sometimes, wanting to bind myself to one as fierce as you."

"It's not too late." My tone sharpened. "I have not agreed. You are free to make your escape."

"I will never be free of you."

Drawn by the warmth in his tone, I tilted my face up to his. He lowered his head, his lips brushing mine tenderly, then pressing harder. His hand cradled my cheek, his fingers threading through my hair. Heat kindled in my veins as he drew me closer. I melted against him, reveling in his touch. Neither of us spoke again but for the language of our tangled breaths, silencing the voices in my mind, burying all thoughts of the perils that lay ahead.

At least for now.

8

OUR MORNING MEAL WAS A quiet affair with no guests to entertain. The sisters from the Golden Desert had left, perhaps sensing our unease or having heard rumblings of the emperor's displeasure. I was glad, in no mood for idle conversation. My mother placed a bowl of congee before me, the rice cooked to a silken texture, dotted with crimson wolfberries, tendrils of ginseng, and tender pieces of chicken. Salted egg slices with vermilion yolks adorned the surface, along with a handful of roasted peanuts and shavings of spring onion.

As I lifted the porcelain spoon to my mouth, the wards pulsed in warning through my mind. I stiffened, turning to my mother and Liwei. "We have visitors."

Liwei set his bowl aside. "How many?"

I pressed a hand to my temple, trying to discern the new arrivals. "A dozen or more."

"We will make our excuses," my mother said tersely. "After that fraud 'Master Gang,' we will shelter none beneath our roof."

I had told her of his true identity, and how he had maligned us to the Celestial Court. I did not want her to be caught unaware by his trickery again.

Footsteps thudded along the corridor, growing louder,

their stride measured and unhurried. How dare they enter our home uninvited? They either felt entitled to, or did not fear the consequences—my gut twisting at the thought.

The doors were thrown open. Celestial soldiers marched into the room, their swords strapped to their sides. At the sight of them in my home, a coldness descended upon me, of old dread merged with new terrors.

A wiry immortal with a pointed jaw strode forward—Minister Ruibing, a high-ranking Celestial courtier. His pupils were ringed with brown like watermelon seeds, his lips thin and wide. Dark-red brocade robes swished around his shoes, an oblong piece of flat jade gleaming from his ceremonial hat.

My mother's face paled as she bowed in greeting. "Minister Ruibing, to what do we owe this honor?"

The minister sniffed as he surveyed her through narrowed eyes. My fingers curled at his lack of civility, even as foreboding plunged through me at the sight of the imperial yellow brocade scroll cradled in his palms. A pattern of twin dragons circling the sun was embroidered across it, the design favored by the Celestial Emperor.

He brandished the scroll with an exaggerated flourish. "I bear an edict from His Celestial Majesty, the Supreme Emperor of the Celestial Kingdom, Protector of the Mortal Realm, Lord over the Sun, Moon, and Stars. May he govern us for another ten thousand years."

As was customary, we sank to our knees upon the ground, pressing our palms and foreheads to the floor. Minister Ruibing took an inordinately long time to unravel the scroll, likely savoring the sight of us kneeling before him. He possessed the pompous air of one who relished the authority ceded to him.

"All present, hear and obey," he recited in ringing tones. "The goddess Chang'e is hereby removed from her guardianship of the moon for the shameful neglect of her duties and the grave insult to His Celestial Majesty. She, and all the moon's inhabitants, will await their punishment here. None of them are permitted to leave its grounds. Defiance of these commands will be considered an act of hostility against the Celestial Kingdom."

His gaze slid toward Liwei, thinned with malice. "Your Highness, if I found you here, I was instructed to convey a message to you. His Celestial Majesty commands that you return to the Jade Palace without delay to await his judgment on your conduct."

A void gaped in my chest, my protest spilling from my lips. "He did nothing wrong, nor did my mother. She meant no harm; this was her first lapse in all these decades. I request an audience with His Celestial Majesty. Let me explain—"

"Thank you, Minister Ruibing," Liwei interjected as he rose to his feet. "I will leave with you in a moment."

Liwei drew me to the far end of the hall. He stood before me, his body blocking out the rest of the room, including the minister's odious presence. "Don't do this. My father will not grant you an audience. Your demand would be seen as a challenge to his authority and will only infuriate him more. He is already angry enough to imprison all of you without hope of release."

I swallowed hard, hating this weight of impending disaster, this numbing futility. I did not want Liwei to go, yet the moon was no longer a haven but the most dangerous place in the realm. I bit down hard on my tongue, relishing the sting. Blood was preferable to tears in moments as these.

"Don't return with the minister." Rash words, ringed in selfishness.

He shook his head. "A refusal would be an admission of guilt.

I must learn what venom has been poured into my father's ears. I must defend my name from the vile accusations flung my way." He smiled, speaking with assurance. "All will be well. I know the workings of the court, my allies from enemies."

I wanted to go with him yet was unwilling to leave my mother. Moreover, my presence would likely do more harm than good; we had been commanded to remain here, and neither the emperor nor his court held me in high regard.

Liwei's expression was grave as he brushed his knuckles across my cheek. "I will put an end to it. I will make it safe for you and your family."

"You must keep yourself safe," I told him, hating the quiver in my voice. This was Liwei's choice, and he was skilled in the maneuverings of the Celestial Court. "If you don't return, I will come for you." This was no hollow claim, nor soft words to ease a lover's parting.

"You must not. The palace will be warded against you soon; you will no longer be able to enter freely as before," he cautioned. "Do nothing to draw attention to yourself."

"Warded?" I repeated slowly. "Why?"

"It is common practice for those deemed a threat, those convicted of any offense against the kingdom."

"Nothing has been proven," I protested.

"Not yet," Liwei said. "But for my father to send the minister with this harsh proclamation is just a formality. His official judgment will follow in a day or two, to give the semblance of this matter being weighed at court. None will gainsay him."

Turmoil raged through my mind, quenching my remaining doubts about Tao's plan. Once we were sentenced, it would be impossible to enter the Jade Palace undetected—even if I could escape whatever terrible punishment the emperor envisioned for us. The elixir would remain forever out of reach. My father would die. Which meant tonight was my only chance, and I would not squander it.

Minister Ruibing scowled as we approached, his hands clasped behind his back. "Make haste, Your Highness," he snapped.

As anger seared me at the minister's disrespect, Liwei raised his chin with the regal arrogance he possessed. "Minister Ruibing, remember your place. I am my father's loyal subject and will obey his command." His words served as a pointed reminder that despite his current disfavor, he was the emperor's son—for whom the tides might swing back in his favor as easily as the wind changed its direction.

"Of course, Your Highness." A brief pause, as Minister Ruibing hastily bowed. He had expected a chastened son crawling back to earn his father's favor rather than the unflinching royal before him—but like any skillful courtier, he adjusted to the situation with repellent ease.

As the minster gestured to the soldiers, eight detached themselves from the rest, moving toward us. I started to recognize Feimao among them, the archer I had fought alongside during my first assignment with the Celestial Army. Relief flickered, abruptly doused by his grim expression.

"These soldiers will remain here," Minister Ruibing said.

"Are we prisoners?" my mother asked coldly.

The minister's lips curled into a smirk. "If you prefer, you can think of them as guarding your safety. These orders came directly from General Wu, and you may raise the matter with him when he arrives."

"Where is the general?" I had thought he would be here; he would have taken pleasure in this.

The minister's gaze flicked toward Liwei before sliding back to me. "General Wu is currently occupied with urgent matters at court."

Undoubtedly the general was one who found much opportunity in Liwei's predicament. A bitterness coated the inside of my mouth as the soldiers surrounded Liwei like he was a villain, instead of the finest immortal in the kingdom. I stared after them until they had gone, fighting the urge to follow, my heart clouded with fear. And despite the sunlight streaming through the windows, it had never seemed so bleak.

9

CREPT THROUGH THE CORRIDORS, KEEPING my steps light. The soldiers were not attuned to my aura, but I masked it nonetheless. As I slipped through the entrance, I halted at the sight of Feimao standing outside. He was clad in his armor, with a bow gripped in his hand, and from memory he was an excellent marksman.

"Why are you here?" He spoke with polite indifference, as though I were a stranger.

"Enjoying the night air," I replied steadily.

"With that?" He stared pointedly at the wooden bow slung over my shoulder.

Fortunately, I had not brought the Jade Dragon Bow, for fear of someone recognizing it. "A habit, just as yours. Why are you asking me these questions?" I met his gaze without flinching. "Minister Ruibing said you were here for our protection."

A short pause. "I think both of us know better than to believe that."

His frankness surprised me. "I hear much has changed in the Celestial Army since I last served there," I said in a warmer tone. A reminder that we had fought together, once, in Xiangliu's cavern.

Feimao nodded, standing a little easier. "There is a divide in the Celestial Army where once there was none. Past loyalties have called into question our current ones. Punishments meted out are swift and harsh, and often without proper investigation."

His words echoed those of Shuxiao's. "Can no one intervene?"

"No one dares to gainsay General Wu; the few who did were relieved of their positions or sent away."

"I am sorry to hear that," I said softly.

"I'm sorry for it too," he replied.

I was tempted to ask more, but he inclined his head to me. "My shift ends at dawn. That is when the rest will awaken." Without waiting for my response, he strode toward the forest.

I discarded the suspicion that his warning might be a trap. Feimao was an honorable soldier, loyal to General Jianyun, and he had stood by me against the Celestial Emperor's wrath. Out of caution, I waited until he had vanished between the trees. Only then did I call a cloud and a brisk wind to spur it along.

The Jade Palace loomed on the horizon, the dragons on its rooftop leeched of color in the night. As a sudden gust tossed my hair across my face, I spun around to find an immortal soaring after me, his eyes as bright as twin stars. I halted my flight to end his chase, wary of alerting the Celestial guards. As Wenzhi drew closer, the violet tendrils of his cloud trailed over mine.

"Why are you here?" I demanded.

"I was on my way to see you, only to find you leaving."

"Did you follow me?"

"Call it 'chasing after' you," he said with a small smile. "You were always the swiftest with the wind."

His praise sparked a flicker of warmth, that I quenched. His opinion meant nothing to me. "What do you want, Wenzhi? I have little time to waste."

"I heard what happened at the Luminous Pearl Lake." His

lips set into a thin line. "I confess to being disappointed. I had hoped he would be a fool, again."

I flushed at his meaning, even as impatience pricked me at this delay. "Your sources are to be commended. I must go now. Do not follow me," I warned.

His gaze swept over me, lingering on the sword strapped to my side, the bow over my shoulder. "You reek of recklessness, Xingyin."

"It is no concern of yours," I returned coldly.

"It is of *great* concern," he corrected me. "It must be a terrible thing indeed if you are here alone. What are you hiding from the others? What are you afraid of your beloved discovering?"

When I did not reply, he strode forward, stepping upon my cloud. As the hem of his dark green robe grazed mine, I fought the urge to move back, refusing to show how much his presence unsettled me.

"Why are you going to the Jade Palace?" he asked. "You can't get in; they will sense you at once."

"What do you mean?" My tone was guarded.

"The wards around the palace have been altered tonight." He paused, adding, "I heard of Minister Ruibing's visit. He was a pompous fool from what I recall. What did the minister want?"

"How do you—"

"I make it my point to know these things," he interjected. "The defenses of the Celestial Kingdom. Your well-being."

The tips of my ears burned. I ignored his earlier question, asking, "Are you telling the truth about the wards?"

His eyes thinned in a familiar look of exasperation. "If you don't believe me, by all means go ahead. You will be stopped before you get a foot through the gates." He cocked his head to one side. "I think I prefer it that way, putting an end to your scheme.

Attempted entry would be a far lighter offense than whatever you have planned."

"I can't be caught. I'm not allowed to leave the moon." I clamped my mouth shut, regretting my words. If I was discovered defying the emperor's edict, it would endanger us tenfold. And if I attempted to break the wards, that might sound an alarm, summoning a trail of suspicious soldiers upon my heels.

Wenzhi lowered himself into a mocking bow. "Perhaps I might be of service. I have some experience getting into places I'm not supposed to."

I stared at him. "Why would you help me?"

"As I told you, I wish to make amends. I also prefer that you remain alive and not locked away in some Celestial prison. It would be much harder to extricate you then." He added with emphasis, "You would owe me nothing. Think of this as recompense for my wrongs."

"Nothing you do will *ever* make up for your wrongs," I said scathingly.

"*Part* recompense, then," he amended, even as an unreadable expression flashed across his face.

I did not like accepting favors from him, nor did I trust him enough to share my plan. Yet I would not risk discovery upon a point of pride; I would not gamble with our lives.

"Help me get into the palace, but you cannot follow me," I told him.

"Will you tell me what you're doing?"

I smiled brightly. "No."

He released a sigh. "What do you want me to do?"

"Break the wards around the Western Gate." Heat glazed my face at my hypocrisy. I had railed at him for such treachery before, and now I was enlisting his aid to do the same.

"Unless you possess an invading army, the palace wards can't be tampered with from outside," he told me.

I had not known this. My assignments in the Celestial Army had always taken me beyond the Jade Palace; I had never guarded its walls.

"Could you draw the guards away from the gate?" I asked. "A diversion to distract them?"

"I would prefer a harder task." When I did not reply, he inclined his head. "As you wish."

"Thank you." Gratitude for him sat uneasily within me.

"If you are not out by sunrise, I will come for you." His eyes shone silver bright.

"I don't need your help to get out," I said curtly.

"Yet you need it to get in." He raised a hand, stalling my retort. "I trust in your abilities, but sometimes luck can get in the way." Without another word, he returned to his cloud, taking flight into the night.

Recalling Tao's warning to mask myself, I wrapped a piece of black cloth across my nose, knotting it at the back of my head. Far from an impenetrable disguise, but I was not adept enough to create an enchantment over my form, much less sustain it. And I had learned not to scorn the simplest disguises, for they were often the most easily overlooked.

A stream of energy coursed through the air, powerful and fierce. Shouts erupted from ahead, a cluster of immortal auras rushing away, drawn to the commotion. Wenzhi had struck the gates with ruthless efficiency. My insides wound tight as I plunged through the unseen barriers, instinctively recoiling from the anticipated discomfort. Yet there was just a coolness grazing my skin like a drizzle of rain—and then I was over the walls, back in the Jade Palace.

No clouds climbed toward me in pursuit as I soared across the lush gardens that divided the Outer Court from the Inner Court, flowers and trees blotting the landscape like spilled ink. A faint rumbling curled through my ears, that rhythmic rush which had soothed me to sleep those countless nights before. I glided lower, inhaling the sweetness of jasmine and wisteria, for a moment lost in the warm echoes of remembered joy. Was Liwei there? Was he safe? I longed to search for him, yet any attempt to do so might plunge us into greater danger, casting more suspicion over him. This was not the time to indulge reckless impulses. The empress would look out for him, and no matter what, he was still the emperor's son.

Beyond the Inner Court lay the heart of the Jade Palace: the Hall of Eastern Light, the Chamber of Reflection, and the Imperial Treasury, spread out across the sprawling grounds. A circular building of red marble rose from the grassy lawn, like a ring of copper dropped onto a bed of silk. Intricate carvings of vines, leaves, and flowers were etched upon its walls. The lacquered doors were studded with gold and flanked by a pair of carved stone lions, while the roof was paved in lapis tiles which slanted into a graceful slope. Glazed by moonlight, all was drenched in silver and white. Celestial soldiers in gleaming armor were stationed at the treasury entrance, the rest patrolling the grounds.

As my cloud landed within a grove of camphor trees, I folded myself into the shadows, making my way quietly toward the lone figure in black.

Tao's teeth gleamed as he gestured at the cloth covering my face. "Have you been reading too many mortal tales?"

"Did you not ask me to disguise myself?" I thrust a piece of cloth at him. "Better this than letting someone catch a glimpse of your face."

"I don't need it." He waved it aside disdainfully as a shimmer glided over his skin, like I was looking at him through the glare of the sun. Except his eyes were more close-set, his lips thinner, his nose squat and broad. If I had not been staring at him, I would have thought he was a different person. Still, his aura remained unchanged, flickering faintly, almost imperceptible.

I frowned. "How did you do that? I sensed no magic."

"It is a skill I was born with, the only useful one I have." His breathing was labored as he wiped the sweat from his brow. "Useful, for my profession."

"Is this like the magic of fox spirits?" I asked.

He shook his head. "Mine is weaker. I can only distort my own form to avoid recognition, while fox spirits can mimic another's appearance. I've also heard of rare enchantments that can mirror not just one's physical attributes, but their aura and voice as well."

"A dangerous skill. Though undoubtedly useful in moments as these." I looked at him hopefully. "Could you disguise my features?"

"No. My powers are not strong, which allows me to avoid detection. It would be a strain for me to maintain two illusions."

I nodded, shrugging away my disappointment. "How do we get in?"

Tao pointed at a panel in the wall ahead, a shade lighter than the rest. I had thought it a shaft of moonlight, only now noticing others were scattered in regular intervals across the marble walls.

"Each of these leads to a different chamber in the treasury. That is the one we want." He handed me a jade disc carved with a peach blossom. "I'll draw the soldiers away. Once you enter, leave the key on the ground for me. Don't draw attention to yourself and use your magic sparingly to avoid alerting the guards."

"What of the other enchantments guarding this place?" It seemed unlikely that nothing else lay between us and the treasury.

"There are none. The items within protect themselves better than anything else could."

The back of my neck prickled. "What do you mean?"

Yet his form was wavering, fading from sight. A distance away, the trees rustled—Tao, already at work. The guards jerked to attention, most of them hurrying over to inspect the disturbance, leaving just two by the entrance.

Bending down, I grabbed a handful of pebbles, flinging them as far from me as I could throw. They scattered with dull thuds, the guards' gazes swinging away. At once, I sprinted toward the entrance, pressing myself against the walls. Just beside the panel was a hollow carved with the same flower as on the jade disc, blending seamlessly into the carvings. My pulse raced as I pressed the ornament against it, sliding smoothly into place. As the panel shimmered, dissolving into nothingness, I tucked the key behind a clump of grass and slipped into the chamber.

Behind me, the door solidified into stone once more. The air within was stale and heavy, like no living creature had entered the room for decades. I examined the vast chamber, larger even than the Silver Harmony Hall of my home. A round mahogany table lay in the center, carved with an elegant floral pattern, books and scrolls stacked in neat piles upon it. There were no stools, perhaps because there were no visitors here—certainly none of leisure. The walls were lined with elmwood shelves, crammed with exquisite sculptures of mythical creatures and ornaments of gold, porcelain, and jade. Along the walls were miniature trees barely knee-high, with spring-green leaves and elegantly curved branches.

As the door shimmered once more, Tao stepped through.

Without a word, he strode to a shelf at the far end of the room. As he ran his fingers across a painted panel, a low crack ruptured the silence. A space appeared behind it, holding a round lacquered box roughly the size of my palm. It was exquisitely carved into a peony, its crimson petals clustered tight. Six jade dragonflies perched over its petals, crafted with translucent wings, iridescent bodies, and golden antennae.

As I reached for the box, Tao grabbed my arm, his fingers like bars of ice. He was trembling as he pointed at the dragonflies. "Those creatures sting. Their venom is excruciating. I barely escaped the last time."

"The dragonflies?" Doubt layered my tone. They were beautiful, so well made, I found myself listening out for the thrum of flight. As I leaned closer to inspect them, they twitched—wings fluttering, rubies flashing from their eyes as sharp stingers slid from their slender abdomens. I leapt back, the stirrings of a gale on my fingertips to sweep them away—

"Careful, the guards will sense magic," Tao hissed, nodding at my bow. "Can't you use a weapon?"

I drew my sword instead, just as the dragonflies shot forth with an ominous whir, the edges of their wings glinting like sharpened knives, a pale liquid glistening from their stingers. They hovered before us, those blood-red eyes fixed on Tao and me. My skin crawled as I forced my arm up, slashing at them— yet they darted aside with startling speed, hurtling toward me once more. I twisted aside to evade them, stabbing frantically at the one nearest to me, its wings breaking off with the clink of sawn glass. My blade flashed in a silvery blur as I hacked at the rest until all that remained were broken shards, strewn across the floor.

I breathed easier—too soon—as the lumps quivered. Bodies

lengthened, wings and heads and limbs sprouting forth until every disjointed fragment had formed a new creature, springing into the air and humming like a plague of locusts.

Tao's eyes went wide. "I had no idea they could do *that*."

"You should have told me about them in the first place," I bit out.

He flushed. "I told you I needed your skills. I . . . I was afraid you wouldn't come. You had enough reservations."

"Tao, we're going to have a long talk after this." I did not look away from the grotesque vision of gleaming stingers and fiery pupils, my ears ringing with that damned whirring and clicking like the gnashing of pincers.

The swarm plunged toward us. I grabbed Tao's arm, racing away, knocking the mahogany table onto its side as we crouched behind it, rolling it to a corner of the room. The dragonflies slammed into the other side, some of their wings wedged into the table—the pointed tip of one already splintering the wood. My throat constricted, my stomach churning violently.

I grabbed a brass urn enameled with yellow chrysanthemums from a shelf, shoving it at Tao. "We must catch them."

His hands shook as he took it. "What? *Why?*" he asked in an anguished tone.

"We can't use magic. They can't be killed. If you have another idea, I would welcome it," I said fervently. "I'll catch, you trap them. Keep the lid shut at all times."

I shook free the binds around my wrists, grateful for Liwei's transformation of them—those creatures would slice through silk in a blink. The cords sprang into the air, weaving into a small net upon my command. Without a pause, I grabbed the net and swung it at the dragonflies. Three caught in the weave, struggling wildly, the rest swerving aside before hurtling toward me once more. I dipped back low, yet their wings scraped my neck and cheeks. My wounds seared like fire, my heart thudding as I emptied the net into the urn, shaking it roughly to dislodge the creatures. As the last one fell in, Tao slammed the lid over the opening, his hold steady though his face was gray.

It was a frantic dance, my net spinning through the air to ensnare the dragonflies, then releasing them into the urn. Once, Tao was too slow—a cluster of them darting out that we had to catch all over again. Another slipped through my grasp, its wing slicing Tao's ear.

"I'm sorry," I gasped as blood trickled down his neck. The whirring grew louder as though the dragonflies thrived on its hot scent.

"Don't miss again," he said faintly.

Finally, the dragonflies were all trapped, their wings scraping against the brass, an eerie, grating sound that tore at my nerves. Tao leaned over the urn, his arms wrapped tight around the lid. Pulling a cord free from the net, I wound it around the vessel, strapping it shut. Once the knots were secure, I shoved the urn away, where it rattled before falling silent.

Tao sank down beside me, trembling as he wiped the blood from his ear. "I'm never doing that again."

Ignoring the heaviness in my limbs, I tugged his sleeve. "Come, we must go."

Rising to our feet, we stumbled to the lacquered box on the shelf. Each peony petal was perfectly formed, curling slightly around the edges. Tao picked it up, a mirror image on both sides. Holding it firmly between his palms, he twisted it apart. The petals quivered, then unfurled to reveal a topaz-studded core. Something clicked, a crack streaking all around like an apricot wrenched into halves. As the scent of honeyed peaches sprang into the air—an intoxicating sweetness—my mouth watered with a sudden craving.

Tao peered into the box, his breath quickening.

"Are the elixirs there?" I asked eagerly.

"Yes." His head swung up as he took in the wreckage of the room. "Best to clean up after ourselves."

I moved swiftly around the room, rolling the table back to its original position, piling the books and scrolls upon it once more. Then I straightened the shelves, finally shoving the shards of broken ornaments to a dark corner of the room. Far from perfect, but hopefully enough to escape a cursory inspection.

"Do you have them?" I asked Tao.

He nodded as he replaced the box on the shelf. As we moved toward the door, light rippled across the stone. Panic clawed me as Tao and I darted behind the nearest shelf, crouching amid the miniature trees, the urn just beside us.

The panel vanished. Two soldiers entered, broad-shouldered and tall. Was this a routine visit, or had someone heard us? The soldiers paused, one slanting his head back like he was listening for something. I drew a shaking breath, the cloth quivering over my mouth as my grip tightened around the hilt of my sword. A loud rattle jarred the stillness, the urn shuddering upon the ground. At once the man swung toward it, his hand locked around his spear.

My limbs froze, yet I shook myself from the stupor. Lunging for the urn, I snatched it up and ripped away the cords—tearing its lid free and hurling its contents at the guards. The dragonflies shot out, whirring louder as though enraged. The soldiers' faces paled, yet they were well trained as their arms flew up, their spears carving the air with rhythmic blows—one of them calling for reinforcements. As the dragonflies fractured—some already re-forming—more guards raced into the room, crowding the entrance. The creatures plunged toward them, stinging their faces and necks. Swollen bumps pushed through their skin, a reddish violet hue, as the soldiers gasped in pain. Tao and I raced toward the door just as a solider leapt forward to block our path, swinging his sword at my head. I slashed at him feverishly, driving him back. We were running out of time. Soon the soldiers would overwhelm the dragonflies, they would stop us . . . the air already stirring with the beginnings of a spell.

Gripping the hilt of my blade with both hands, I flung it up to meet the soldier's blow—my arm throbbing as I shoved his weapon away. He staggered back, weaving to catch his balance, his sword arcing toward me once more. I twisted aside, his blade sliding across the air where my chest had been. Crouching lower, I kicked at him, my foot colliding with his stomach. He gasped even as he dove forward to grab at my face covering. I darted out of reach, dragging my blade across his arm, slicing his flesh. Blood gushed out, a cry wrung from his throat—the whirring from the dragonflies escalating into a frenzied pitch.

My energy surged, summoning a gale to knock him aside—no need for subterfuge or caution now. At least our faces were still concealed; we had a chance of escaping unscathed, though the odds were rapidly diminishing.

"More soldiers are coming!" Tao yelled.

We bolted from the chamber, sprinting across the grassy lawn. Magic flowed from my hands, calling down a cloud as we raced onward in a jagged path to evade the soldiers. As we scrambled upon our cloud, an ominous whistling sliced the air. Tao and I ducked low, holding our breath as arrows hurtled over us. Sweat dripped from my brow, my limbs ached—yet I dared not pause, channeling more energy into the wind that swept us upward in a twisting route to throw off any pursuers.

We soared in silence for a long while, our eyes searching for any sign of danger. Only once the luminous glow of the moon lit a path through the night did I tug away the covering from my face. It had seemed a foolish idea before, but I was grateful for it. If someone had recognized me . . . I shivered at the thought.

Tao's arms were wrapped around his body. "We were lucky. Beyond lucky, to have escaped."

I nodded, inspecting the cuts from the dragonflies crisscrossing my skin in a bloodied web. Tao, beside me, nursed a deep gash across his arm, blood still dripping from his ear.

"Does it hurt?" I asked.

"No." There was a slight tremor in his voice.

"Let me imagine your wound," I offered, wondering if it went deeper than it appeared.

He shook his head. "It's not severe."

"Do you have the elixirs?" I was already imagining my father's face alight with pride. My mother's joy when I brought him home.

Tao slipped his hand between the panels of his robe, drawing out a small bottle the size of my thumb. It was crafted in translucent white jade, with delicate gold filigree adorning its stopper. A glowing liquid swirled within, its honeyed scent almost drowning my senses.

I smiled, reaching out for it—but then Tao's shoulders slumped as the air around him shimmered, his face and body blurring like he was shrouded in mist.

"What's the matter? Are you all right?" I reached for his arm to steady him, but my fingers passed through his flesh like smoke.

"I . . . I'm sorry. There was only one." His face crumpled, his voice cracking with remorse as it melded into the rushing wind.

I stared numbly back at him, dread crashing over me. To

have risked so much and come this far! Anger blazed as I sprang at him, clawing at the shadow of the bottle in his hand, but it was like trying to grasp a shred of sky.

It was too late; he had gone. I had been played for a fool, risked myself for nothing—and worst of all, I had failed my father.

10

DAWN STREAKED ACROSS THE SKIES as the last flickers of light dwindled from the moon lanterns. I almost longed for the return of night, as dark as my thoughts. I had come so close to bringing my father home, and now . . . the elixir was gone. My fingers curled as I cursed Tao and his sister, and myself for trusting them. Yet Tao's distraught expression as he had vanished tugged at me. Had he expected two elixirs, only to find one? Would I have chosen differently—sacrificed my father's life, my mother's happiness, for a stranger's? Regardless, if I ever found him again, I would repay his selfishness in kind. I had risked my life as he had; the elixir was no less mine, and his theft had nullified all claim he once had upon it.

The Celestial soldiers standing guard outside were unfamiliar to me. Feimao's shift must have ended. Just yesterday I had strode through these doors without hesitation, and now I was forced to break in like a thief. Stealthily, I made my way to the back, clambering up a mother-of-pearl pillar, then swinging myself onto the balcony. As I discarded my garments and pulled on a lilac robe I had hidden there, my gaze fell upon the realm below, awash in the soft haze of morning. A heaviness sank over me as I recalled the nights spent in idle contemplation here. Would I ever regain the peace I had known then?

The corridor was deserted as I made my way to my room. Sliding the doors apart, I entered—startled to find Shuxiao sitting at the table, along with General Jianyun. Their teacups were drained, Shuxiao's sword lying on the floor. Had they been waiting for long?

"You shouldn't be here," I blurted. Recalling my manners, I bowed to General Jianyun. "The emperor's edict—"

"I heard," Shuxiao said, her forehead wrinkled. "Where were you? You weren't supposed to leave."

I glanced at General Jianyun. He was still one of the emperor's advisors, moreover it was safer for him to not know. Though his unexpected presence here sent a sliver of trepidation through me.

"Do you have news of Liwei?" I asked, evading Shuxiao's question.

"No one is permitted to visit His Highness. The emperor has commanded that he remain isolated in his quarters," General Jianyun said grimly.

My teeth gnawed the soft inside of my cheek. "Has Liwei spoken to his father?"

General Jianyun shook his head. "His Celestial Majesty refuses to grant him an audience until His Highness apologizes—which he has not done. Nor will the emperor hear reason from the few advisors who voiced their concerns regarding the treatment of the prince."

"But that's not why we're here." Shuxiao's expression was somber. "Soldiers are assembling as we speak. They are coming here, led by General Wu."

Fear jolted down my spine. "Why?"

"The emperor has passed the sentence for your mother. For all of you." She released a drawn breath. "Confinement in the tower."

My insides hollowed at the thought of my mother, Ping'er,

and me trapped in such a place. The tower was a Celestial prison on the outskirts of the kingdom, where vicious monsters as the Bone Devil had been confined. It was a place of utter desolation, sheathed in darkness for there were no windows or doors within its walls, nothing to yield a glimmer of light.

"How long?" I choked out.

It was General Jianyun who replied. "No length of time has been set."

"It could be forever." Despair writhed in my gut, burrowing deep. The emperor had done this to my mother and to the dragons, their punishment dragging on indefinitely without a chance for clemency. Our names would be buried, forgotten, as the years flew by—becoming no more than another cautionary tale of defiance against the Celestial Emperor.

"Some tried to argue on your mother's behalf. Chang'e had never failed in the performance of her duty before; it must have been an innocent slip." General Jianyun's face darkened. "But others twisted our words, arguing that her unprecedented lapse that day, on His Celestial Majesty's birthday, must have been intentional. Some took it further, claiming the insult to His Celestial Majesty was treason to weaken his standing, embolden his dissenters, and bring misfortune to his reign."

"They think too highly of us. It was just a harmless mistake."

"No mistake is 'harmless' in the Jade Palace. Particularly none which earns the emperor's wrath," Shuxiao said.

"What will you do?" General Jianyun asked.

"How many soldiers? When are they coming?" I made myself ask.

Shuxiao's face darkened. "Over a hundred. They will come today or tomorrow, at the latest."

"A *hundred*?" I repeated numbly. Did they expect us to fight? This was no invitation to yield but a troop sent to subdue an enemy and to seize what would not be surrendered. A year ago, Celestial soldiers had stood by me and now . . . they were marching upon my home.

My deepest fear, my worst nightmare, come to life.

"I can't let them take us." I spoke on instinct.

A brief silence followed, before General Jianyun cleared his throat. "What of the laurel?"

"They can have it if they leave us in peace." Rash words spoken with a child's terror, offering a futile bargain to delay inevitable punishment.

"In the wrong hands, who knows what the laurel can be used to do," General Jianyun argued. "While we don't understand its power, neither can we ignore it."

"How can we fight them? Not just because we're outnumbered, but the soldiers helped me once." I was sickened by the thought of attacking those I had fought alongside before.

"The Celestial Army is not what it used to be." General Jianyun's tone was heavy. "The soldiers who came to your defense that day have been sidelined, their loyalties cast in doubt. Many have left, and the ones who remained were sent to distant borders."

Their support of me had cost them dearly. A simple gesture rooted in gratitude, yet striking a keen blow to the Celestial Emperor's pride. It had been one of the greatest moments of my life, and now it was tainted with guilt.

Precious seconds were slipping away, the emperor's soldiers drawing closer. I searched General Jianyun's face, hoping for guidance—yet he remained silent. Sometimes there were no answers, sometimes we had to make them up as we went along.

Cupping my hands before me, I bent low from my waist. "Thank you for warning us. I apologize for the discourtesy, but it might be safest for you both to depart before the soldiers arrive."

Lines deepened across General Jianyun's brow like fingers trailed in the sand. "What will you do?"

I did not answer, my nerves strung taut. All I ever wanted was to be left in peace with my family, and yet all I did plunged us into more danger.

No, my mind whispered. *You wanted more than that. You wanted to help the dragons. You defied the emperor by attempting to force his hand. You tried to steal the elixir. Even now you're trying to think of a way to stop this attack. You were never content to leave things as they were . . . always wanting more.*

Peace does not flow in your veins.

My teeth sank into my lip, tearing at the soft flesh. I had kept quiet before, trying to avoid the emperor's wrath, foolishly thinking that past grudges would be forgotten in a decade or so. What did I care for the politics of the realm, these shifts of power? Such things were beyond my paltry influence. However, the seeds of betrayal had been sown and its harvest needed to be reaped. The emperor did not trust me, nor did I him. My stomach roiled at the thought of the laurel in the emperor's possession, all the more terrifying because I did not know the consequences.

If only we had allies of our own, those we might seek refuge with. Prince Yanxi could not harbor us; they would not risk their alliance with the Celestial Kingdom. I still possessed the scale the Long Dragon had gifted me. Could I ask the dragons for aid—not to attack the soldiers, but to flee? Yet their presence would be detected, and the dragons had no desire to be pitted against the Celestial Emperor again. I would not endanger them lightly, not before exhausting every other path.

Doubt clouded my resolve, wavering like a flame caught in a crosswind. Each path before us was fraught with peril. If we fled, the emperor would not forgive us, he would hunt us across the realm. Nor could we fight, outnumbered as we would be. The only alternative was to remain and accept our punishment—yet dare I trust in the emperor's benevolence, that he might eventually relent and set us free?

The Celestial Emperor's words surfaced in my mind, what he had warned me of the day I won my mother's freedom: *As the Moon Goddess it still falls upon her to ensure the moon rises each night—without exception.*

This was my mother's second offense against the Celestial Emperor, and the insult paid a personal one. There would be no mercy, not that he was ever inclined to it. Their Celestial Majesties had no love for my family, and this was an ideal opportunity to rid themselves of us.

Part of me was glad that Liwei was not here. He would have supported us against the Celestial invasion, setting himself against his father who would view it as an unforgivable betrayal. This way, Liwei could claim ignorance of my plans—for in truth, they had only just formed.

"We will flee." My heart was laden with regret, pricked with shame. But I had little faith in the justice of the Celestial Kingdom.

Disappointment shadowed General Jianyun's face. Perhaps he had hoped I would take a stand to defend the laurel. Perhaps he imagined that a spark of my father's heroism burned in my spirit. I was neither so noble nor valiant. Some might call me selfish, but I would look out for my own. I had done my part for the realm, and been repaid by mistrust at every turn.

"I understand. Be careful," he said at last.

"We must prepare ourselves," Shuxiao said.

"We?" I asked.

She crossed her arms in seeming challenge. "I'm not leaving until you get away safely."

"How can I let you stay?" I countered.

"This is not your choice," she said fiercely.

I hesitated, wanting her by my side yet dreaded exposing her to danger. "Thank you," I managed through the tightness in my chest. I would have done no less for her.

"General Jianyun," Shuxiao addressed him. "Could you send word to my family? Tell them to go into hiding until they hear from me again."

Bitterness seared me that she had to do this, that we were forced to flee. But there was no shame in flight; I had done it before. I would not sacrifice us to a cause we cared little for. What mattered most was our freedom and our lives—upon which hope was borne, along with the promise of new beginnings.

I RAPPED UPON MY mother's door—short, hard knocks. She emerged from her room, clad in her white robe. I was glad to find Ping'er with her, sitting by the table, pouring tea into two cups.

I wasted no time, speaking urgently, "Celestial soldiers are on their way here. We must flee."

"Flee? Why?" Her eyes were wide with shock.

"The emperor has sentenced us to imprisonment in the tower. We have been accused of insulting His Celestial Majesty, of treacherous intent for the lapse in lighting the moon."

A shudder ran through her body. "They are mistaken. Can we explain?"

"It would not matter. You cannot change the minds of those who do not want to be proven wrong." I took her hands in mine, inwardly flinching from their chill. She was afraid . . . as was I. "They want to believe this of us. Forgetting to light the lanterns was a harmless thing, just as taking Father's elixir, or the dragons bringing water to the suffering mortals. The Celestial Emperor will tolerate no threat to his pride or standing. To him, appearances matter more than intent." It struck me then how much he must despise me—the girl his soldiers had bowed to, whom he would have killed that day.

"Must we flee?" My mother's voice broke. This place was all she had known of the Immortal Realm—once, her prison, and now her home.

"Yes. His Celestial Majesty will not rescind his sentence, nor will anyone plead on our behalf—at least, none he will listen to. We are a thorn in his side that he is eager to pluck. Moreover, he wants our home, and this is the perfect excuse to seize it."

Ping'er frowned. "Won't disobeying his edict anger him further?"

"Undoubtedly." Reckless satisfaction flooded me at those words. "Though we have little to lose at this stage."

Beyond our lives. Was I being a fool to risk us all? Was imprisonment not preferable to death? Yet that was not the choice; we were fighting for our freedom, for the chance to live as we chose. And I did not trust our safety in the emperor's hands.

My mother lifted her head, her expression calmer. "We will be ready."

"You must go first, with Ping'er. I will follow shortly, with Shuxiao. We will distract those standing guard here so you can escape safely."

My mother's gaze bored into mine. "I won't go without you."

"Mother, if the Celestials capture you, you will be their hostage. I can't do what I must if you're in danger. And if we flee all at once, they will sense our absence and give chase. Shuxiao and I can evade the soldiers, but as for you and Ping'er—"

"I am weak, I know." My mother looked away. "I wish I could help. If only I had magic like yours."

Perhaps my mother's power was a quieter magic, like Tao's, or one she was unaware of. Regardless, there was a core of strength in her that I had not understood as a child; I had thought her frail and delicate then. However, when I had left my home the first time, I had been a muddle of terror, while her mind remained clear, her resolve unclouded. It was as Ping'er had said: *She is stronger than you think.*

"No, Mother," I told her gently. "Magic is not the only power; we are strong in different ways. You have kept me safe all these years, it is my turn to protect you now. Both of you," I said, reaching out to take Ping'er's hand.

My mother drew a deep breath. "Don't do anything rash. You must be careful and don't get caught. Promise me this."

"I promise," I agreed at once, ignoring the guilt that pierced me.

There was another part to my plan that I had not revealed, one still forming as we spoke. Shuxiao and I planned a diversion, but what if we were to set a trap for Wugang instead? Not from spite but the instinctive desire to end this ominous threat— for who but Wugang could harvest the laurel seeds?

My mother and Ping'er moved around the room, gathering a few possessions. At the doorway, my mother embraced me tightly. I closed my eyes, inhaling her fragrance threaded with the sweetness of osmanthus.

"Be careful, Little Star." Ping'er's hand touched my cheek gently. "The darkest of nights is when the stars shine brightest."

A lump rose in my throat to hear my childhood name. I breathed deeply, holding my emotions in. Only after they had left, did I crumple to the floor, brushing my fingertips along the stone tiles. A final farewell.

That was all I allowed myself. Rising to my feet, I stalked to my room. The Jade Dragon Bow was the first thing I reached for. My sword was strapped to my side, a dagger tucked in my sash.

How arrogant I had been, thinking I would never run again. But this time, I would be ready . . . and I would take my loved ones with me.

11

THE MOON SHIMMERED LIKE A sea of silver, my mother having completed her task. Leaving the lanterns dark would have been a beacon for trouble, arousing the soldiers' suspicions. As she emerged from the forest, walking toward Shuxiao and me, thin trails of smoke drifted from the splint of wood in her grasp.

"Mother, are you ready?" I asked quietly.

She nodded, her eyes bright with tears, yet it was not from fear or the impending loss of our home. For as long as I could remember, it had been her nightly ritual to wander the forest, weeping for my father—the only time she allowed her grief to unravel instead of knotting tight in her chest. As a child, I had been hurt by her seeming coldness when I interrupted her during those times, realizing only later it was because she did not want me to see her cry. The urge to confess my father's existence gripped me, a hard secret to keep when it was what she longed for most—yet I stifled the words. The bond between my father and me was new and untried, but I had given my word; I would respect his choice. And my mother had suffered enough from their parting. I would not revive her hopes only to have them crushed again. Not until I found a way to restore him. Not until I found that duplicitous, backstabbing Tao.

"Make sure the soldiers see you enter, then leave through the balcony with Ping'er," I instructed her. "Clouds have been summoned just beyond the forest. Shuxiao and I will meet you on the shores of the Southern Sea."

"Come as quickly as you can," my mother reminded me, her lips pursed as they did whenever she suspected I was up to no good.

But I no longer crumbled beneath her glare, the truth tumbling out in a stammer. "We will," I replied steadily.

She left then, the Celestial soldiers by the entrance paying her no more than a cursory glance. Their eyes darted toward me instead, cautious and assessing, before shifting away. My gaze lingered on the luminous walls of my home, its iridescent pillars— pressing each tile and stone into my mind, just as when I had left the first time. My chest ached with suppressed grief. How I would miss this place. Yet as long as we remained alive, so would the dream of returning . . . no matter how frail it seemed right now.

The wind surged, the air quivering with a rush of immortal auras. Clouds veiled the once-clear night. I locked my hands together, cold yet slicked with sweat.

"They are coming, sooner than anticipated," Shuxiao said in a low voice.

Something hardened within me. "Then we must go."

Sensing the soldiers' eyes upon us, we strode with deliberate measure into the forest, only then breaking into a run, our feet sinking into the shining soil. We halted by the glittering laurel, its leaves clinking like pieces of silver. It was beautiful, yet in that moment I had never hated anything more. If this tree did not exist, the emperor would never have set his sights on my home, and we would not have been forced to flee.

As I raised my hand, a breeze rippled from my fingertips. It wound through the osmanthus trees at the other end of the forest, encircling them and rattling their branches. A decoy, to draw the soldiers' attention, allowing my mother and Ping'er to escape unhindered. As we sensed their auras rushing away, Shuxiao and I wove delicate threads of air coated with translucent flame, braiding them into a snare around the laurel's trunk—to be set off with a single touch.

A heaviness crashed against my consciousness like I had slammed my head against stone. I shuddered as the wards that Liwei and I had so painstakingly constructed were ripped apart like rice paper, the roaring in my mind fading to a deep stillness, the type that plunged ice down my spine.

Tremors rippled through the ground, soil scattering over our shoes. Shuxiao's eyes rounded as she gestured ahead. Pale tendrils streaked the night like fingers clawing at the sky, the smoky bitterness of ash entwined with the sweetness of charred cinnamon. My home . . . it was afire. Flickering flames devoured the once-white walls, gray smoke spiraling high. A writhing anguish took root within me, choked gasps wrung from my throat.

Shuxiao's hand gripped my shoulder. "Grieve later."

Steeling myself, I nodded, turning from the hellish sight. A flash of brightness splintered the dark as a bolt of light shot past me, striking Shuxiao's ribs. She gasped, reeling back as I grabbed her arm—my turn to steady her—as she pressed a palm to her wound, her magic streaming forth to close it. Grasping my energy, I wove a shield over us just as another wave of malevolent light plunged forward, crashing against our barrier.

An immortal appeared, clad in the Celestial armor of white and gold, wielding a great axe in his hand. His brown eyes gleamed, his hair slicked into a glossy topknot. Wugang, without his soldiers—an opportunity I would not waste.

His lips tilted into a mocking smile. "Still here? You're not as clever as I thought."

"Alone?" I shot back. "*You're* not as clever as you think."

I drew my sword—not the bow, as its light would draw every Celestial from the skies. Yet he did not move to defend himself, letting his axe blade rest upon the ground as he leaned upon its handle.

"Why do you hate us?" The question burst from me, one I had longed to ask before. "We did nothing to you."

He shrugged. "My dear girl, I don't hate you in the least. Call it a misalignment of fates; you stand in the way of what I want."

Rage seared me at his callousness, his indifference as venomous as malice. My fingers tightened around the hilt of my sword. *Make this quick*, my mind urged, the part not incapacitated by terror, sickened by this needless destruction of my home. What did it matter if he refused to fight?

I lunged at him, my weapon thrust out as he swung his axe high. Our blades collided in a shrill scrape, my wrist throbbing from the force. Shuxiao leapt up, slashing at Wugang from the side, his body curving inward to evade the blow. Shoving his full weight against his axe, he flung me off, a bright flare of his magic streaking toward us. At once I pushed Shuxiao to safety, spinning aside to avoid his attack.

Wugang raised his palms, alight with power, a shield gliding over him. "I was right to doubt your loyalties, Lieutenant."

"You did nothing to earn them," Shuxiao retorted.

"Disloyal. Disobedient. Untalented. It's time to purge the Celestial Army of such worthless recruits."

Anger throbbed as I swung at him again. Shuxiao's sword flew beside mine, swift and ruthless—yet Wugang moved with startling deftness. He dodged Shuxiao's next blow, spinning around to slam his foot into her gut. She went sprawling but scrambled up at once, flinging a bolt of ice into his shoulder. As Wugang staggered back with a gasp, I dove forward, driving my sword into his chest. The metal tip ground against the scales of his armor, yet his shield held fast. Grasping the hilt of my sword with both hands, I threw all my force against it, magic sliding from my palms to sheathe the blade. Wugang's shield fractured, my sword sinking deeper to penetrate his flesh—

A cry jolted me, ringing between my ears. My mother's voice. Why was she still here? As I froze, Wugang shoved my sword aside, springing out of reach. I started after him at once, but Celestial soldiers spilled from the trees like rivers of gold. My heart sank as Feimao dragged my mother forward, while another soldier built like an ox held Ping'er fast.

"They found us," my mother whispered. "I'm sorry."

"Drop your weapons," Wugang commanded, a slick smile upon his face—when barely a moment earlier, my sword had been pressed to his chest. "Any foolishness on your part, and your mother will pay the price."

Feimao shoved the edge of his blade to the back of my mother's neck. One upward thrust, and it would sever the core of her lifeforce. I searched his face, hoping for a flash of doubt, a sign of assurance—yet his expression remained blank.

Fury burned within me, enmeshed with the ice of fear. The temptation surged to unleash a gale upon them, sweeping Wugang to the ground . . . yet I forced myself to release my power, letting my sword fall from my grasp. How I hated this feeling of helplessness; these binds of futility.

Wugang inclined his head to my mother with unexpected courtesy, as though he were the genial Master Gang once more. "Chang'e. It saddens me to repay your hospitality in this manner."

"You could release us and spare yourself the grief," I bit out.

"That is out of my hands." His voice was tinged with regret.

My mother glared at him. "What do you want with us?"

"You should not have attempted to defy His Celestial Majesty's orders. You were commanded to remain here to await his justice. Disregarding his edict is a grave offense, as is attacking the emperor's chosen general," Wugang said solemnly.

"Justice?" I repeated with scorn. "Should we have waited here to be imprisoned?"

"It is not I who passes judgment," he replied. "I am but a servant to His Celestial Majesty."

"False pride does not suit you." I jerked my head toward the laurel. "*You* told the emperor of this place. You turned his gaze here and poisoned him against us."

He did not deny my claims, addressing my mother instead. "Those who rebel will face worse punishment. Rest assured that I will beseech the emperor for clemency on your behalf. However, your daughter possesses a rebellious streak that must be quelled."

"I need no favors from you," my mother said in glacial tones. "Especially those that will harm my kin."

Wugang spread his hands wide. "Come, Chang'e. Let us not be at odds. There are not many of us in existence—mortals who ascended to the skies. Who else might we trust if not each other?"

A strange note rang in his voice: Cajoling. Almost hopeful. I did not think it was lust; he did not look at my mother with desire. Did he feel a connection with her because of her mortal heritage? Was he lonely? After all, he had little reason to think well of immortals, his sole company in all these centuries. And everyone he had cared for in the world below had died.

"Trust?" My mother's chin tilted up. "When you attacked my family, lied to us, and seized our home?"

He stiffened, his fingers tightening around the bamboo handle in his grip. Was this the same axe he had stolen from the immortal? The one stained with his wife's blood?

"Why do you use the flute for the handle?" While my question stemmed from curiosity and the urge to divert his attention from my mother, I wanted to glean some insight into his mind. The surest way to defeat an enemy was to learn how they moved, their innermost thoughts and fears.

"It was a gift from someone unworthy. A reminder to never place my trust in another again." Bitterness thickened his voice, along with something else—a tinge of regret?

"You said your wife liked to hear you play. She gave you the flute . . . and you killed her with it," I said slowly, my stomach roiling with revulsion.

Wugang's lips pulled into a taut smile. "You seem curious about my weapon."

"I heard you spent a long time chopping a tree with it." I spoke with deliberate insult, trying to goad him into rashness.

"How would someone like you hear of such things?"

"The tales are told far and wide, sung in the mortal teahouses even," I lied. "How they must pity you."

"They would not dare!" His face twisted before it smoothed over, a mask slipping back into place. "Do you know, the mortals tell their own stories of the Moon Goddess? How she stole the elixir won by the noble Houyi, out of selfish desire to become a goddess. Some said she broke her pact with him to share the elixir, taking it all for herself. The entire one grants immortality, yet half of it would have bestowed them a long life beyond the mortal span. I would not have imagined such a ruthless heart to beat beneath this gentle exterior. How I applaud your choice, to disdain love." His smile was sharp with malice. Repayment tenfold for her hostility.

"You know nothing of me, nothing of love." My mother's voice was hard and cold. I had never seen this side of her before, radiating ice and snow—the goddess the mortals knelt to worship.

"Love is worthless," Wugang sneered. "Fleeting, inconstant,

and shifting like the wind. All it yields is sorrow in the end, whether through indifference, betrayal, or spite. Those truly powerful have no need for love—a weakness, as it brought you all down today."

His taunt seared. "Perhaps you've never truly been loved. Perhaps you've never really loved another." A low blow as I wielded his pain as a weapon.

He laughed, though there was no joy in it. "What is love to eternal life?"

"Is that why you serve the Celestial Emperor even after he treated you so?" A part of me still hoped to sway him from the emperor's side. To make him question his allegiance.

"Those of you who are born immortal take death for granted. You can't comprehend the dread of an inevitable end, whether emperor or slave. That's why your mother was banished instead of lauded, until you—her conniving offspring—tricked His Celestial Majesty into making a bad bargain. You were fortunate not to have died that day, a mistake that will be thoroughly remedied this time."

"Not by you." I fought for calm. Oh, he was skilled at deflecting my attacks, turning them upon me instead.

"His Celestial Majesty has been most generous to me. Immortality is the greatest honor any mortal could wish for. Worth any price, any insult, any *betrayal*—is it not, Chang'e?" His lips twisted into a cruel smirk.

An urge gripped me to lunge at Wugang, to attack him with my fists if need be. But my mother's face contorted with fury as she rammed her elbow into Feimao's gut. He released her, stumbling back—though he was a seasoned soldier and should not have been so easily overcome. As his eyes met mine, a flash of knowing in them, I dipped my head in silent thanks.

As Shuxiao and I rushed toward my mother, a soldier leapt

into our path. Another swung her spear at my mother, slashing her arm. A deep gash split her skin, crimson blood oozing from it. My scream erupted just as Wugang shouted a furious reprimand. At once, the soldier lowered her weapon, seizing my mother's arm. As she struggled, more blood spilled from her cut, scattering over the laurel's undulating roots. A drawn-out sigh rustled from the tree, wistful and filled with longing—if such a thing were possible. The tree quivered, flinging its branches wide like a fan, its seeds showering upon the ground like rain.

I sucked in a ragged breath as I stared at them, nestled in the grass like luminous pearls of ice. Hundreds. Thousands, perhaps, yet countless more clung to the branches.

"Bind them," Wugang barked at his soldiers, his eyes alight with sudden avarice.

Before I could move, glowing coils shot out from the Celestials' palms, snaring my mother, Shuxiao, and me. They seared against my skin, biting deeper as I writhed against them, welts forming across my wrists. Fighting for calm, I channeled a burst of energy to break the restraints—yet more ropes whipped out, twining around my arms and legs.

My mother kicked out hard. Her head flew back, slamming into a soldier's face. He swore but did not loosen his hold. I wrestled with the shimmering cords, a task made harder through my swelling panic. Sparks flared from Wugang's hand, scattering over my mother. Her limbs went slack as her eyes rolled back, her body crumpling onto the ground, where her skirts pooled like water.

Terror jolted me at the sight of her so lifeless and limp. *She's alive*, my mind cried, trying to rouse me from my stupor. *She breathes; her aura shines.*

Wugang crouched down beside her, his fingers clenching

harder around his axe. As he raised it above her, fear shot through my veins, magic flaring from my skin, dissolving the cords that bound me. Rolling to my feet, I rushed toward Wugang—just as Ping'er threw herself forward, covering my mother's body with her own. Wugang cursed, flinging a blazing bolt at Ping'er's head—the force of his blow hurling her against a tree, osmanthus petals cascading over her like a shroud.

"No!"

My scream shattered the silence. I raced to Ping'er's side, wrapping my arms around her, her body spasming in a broken rhythm like a puppet wielded by a novice. A warm wetness spilled over my palms, her blood streaming from the wound at the base of her head. At once I channeled my energy into it, sealing it as well as I could, though a thin trail of blood still trickled forth, her aura shuddering uncertainly.

My mother stirred then, blinking wildly as she pushed herself up. As her head swung toward us, the color drained from her face. "Ping'er! What happened?"

I could not speak, raising my hate-filled glare to Wugang. He showed no remorse, gesturing impatiently to the guards who closed around us. Rage spiraled unbound, loosening something deep inside me as I grasped my magic—a gale surging from my palms, crashing into the nearest soldiers. More rushed forward, but my caution had disintegrated, violence burning unquenched within. I whipped my bow free, releasing a bolt of Sky-fire at Wugang—even as his shield flared between us, my arrow fracturing into shining shards.

Wugang thrust his hand out, streaks of blazing light lashing forth. I ducked low, his attack searing the emptiness above me, crackling with malevolent heat. As I swung back up, Wugang was already moving toward me, the shadow of the laurel falling over his face.

An idea struck. "Run, Shuxiao! Take them with you," I called to her, slanting my head at the laurel.

She nodded once, spinning to my mother, who lay crouched over Ping'er. As Shuxiao pulled her away, casting a breeze to bear Ping'er along—I drew the cord of my bow, a bolt of Sky-fire blazing between my fingers. Wugang's expression tensed as his shield shimmered brighter, bracing for my attack—yet I aimed at the laurel instead, letting the arrow fly.

White light hurtled into the tree, coiling around its trunk like glowing chains—scorching the pale bark, hissing with smoke . . . yet the marks were already fading, the golden sap spilling across the wood once more.

As Wugang's lips stretched wide, my pulse quickened in anticipation. He thought he had the upper hand, that he alone knew nothing could destroy the laurel. He was mistaken; that was not our intent. As I bolted after the others, a sharp snap ruptured the stillness—the snare triggered. Waves of translucent fire cascaded down, showering those beneath in a torrent of agony. Celestials screamed, casting gleaming shields that arced over them—as Wugang raced to safety, his instinct for survival ever acute.

As I ran, the air stirred, pulsing with power. Streaks of flame and ice shot past, narrowly missing me. Breathing heavily, I grasped my energy to weave a shield—yet one glided over me, its powerful energy cool and familiar. Unwelcome, even as a small part of me was undeniably relieved.

Wenzhi stalked from the trees ahead, his black robes swirling, his eyes churning like the storm-lashed sea. With a flick of his wrist, spears of ice plunged toward my attackers. As they struck their mark, cries broke out behind me, some falling to the ground.

Clouds descended from the sky, the Celestials running toward them—if mounted, they would catch us. Stumbling to a halt, I channeled my energy into a fierce wind that swept around the soldiers, halting their advance. Beside me, Wenzhi's magic flowed, summoning a blizzard of hail, the jagged shards riding upon my gale, striking down those in pursuit. We moved as seamlessly as we used to, when we had fought together in the Celestial Army—when I had believed him honorable and trusted him with my life.

"The traitorous Captain Wenzhi," Wugang called out in a gloating lilt from where he stood, a distance away. "No surprise, that you'd keep such treasonous company. The emperor will be most pleased at this proof of your treachery. Those who consort with the Demon Realm are our enemies too."

"Better a Demon in name than one by nature. Striking the innocent, preying on the weak." I did not deny his false accusations; it would do no good.

"Those who get in my way only have themselves to blame," Wugang taunted. "A lesson you would do well to remember, as should your unfortunate attendant."

A vicious darkness engulfed me, seething with hate. Perhaps this beast existed in us all, roused once we were driven to its depths. One thought blazed clear, that Wugang would pay for what he had done. As I grasped my magic, stalking toward him—Wenzhi caught my arm, his fingers searing like frost.

"Let's go," he commanded, in the voice that countless soldiers had obeyed unquestioningly.

"No. He hurt Ping'er," I bit out.

"And he will hurt *you*. He wants you to retaliate; it's a trap." Wenzhi nodded toward the Celestials who were already stumbling to their feet. Too many for us to fight.

Swallowing my rage, I wrenched free of his hold, racing away from the soldiers until my calves burned. Wenzhi kept pace beside me as we barreled through the trees, ducking beneath the low-hanging branches. Outside the forest, my mother and Shuxiao were waiting upon a cloud, Ping'er lying beside them. As Wenzhi and I leapt upon it, Shuxiao cast a swift wind to bear us along. A dark mist flowed from Wenzhi's palms, thickening as it closed behind us, concealing our path.

A low groan broke from Ping'er's throat. I fell to my knees beside her, clasping her hand, so ashen and cold. More blood leaked from the wound at the base of her skull, my throat tightening at the sight of the torn flesh.

Closing my eyes, I released my power into her, just as Liwei had done for me before—letting it surge unbound, not halting even when a weariness sank into my limbs, darkness toying at the edge of my consciousness. She could not die; I would not let her. But there was no echoing warmth, the lights fading from her blood until it grew mortal-dull. I gathered more of my magic, hurling it into her—again and again—even as something pierced my daze, the sound of my name repeated in an endless refrain, each time more urgent than the last.

"Xingyin, stop! Don't drain yourself." Wenzhi's voice rang out. Had he been calling me all this time?

"I can't let her die." Such anguish wracked me that I would fail, that there was nothing I could do to save her. Wenzhi's hand clasped mine, and I had not the strength to tear myself away—numbed from exhaustion, from the agony that burrowed a hole through my chest.

"Let me try." He released me to press his fingers to her brow. His eyes narrowed, as a bleakness settled over his face. "The wound is fatal; her lifeforce is destroyed. No matter how much of your energy you give her, it is hopeless."

He spoke gently, yet each word hit me like a blow. As my

mother's sobs stabbed my ears, I took Ping'er's hand again, refusing to yield.

Her eyes opened wide, startlingly bright like they were lit by some inner fire. Her chest convulsed, her lips parting, a labored breath slipping out. I leaned closer, placing my ear just above her mouth.

"Little Star, no more. I am tired."

Fear was a dagger plunged deep through my heart, and twisted once to tear it anew. A hopeless wish wound through my mind: That *this* was not real, that I had not failed her, that she was not dying.

She reached for my mother with a shaking hand. "Mistress, it was my greatest honor to have served you. My honor and my joy."

My mother clasped Ping'er, tears sliding down her pale cheeks. "The honor was mine, my dearest friend."

Ping'er's mouth worked as though she had more to say, though not the strength to voice it. She squinted like she could not see, darkness beginning to cloak her vision. As her grip tightened around mine, I squeezed back with all the love in my heart . . . but then she broke free to fumble at her neck, unlatching something that she pressed into my palm—the pearl I had seen once before. It had been warm then, yet was now glazed with a wintry chill.

"The daughter I never had. The light of my days." Her words rang clear, a radiant smile upon her face. "Would you bring me home?"

I nodded violently, eager to do anything to lighten her cares. Hope burst in me at this show of strength, dissipating abruptly when she fell back down, as though she had struggled against the shackles of her broken body and could fight no more.

"The sea," she rasped. "It is beautiful there." Her body shuddered, eyelids fluttering in a frantic rhythm before going still.

Soft cries punctured the silence, those of my mother's, as I stifled the screams that surged up my throat. I crumpled over Ping'er, clasping her tight—as she had held and rocked me in her arms when I was small enough to fit in them. But she was no more, forever gone . . . taking along with her a part of me.

PART II

12

THE RUSH OF THE WIND was a mournful lament as our cloud soared onward. My mother's eyes were veined red, the coils of her hair undone, falling over her shoulders. As my gaze rested on Ping'er's body, a wrenching pain suffused me. Without her vitality and warmth, it was nothing but a shell.

Memories flooded me: of Ping'er correcting the fingering on my flute, of her showing me how to pluck the strings of a qin, of her stories that gave me my first thrill of adventure. The times she had tucked me into bed and pressed a kiss to my brow when my mother had lingered too long in the forest. The tears came then, sliding down my cheeks. I would not wipe them away or flinch from these recollections, because they were all I had left of her. There was an aching finality to this moment, this immutability of death. For gone were the days that Ping'er would hug me, never again would she call my name. How did the mortals bear such anguish, knowing all they loved would meet this end?

A gust of wind ruffled Ping'er's sleeves. I smoothed them down, my knuckles grazing her skin—so cold and still. I was a selfish creature to think of just myself. What of Ping'er's family? My mother? This loss was not mine alone.

I touched my mother's arm. "Are you all right?"

"Pain is no stranger to me." Her eyes were dulled pools of despair. "At least we have each other."

I wanted to tell her of my father then, to let hope spark in this impenetrable darkness. Yet my vow bound me fast, as did my shame. How arrogant I had been to think I could have helped my father, how reckless to steal from the Celestial Emperor, to have imagined we could escape his wrath, to have ever challenged him in the first place. For now Ping'er was dead, our home was destroyed—and I was lost.

Wenzhi bowed his head as he intoned formally, "May she find peace in eternity. May you and your mother find the strength to overcome your sorrow." He reached out a hand to me, then pulled it back, his fingers closing into a fist.

Shuxiao hugged me tightly. "I'm so sorry. I'll miss her too."

Grief clawed me, endless recriminations ringing through my mind. If only we had fled sooner, if only I had been swifter—I might have killed Wugang before. Had I treated him with the same mercilessness as he showed Ping'er, his blood would be bathing the laurel and Ping'er would be alive.

"Where should we go?" Shuxiao asked as she released me.

"To my home. You will be safe from the Celestial Emperor there," Wenzhi offered.

I recoiled from his suggestion, despite the sense in it. Once, he had brought me to the Cloud Wall against my will, and I had no desire to ever return. Even if Wenzhi truly wanted to aid us, what of his ruthless father? His vile brother? My nails dug into my palm. No, I would not thrust us into that nest of vipers. I would not lay Ping'er to rest there, in a strange place she had feared all her life.

Would you bring me home? Her words echoed through me, cutting through the fog of misery.

"We have to bring Ping'er back to the Southern Sea," I said flatly.

Wenzhi frowned. "Queen Suihe is neither benevolent nor tolerant. She will not harbor you if she knows you are wanted by the Celestial Emperor; she will see you as a threat to her people."

I did not expect a warm welcome from the queen. Fugitives, with neither friend nor kin there. The bearers of ill tidings. Yet Ping'er had never asked for anything before. This was a paltry request when she deserved so much more. While she had never expressed a desire to return, she always spoke of the sea with such warmth and longing, even with her final breath. No matter how far we had traveled from our home, it was a bond impossible to sever—rooted deep into what we were, entwined with all we would become.

My resolve hardened. "We will fulfill Ping'er's last wish," I replied, as my mother nodded in agreement.

"You must be careful," Wenzhi said gravely. "Fortunately, the queen will not have heard the news yet. The Celestial Emperor will be keen to keep this quiet as your escape would be seen as another weakness, a failure. Do what you must, then leave as soon as you can."

"We will," I told him, even as I longed for a few precious days to recoup our strength, to plan our way forward. To mourn.

"I know you blame yourself," Wenzhi said in a low voice. "Don't forget, it was *Wugang* who struck her. The *emperor* who ordered the attack on your home."

I glanced up, catching the tautness in his expression. "How did you learn of the attack?" I asked numbly.

"We have our informants at the Celestial Court. Unfortunately, this matter was so closely guarded, I only learned of it after the soldiers had left. I came as soon as I heard."

"Thank you for your aid." I spoke formally, listlessly, unable to muster the energy for more.

Kneeling down beside me, Wenzhi laid a hand on my shoulder. I had always thought his touch cool, yet now it burned through my robe. Or perhaps it was because I was frozen all the way inside, nothing but a brittle layer of ice holding me together.

"Cry. Shout. Strike me if you will. Just don't treat me like a stranger. Don't pretend to be all right when you are not."

His blunt compassion was my undoing. My chest caved until I was fighting for breath, my emotions churning within. Strong arms went around my shoulders; my head folded against his steadiness. My hands moved of their own volition, instinctively seeking comfort, my fingers clutching at the lapels of his robe as though I were falling. I did not draw closer, nor did I push him away. How familiar his embrace and the comfort it yielded . . . and how I craved it in this moment, drowning in this void of despair. A part of me wanted to stay there, locked away from the devastation of my reality—even as my pride urged me to pull away, to protest his touch. And though I despised myself for this weakness, I sensed he understood my pain—and so I remained still until my tension eased, my body going as limp as a vine as the last of my strength dispersed. Ragged breaths and bitter tears spilled from me until somehow, I was no longer stretched to breaking, exhaustion crashing over me as my eyelids sank shut into merciful slumber.

WARMTH GRAZED MY SKIN. My mind stirred from oblivion, but I did not want to awaken. Already, the ache within was returning, relentless and sharp—each breath a strain. A breeze swept against my face then, cool and fresh, stirring something in me . . . something that was not laden with sorrow, pain, or regret. Fragments of memories, good ones—of my first glimpse of the Eastern Sea and the wonder I had felt then, along with the lightness of hope.

Flicking my eyelids apart, the brightness of day crowded my vision. I blinked, making out my mother staring blankly ahead, Shuxiao sitting beside her. Instinctively, I glanced around to check no one was in pursuit. As I recalled my lapse into a weeping wreck last night, shame coursed through me. How could I have wept in Wenzhi's arms, the arms of my enemy? A betrayal of Liwei and myself.

Except, Wenzhi was not my enemy. At least, not anymore.

"Where is he?" I asked.

"Your friend said he needed to go home but would return to find us," my mother replied.

"You seemed on good terms with Wenzhi. Better than I expected after what he did," Shuxiao remarked curiously.

My mother's eyes narrowed as she sat straighter. "Is he the one who betrayed you? The Demon you hate?"

A few days ago, I would have agreed at once. Yet the things Wenzhi had said, how he had come to our aid so unflinchingly . . . these went deeper than I wished. While it did not make things right between us—nothing ever would—it was no longer pure bitterness in my heart when I thought of him.

"He did betray me. I despised him and worse," I said haltingly. "But he also helped us, more than you know."

"Have you forgiven him?" Shuxiao asked tentatively.

"No," I said fiercely. "Nor will I ever trust him again. But I don't hate him anymore either."

"Anyone who deceived you in that manner cannot be trusted." My mother paused, shaking her head. "However, some tales told of me are little better. It was as Wugang said—many believe that I wanted the elixir for myself, that I stole it to become immortal. Is that not a vicious betrayal? Was I not a selfish coward, regardless of my reasons?"

I had never heard her speak with such raw anguish, her expression haunted with grief both old and new. Perhaps Ping'er's death had wrenched her heart apart, and all the sorrow within had spilled forth.

I reached out to take her hand. "You did it to save us."

"Only we know that." Her smile was sad and thin. "While the story remains the same, the picture painted is so vastly different. Your father must have hated me, and the mortals should despise me too."

"They do not," I assured her. "Perhaps because they sense your pain. As do I."

"This is what matters." She pressed my hand tight. "That those we love understand what we did, and why."

It would comfort her to learn that my father understood, that he forgave her—but I kept silent. Wenzhi's reasons for his deception slid into my mind: his brother, a twisted monster, the vicious games of power where only the strong survived. Yet it was not the same—one driven by despair, the other, a calculated betrayal. Wenzhi had asked for us to start over, but it was impossible. All that had been precious between us could never be remade. It was gone, as irrevocably as an incense stick burnt to ash.

On the horizon, white sands rippled as bolts of pale satin, billowing with the breeze. The turquoise ocean mirrored the skies, its waters flecked with pearlescent foam. Coconut trees with leafy fronds and golden globes of fruit swayed at the far end of the shoreline. Yet unlike the beach of the Eastern Sea that flourished with life, this place was starkly desolate.

"Where is the city?" my mother asked, as our cloud descended.

"I heard it lies beneath, upon the seabed itself," Shuxiao told us.

I stared at the waters, shifting in a ceaseless rhythm. "Can you swim?"

Shuxiao shook her head. Celestials did not take naturally to the water; their lakes and ponds were purely ornamental, brimming with lotuses, adorned with waterfalls and fountains. What need was there to swim when one could fly?

"I will go. My father was a fisherman. I could swim almost as soon as I could walk." It was my mother who spoke.

Her father; my grandfather. It was the first time she had mentioned him. She spoke so rarely of her mortal family, the one she had left behind.

"Be careful, Mother." My stomach knotted at the sight of waves, deceptively mild one moment, cresting violently in the next.

Without hesitation, she strode into the waters until they lapped around her thighs. Diving in, she cut a path through the waves with smooth, sure strokes. I shaded my eyes, staring after her until she was a speck in the distance. As a wave swelled, lifting her high, she vanished abruptly from sight. Dread coursed through me as Shuxiao and I urged our cloud onward, soaring to where she had disappeared. My nerves were frayed thin; I had lost too much already.

Waves churned beneath us, their tops aglitter with the gold of the sun. The opaque waters masked their secrets well; there was not a trace of my mother or the fabled city of the Southern Sea. My heart thudded in a frantic rhythm as I grasped my magic, twisting the air into a translucent spear that burrowed through the waters, plunging to its depths.

An arm flailed up, my mother emerging as she floundered amid the turbulence. The wind dispersed at my command, the waves calming as I grasped her hand to pull her up onto the cloud.

She coughed, scattering droplets of water as I slapped her back. "Xingyin, what did you do?"

"I couldn't see you. I thought you were in trouble."

"I *am* capable of looking after myself."

She wiped a dripping sleeve across her face, then wrung her hair out, coiling it into a simple knot. Her face was drawn and pale, yet she looked younger somehow, as though the seawater had washed away a carefully cultivated veneer, that of the immaculate goddess. I caught a glimpse of the girl she had once been, echoes of her carefree youth in the quiet seaside village. My mother had ascended to the skies, becoming a goddess— and given up her parents, her husband, her future. And now she had lost her steadfast companion throughout the long years of solitude and despair. Some might think this was a small price to pay for immortality, and yet for us, grief was eternal.

A breeze fluttered from my fingers, drying her clothes and hair. "What did you find, Mother?"

"It's colder, the deeper you get. The current turned stronger, almost like it was pushing me away."

"Xingyin, over here," Shuxiao called urgently, pointing at something below.

I followed her gaze—was it a trick of the light or did the waters here gleam brighter, the foam possessed of a glowing iridescence? Passing my palm over it, I released a surge of energy across the waves, shimmering as though a shaft of sunlight had pierced their depths. A line of characters formed before us:

Enter our waters with no fear,
for those who possess an eternal tear.

"What does that mean?" Shuxiao glanced doubtfully at the churning waters. "Tears are lost as quickly as they are shed."

"Ping'er told me the tears of her people can transform into

pearls." I brushed my thumb over the pearl clasped around my neck, the one she had given me. This was not just a gift but a key.

"I miss her," my mother said in a hollow voice.

I unclasped the pearl from my neck, wrapping the gold chain around my fingers. "Let's bring her home."

As I lowered the pearl into the sea, a whistling sprang up, luminous streams of bubbles spiraling forth—twining and melding to form a slender corridor through the waters. Light blazed from the murky depths, surging up to illuminate the pathway.

I wrapped Ping'er's body with coils of air, tethering her to me. Taking my mother's and Shuxiao's hand, we leapt into the passage together. My body braced for a violent descent, but we glided through the tunnel like drifting feathers. At last, my feet sank into the tawny sand, a dampness soaking through my shoes. The air here was heavier, thick with the salt of the sea.

We stood in a circle just wide enough for one to lie across, surrounded by walls of water. The crash was thunderous yet soothing, reminding me of the waterfall in the Courtyard of Eternal Tranquility. Was Liwei there? How I hoped he was, and that he was safe. A cowardly part of me hoped that he would never learn of how I had wept in Wenzhi's embrace. It would hurt Liwei, when it meant nothing—less than nothing, I told myself fiercely. I had been desperate for comfort, weak with grief. I had done nothing wrong, and still . . . I was ashamed.

A silhouette appeared on the other side, the water parting like a curtain to reveal a guard. He was not drenched, but dry, down to each strand of his flowing hair. His black eyes were ringed with pale blue, startling against his yellowed skin. A spear was clutched in his hand, a shimmering translucent cloak flowing over his armor of turquoise scales, rimmed in gold. A pearl ring gleamed from his thumb, set in a thick band of silver.

The guard's chin jutted out. "Who possesses the pearl?" he demanded.

Wordlessly, I held it out in my hand.

"You are not one of us." An accusing note slid into his tone as the point of his weapon swung toward me. "How did you obtain this?"

"It was a gift."

As I gestured toward Ping'er's body, the guard stiffened. He studied us for a moment, finally jerking his head toward us. "Come with me. Queen Suihe will want to meet you."

13

W E TRAILED THE GUARD ALONG the passage that tunneled through the inky depths, the waters merging behind like it was sealing us in—a chill running through me at the thought. The shimmering liquid walls reminded me of the crystal panes in the Fragrant Coral Palace, except here my skin was damp with spray, my pulse racing each time a stray fin or tentacle lashed through the surface. I studied the guard, curious at how the water slid off him instead of soaking his garments. His cloak gleamed brightly, infused with some enchantment. Dragon yarn, the fabled cloth of the Sea Immortals that kept its wearers dry.

At the end of the passageway gleamed a circular door paved with mother-of-pearl and studded with turquoise. Coiled around the frame was an intricate carving of a sea creature. Golden horns curved from its head and bulbous eyes protruded from its face, its spiked tail curling along the ground. As I pushed the door, it held fast, a stinging pain shooting across my palm. I leapt back, smothering a cry.

"Use the pearl," the guard barked, as though such knowledge were commonplace.

"Does it also control the passage formation?" Shuxiao gestured toward the watery wall that had formed behind us.

He nodded, pressing his ring into the small hole dug in the creature's pupil. The door swung open, its other side adorned with the same carving. Guards stood by the entrance, uncrossing their spears at the sight of us.

"How does the door open from the other side?" I asked.

"The same way," he said curtly. "Unless it's sealed."

"Why would it be sealed?" Shuxiao asked with a wide smile, one which invited the sharing of confidences.

The guard blinked, a little of his hostility easing. "Upon Queen Suihe's command, whether in times of peril or when we need to capture an intruder. No one leaves here without Her Majesty's permission."

A disconcerting thought. As I glanced ahead, my caution dispersed. Silver flecks dusted the sands, the pathway lined with swaying fronds of emerald seaweed. The seabed was littered with shells in cream, lilac and rose, a few agleam in copper and gold. Some were shaped as fans and stars, others boasting elegant spires atop slender cones—as wondrous as those from the merchant at the Celestial market, all those years ago. A translucent barrier arced above, shielding the city from the sea—and this deep in, the lapping waters were midnight black.

As I stepped through the doorway, a slippery softness clung to my skin like I was walking through a bubble. The air was unexpectedly crisp, and if I closed my eyes, I might imagine I was on the beach instead of hundreds of feet below. Silk lanterns were strung up along the path, casting their luminous glow all around. We walked past rows of honey-colored stone houses with sweeping roofs of lapis and agate, glowing coral springing up between them, as vivid as wildflowers.

The Sea Immortals were pale, their skin a light yellow, perhaps because the sun could not reach this place. Their dark hair was braided and coiled around their heads, both men and women alike, and the eyes that turned to us in curious speculation were ringed in shades of blue. Shimmering cloaks of dragon yarn were draped around their bodies, falling to their ankles like sheets of starlight.

At the center of this glittering jewel of a city rose the Bright Pearl Palace—shaped like a magnificent shell, its conical spires stretching out like the rays of the sun. Pearls of white, rose, and black studded the golden walls, and verdant seaweed towered as tall as trees, their fronds undulating in a graceful rhythm.

The guard led us into the palace, through a long corridor that seemed to curve once around the grounds before opening into a grand hall. Amber pillars climbed from the floor to the ceiling, encircled by strands of jade beads. Exquisite carpets of blue and emerald silk were strewn across the floor, woven with swirling patterns in silver, evoking images of the waves above. The immortals were magnificently attired, their robes shimmering with threads of gold, shining jewels plaited into their hair. They formed two lines that led to the dais at the far end, where a woman sat upon a throne of crimson coral, its delicate branches flaring wide. Queen Suihe, as regal and forbidding as when I had last seen her at Liwei's banquet.

"Kneel, foreheads to the ground," the guard ordered brusquely. "Greet Her Majesty before you dare look upon her."

I tempered a flash of annoyance as I dropped to my knees, performing an obeisance. Prudence was advisable when one was a stranger to the court.

"Rise." A command, yet the queen's rich tones cloaked it in an invitation.

This close to the dais, Queen Suihe's aura rushed over me— formidable and aloof, her power grasped at the ready like a spring coiled taut. Her violet robe pooled by her feet, banded around her waist by a rope of sapphires. An exquisite headdress rested on her black hair, wrought of jade leaves and turquoise flowers, a short fringe of coral beads falling over her brow. Her face possessed the soft curves of an apricot, though devoid of its warm blush.

"It has been a long time since Celestials graced our court. What brings you here, particularly in such . . . disarray." Her lips stretched into a smile, jarring against the speculation in her eyes.

I resisted the urge to brush the loose strands from my face, raising my head higher. What was this monarch's disdain to the Celestial Emperor's wrath? I would mind my manners as my mother had taught me, but I would not cower.

Before I could speak, my mother stepped forward. Her hair was damp and tangled, her white robe stained, yet she bore herself with as much dignity as the queen. "Your Majesty, we are not from the Celestial Kingdom. I came to bring my friend to her final resting place."

The queen's gaze swung to Ping'er's body. "This grieves me. Her mother is my chief attendant, a loyal servant." She gestured to a young immortal, who rushed to her side. "Summon the chief attendant."

She turned back to my mother. "Welcome, Goddess of the Moon. You have traveled far from your home."

My insides curled, though it was no secret that Ping'er had been my mother's attendant. It was unlikely the Southern Sea would have learned of the emperor's attack, yet the fewer who knew of our presence, the safer it would be.

My mother inclined her head. "Thank you, Your Majesty. We are grateful for the kindness of the Southern Sea."

Queen Suihe smiled warmly. "I congratulate you on your pardon. It was a tale that only recently made its way to our ears, isolated as we are from the rest of the realm."

"Isolated, Your Majesty?" I tried to conceal the lift in my tone, my surging relief.

"The path here is not easy to traverse, and we have ways of keeping out unwanted guests." Queen Suihe searched my face as she spoke to me, her curiosity evident. She did not know me; it had been years since Liwei's banquet, and I would have been beneath her notice.

"This is my daughter, Xingyin, and her friend Shuxiao," my mother said.

"The Celestial archer." Recognition thrummed in the queen's tone. "Prince Yanxi of the Eastern Sea spoke highly of you."

"His Highness is too kind. I was glad to be of aid." I breathed a little easier. "I no longer serve the Celestial Army, Your Majesty. I left to return to my mother." I hoped she would not probe further.

"A dutiful daughter." She settled back against her throne, satisfied that we were figured out, no longer a riddle where danger might lurk unseen. "The monarchs of the Four Seas are gathering here soon. If you wish, you may remain as our guests until then."

I was tempted to accept, my exhaustion reaching deep—but I recalled Wenzhi's warning. "We are honored by your invitation, Your Majesty, but we cannot stay. We do not wish to impose on your generous hospitality and—"

"It would be no imposition," the queen interjected, a frown flitting across her brow. She was unused to being refused. She leaned forward, addressing my mother instead. "Your loyal attendant's funeral will take place in a few days. Do you not wish to pay your final respects to her?"

My mother's throat worked, her fingers gripping her skirt. The eyes she turned to me were bright with hope. Oh, I wanted to stay too, to see Ping'er laid to rest. But would we be safe until then? Yet another refusal might rouse the queen's suspicions, for who would turn down a royal invitation without good cause? Moreover, I believed the emperor would conceal the attack for now, given he had acted so furtively before. Which meant we had a few days respite, to regather and grieve.

"Thank you, Your Majesty. We are grateful for your consideration," I said, as my mother and Shuxiao lowered themselves into another bow.

Two immortals hurried into the hall then, clad in indigo robes, their hair tucked into silver headpieces. At the sight of the younger immortal, shock coursed through me. There were echoes of Ping'er in the set of her eyes, the arch of her nose, though her chin was more pointed and her face leaner. Was this her sister? An urge gripped me to embrace her, for no other reason than she was Ping'er's flesh and blood . . . and that she shared our pain.

The pair knelt on the floor to greet the queen, who gestured for them to rise. "Chief Attendant, this is Chang'e, the Moon Goddess, and her daughter."

As the woman's face brightened, her lips parting to speak—a sharp cry rang out from the younger girl.

"Sister!" she gasped, falling to her knees by Ping'er's body, holding her in a futile embrace.

The chief attendant staggered back, her gaze swinging to us, hard with accusation. "What happened to my daughter? What did you do to her?"

"Chief Attendant, compose yourself." The queen's tone was a knife sheathed in silk. "Allow our honored guests the chance to explain."

Tears shone from my mother's eyes, spilling down their corners. She did not wipe them away. "I am grateful for your daughter's company for all these decades. Ping'er has been a loyal companion and . . . my dearest friend. She died, protecting me from a heinous attack. We brought her here to be laid to rest because it was her final wish."

Queen Suihe shook her head. "A great tragedy for her family and you. Chief Attendant, you have leave to proceed with the funeral proceedings."

The chief attendant's chest heaved, her throat working with unspoken words, but a stern look from the queen silenced her. "Ping'yi, bring your sister's body," she called out harshly.

Without another word, the chief attendant bowed to the queen and left the chamber, her steps unsteady and hurried. I wanted to call to her, to explain, to tell her what Ping'er had meant to us, to share our memories—except that would be a cruelty rather than a kindness. For the life Ping'er had with us was only possible because she had been parted from her family. Foolishly, I had imagined we would weep over our shared sorrow, a release to the anguish coiled tight in my chest. After all, Ping'er had intended to leave me in her family's care here—this was where I might have spent my years if we had not been chased by the soldiers, if I had not leapt to the Celestial Kingdom.

As Ping'yi stared at her sister's body, her nose reddened, a tear sliding down her cheek. The clear liquid shifted to a milky white, gleaming as it morphed into a pearl that fell to the ground.

Bending down, I picked it up. Smooth and warm between my fingers, it looked just like the one around my neck. Its luminosity reminded me of the laurel seeds, but with a softer glow instead of their harsh glitter. Silently, I passed it to her.

"Thank you." As she raised her hand, light surged forth to envelop Ping'er, her body rising into the air.

"Wait! Where are you taking her?" I was not ready to let go.

"My sister will be laid to rest with the spirits of our ancestors, eventually becoming part of the ocean we love." Her gaze flicked to me, lingering on the pearl around my neck. Unlike her mother, there was no animosity in her expression, just a deep sadness, which hurt more.

"Why did she leave?" I wanted to learn everything I could; the stories Ping'er never had the chance to share with us.

Ping'yi hesitated. "It was my fault. I was in love with our childhood friend, though he offered for Ping'er instead. We fought that day. I accused her of selfishness, of scheming to have him for herself. She left the next day." Her shoulders hunched inward. "I thought she would return after a year or two. Ten years passed, then decades more. When she finally wrote to us, she said she was happy to serve the Moon Goddess and that she had found her place in the world."

"She was better than we deserved." My sight blurred, tears catching in my lashes.

Ping'yi studied my face. "Your tears . . . do they contain a part of you too?"

"No. Why would you think so?"

"Is that so surprising?" Her smile was pensive. "Tears are born of our deepest emotion, whether joy or grief. They are a part of us, just like our blood through which our magic flows. It is said the tears of some immortals possess great power, that manifests in unexpected ways. For us of the Southern Sea, our tears can transform into pearls—though it is a rare occurrence, perhaps only once or twice in our lifetime. A gift to our loved ones and also a key to our realm, so they can always find their way back to us."

My hands moved to my necklace, unclasping it. Cradling it in my palm, I held it out to her, though it pained me to yield it. "I was unaware of its meaning when Ping'er gave it to me. Please take it."

Her fingertips brushed the pearl's lustrous surface. "She must have loved you greatly. And no, I will not take my sister's gift to you." She inclined her head to me. "I must attend to my mother. She is distraught."

"I am sorry." The words were torn from deep within.

"I'm sorry too. For driving her away, for not telling her how much I loved her, and most of all, for not asking her to come home." Her shoulders tensed, her fingers curling. "I don't know how she died or why, but don't let it be for nothing."

I nodded in silent assent, holding fast to this fragile solace. I would not flinch from the hurt or tuck Ping'er away in some untouched part of my mind. I would embrace the pain, for it meant that I loved her—and I would never forget.

14

I PULLED THE GOSSAMER CURTAINS AROUND the bed, sinking upon the soft mattress. Exhaustion pressed upon my limbs, yet sleep eluded me—the pain in my chest sharpening each time I shut my eyes. A gentle clinking broke the stillness, the strands of beads that fringed our doorway knocking together with the breeze. This deep underwater, how could there be a wind? Perhaps it was some enchantment like the glowing coral that illuminated our room, or the floor, speckled like sunlit sand.

Finally, I rose and headed to my mother's chamber, just down the corridor from mine. She had changed into a fresh set of garments, provided by the attendants. The pure white brocade was a color my mother often wore, yet devoid of her usual vivid underrobe and bright-colored silk ornaments. She was winter, snow, and ice. The moon in mourning.

"Could you not sleep?" I asked.

A shudder ran through her. "There would be no rest in it."

She was right, for too many nightmares would haunt us tonight.

We sat by the table, crafted with flat pieces of mother-of-pearl layered together like the scales of a fish. Small plates of food were laid out: tarts brimming with yellow custard, pastries of crushed almond and honey, glistening discs of sweetmeats. Though I had not eaten all day, their rich scents turned my stomach.

As my mother lifted the teapot, her hands trembled, the amber liquid spilling.

"Let me, Mother." I took it gently from her, filling our cups. My training had taught me to feign strength when there was none, and to strike with a steady hand even when fractured within.

Someone knocked, sliding the doors apart. Shuxiao entered, Wenzhi following her, as he stooped to avoid colliding with the beads.

"What are you doing here?" His presence startled me, though I should have grown accustomed to him appearing when I least expected him to.

"He came looking for you and found me instead," Shuxiao said with a smirk. "A careless mistake."

His lips formed a sardonic smile. "I asked the attendant for the room of the fierce one, the one who looked ready to attack upon the slightest provocation."

"Only those who deserve it." I glared at him, even as a part of me was relieved to feel *anything* other than this hollow ache. "How did you get here?"

Wenzhi lifted an ornament by his waist, a black pearl adorned with an amethyst silk tassel. "A gift from Queen Suihe so our messengers could enter her domain. When we challenged the Celestial Kingdom, we rose in her esteem. Since then, she has cultivated cordial relations with us."

"Are they your allies?" I asked, surprised.

"The Southern Sea has no formal alliance with us, nor with any kingdom in the Immortal Realm. While they did not come to our aid in the war, neither did they rise against us. Queen

Suihe has kept the Southern Sea free of many a battle. Yet while they have few enemies, they have fewer friends."

"Which are you at the moment?" I asked.

He shrugged. "Neither. Both. Queen Suihe is a consummate diplomat, something my father appreciates. She switches directions as ruthlessly as the wind, with a keen sense for the winning side."

My gut churned. Such shifting loyalties gave me little comfort.

My mother fixed Wenzhi with a cold stare. "I thank you for your aid. However, you have much to answer for in your treatment of my daughter."

"It is my greatest regret," he said gravely.

A tense silence fell over us, but I would not let myself dwell on his words. "Do you have news?" I asked him.

"Just that you can rest easy for now. No official proclamation has been issued regarding the attack on your home—if the Celestial Kingdom wanted their allies' support, they would have sent word by now. Nevertheless I wanted to ensure Queen Suihe had not tossed you into prison upon a whim; she will not hesitate upon the slightest whiff of suspicion. There are many cells hidden within this palace, impervious to magic, impossible to escape from."

"I trust you know such places well," I remarked.

He smiled. "Well enough to know that you'd find my home far more comfortable, and infinitely safer."

"I will not go to the Cloud Wall," I told him bluntly. "I do not trust your kin."

"Neither do I," he agreed. "But an enemy in the open is safer than a friend who might turn on you at any moment."

"The Cloud Wall?" My mother repeated in a dazed voice. "Where is that?"

"The Demon Realm," I said.

My mother recoiled. All she knew of the Demons was how they were depicted in the tales—as evil, vicious, hideous creatures who feasted on the flesh and suffering of others. In my childhood, it had been a comfort to believe such monsters were tucked away on the outskirts of the realm, where only the overly brave and foolhardy ventured. I now knew that was an illusion. Demons were everywhere, by deed if not by name, and they did not wait for you to seek them out.

"The Demon Realm used to be called the Cloud Wall, part of the Celestial Kingdom. They were exiled for their magic, which the emperor had decreed forbidden. They are . . . just like other immortals," I explained.

I had not told my mother much of my time there, eager to forget it myself. Moreover, few spoke of this, particularly in the Celestial Kingdom. History was rewritten as it pleased the victor or buried when it was an inconvenient truth. Those of the Cloud Wall had done terrible things; they had destroyed and hurt others—but who had not in a war? The Celestial Kingdom was not blameless either, and fighting for one's home was something I could comprehend.

"Was this magic so dangerous?" my mother asked.

"All magic is dangerous, particularly when wielded as a weapon," Wenzhi said.

"Though some can cause far greater hurt." I repressed a shiver as I recalled Liwei's blank gaze, the moment he had thrust his sword into my heart.

No, I could not forget what Wenzhi had done, these unseen wounds he had inflicted—the fruits of his devious schemes. A fragile truce was the only thing I would allow us, as far as forgiveness went on my part. I would trust him only when our interests were aligned, and I would not hesitate to use him to our advantage just as he had used me before. And if he was to turn on me again . . . this time my arrow would find its mark.

"We will leave right after Ping'er's funeral," I told him. "Have you heard any news of Liwei?"

A line creased Wenzhi's brow. "His Highness has been moved from his courtyard and is being held under guard."

The fear caged within me broke free, images flashing through my mind of Liwei locked in a windowless cell, tormented into some baseless confession. "Why would they do this?"

"His Highness has recently acquired a startling number of enemies. His position has never been so vulnerable, and many see a rare opportunity in the tussle for power."

My insides twisted, imagining assassins dispatched to murder Liwei, poison in his cup, carefully orchestrated "accidents."

Sensing my distress, Shuxiao wrapped an arm across my shoulders, hugging me to her. "No one will dare to harm him."

"Because of his position?" My tone was hopeful yet dulled.

"Because of his mother," she said wryly.

I found no levity in this wretched situation, that the Celestial Empress was now my best hope to keep Liwei safe. For once, I was glad for her devious cunning and ruthless spite. Few in the Jade Palace would dare cross her.

"Can she protect him?" I asked Wenzhi.

"The empress is trying but her hands are tied. The true power lies with His Celestial Majesty and she cannot be seen to defy him, for it would endanger her own position and safety."

"Where is Liwei confined?"

Wenzhi's eyes narrowed. "You can't get into the Jade Palace. Not even with my aid."

"Why not?" I asked.

"After the Imperial Treasury was breached, new wards have been woven around the palace, barring entry to all outsiders except those allowed by General Wu." Wenzhi threw a cautious glance my way. "More guards have been stationed around the walls. They will not be easily led astray, when the threat of whipping or worse hangs over them."

"I must rescue Liwei," I said flatly.

"How, if the palace is so tightly guarded? If you are captured, they will never let you out again, and you will make things worse for His Highness," Shuxiao warned.

"I need someone inside the Jade Palace to help," I said slowly. "The wards cannot be broken from outside."

"Can your informants aid us?" Shuxiao asked Wenzhi.

"Not for so dangerous a venture; they will not risk their position. I am privy to their briefings, but they answer to my father alone. He will not lift a finger to aid the Celestial Crown Prince." He added contemplatively, "It would not help anyway. You need someone of sufficiently high rank to breach those wards."

General Jianyun might help us, but his own position was precarious. Unease crawled over my skin as just one other idea surfaced—repellent, yet it offered the best chance of success.

"I need your help to get a message to someone in the Celestial Kingdom," I told Wenzhi.

"Who would that be?" he asked carefully.

I paused, holding his gaze. "The Celestial Empress." My steady tone concealed the uncertainty that shook me.

As my mother paled, Wenzhi studied my face. I swallowed to moisten my throat, showing none of the doubt which beat through me. "Will you do this?" I pressed when he did not reply.

He leaned toward me. "If this is what you want. If you have thought this through."

"Xingyin, is this a joke?" Shuxiao asked. "The empress will never meet you, much less help you."

"Not for me," I said. "For her son."

I was not so deluded as to imagine the Celestial Empress would grant me a favor, when a year ago she had clamored for my death. Yet something bound us that went deeper than hate—our love for Liwei, for we would do all in our power to save him . . . even stooping to deal with those whom we most despised.

15

NEVER DID I IMAGINE I would be meeting the Celestial Empress in a mortal teahouse. I almost did not recognize her—stripped of her splendid garments and ornaments, her dazzling aura muted. She was dressed as any other villager, wrapped in a cotton robe, a wooden pin tucked in her hair. Gone were the gold sheaths that covered her fingers, but her tapering nails, ending in sharp points, looked no less threatening.

"You came." An inane thing to say when she stood before me.

She did not deign to respond, disapproval puckering in her brow as her gaze fell upon the worn wooden floor, the bamboo stools, the unvarnished ceiling beams. Her nose wrinkled as a serving man scurried past, bearing a tray filled with bowls of steaming soup and plates of fish and vegetables. Had I chosen this place to irk her, who clung to pomp and grandeur like a second skin? Perhaps, without even knowing it, but mainly to avoid any trap she might have devised in the Immortal Realm, where she had the upper hand. A test, to gauge how far she was willing to go to save her son—and the fact she was here meant she was as desperate as me.

I lifted the heavy porcelain teapot, pouring her a cup. Not from respect, but my mother's teaching that I had to show courtesy to an elder, a guest who had accepted my invitation.

She ignored it, lowering herself upon a stool. "Why did you want to meet me here?" Her voice reeked of hostility.

"Where else might we go, Your Celestial Majesty? To the Jade Palace? This meeting is best left unseen. Moreover, this place gives us *both* comfort, since magic is forbidden here."

Her cheeks flushed so dark they appeared speckled with blood. "How dare you speak to me as though you are my equal? You are nothing, whereas I am the empress of the earth and skies. Do you forget who judges what is permissible here?"

"Your husband. And I trust you do not wish him to learn of this." Somehow, I managed a semblance of civility. To show my contempt would gain nothing except fleeting satisfaction and lasting enmity.

Her gaze slid to the window. Was she searching for her guards who waited outside? They were hardly inconspicuous, standing stiffly apart from the mortals, a sneer on their faces despite the humble garments they wore. The thrum of immortal auras pulsed through the air, rising above the efforts to muffle them. Why had they not attacked? What was the empress waiting for?

"I know you hate me," I said without preamble. "My father killed the sunbirds, but he did it to save the mortals."

"He could have stopped them without killing them," she snarled.

"He had no choice. It was that or let the Mortal Realm be destroyed. Deep down, you must suspect who aided him, who had the power to do so." I said no more, unwilling to break my father's confidence.

Her gaze fixed on her cup though she made no move to take it, likely disdaining the coarse stalks of tea floating on the murky surface. "You asked me to come here. Why?"

"For the same reason you came. For Liwei."

Her fingers curled on the table. "This is *your* fault. Because of you he has become defiant, turning his father against him. You brought him to this pitiful state. Fool that he was, he even refused the betrothal with Princess Fengmei—for you."

Her words stabbed like knives. Worse, because I could dispute nothing. No one could deny that Princess Fengmei was a far more eligible bride, who would have brought along with her considerable charms, an army to defend her betrothed and an unassailable place on the Phoenix Throne. Unlike me, who had antagonized his mother, stolen from his father, and fled like a criminal.

"Is Liwei in danger?" I went cold inside, my only assurance that the Sky-Drop Tassel had remained still all this time.

She slanted her head back, staring at me down the length of her nose. "He is safe for the moment. My personal guards are keeping watch to ensure there is no foul play. Now, stop wasting my time and tell me what you want."

"To get Liwei out of the Jade Palace," I said.

"What if I think he should stay? Beg his father for forgiveness? Accept the betrothal with Princess Fengmei in exchange for his freedom?" She spoke slowly, savoring the barbs in her words.

I stifled a spurt of anger as I met her gaze. "I am sure you have attempted that, and the fact you are here means Liwei refused."

"Sometimes, it depends on the stakes." Her lips curled into a crimson crescent. "Ask yourself, *why* do you think I came today? To barter with some useless girl who can offer me nothing, or to gain something I did not have before?"

There it was, her game revealed. I had invited her in good faith, yet she had devised a trap. She wanted to take me hostage, to trade me for Liwei's compliance. My stomach roiled in revulsion, and I was relieved for the absence of fear. And most of all, that I had anticipated her deviousness and was not quite the fool she had expected. In dealing with vipers, I had learned to think like one. I swung with deliberate measure to the corner of the teahouse where Wenzhi sat, his great sword lying on the table in full view. As my gaze collided into his, he raised his cup in a mocking toast—even as his other hand clasped the onyx scabbard of his weapon in a barely veiled threat. He need not fear offending the Celestial Empress; she had no hold over him or his family, which was why I had asked him to come instead of Shuxiao.

The empress's eyes blazed. "The traitor. Is my son aware of this?"

"Is he aware of your scheme to force his choice?" How liberating to not mind my words, to discard the mask of humility I had been compelled to wear in her presence.

Shoving back the stool, she uncoiled to her full height. "I have nothing more to say to you."

"I have *plenty* more to say to you." I bit back several choice insults. "Tell me, what happened to Liwei?"

A long pause. I thought she would leave, but then she sank back onto the stool. "He's being held captive, under watch by those who should rightfully bend their knees to him. It would have been prison had I not intervened, he had infuriated his father so."

"Liwei did nothing to deserve such treatment," I said fiercely.

"It's that vile pretender, Wugang, pouring venom into my husband's ear about our son."

"Wugang?" Hatred seared me like a burning coal. I drew a long breath to calm myself, to focus on what might be done. "What of General Jianyun? Can he intercede?" Selfish of me to ask, with the general's own troubles.

"General Jianyun has been retired with an honorary title. Wugang convinced my husband to grant him full control over the Celestial Army. I always believed that was the pinnacle of that upstart's plans. It is now clear he intends to usurp my son's rightful position as heir—to taint the throne with his mortal blood, and rule after my husband."

Did she despise me for my mortal heritage too, that I was not merely low-born but "tainted"? I did not care. The empress was of the noblest blood in the realm, and yet I could not stand her.

"Would the emperor displace his own son for Wugang?" This seemed a step too far, even given his unforgiving nature.

Her lips peeled back into a snarl. As much as she detested me, it was clear she hated Wugang more. "Wugang once endangered himself, performing a great service for my husband. Since then, honors have been showered upon him. My husband treasures loyalty above all, and Wugang was ever compliant, fulfilling his every command. I favored him, too, until his ambition grew clear: his desire to rule instead of serve."

"Why would Wugang serve your husband after the humiliation heaped upon him?" I probed.

"Would not *any* mortal be eternally grateful for the gift of immortality?" she asked scathingly.

As the empress glanced at the doorway impatiently, I stifled my curiosity. The answers I most wanted were for myself. "Why did the emperor send his soldiers to the moon? What does he want with my home?" The official reason—that my mother had slighted the emperor's pride—felt hollow, incomplete. There was little reason nor justice in this, beyond the fact he wanted us gone. It would not have changed our decision to flee, but I wanted to learn what else we might have to fear.

The corners around the empress's mouth creased. "What does it matter, now that it's done? You do not need to know," she replied harshly, yet I caught the crack in her tone. She did not know, and that unnerved me, for the emperor's ambitions were a mystery even to those closest to him.

"It does matter," I ground out. "My home was destroyed, my loved one killed. It means nothing to you, but it is everything to me."

"Blame yourself for all that happened."

"This was *not* my fault." I had done all I could to steer clear of court politics; I wanted no part of it.

"You disrupted our peace. The army bowed to *you*. General Jianyun came to your defense. Liwei defied his father's command before the court, as he had never done before. One by one, you destroyed my husband's pillars of support until just Wugang remained—and now that ambitious pretender is the only one he will listen to."

My gut twisted yet I did not look away; to show her any weakness was to invite retaliation. "None of this was intended as a challenge. When greatness runs deep, it need not fear such shallow ripples."

Her eyes narrowed to slivers of loathing. "Ripples turn into waves."

"Sweeping them away will only create more. No power is absolute, nor is obedience."

She drew herself up, her movements taut with fury. "I did not come here to listen to your foolishness. You say you want to help my son. How?"

"Liwei can't remain at the Jade Palace. Wugang will kill him to secure his position." Speaking these words sickened me, but I laid them bare in hopes of convincing her.

The empress's hands clenched on the table. She knew I spoke the truth, perhaps she had suspected it herself but not given it voice. Our worst fears were those we most wanted to silence.

I pressed on. "With the soldiers under his command, Wugang could strike at any moment. He is both ruthless and cunning; he won't let this opportunity pass. How long can your guards protect Liwei? Can they stand against the Celestial Army?" I leaned across the table, close enough to see my reflection in her eyes. "Help me get him out."

She did not reply. I could almost hear the scales in the empress's mind weighing the tallies, calculating how to swing this to her advantage. She wanted to save her son, but she would not let me off unscathed.

"Why do I need you?" she demanded.

How she despised the very idea. Yet this question was more than spite—a tool to make me plead for her aid, to turn me into the supplicant. There was little need for that; I would promise her anything I could, for I needed her too.

"The great Celestial Empress should do nothing to risk her position." I kept my expression blank, masking the contempt in my words. "You don't want to oppose your husband openly. Help me and I will get Liwei away, while you remain blameless."

As her pupils gleamed brighter, I continued, "We both want him to be safe. We want the same thing."

"We do *not*," she seethed.

A mistake, to speak of us together. She would hate the association; she would think it beneath her.

Her nails dug into the table, carving fresh marks on the pitted wood. "I want him to rule the Celestial Kingdom as the most powerful monarch across the realms—his name revered by immortals and mortals from the moment their tongues form words till they fall silent in death. I want him to become the greatest immortal who ever lived, while you just want him for yourself. You will diminish him, as you already have—before his father, the court, and the realm."

I shook my head. "I never asked him to give up anything for me."

"Yet you would have let him turn his back on his position,

his heritage and family." A cruel smile lit her face. "You would not be happy though. Liwei is not meant for the type of life you crave. My son is used to greatness, to being adulated and revered. His heart is soft; he would not outwardly blame you, but know this—you, alone, will never be enough for him. Dissatisfaction would sink in, morphing into resentment. And finally . . . hate."

Her words bore the malice of a curse. She had seen into my deepest fears and most selfish desires, casting them in a shameful light. Nor could I object when she spoke the truth—I *would* have let him. I had almost convinced myself that this was what he wanted, rather than a sacrifice for my sake alone. A cowardly act, for it was easier this way, rather than undertaking a burden I would bear for the rest of our lives.

"I don't trust you," she hissed. "You say you want to help him, but you are just afraid to lose your hold over him."

"I could say the same of you." I leashed the more vicious responses that surged to my tongue. It did not matter what venom she spat; Liwei's safety was at stake. "What will it take for you to believe me?" I braced myself, for I had bargained once with her husband and nearly lost everything. I would tread carefully this time, though I was certain her price would not be to my liking.

"One condition. Just one, and no other." Her smile radiated genuine pleasure. "He proposed marriage to you. Swear to me that you will refuse, that you will break it off with him forever."

"No." The refusal sprang from my lips, born in the heat of anger yet tempered by a rush of dread.

"You must have your doubts. Why else have you not accepted?" Her tone was silken, her gaze pitiless—a predator secure in its prey. "You are ill suited for the demands of an empress, unworthy of the honor. The Celestial Court will not let you forget that every day of your existence. They will scorn you behind your back, sneer at you beneath their smiles, eagerly awaiting the day that you will be displaced by another—the inevitable fate of an empress."

Spite coated each word, yet beneath lurked pain. The Celestial Emperor's infidelities were known far and wide. I ignored the pity stirring in me; she did not deserve it.

"I will not agree." Strong words, if only my voice had not quavered.

"Then I will keep my son close to me in the Jade Palace."

The empress was wrong, she could not protect him. However, she was arrogant and vindictive enough to convince herself that she could. "You would sentence him to death," I made myself say. "How long until Wugang moves against *you*? What will happen to Liwei then? If you defy your husband openly, it will only strengthen Wugang further."

Her lips pursed. Although I had foiled her plan to capture me, I was still the perfect piece for her to play. All she had to do was feign innocence and malign me, both of which she was adept in doing.

"What choice do you have?" I pressed. "You can't send Liwei to your kin in the Phoenix Kingdom, not while they're allied with the Celestial Kingdom."

"He would have been safe there had he wed Princess Fengmei. Do not presume to tell me what I can or cannot do. I don't need *you* to protect my son."

She jerked to her feet again, flicking down the skirt of her robe contemptuously. I had thought the urgency of the situation and her love for Liwei would suffice to persuade her. I had miscalculated, misjudged, tripped myself in my haste by bruising her pride. She would never let me—a *nobody*—appear to get the better of her. She would leave, for spite was a well that ran deep in her, and she would tell herself this was for Liwei's sake.

Despair sank over me. Part of me wanted her to go, to reject her loathsome terms. Yet she had read me better than I had read her. She wanted Liwei to be free of me, and nothing else I offered would suffice. And despite my protests, she knew I would yield—for I could not toy with his life.

"Wait." My voice was low. Unwilling. "For this to work, you must break the palace wards which bar me from entering."

She turned around, her face alight with triumph. "Swear that you will end your relationship with Liwei forever. Swear to never tell anyone of this. Swear this on your mother's life," she demanded with ruthless cunning, "and it will be done."

Fury seared me, edged with pain. Yet her gloating expression roused me from the depths of defeat. I would not be a fool; I would salvage whatever I could from this wreckage. I would make her surrender something of value in return.

"I have not agreed to your terms," I told her.

"You have no choice."

"I do. I can do nothing, and trust in your claim to keep Liwei safe. If he dies, *you* will have failed him, you will have killed your own son." I almost choked upon these vile words, but it sufficed that she flinched.

"What do you want?" she demanded. "I will not relent on my terms."

"Swear this, then: to never harm my kin and me without just cause." When she did not reply at once, I added quickly, "One other thing. A small ask, compared to yours."

"What is it?" she hissed. "My patience is wearing thin."

It must seem an innocuous request, not one driven from true need. "There is someone in the Celestial Kingdom who offended me greatly. I want you to find him and secure him in the same place as Liwei. I will deal with him myself."

"What did he do?"

"You do not need to know." A petty vengeance, to return her earlier words. "But you cannot harm him."

A curt nod, her mood more agreeable. "Who is he?"

"Tao," I told her. "His sister is the Keeper of Mortal Fates' apprentice, but she is ignorant of this matter." I did not want to implicate her. All I wanted was the elixir, and I hoped it was not too late.

"A known troublemaker." A speculative gleam shone in her eyes. "I have heard of this one."

She had agreed too readily. I searched for something to bind her as irrevocably as she had done to me. Liwei was whom she loved the most, but I could not ask her to swear on his life. So, I would hold her instead to what she most despised.

"Do this, and I will honor my promise to you. However, if you break your word to me, our deal is void and I will be free of my vow. I will be free to marry Liwei, to take your place as the Celestial Empress." She would hate the thought of me upon her throne as much as I would; she would do anything to prevent it from happening.

Her chin jutted out. "I will keep my word. You are a fool for ever imagining that you are good enough for him. You will *never* be the empress."

"I have no desire to be one, especially seeing the joy it gives you." A brutal jab, but she had taken enough from me already. I had driven the hardest bargain I could, and still she had won.

Her face went pale, then flushed darkly. "Are we agreed?"

"Yes." The word left a bitter tang in my mouth.

It was done. Her lips stretched wide like those of a well-fed hyena. "Tomorrow evening. I will weaken the wards and you can enter the palace without fear of discovery. You may mask yourself in invisibility, do whatever you need to get to Liwei. I will keep my husband and Wugang occupied, but you must dispatch the soldiers guarding my son. I cannot dispose of them without suspicion. Be warned, I will offer no aid should you be caught. No one will take your word over mine."

Her gaze shifted to the back of the teahouse where Wenzhi sat. "The Demon must not accompany you into the palace; I can do nothing about the wards against his kind, for those are crafted by my husband. Moreover, he cannot be linked to my son; they will accuse him of treachery and worse. You must take no chances with Liwei's life, nor can there be any doubt that this is your doing."

I forced my mind to clear, to untangle it from my emotions. "Where will Liwei be?"

"He has been moved to quarters east of the palace. I will ensure the thief will be placed with him. You must move swiftly, plan your escape well; you won't have much time once the alarm is sounded." Her tone pulsed with warning. "If anything happens to my son, you will pay a hundred times over."

I bit down on the inside of my cheek, reining in my temper. "Do your part and I will do mine."

Without another word, the empress stalked through the teahouse, disappearing through the doors. Only then did the tension inside me loosen, my forehead dropping onto my palms, pain clawing my heart like she had raked her talons across it.

16

OUR CLOUD CLIMBED THE SKIES toward the Southern Sea, leaving the Mortal Realm behind. The night was sunken in gloom, devoid of moonlight, for who would tend the lanterns now my mother had gone? Certainly none who could do it as well. While I had helped her on occasion, the lanterns flared brightest upon my mother's touch, their light purer and more luminous. What did the mortals make of these dark nights? Soothsayers and fortune-tellers must have been summoned to many a royal court to decipher this mystery, all likely concluding that such a thing was an ill omen indeed.

They would not be wrong.

"That went well." Wenzhi's mouth tilted into a wry smile. "By well, I mean the empress did not command her guards to arrest you, nor did you draw a weapon."

"It was close," I said tightly. "We were always a breath away from attacking each other."

"You might want to reconsider the family you are marrying into."

"I will not be marrying into that family."

As he stilled, his eyes darkening—I added hastily, "Don't be so quick to judge when your family has their own *charm*."

"I don't recall offering my family as an alternative," he countered lightly.

I flushed, turning from him. "The empress agreed to help Liwei escape. I will get him out."

"*We* will get him out," he corrected me.

"No, I must go alone," I told him flatly. The empress would not have lied, not for this—she would want me to succeed, especially after securing my vow. "The palace is warded against your people. I can't risk Liwei being accused of conspiring with the Demon Realm."

"You would rather get caught? Because of what people might say?" he asked tersely.

"Your presence might be what gets us caught," I told him.

"You can't do this alone. Every soldier will be on the alert. Who will speak for you should trouble arise?" He stepped closer to me, and I made myself hold my ground. "Don't punish yourself for what happened on the moon, for what you think were your mistakes. You don't need to save everyone in some misguided attempt to right these wrongs, out of a sense of obligation."

"I'm not doing this out of duty. I want to save Liwei, more than anything." My voice was hoarse with suppressed emotion.

His expression shuttered. "I spoke out of turn. I know your feelings for him."

I looked away, the hurt inflicted by the empress still raw. For even if I succeeded, she had ensured that I would still lose. "I have a plan. There will be no danger."

When he stared at me, unspeaking, arms folded across his chest, I added, "Maybe just a little danger."

"Don't be a fool." Wenzhi's tone dropped dangerously low.

"Don't call me a fool when the worst thing I ever did was to trust you," I hissed through gritted teeth. "Don't imagine you alone have all the answers. I have seen and done as much as you, I have guarded your back as you did mine. I tricked you once, and would do it again."

We glared at each other, our robes fluttering in the breeze, the wind teasing our hair. His eyes shone so brightly, the only stars in this bleak night.

"You are right. I am the fool for imagining anything could change." He held my gaze. "Tell me, then, how you will invade the Jade Palace singlehandedly with *just a little danger.*" A shred of humor lifted his words.

"There will be no invasion. I intend to draw their attention away, like you did the last time, except within the palace grounds."

"If only I had not helped you then," he said with feeling. "Causing a small diversion at the gate is not the same thing as wreaking turmoil in the heart of the Jade Palace. What will you do?"

"Shoot a few arrows into the Hall of Eastern Light?" I stifled a laugh at the expression on his face, equal parts incredulous and anxious. While the thought had crossed my mind—undoubtedly satisfying—it would be dangerous beyond measure. "I don't have a plan yet," I admitted. "But I will."

He inclined his head. "I did not mean to offend you earlier. You might be somewhat reckless at times, though never a fool."

Something stirred in my chest that I quelled. Silence fell between us as we entered the Southern Sea, making our way through the watery tunnel. The guards at the entrance did not question us when we displayed our pearls for their inspection. As we strode to the palace, a shell caught my eye. Snow white, spiraling into a cone, just like the one I had given Liwei. As I crouched down to pick it up, a memory surfaced, of the vendor proudly displaying his wares in the Celestial market.

These were picked from the deepest waters in the Southern Sea . . . enchanted to capture your favorite sound, music, or even a loved one's voice.

My mind spun with the beginnings of an idea. I stopped the first Sea Immortal passing by, a plump woman draped in lilac brocade. "Is there a merchant here who sells shells? Enchanted ones?"

She blinked, taken aback by my urgency. "Master Bingwen owns the shop by the coral fountain. You will recognize his store when you see it."

As I thanked her, Wenzhi stared dubiously at the shells strewn around us. "Why would anyone want to buy one of those here?"

"Not everyone can do what he does."

Away from the palace, the streets widened, lined by undulating fronds of jade-green seaweed, interspersed with coral in jeweled tones. The walls of the buildings shimmered with a pearlescent hue, their arched rooftops adorned with delicate sculptures of sea creatures in turquoise, gold, and silver. Circular gateways opened into lush courtyards, though a few remained locked behind gates of lacquered wood. As a soft rush of water drifted through the air, we followed its trail to find a fountain formed of azure and lilac coral.

An elegant building was situated beside it, its mahogany pillars carved with a pattern of shells. The latticed windows were shut as was the door, but I rapped on it, my nerves frayed. When there was no response, I pushed against the wooden panel that swung open smoothly. At the entrance, I hesitated—reluctant to enter without an invitation, yet I had little time to waste. It was dark within, a damp heaviness clinging to the air, clogging my lungs with each breath. Glittering flecks darted through the air like fireflies, and red lacquered chests of drawers were pushed against the walls. Glancing down, my eyes widened to find the floor submerged beneath a layer of luminous seawater. Its glowing tendrils crept up the sides of the drawers, seeping into the wood like shining veins. Bracing myself, I stepped into the room, the ice-cold water sloshing around my ankles. At once, a brightness suffused the chamber, the lanterns hanging from the ceiling flaring to life.

"The store is closed. Who are you?" an irate voice demanded.

An immortal strode in from a doorway at the far end, the broad-faced merchant from the Celestial market. As he caught sight of me, his forehead furrowed like he was trying to recall something.

"The musician!" A smile broke across his face as he came forward, wading easily through the water. "I never forget a face. Especially not someone I made a good trade with."

I had met him only once, years ago. Yet his features were etched in my memory too—one of those encounters that left a mark, no matter how fleeting. I raised my cupped hands to him in greeting. "Master Bingwen, I hope you will excuse our intrusion."

"Customers are always welcome." He waved at the water lapping around us. "I apologize for the inconvenience. It is necessary for the enchantment to take root, how the shells retain their sound. This was why the store was shut today." He paused. "Now, tell me, how may I help you?"

"I have urgent need of a few shells."

His eyes twinkled beneath raised brows. "Urgent need? I can't recall anyone ever requiring my wares so pressingly. What do you have to exchange today?"

If only I had kept a little of the gold, silver, and precious stones that found their way to me. But there were few needs immortals could not satisfy on our own, whether coaxing a tree to bear fruit or conjuring water from the purest spring. It was whether we chose to make the effort, as drawing upon our magic was often more tiring than using our hands.

I pulled my flute from my pouch, twirling it once between my fingers. "The same trade as before?"

"A song for a shell," he agreed. "How many do you need?"

"Eight. The smaller and plainer, the better."

"Done." Master Bingwen clasped his hands as he hurried to a chest, tugging its drawers open.

"What enchantment is in these shells?" Wenzhi asked.

"They can retain any sound that can be replayed at will."

"How did you learn of it?"

I did not answer right away. The morning Liwei and I had spent wandering through the market was one of my most cherished memories, one of our few days of unsullied happiness together. "I met Master Bingwen at the Celestial market, where I exchanged a song for a shell."

"He got the better end of the deal," Wenzhi remarked.

Master Bingwen returned, balancing two trays in his hands. "For your selection." He offered me one of the trays crammed with shells of white, gray, and pink, each no larger than my thumbnail. The other, which he set aside, had only eight exquisite shells, with elegant curves and graceful spires. Some were spiked or dusted with gold or silver, others with the radiant blush of a sunset.

I drew out my flute, my gaze sliding to Wenzhi's. "You don't have to listen."

"It would be an honor." It was what he had said when I offered to play for him the first time. He spoke with no anger, just a small smile on his face as he added, "Though I will be more cautious about accepting a cup from you."

My eyes narrowed. "Caution, is a lesson we have *both* learned."

As he settled himself upon a wooden stool, his palms resting upon his knees, I looked away from him, drawing my attention inward. The song must be flawless, for I would earn this trade. As I lifted the jade instrument to my lips, its familiar touch calmed me. Taking a deep breath, I released it to flow into the flute, the melody thrumming with the joy of spring awakening, the warmth in the air, the birds bursting into song. The next was a plaintive melody, each note ringed with sorrow, reverberating with loss. I kept my mind on the tune, not daring to think about its meaning, for then the frail hold over my emotions might snap. Eight songs I played, into the eight shells before me, my emotions swelling and crashing with the rise and fall of the melodies—until at last, I was spent.

As the final note faded, the merchant bowed. "Thank you. I confess I have obtained the better bargain once more."

"That you did," Wenzhi agreed, his eyes alight.

I returned Master Bingwen's bow. "It was a fair trade. The best kind."

As Wenzhi and I left the shop, heading back to the palace, I clutched the silk-wrapped package of shells in my hands.

"What will you do with them?" he wanted to know.

"A decoy," I said slowly, unraveling the plan in my mind. "To make the soldiers think I'm where I am not."

He halted in his tracks, facing me. "Let me help. Let me go with you," he asked again.

"You can't. And I find it hard to believe you're eager to help Liwei," I said, concealing my own trepidation.

He made an impatient sound. "Not for him; for *you*."

"You must not follow me," I told him.

"If that is what you wish. Though there is one thing I want in exchange for my . . . compliance."

"I would rather—"

"Just a promise, in exchange for mine. That you'll stay alive." A corner of his mouth lifted. "What did you think I would ask for?"

Heat crept across the back of my neck. "I fully intend on staying alive."

"If anyone hurts you, they will regret it," he declared ominously. "But it is a good plan," he conceded.

High praise from one who had plotted each step so meticulously that he had fooled the Celestials for years, and betrayed me so thoroughly. We were on civil terms, now. Allies, almost? Yet whenever he spoke, I could not help weighing his words for deceit. Trust was infinitely easier to destroy than restore.

Still, I had to know one thing that ate away at me whenever I saw him. "The Celestial soldiers who marched to your border—would you have killed them all?"

"No," he answered without hesitation. "The mist was meant to confound them, to make them easier to subdue. Hostages are of greater use, to force the Celestial Kingdom's surrender. Some would have died, an unavoidable circumstance of war, but I would have spared those I could. The effects of the mist were unexpected in the chaos of battle—inflaming bloodlust, inciting violence. I take no pleasure in tormenting others. That is my brother's specialty."

The mist had affected me too. I had been disoriented, frightened, confused, until the Black Dragon bore me to safety—but felt no urge to hurt another.

His gaze bored into mine. "Did you really think I intended to kill them all?"

"Yes," I said bluntly. "For I did not think you would lie, steal, and imprison me either."

"I would have released you after the battle with the Celestials; I could not risk our soldiers' safety before." He paused, speaking with emphasis, "I am sorry, Xingyin."

"Would you do it again?" I demanded. "If so, you do not truly regret it."

"I am glad to be free of my brother's control, that those I care for are safe. I feel no remorse in betraying the Celestial Kingdom—they are my enemy; they have hurt and threatened us. In the end, both our kingdoms have wronged each other and there were no true heroes in that war." His expression turned contemplative. "The Celestials are the glittering saviors of the realms, sweeping in to destroy monsters, graciously lending a hand to allies, dispensing aid which varnishes their glory—yet how often have they ignored those no less in need? Why do they get to dictate who is evil and not? While there is good in what they have done, as much wrong has been concealed."

His words struck deep. I thought of my mother's punishment, my father's exile, the dragons' imprisonment—of how long Xiangliu had been left to terrorize the villagers, the sunbirds destroying the Mortal Realm. Was it a callous cruelty or indifference? To cultivate desperation, so the savior might be twice as celebrated? Yet I said nothing, giving no hint that our thoughts might be aligned—not liking these unsettling emotions he roused in me.

"Yes, you know well the power of perception. How easily you vilified me when it suited your needs," I said instead. Scorn was a useful shield.

"If they believed ill of you so quickly, their good opinion is not worth having."

"You should hear what they say of you." A petty response for I had none else.

He shrugged. "It does not bother me. The only opinions that matter are from those I care for. Yours, for one."

"You would not like to hear my thoughts."

He tilted his head toward me. "Is that an invitation?"

I recoiled at once. "Never."

"I would not, without your consent, but I confess to being most intrigued."

"You would be sorely disappointed," I retorted.

A faint smile. "Perhaps. Though I hope you are mistaken."

As my throat went dry, I forced my mind to safer ground. "The Celestial Emperor might be wrong, but that does not make you right."

"At least we do not portray ourselves to be the heroes we are not." He added pointedly, "I feel no shame for defending ourselves, just as you did not when fighting against those invading your home." A breath slid from him, soft and drawn. "I do not regret the fruits of my endeavors, but I wish I had done it differently."

"Why?" I asked without thinking.

"You know why. As much as you try to ignore it, to pretend what lies between us does not exist." The ache in his tone caught at me against my will, against all sense.

"You say these things because you want what you can't have. You just want to 'win,'" I said harshly, echoing what Liwei had said once.

"Oh, I could have had you." He spoke with infuriating assurance. "I could have taken you and your beloved that day by the Jade Palace. A tempting thought, and I would have done it, if all I had wanted was to 'win.' I want so much more than that; I want you to want me, too."

I swallowed hard, reminding myself of his capacity for deceit. "You want the impossible."

"You are stubborn, Xingyin. Except you are not as indifferent to me as you claim to be."

Anger seared, and I was glad to cling to it. "Even if I felt anything for you, it would not matter. I could never trust you again."

"You trust me enough to guard your back," he pointed out.

"I trust that you do not want me dead. At least, not yet. When we want different things—that is the moment when trust really matters, when its true worth shines," I said fiercely.

He stepped closer, his sleeve grazing mine, his voice deepening with intensity. "Believe this, then—for I swear it upon my family, my kingdom, and my honor. When I won the crown and lost you, it was a hollow victory. I regretted all that was lost between us, all I had destroyed—for nothing was worth losing you."

He spoke with such fire and passion, so different from his usual restraint—kindling something in me that I struggled to suppress. And though the walls I had built against him went wide and high, his words still pierced my heart. I rebuked myself for my wavering resolve. If I had learned anything from the past, it was that promises were easily made, twisted, and broken. I was no longer an easy dupe; I would accept his help, and no more.

"Don't speak to me of such things. They belong in the past." The barest quaver shook my voice, which I hoped he did not hear.

His eyes searched my face. "Can't we leave the rest in the past, too—the hate, mistrust, and lies?"

"No, we cannot. Do not ask me for more than I can give."

"I will be happy with any part that you will give me. Though it will not stop me hoping for more, for all of you, however long it takes."

I did not reply, ignoring the quickening of my pulse as I strode ahead. And though I could feel his gaze upon my back, I did not turn. I would not allow such emotions to cloud my heart or dull my resolve. For the path before me was fraught with danger, and even should I succeed, rife with pain.

Yet one thought burrowed into my consciousness, that while nothing Wenzhi said or did could excuse what he had done, while he had never been the honorable immortal I had once thought he was . . . neither was he quite the monster I had believed him to be.

17

CLOAKED IN INVISIBILITY, I FLEW above the walls of the Jade Palace. I held my breath, half expecting a trap—for the guards' heads to snap up, their eyes squinted with suspicion. Yet they remained at ease, fingers loosely clasped around their weapons. The empress had kept her word; the wards were down, though escape would be infinitely harder.

The rosewood lanterns were extinguished at this hour, the corridors bathed in shadow. With each step, the shells in my pouch clinked softly. I worked swiftly, placing one in the soldiers' quarters near my old room, one in the garden beyond. Another in the Outer Court, nestled between the flat gray stones that formed the path. My chest tightened as I slipped into the Courtyard of Eternal Tranquility, achingly still without Liwei except for the crash of the waterfall. Memories beckoned, but I dared not linger, tucking a white shell between the roots of a peach-blossom tree. I left quickly to hide another outside the empress's courtyard, then two more in the Chamber of Reflection and the Hall of Eastern Light. One last shell I clutched in my sweat-slicked palm. With careful steps, I made my way to the Eastern Sun Courtyard, the Celestial Emperor's quarters. During my years in the Jade Palace I had never ventured there, only too glad to keep my distance.

The doors were adorned with gold filigree in an ornate scroll-work pattern, interspersed with discs of jade. I scaled the pale stone wall, dropping into the garden. The air seemed cooler, infused with threads of the emperor's power. Gingko trees shaded the vast garden, yellow lotuses blooming upon a large pond. Crouching down, I tucked the final shell—a small crescent of ivory—between the satiny petals of a lotus. Rising to my feet, I summoned a cloud. Soldiers would flood this place in a moment.

Raising the Jade Dragon Bow, I drew its cord, an arrow shining between my fingers. I silenced the caution in my mind, that of Wenzhi's scathing disapproval—letting the arrow fly, blazing a trail through the dark. It struck a tree, light crackling over its bark, the leaves shivering as they fell. Power tingled through my veins, surging free as a gale hurtled through the courtyard, tearing through the branches, rippling the pond until the lotuses trembled. A spectacle, impossible to ignore. It had been a wild idea, uttered in jest—but what better way to draw every soldier in the palace? I would stir a tempest of chaos to mask our escape.

Shouts broke the stillness. Slinging my bow over my shoulder, I whisked the flute to my lips, a song flowing through the jade—the one I had gifted to Liwei. As footsteps pounded toward me, terror clung to my insides, my feet instinctively lifting for flight. I dug my heels back into the ground. *Not yet.* I would keep my promise to be the empress's willing scapegoat.

Stemming my breath, I halted the song. Boots thumped louder, a rush of auras descending as soldiers streamed into the courtyard, thankfully none of whom I recognized. Shouts rang out as they lunged at me, swords and spears glinting, hands raised to summon their power.

Magic surged from my fingertips, concealing my presence as my cloud shot into the skies. Below, the soldiers mounted their clouds, the quickest already soaring above in pursuit. Plucking a tendril of air, I hurled it into the shell by the lotus pond—my song flowing from it, each note as clear as when I had played it earlier.

The soldiers closest to me stared at each other in confusion, one gesturing wildly below. "The emperor's courtyard. She's there!" he cried.

"We saw her fly above," another argued.

"A decoy! She must intend to harm His Celestial Majesty!"

I uttered a prayer of thanks for the last soldier's misplaced conviction—as the rest swung around, their clouds descending once more. They raced back into the courtyard to join those who had remained. Together, they trooped through the garden, hunting beneath the trees, trudging through the flower beds. A diligent soldier even wove threads of magic into a glowing net to comb the pond, perhaps imagining I was submerged within the dark waters.

The emperor's elegant courtyard was utterly ravaged; mud slopping from the pond, lotuses ripped from their stems, rough holes pitting the ornamental path. A rash urge to laugh gripped me as I imagined His Celestial Majesty's wrath, though this was small recompense to what we had suffered at his hands.

As the song ended, the soldiers stilled, muttering among themselves. Some stalked toward the entrance once more, others clambering onto their clouds. Ten long seconds I counted silently, before flinging a dart of air into the shell in the Courtyard of Eternal Tranquility. The melody burst forth again, fainter this time, from farther away.

"His Highness's courtyard! Quick!" Someone called out.

Footsteps thudded below, heading to my former residence. More soldiers followed, drawn by the commotion, some of their clouds brushing so near, I dared not breathe. Only after they had all descended and the skies were clear did my tension ease.

I strung the Celestial soldiers on this frantic chase, triggering one shell and then the next—my song winding in a ceaseless refrain through the courts, circling the palace walls itself. A dangerous game; one I could not afford to lose, and I was running out of time. Someone would figure it out, or I would make a careless slip. Exhaustion was stealing upon me, dulling my senses, weighing down my limbs. As the soldiers swarmed toward the western side of the palace, I made my way east, to where Liwei was held.

I slipped into the small courtyard lined with clusters of bamboo, a lone crabapple tree shedding its pale petals upon the stone table beneath. Several guards were clustered outside the entrance of a low building, more patrolling the grounds. They exchanged curious whispers, wondering at the chaos, yet remained at their posts.

A lantern within the room threw the silhouette of a man across the window. Liwei. My heart leapt at the sight of him. I studied the courtyard, counting twelve guards on duty. I would have to move swiftly, mercilessly, to dispatch them before they had a chance to cry out. A risk even then, as I quelled the remorse that rose in me. As I gathered my magic, a hand clamped down over mine. A stranger's. I grabbed her wrist to throw her off, but she twisted out of reach, catching my arm from the other side.

"Wait," she whispered urgently. "It's the change of shift; more guards are coming." As she spoke, another dozen soldiers entered the courtyard.

I shook off her grip and faced her. Arched brows, a delicate mouth, a slight flush to her skin. She looked like she had stepped out from one of those scroll paintings depicting the classic ideals of beauty. Something about her face seemed familiar, though I could not place her. A sword was strapped to her back and her dark garments blended into the night. As her head darted up, she raised a finger to her lips in warning. Her movements were deft, with a fighter's grace, which meant she must be trained. Yet she was no Celestial soldier, as eager as I was to avoid detection.

"Are you one of the empress's guards?" I asked carefully.

The woman's nose wrinkled. "The Celestial Empress would rather see me dead."

Something we shared. I warmed to her, though my suspicions were still roused. "Why are you here?"

She glanced at the silhouette by the window. "To get him out. Isn't that why you're here?"

I nodded. "How do you know him?"

"He's an old friend."

At the affection in her tone, my tension eased, though curiosity pricked me. I wanted to trust her, yet some alliances were a fragile bond, snapping beneath the slightest weight.

Her gaze fell on my sword. "Now that we've decided not to kill each other, shall we work together?"

There was an arrogance to her manner like she had been born to privilege. "I have not decided anything," I said carefully.

She shrugged, folding her arms across her chest. "Very well. You may dispatch all the guards on your own."

I glared at her. "Can you handle your weapon?"

"As well as you," she returned.

"A battle, even a quick one, will draw attention. Someone might call for aid."

"If you hold them steady, I can handle the rest," she said confidently.

"Will you kill them all?" A slight tremor in my voice.

She sighed. "Keep them still, and I will *try* not to."

We waited till the first group of guards left the courtyard. Only then did I unleash my magic, forming coils of wind, encircling the guards and binding them tight. Their mouths gaped, their cries stifled as more layers of air wound around them like a cocoon. A struggle with twelve; my body tensing from the strain. I glanced impatiently at the woman, streams of glittering energy already flowing from her palms and swirling over the guards. They lingered across the centers of their foreheads, the hollows of their necks, their wrists and knees. The guards struggled wildly at first—soundlessly—before going limp, their bodies slumping to the ground, their chests rising and falling in a steady rhythm.

"What did you do to them?" I asked.

"An enchantment on their meridians. If they had so much as twitched, it would have struck the wrong place." Her nose wrinkled. "It would not have been pleasant."

She was skilled in Life magic. Before I could ask her another question, the hairs on my skin sprang up, the sudden awareness of danger pressing upon me.

When had the music stopped?

"Quick!" I urged her. "We must hurry."

Together we ran to the room, throwing the doors apart. Liwei was there and Tao too, his eyes widening in shock. Relief crashed over me as Liwei crossed the chamber and reached for me—but I reigned in my emotions, shaking my head.

"We must go."

"You!" Tao gasped, his face ashen. "How did you—"

I stalked to him, grabbing his arm. "Do you have the elixir?"

Before he could reply, the woman's voice rang out from behind me. "Release him!"

Her magic flashed, streaking toward me. Taken aback, I swung aside—too slow—as it struck the side of my neck, blisters erupting over the skin with stinging pain. Tao wrenched himself free and darted away, cowering behind the woman. As Liwei pressed his palm to my wound, channeling his power across it, the pain eased at once. My breathing came labored, shock mingling with anger at her unprovoked attack—along with a dawning realization.

I pointed at Tao. "You're here for *him*."

She opened her mouth, but then her head snapped to one side. I sensed it, too, the swell of auras beyond the courtyard. The woman bolted outside, pulling Tao after her, Liwei and I racing after them. As a large cloud swooped down, summoned by Liwei, we sprang upon it. Celestial soldiers called out, gesturing at us—a few already climbing upon their clouds to give chase. My energy flowed forth as I wove an invisibility enchantment, shielding us from sight as we soared toward the eastern gate. Turning around, I hurled eight bolts of flame into the shells across the palace, burning them to cinders and ash. I would not draw the emperor's wrath to Master Bingwen and the Southern Sea.

Liwei's power merged with mine, channeling a gale that sped us onward. As we neared the eastern gate, I braced for battle, for the guards there to try to stop us—yet it was strangely abandoned, no one rushing forth in pursuit as we shot into the skies. If this was the empress's doing, I was glad for her foresight.

Only after the Celestial Kingdom's borders were far behind us did I allow myself to relax. My heart was beating much too quickly as my gaze met Liwei's. Without speaking, he closed the distance between us and pulled me into his arms. I softened against him, inhaling his scent. A lightness spilled through me, the relief of being with him again, though it was speared by dread of what would come.

I pushed away from him, ignoring the sharp pang in my chest—my vow to the empress ringing through my mind. I dared not allow myself even this indulgence. Liwei dropped his arms and stepped away, his eyes shadowed with hurt. Reluctant to answer his unspoken question—to lie—I turned to Tao, only to find a cloud sweeping beside ours as the woman leapt upon it, Tao's hand clasped in hers.

I lunged forth, seizing Tao's other wrist. "Who are you? What do you want?" I demanded of her.

"It's none of your concern."

"It is, when he stole from me," I shot back.

"You must be angry at me," Tao began.

"*Angry* does not capture it when I have been lied to, cheated, and left with the blame." I rounded upon him. "Why did you do it?"

"I didn't intend to! I believed there were two elixirs, not one," he stammered.

As I recalled his strange reaction when he opened the box, a little of my anger dissipated. "Where is the elixir?"

"I . . . I no longer have it."

I breathed deeply, fighting for calm. I had earned the elixir, bled for it as he had. Perhaps, if he had not tried to cheat me . . . it was no use thinking of that; the only thing that mattered was retrieving the elixir, if it was not too late. "Tell me where it is."

Tao's tongue flicked over his lips as his eyes darted toward the woman. I swung to her. "He gave it to you. Is that why you're helping him?"

"Release him, before I make you regret it." Menace coiled in her voice as she raised her hand, a wave of glittering magic rushing through the air.

I sprang back to evade it, letting go of Tao. At once the woman pulled him over to her cloud. As they soared away, I whipped the Jade Dragon Bow free, training it upon the fleeing pair, a beam of light pulsing between my fingers—

"No." Liwei moved in front of me.

"What are you doing? They're getting away!" I cried out in frustration.

"Xingyin, I know her." An unfamiliar eagerness pulsed in his voice as his magic surged forth, ropes of flame lashing around the woman's cloud and dragging it back to ours.

As her face contorted in fury, she raised her hand to attack us again—just as Liwei called out, "Sister Zhiyi, it is good to see you again."

18

ISTER?" I REPEATED IN DISBELIEF, examining the woman more closely.

After Liwei's greeting, she had frozen, eyes widening as she stared at him. Something nagged at me just as before, an elusive twinge of recognition—a memory surfacing in my mind like the chords of a forgotten song.

"Liwei, is she the woman in your painting? Your childhood friend who moved away?" I had wondered about the scroll by his desk, when I first came to the Courtyard of Eternal Tranquility.

"Yes." He smiled with such joy, despite the strain of the night, my spirits lightened. "I did not see her clearly at first, and it has been many years since we last met."

The woman—Zhiyi—strode onto our cloud, searching Liwei's face. "Liwei?" His name came out tentatively yet with undeniable tenderness. "There was only one person who called me 'Sister.' It has been so long . . . you were a child when I left."

I lowered my bow, the arrow vanishing. Whoever she was, she was dear to him and no enemy of mine. "Is she truly your sister?" I asked Liwei.

"We are not really siblings. I was a child when I knew her. It seemed impolite to call her by name, as she was my elder, yet 'Aunt' did not seem to fit."

Zhiyi shuddered. "Definitely not 'Aunt.' Now you are grown-up, just my name is fine." Her gaze slid to the ground. "How are your parents? Your father, His Celestial Majesty?"

"In good health when he ordered my imprisonment," Liwei said tersely.

"But you are his favorite; the one who can do no wrong." She pressed a fist to her mouth, as though fearing she had said too much. How readily she spoke of the emperor's relationship with Liwei, like she had turned it over in her mind countless times before.

"Who are you?" My tone was quiet but firm.

"Tell them," Tao urged her. "Maybe she won't kill me then," he muttered, throwing a wary glance at me.

Zhiyi hesitated. "Liwei, I should have told you this before. I wanted to but was afraid of her."

"Who do you mean?" he asked.

"The Celestial Empress. Your mother. She ordered me to not speak of it."

I kept my gaze on her as I gathered my energy stealthily. I did not think she meant us harm *now*, yet my instincts had failed me before. I would balance them with what I knew: that for some reason, the empress had deemed this person a threat to her son.

Liwei frowned. "Why would she do that?"

I stared at her face, those eyes—the same shape as Liwei's and as dark as midnight. I was a fool to not have noticed before. "She *is* your sister," I breathed.

"Half-sister," she corrected me, turning to Liwei. "Your father is my father too. Ever since I was a child, your mother detested me. It was partly my fault. I was stubborn, and not as respectful as I should have been to my stepmother. You and I weren't close at first. You were the favored one, the precious heir." Her words fell out like they had been held in for a long time.

"I must have been insufferable," he said wryly.

"You were not. I envied you for taking what I thought was mine, for our father's attention. I was young. Foolish, in so many ways." She touched his arm. "Only later did I grow to love you. It pained me that I could not tell you who I was."

"Why did you leave? I searched for you, but no one would tell me where you had gone," he told her.

She dabbed the corners of her eyes with her sleeve. "Cursed tears, this is a happy day. They did not tell you because of the disgrace. I could not remain in the Immortal Realm after I chose to wed a mortal. Even if Father had permitted it, the Celestial Court would have made life a misery for us."

"A mortal," Liwei repeated with surprise. "Are you . . . happy?"

"More than I ever imagined." A radiant smile lit her face. It vanished abruptly when she bent her head toward me. "And who are you? What claim do you have on the elixir?"

I pushed aside my reluctance to disrupt this tender moment, my fears for my father roused anew. "Tao and I stole the elixir together, then he stole it from me. Now it is mine," I said plainly.

Beside me, Liwei stiffened. "You stole it?"

"I did not tell you. I was afraid you would stop me," I admitted to him.

"I would have tried," he said grimly. "What if you were caught?"

"I had to do this. My father is ill," I explained.

As Liwei's face darkened, Zhiyi shook her head. "I need the elixir for my husband. His mortal years are running out."

Guilt assailed me, mingled with stark hope. "You have the elixir still? You haven't given it to your husband?"

"Oh, I tried," she ground out. "He would not take it, sensing something awry from Tao's expression. The thief is not quite as skilled a liar."

"Would you return the elixir to me?" I hardened myself, for my need was no less great. An amicable agreement seemed impossible when neither of us could be impartial, weighing my father's life against her husband's. But could I really fight Liwei's sister for the elixir?

"Why is the elixir not Tao's if you stole it together?" she countered.

"He forfeited his rights the moment he took it from me," I replied.

Her mouth drew taut. "Do you know how long I've waited for this? Do you think immortal peaches and elixirs grow on trees?"

"Immortal peaches do grow on trees," Tao interjected.

She glared at him, so ferociously, he shrank back. "I mean growing wild, on trees like those." She flung her hand out at the forest we were flying over. "My husband and I are on borrowed time."

"I risked my life for the elixir; I earned it. If you wanted it, you should have gone yourself." I did not speak unkindly but merely recounted the facts, appealing to her sense of fairness—innate in Liwei, perhaps it lay in her as well.

She bit her lip. "I could not enter the Jade Palace; I am no longer permitted to."

We stared at each other, unrelentingly—I could be selfish too. After a long silence, she reached into her sleeve, pulling out the white jade bottle. It gleamed in her hand, its gold stopper catching the sunlight. Her jaw clenched as she thrust it at me. "Take it. He will not drink it anyway, not if it was tricked from another. Cursed honor."

I accepted the bottle, clutching it tight. My spirits lifted, even as a new weight sank over them—a heavy burden to have taken the one thing that could save her beloved. And in truth, she did not have to return it to me. Despite her harsh words, this was a gift.

"Thank you." My voice was raw with emotion. "My father is dying in the world below, and I am almost out of time."

"Time," she repeated, with a trace of sadness. "How strange, that we are fighting over what every immortal is born caring nothing for. While for the mortals, wars are waged, lives lost in the pursuit of eternity. An impossible dream for all except a handful."

"I wish we could both have the elixir," I told her honestly.

"I don't blame you. Make no mistake, if my husband had fewer scruples, that elixir would be gone and I'd have felt little remorse." Her tone softened. "But he would not be who he is, either, and I have some time yet."

"I will repay you," I promised, without having the faintest idea how. "If there is another elixir, I will help you obtain it."

"Thank you," she said gravely.

We both knew it was an unlikely pledge, yet I did not mean it any less.

"I must go," Zhiyi said. "The chickens and cows will not feed themselves. I came because Tao's sister sent a message that he was in danger."

"Chickens? Cows?" I had imagined her living in some palace or grand manor as befitted the emperor's daughter, even one in disfavor.

She laughed. "Does it sound so terrible? I do not mind my life. Titles, crowns, and palaces come with a price of their own," she added darkly.

Her words resonated with me. Once I had dreamed Liwei and I might be so free, and now . . . we never would.

Shortly after, she left with Tao upon her cloud. Alone with

Liwei, emotions flooded me—relief that he was safe, punctured by despair.

"Are you glad you found your sister?" A clumsy attempt to delay the inevitable.

"Yes. To learn I have a sibling is a precious thing." He studied my face. "You seem sad, Xingyin. Aren't you happy about the elixir?"

"I wish it had not come at the price of her happiness." It was one part of the truth.

"As do I. But she would not want your guilt," he said gently. "Reach for the joy you have, revel in it. For it is scarce enough in the world."

If only I could.

"How are your mother and Ping'er?" he asked.

Grief surged, crowding my throat and eyes. "Ping'er is . . . dead."

He grasped my hands. "What happened?"

"Wugang led the Celestial attack on the moon. He killed her." I breathed deeply, fighting for calm.

"I am sorry, Xingyin." He bent his head to graze mine. "She was like family to you. I will miss her too."

"She *was* family."

Shadows crept between us—slithering, dark, and opaque. Yet again, his father's command had torn my family apart.

"Where is your mother? Is she safe?" Liwei asked.

I nodded numbly. "She is in the Southern Sea. We took Ping'er's body to her family there."

"She would have wanted that." He hesitated, before saying, "Thank you. You saved me again."

"Did you not say we should not thank each other?" I smiled, my first real one in a long time.

202 SUE LYNN TAN

He thought for a moment. "Perhaps I was wrong. Thanking you brings me joy too."

His hands slid up my arms, drawing me close. I should have pulled away, but I was weak after the turmoil of the past days. Leaning against him, my head settled into the curve of his neck. The feel of him, so familiar yet thrilling, almost undid my resolve. Blood rushed to my head, my skin tingling with the awareness of him. How I wanted to press myself against the warmth of his skin as we fell upon the soft folds of the cloud. My heart quickened, my arms tightening around him, before I forced them to loosen.

It would be nothing more than a final farewell, delaying the inevitable hurt. I pulled away, hating myself for the confusion that flashed across his face. His body tensed as his hands fell to his sides. Surely he wondered at the change in my behavior, so different from how I had been on the moon.

As loose strands of his hair fell across his brow, I suppressed the urge to brush them away. He was not mine; he never would be again. His mother had made sure of that. I thought I could bear it as long as he was safe, but this was far harder than I had imagined.

I braced myself, my skin damp with dread. "I cannot marry you."

His eyes went wide and dark. "Why?"

I stumbled over the words, for the empress had bound me to lies. "The rift between our families. I thought we could overcome it, but I was wrong." The empress's accusations held a grain of truth that I had never let myself examine, afraid of what I might find. These seeds of doubt had been sown long before, from the moment I fell in love with my enemy's son.

"Our parents are not us. I will find a way to make things right."

As he stepped toward me, I moved away. "Your father tricked

mine into surrendering his immortality. Trapped him into a mortal existence." Anger seared me as I forged onward, using the truth as a shield. "What of my mother's imprisonment? The attack on my home? Ping'er's death? How can I marry into your family when yours only wants to destroy mine?"

The cold vehemence in my voice was that of a stranger's. I had never spoken to him this way before, not even when we had fought in the Willow Song Pavilion—when he accused me of deception and worse. It was not easy; I hurt too. Yet I used every remnant of resolve, every scrap of resentment I ever bore against his kin to bind myself together—my nails digging into my palm, stinging, as the skin broke.

Liwei shook his head. "This is not like you, Xingyin. What is the matter? There is nothing you can't tell me and whatever it is, we can work it out together."

He was wrong; there was no way forward for us. I had sworn on my mother's life, and I had done so to keep him safe. I racked my mind for something more to say, something that would irrevocably destroy all we had fought for, all that we were—even though it would break my own heart.

"The way things are . . . we can never be together." My words emerged fractured.

"Is it him?" Liwei's voice was low.

Wenzhi. Who else could he mean?

Liwei's expression hardened as he leaned away to study my face. "You can't forget him." A statement, not a question. Laced with sadness and irrefutable knowing.

My throat went dry. I smothered my instinctive protest as my mind raced. A torment to see his pain, even as I hurt too—yet this might be the only way I could fulfill my vow to the empress. Even then I could not choke out the false admission . . . in the end, my silence serving as a louder confession than anything else might.

"It is why you let him visit you, why you kept your distance from me in the past year. You did not pull away but neither did you come forward. Even after all he did"—he paused, holding my gaze—"you still want him."

I flinched inwardly, looking away—whether from confusion or guilt, I no longer knew. Lies and truths, interwoven so tight I could no longer tell them apart.

"I'm sorry." Somehow, I managed to keep myself steady, watching the light in his eyes dwindle until the black was all that remained. How I hated myself for giving Liwei cause to believe this so readily of me, for hurting him, for hurting us.

"What will you do?" he asked.

"Nothing. I cannot be with him after what he did." A relief, to speak honestly at last. "But you deserve better than a divided heart, as do I."

"It would be enough for me." He spoke with such intensity, it stole my breath. "I could help you forget him. We could go back to what we were."

"No," I made myself say. "We cannot rewrite the past, nor can we foresee the future. It would not be fair to make promises we cannot keep."

He raised a hand to my face, his fingers trailing slowly down my cheek. "I told you once, my heart is yours, that it will always be yours. I hope one day you will want it again."

He moved away from me then, clasping his hands behind his back as he stared into the horizon. The ache in my chest sharpened, almost splintering apart. Just ahead, the curve of the Southern Sea glittered. Before entering its waters, Liwei cast an invisibility enchantment over himself, disguising his aura. Perhaps the guards had grown accustomed to my presence, for they no longer appeared to escort us through the passageway. Yet I would take no chances, channeling my magic to mask Liwei's presence from those guarding the entrance.

One of them halted me. "What spell is this?"

I stared pointedly at his cloak of dragon yarn. "To keep myself dry. I am tired of getting drenched every time I come through here."

He waved me aside, his eyes glazing over with disinterest. I strode past him, hiding my relief. The grounds were not as well secured as those of the Jade Palace, because few made their way here without Queen Suihe's permission.

In the Bright Pearl Palace, I led Liwei to my chamber, halting outside the door. "You may have my room."

"We are not strangers," he said with cool civility. "Surely we can stay in the same room together. Take the bed, I will not disturb you."

I shook my head. It was not him but myself I did not trust. I left then, making my way to my mother's room.

Her smile vanished when she saw me. "Xingyin, what is the matter? Why do you look so upset?"

I said nothing, just hugged her tight, catching a trace of the osmanthus that somehow clung to her still. Her arms went around me, her palm stroking the back of my head, just as she used to when I was a child in need of comfort. She did not ask again, nor did I speak—silence was our language of grief.

I had slain monsters, fought vicious enemies, been stabbed and speared and burned—yet the torments of the heart were no less excruciating. Perhaps those who brought us greatest joy, also wielded the power to inflict the most suffering. I did not know how long I wept, until at last my breathing calmed and I lay still.

My mother brushed aside the damp strands of hair from my face. "This pain you feel . . . you might believe that you

206 ~ SUE LYNN TAN

will never recover. And while it might always hurt, the pain will fade a little more each time—until one day, there will be no more tears. Just the memories and the hope, that you might find some joy in them again."

She was well schooled in suffering. What anguish she must have endured when she first came to the moon, separated from her husband, knowing she would never see him again.

I pulled myself up, wiping away the last of my tears. This was no time to wallow in self-pity. My father needed me. The world below held countless dangers for a mortal: accidents, wild beasts, illnesses that swept in like dust carried by the wind. My fingers brushed the jade bottle tucked into my sleeve. Something stirred in my veins, a precious hope blooming within the void of my chest, one that had haunted all the days of my life. Too fragile to be spoken aloud as I dared not tempt the vagaries of fate—that even as my own heart was broken, I might be able to heal those of my parents.

19

THE SKY WAS AGLITTER WITH stars, as though the heavens were trying to distract from the absence of the moon. Following the directions my father had given me, I made my way to his home—the whitewashed walls gleaming against the slate gray roof. As I approached, light flared from a window, throwing my shadow across the ground. Had he sensed me, though I'd made no sound? After all, he was no ordinary mortal.

The wooden door swung open. He stood in the entrance, the glow from the lantern casting a sheen of gold over his silver hair. At the sight of me, he blinked as though taken aback, even though few things could catch him unaware.

"You came." His tone lifted with surprise as he stepped aside to let me in.

Did he think I would not? Eager to shed the burden of a mortal parent, easily forgotten in the realm where the years had no meaning and illness dared not trespass? He did not know me, but we had time. All the time in the world.

His house was furnished with an elegance that was unexpected, given its unassuming exterior. A blue-and-white porcelain tea set was laid on a table of prized zitan wood, its barrel-shaped stools tucked beneath. Scroll paintings hung from the walls, some depicting scenes of temples and pavilions amid lush pine forests. One caught my eye, of a woman—my mother—I realized with a start. Not the goddess flying among the clouds in ornate silk robes, as the mortals often depicted her—but clad in a plain robe, standing in a garden of peonies. The artist had captured the graceful curves of her face, the tilt of her eyes, and more than that, the radiance in her expression. Mortal and incandescently happy.

I inhaled sharply, catching the scent of incense in the air. Only then did I notice the lacquered altar before the painting, laid with plates of pears, oranges, and sponge cakes. A brass burner sat among them, crowded with incense sticks already burned down.

"Why this? Mother is alive," I blurted.

He stared at the painting, his shoulders hunching inward. "They say the incense smoke carries our prayers to the gods. I did not think it was true, yet I lit them every day in hopes my words would somehow find their way to her."

It was a trait we both shared: dreaming of the impossible, reaching for it all the same. Something caved in my chest. For all these decades, despite the irrevocability of their parting—my parents had yearned for each other. The sorrow, regret, and misunderstanding that tainted their past had not diminished their love.

"Father, you do not need the incense. You will see Mother again soon. You can tell her yourself."

Light flared in his pupils, impossibly bright. "Did you find the elixir?"

I pulled the jade bottle from my sleeve and offered it to him with both my hands. As the filigree goldwork in the stopper caught the candlelight, it glowed like it was afire.

"This belongs to the Celestial Emperor. How did you get it?" he asked hoarsely.

"I stole it." I felt no shame in taking the elixir from the emperor, though I had been drowned in remorse to accept it from Zhiyi. His Celestial Majesty had taken enough from my family: my father's immortality, my mother's freedom, and now our home.

"It was a great risk, my daughter," he said gravely.

I smiled in reply. I would not tell him what I had risked for this; there was no need to burden his conscience. It was enough that he would be restored to us.

He took the bottle and tugged out its stopper. The scent of peaches wafted forth, so lush and indulgent, my senses were drenched in it. Closing his eyes, he lifted the bottle to his lips and tipped it all the way back, his throat convulsing with each swallow. He moved without hesitation, with an eager impatience. After all, he had waited over half his life for this.

Silence fell, punctured only by our breaths. I kept my head down, almost afraid to look up. Light stroked the walls in rich shades of amber. Had the sun risen? My gaze darted to the windows. No, it was still dark, not a glimmer of dawn on the horizon.

As my father's breathing quickened, I swung toward him. He was stooped over the table, shaking his head as though dazed. "Bitter, when its fragrance was so sweet." His head darted up to mine, a shiver rippling through his body. "Is it cold?"

Springing to my feet, I searched for a cloak, doubts raging through my mind: Was this some mortal ailment? Could the emperor have planted a decoy in place of the elixir? Yet the fragrance of those peaches was unmistakable.

Tossing open the cupboard doors, I grabbed a heavy cloak from within. I spun to my father—finding a stranger before me. The lines on his face had vanished like sand smoothed by the tide. His eyes were clear, their whites brilliant, the mark in his chin more prominent than before. Yet his jet-black hair was winged with white at his temples, marks of mortality that even the elixir could not erase.

"It worked. My aches, my pains are gone." He clenched and unclenched his fingers, raising them to his face in wonder. "Daughter, only those who have lived a mortal life till its tail know never to take this for granted."

Relief flooded me, thawing the stiffness in my limbs. "Father, immortals fear death too. We can be weak, we can die," I reminded him.

"You are right. Danger lurks in both realms, but time is a faceless and merciless foe. It is no fair battle when the enemy is inexorable, and your defeat inevitable."

I searched him for any sign of injury. "Did the elixir hurt?"

He crouched down to pick up the empty bottle. "Like a hundred thorns were scraped across my skin. Your mother must have suffered, too, yet she is strong." His tone softened.

I thought back to when my mother had taken the elixir, the fear that must have shadowed her heart. Though some claimed she had been selfish, there had been bravery in trying to save us—in reaching for a new life and plunging into the unknown, leaving behind all that she loved. For I knew better than anyone, despite becoming immortal, a part of my mother had died that day.

Pain is no stranger to me, she had said. That did not mean it hurt any less.

Soon, I would bring my father back to her. Such lightness swept through me that, for a moment, all my sorrows receded. They would return, but for now, it was a relief to be freed.

"Daughter, I thank you."

I bowed, searching for the words that would not come, my

chest swollen with emotion. It struck me then who he was: *Houyi, Slayer of the Suns. The Dragon Lord. My mother's husband. My father.* We were little more than strangers, bound by name and an intrinsic connection. But then he reached out and wrapped his arms around me . . . my father, holding me just how I had dreamed all those years.

Sunlight streamed through the window in shafts of pale gold. Morning had crept up; this was no dream that would vanish with the night. I dared not linger any longer. What if someone had sensed our presence? The elixir's power?

A guttural sound broke the quiet, throbbing with anguish. My head snapped up to my father, who was shaking, the veins protruding from his neck.

"Are you ill?" I took his arm to help him to a chair, but he stiffened, his palm pushing me aside.

"Stay back!" He staggered forward, almost falling over the table. His hands tightened around its sides, knuckles whitening as he struggled against some unseen foe. The door rattled as though assailed by a storm, yet the skies beyond were calm. Ignoring his warning, I gripped his arm—his body lurching into the air like an invisible fist had snatched him up by the ankle. As his hand slipped from mine, I squeezed harder, holding fast.

"It's the elixir," he rasped. "All mortals who ascend to the skies must attend the Celestial Emperor."

I dared not imagine what would happen if my father were to appear in the Hall of Eastern Light. "It's too dangerous. The emperor attacked our home. He's hunting Mother and me."

His jaw clenched, his throat working. "I can't hold on. It's too strong."

"Your magic!" I cried, even as I grasped my own.

He shook his head. "There's nothing." Shock flushed his tone.

Was the elixir not complete? Had the emperor left it unfinished, missing some vital step only he could perform upon its gifting? My power surged forth, seeking the force that had ensnared my father. I was careless of discovery, of the Celestial soldiers who might be on their way to us, of everything except halting my father's ascent. What did the laws of heaven matter at a time like this? As my energy flowed, fatigue locked my limbs, my power already tapped by the events of today.

"Don't let go." Each word was uttered in a disjointed rhythm.

Silver light streamed from my fingers, enveloping him in a gleaming shield. It was not enough, the enchantment that dragged him away strengthening. His eyes rounded like marbles, his hair streaming wildly across his face. I clasped his hand harder, numbed from the strain.

"This pull . . . it's coming from *inside* me," he said breathlessly.

Of course. This was not some force that had swooped in from the heavens but flowing through his veins, from the elixir consumed. I chided myself for thinking it would be a simple matter of my father drinking it and us returning to the skies to reunite with my mother. I should have learned by now that things were never that easy.

Closing my eyes, I reached for my magic again, casting it down his throat this time, after the trail of the elixir that glistened like a shimmering serpent. A thudding filled my ears—his heart, beating much too fast, pumping the elixir through his blood. Gold threaded through the crimson, brighter than any mortal's blood—suffused with that honeyed fragrance, grown sickly sweet like fruit on the cusp of spoil. My power rushed through his veins, prying him free of the elixir's hold. A painstaking effort, like trying to untangle a folded cobweb. Choked sounds wrung from my father's throat, still I pushed on. Was I hurting him? Undoubtedly, in the way he flinched, yet I dared not stop. A moment's pause and he would be ripped from my grasp, hurtling toward the Celestial Kingdom and into utmost peril. Fatigue sank into my bones, an ache crawling from the base of my spine to my neck, until I could barely stand.

Clamping my jaws, I quelled the instinctive urge to halt my power, streaming forth untamed, burning the taint of the elixir away—until at last, the pull on my father eased. The blazing gold that ran through his veins dissolved into pinpricks of light, his blood now shining as that of any other immortal's. The scent of peaches faded, leaving only that of wood and earth.

My father's body shuddered as it descended, his feet sinking to the ground. Still, I would not let go.

"Do you want to bring anything?" I asked.

He shook his head. "All I have longed for is in the realm above."

Together, we dashed outside into a clear morning, the sky a vivid aquamarine, the air glazed with warmth. I summoned a cloud, which we leapt upon, a rush of wind spiraling down to bear us along. Neither of us spoke, our breaths unsteady—the anxiety of the night only just beginning to subside as the shores of the Southern Sea glistened ahead.

Before entering the waters, I cloaked my father in invisibility, just as Liwei had done before. The guards at the palace entrance cast only a cursory glance our way, and we slipped into the Bright Pearl Palace without incident. Yet the farther we walked, the more his steps lagged.

"Father, are you all right?"

His lips lifted into a smile, as bright and fleeting as a shooting star. "It has been a long time since I felt this way." He brushed a shaking palm over his hair. "How do I look?"

His question surprised me. I almost laughed aloud, suddenly as giddy as he was. "Don't be nervous. Mother will be overjoyed."

"I'm not nervous." The slightest tremor shook his voice. "Does she know about me?"

"I didn't tell her. I kept my word."

His fingertips brushed his cheek, as though tracing the lines that had once creased their surface. "My face," he said haltingly. "A foolish thing to worry about."

I picked up a silver plate from a table, inlaid with coral along its rim. Wordlessly, I lifted it to him so he might see his reflection— a face more strong than handsome, the one my mother loved still. He stared at it for a long while, though I did not think him vain. There was no pride in his expression, just—wonder.

His eyes darted from the mirror to my face. "I see *us*, my daughter."

My heart soared. Now that we were safe, it finally sank in: my father was home.

He rapped his knuckles against my mother's door. As it swung open, she stood in the entrance, her gaze moving from me—to my father.

No one spoke, no one moved, as though we had been turned to stone. In all my fantasies of reunion, I had not imagined this stillness. And I *had* dreamed of this day, dreams so secret and burrowed so deep, I had never dared to speak them aloud. There was none of the violent joy I had anticipated—of tears and gasps and loving embraces. Had too much happened? Fifty years to an immortal was gone in a blink, and yet to a mortal it was over a life half-lived. They had spent more time apart than together; perhaps they needed to learn to be with each other again. And though I could not bear to think of it, there lay too, the unspoken rift between my parents, as vast as the skies that had once divided them. My mother's theft. My father's anger. His deception in not revealing himself, letting her weep by his grave. The decades of regret, recrimination, and sorrow, which might not be so easily forgotten.

"Houyi?" At last she spoke, the frail whisper rising from her throat. "Is it really you?" Her shock morphed to disbelief, and then . . . rapture.

"Chang'e, my wife. I have returned at last," he said quietly, an unreadable expression on his face.

Her cheeks flushed like camellias, her eyes glistened like dew. But then she froze, bending her head. "I'm sorry, Houyi. I took the elixir, *your* elixir. I was so scared . . . I thought I was dying, and our child too. The doctors frightened me, and the pains came too early. I was all alone." Her words tumbled out in fragments. Her anguish as raw as though it had been yesterday.

He did not speak. Was he still angry despite what he had said? Could he forgive her? Perhaps a spark of his rage had remained unquenched, flaring to life when confronted with her. Perhaps he blamed her still, even without knowing it. And a part of me wondered, how could he not?

"I was furious," he began in a low voice. "Wretched in my grief. Those were my darkest days, worse than any battle I had fought, any loss I had suffered. Betrayal cuts deepest when it stems from those you love. For then you feel twice a fool, broken and hurt—all at once. For then you do not even have the solace you most crave. I tormented myself, wondering if that might have been your scheme all along, that you desired immortality more than me." He spoke slowly, as though these words were wrenched from him. "And when years passed without a sign from you, a single message—I almost hated you then."

A strangled sob erupted from my mother, the back of her hand flying to her mouth. I stiffened at my father's harshness, yet I also wanted to weep for the suffering knotted in his heart all this time. While my mother and I had each other, it was he who had been left alone. And I understood how he felt, his words stirring in me an echo of my own betrayal at Wenzhi's hands. Yet I had seen my mother's suffering and anguish, and no matter what my father had gone through, I would not let him hurt her.

Before I could speak, my father took my mother's hand. "I first saw you at my grave a year ago. I restrained myself from confronting you, for I believed you faithless. A part of me was also ashamed of what I had become, while you remained as luminous as the day we wed. I told myself it was enough to know you were well, that you remembered me. That you wept for me still. At last, I would find peace."

He paused. "I was wrong. It was then I realized the last of my anger had vanished, and only the sadness remained. I told myself not to go again, for it was a cruel torment—one I could not resist. To feel both relief and disappointment on the days I did not see you, elated and desolate whenever I did."

"I could not come," she wept. "I could not leave. And even if I could, I did not know where you had gone. Whether you were alive."

He reached for her then, embracing her so tightly it was as though they were one. "I am sorry too," he whispered fiercely into her hair. "For leaving you alone and not listening to you. I was thinking of myself and what *I* feared and wanted to be true. I would have given the elixir to you. I should have offered it to you before. I would *never* have let you or our daughter die. You made the choice I was too selfish and afraid to make."

Silence stretched wide and deep. Lightning could have struck the ground, wild beasts could have rampaged through the corridor—yet nothing could have torn them apart. My mother gazed at him like he was light and warmth. The sun, moon, and stars. As though everything else, including me, had receded into the shadows . . . and I was glad for it.

I left then, trying not to make a sound. Behind me, no more words were spoken, there was just the creak of the door as it slid shut. This was a moment for my parents alone. I would have my chance later, with the three of us together. For the first time in my life, a profound and unfamiliar sense of oneness filled me— that we would finally have time enough for us to be a family, to know one another as we would have done had we lived in the Mortal Realm without the sunbirds, capricious gods, and enchanted elixirs.

20

IT WAS EARLY AFTERNOON WHEN I made my way back to my mother's room. I was reluctant to intrude upon my parents' reunion, but dared not remain in the Southern Sea any longer. With Liwei's escape and my part in it known to all, the emperor would be furious. He would retaliate, I had no doubt, my stomach churning at the thought.

Moreover, Ping'er had been laid to rest according to the customs of her people. Just this morning, my mother and I had knelt before her ancestral altar to pay our final respects. A lump had clogged my throat to see the ebony tablet inscribed with Ping'er's name in gold. While there was a solemn peace in knowing she was among her people again, the ragged cries of her family and friends wrenched my heart.

We no longer had a reason to linger here, beyond the fact we had nowhere to go. As I entered my mother's room, I found my father sitting by the table, his hair unbound, falling loosely over his shoulders. There was an ease to my mother's smile, a new lightness to her movements. How strange it was to see my parents together, strange and utterly wonderful. Yet a slight uncertainty edged their interactions as though they were discovering each other again, as indeed they were: the way my father glanced at my mother to assure himself she was still there, the slight widening of her eyes whenever she looked at him. And when their fingers brushed, that moment of hesitation before my mother clasped his hand in hers.

"Daughter, I'm grateful." My father inclined his head to me. "For your trust, for restoring my life. I had thought it impossible."

"She is your daughter, Houyi," my mother said with pride. "She does not walk the path before her; she forges her own."

"*Our* daughter," he corrected her, rising to place his palm on my shoulder. "All those years I've lost."

I blinked away the prickling in my eyes. "We have time now, Father."

"Houyi, you are so somber," my mother teased him before her expression darkened. "While we speak of years 'lost,' how could you let me think you were dead? Did you enjoy watching me weep at your grave? Hearing my prayers for you? If I had known, I would have put salt instead of sugar in the cakes I made for your offerings."

He laughed, a full sound that warmed me deeply. "They would have tasted just as sweet. I ate them all after you had gone, though the familiarity of their taste was a bitter consolation." He paused. "As for your prayers, I heard nothing from where I hid. They would have been a comfort to me, they would have given me hope that you still cared."

"Why else did you think I went to your grave?" she demanded.

"From duty? Guilt? After decades of disappointment, I had no reason to hope. I didn't know you could not come. I tried to stay away, but I confess to going whenever I could. When I saw you again, part of me dared to dream once more. However, too much time had passed; I could not bind you to an old man." As he cupped her cheek with his hand, she leaned into it.

"I would not have cared. I would have known you anywhere," she whispered. "If we were old and gray, it would be the mark of a life well spent."

"Yes, if we grew old and gray *together*—but we did not. With the little time I had left, I believed it better that way, rather than reopening old wounds. I wanted you to remember me as I was."

It was a hard choice he had made, to cut himself from us like the ailing part of a plant without which the rest would thrive. And I understood how he had felt, because his pride lay in me too.

Someone knocked. Unexpected, as we had few visitors. Since our arrival, Queen Suihe had left us alone, as though she had forgotten we were here. We had gladly kept to ourselves, shunning all banquets and festivities, only emerging today for Ping'er's funeral. As I probed the auras before opening the doors, relief and apprehension swirled through me.

Liwei and Wenzhi entered. From their hostile expressions and the way they stood stiffly apart, this was a wholly unwelcome coincidence. Liwei's gaze slid from my father to me, his expression solemn. A sudden realization sank over me that while I had been reunited with my family, he was torn from his and hunted by his own father.

Liwei inclined his head in greeting, cupping his hands before him. "Master Houyi, it is an honor to meet you."

Wenzhi shot me a sidelong glare, an unspoken reproach for keeping him in the dark—then he bowed too. "Master Houyi, your return brings great joy to your family."

My father said nothing, his eyebrows drawing over narrowed eyes in a look that had undoubtedly struck fear into many a soldier's heart. What had my mother told him of them? Under other circumstances, he might have inquired after Liwei's parents, or that of Wenzhi's family. However, I doubted my father had any concern for the Celestial Emperor's well-being or that of anyone in the Demon Realm.

"I should have believed you when you told me of your father," Liwei said. He did not come toward me, and while this new reserve in his manner hurt, it was what I had sought.

"You did not?" Wenzhi's tone was scathing.

"It seemed improbable even to me," I said at once.

Liwei ignored him, speaking to me alone. "I am happy for you. I will always be happy for you."

Was there an additional meaning within his words? Such lies I had told him of Wenzhi, which he had so readily believed—perhaps because he had harbored suspicions from the start. I glanced at Wenzhi, finding his eyes upon me, questioning and bright. Did he wonder at the distance between Liwei and me? If so, it would forever be a mystery, for I would never tell him the truth.

"Why are you here?" I asked Wenzhi.

He shook his head as though disappointed by my question. "Such paltry thanks from you, after I led the Celestial guards away from the eastern gate last night."

I stared at him. "*You* did that? You promised you would not interfere."

He shrugged. "I promised not to follow you. I did not."

"Did you run into any trouble?" I asked.

"Are you concerned for me, Xingyin?" he tilted his head toward me.

I scowled. "Not in the least. Such a trivial task should be unworthy of your talents."

"I am glad you think so highly of them."

As I choked back a rude retort, he smiled. "It was not quite as easy as you would think. These soldiers were far more dedicated to their posts, nor could I enter the Jade Palace in case it roused an alarm. I had to resort to more creative means to draw them away, leading them on a merry chase halfway across the Celestial Kingdom."

I stifled a flicker of concern for his safety. "Thank you," I told him, somewhat stiffly.

"I would do that and more for you."

"Just as you took her captive?" Liwei taunted.

My father's head jerked up as he rose to his feet, but then Mother tugged his sleeve, until he sat back down—though his expression remained thunderous.

Wenzhi's eyes glittered dangerously as he turned to me, ignoring Liwei. "I'm beginning to wish you had not succeeded quite so thoroughly last night."

"I am delighted to have disappointed you." Liwei's lips parted in an almost feral smile, one I had never seen before. "If I had known, I would have returned sooner."

"Without Xingyin, I doubt you could have."

"Enough." I glared at them. "My father has returned. Do not ruin this occasion."

A brief silence before Wenzhi bent his head. "If anyone could bring a mortal back from the dead, it would be you."

"The Black Dragon was mistaken; Father was not dead. If he was, no elixir in the realm could have restored him."

Liwei did not look at me, nor did he speak. He must think me heartless, to speak so familiarly to Wenzhi. To him, Wenzhi was the Demon who had infiltrated his kingdom, tried to destroy his army, and captured me. I would never forget that—just as I could not forget the times he had come to my aid, and the circumstances that had set him along this path. With Wenzhi, the good and bad were woven so tight, it was impossible to pick them apart—a confounding knot of our past and present, all he had been to me and what he was now.

"We must leave," I said firmly. "With Liwei's escape, the emperor might summon the other kingdoms to aid in his search. Word will reach Queen Suihe soon."

"The queen will look to the safety of her own people, as any monarch should," Liwei said. "She would not hesitate to surrender us to gain any advantage."

My mother paled. "Where can we go?"

"My home is open to you," Wenzhi offered. "No Celestial will set foot in the Cloud Wall."

"No Celestial would want to," Liwei said with distaste.

Wenzhi surveyed him coldly. "*You* are welcome to remain here. I would prefer it if you did."

"No, not the Cloud Wall," I interjected. Even if Wenzhi wanted to protect us, would he be able to from his family?

"The Eastern Sea," my father said. "The dragons will keep us safe."

Though the dragons were no longer bound to the pearls, they still bore great respect and affection for my father. Their wisdom would be invaluable, even though they could not fight the Celestial Army.

"The Eastern Sea is allied to the Celestial Kingdom," I said carefully. "Will it be safe?"

"They will not countermand the dragons' wishes," Wenzhi assured me. "They revere them greatly."

"Will we bring trouble to them with our presence?" I asked.

"In times as these, there is no perfect solution," my father said decisively. "We must make hard choices, do what we think is right, and not regret the consequences."

As a leader of mortal armies, my father must have had to make such impossible decisions every day, those that ate at his conscience. How many soldiers had he sent to their deaths? How many families had been broken? No war came without a cost, and the highest price was often paid by those who had the least.

A loud rap on the door startled us. "Goddess of the Moon. Queen Suihe requests you and your daughter to attend to her in the great hall," a voice called out.

I exchanged a guarded look with my mother. "We will gladly attend to Her Majesty. What is the occasion?" I spoke steadily, to avoid arousing suspicion.

"Our honored guests have arrived, and they wish to meet with you," the messenger replied.

"Guests?" My mind leapt to terrifying thoughts of the Celestial Emperor.

"His Highness Prince Yanxi of the Eastern Sea."

My tension eased as I sagged against the table. Had he accompanied his father for the meeting of the monarchs of the Four Seas? Prince Yanxi was a friend, while his brother Prince Yanming had been in my care during our campaign in the Eastern Sea. Despite the danger and my near death, I had cherished those weeks—for the first time experiencing what it might be like with a younger sibling.

"We will come shortly. We must change our garments first," my mother replied, buying us a fragment of time.

"Send word to Shuxiao," I told Liwei and Wenzhi, after the messenger had gone. "Don't let anyone see you, and wait for us outside the palace." I hesitated, thinking this was an undeniably bad idea to leave them together, but my father would prevent any foolishness.

"Xingyin, be careful." Liwei warned. "Make haste, but do not appear to be in a rush."

"Queen Suihe is most astute; little escapes her notice. You must give her no reason to suspect you," Wenzhi cautioned.

I nodded grimly. "We will leave as soon as we can."

As soon as the queen allows us to, my mind whispered.

21

W E WALKED TOWARD THE THRONE room, our measured steps masking our trepidation. As a close ally of the Celestial Kingdom, would Prince Yanxi be aware of our situation? Would he be obligated to inform Queen Suihe? I could not refuse the queen's invitation, though my bow, wrapped discreetly in a piece of silk, was a comforting weight against my back.

The queen's throne was flanked by brocade-lined chairs and red-lacquered tables. Porcelain tea sets rimmed in gold were laid upon each table, alongside plates of crisp seaweed, glistening walnuts roasted in honey, sesame-encrusted pastries, and almond cakes topped with a flaky crust. The amber pillars shimmered like sunstruck gold and the carpets were newly enchanted, the embroidered silver waves undulating in a soothing rhythm. Crystal vases were filled to the brim with glowing shells, emitting a sweet floral fragrance underlaid with the opulence of musk. A haunting ballad was sung by the performer in a corner of the hall, her painted nails expertly plucking the strings of her pipa, its rippling strains the perfect accompaniment to her pure tones.

Queen Suihe was resplendent in rich folds of amethyst silk, embroidered with orchids in copper thread. The filigree gold and ruby flowers on her headdress quivered as she nodded to us in greeting.

"My honored guests are eager to meet you," she said in her melodious voice.

Before I could reply, someone hurtled into my side, small arms locking around my waist. Staggering back, I caught my balance. "Prince Yanming!" I bent down to hug him tightly. "You've grown taller, Your Highness."

"Maybe you shrank." He laughed as he released me. "I hear that happens to the elderly."

"If I'm elderly, you need to treat me with a lot more respect," I replied, prodding him lightly in his shoulder.

"Yanming, behave yourself. What would Her Majesty think of you?" Prince Yanxi chided him.

As we both straightened, I cupped my hands to bow to the prince, conscious of Queen Suihe's watchful stare. "Your Highness, this is a welcome surprise."

"My father sent me in his stead. I would have left my brother at home, but he begged to come, and I had no peace until I agreed."

From the corner of my eye, I caught Prince Yanming twisting his lips into a mock scowl, which vanished the moment his brother turned to him.

Prince Yanxi's face softened as he ruffled his younger brother's hair. "Yanming, enough. What would Father say?"

I envied them, their unrestrained camaraderie. Their close bond, knitted with affection and the familiarity of a shared past. "I am glad to see you both, though much has changed since our last meeting." More than they knew, I hoped.

Prince Yanming sighed. "It's been so dull since you left. No one will spar with me or tell me any good stories. Lady Anmei shrieks whenever I touch a sword, even the wooden ones."

Prince Yanxi turned to my mother and inclined his head. "Moon Goddess, this is an unexpected honor. I had heard of your release but am surprised to find you here, so far from home."

The prince was sharp, not easily duped. He had aided me before when I sought to help the dragons, though I suspected that stemmed more from his reverence of them than any desire to foil the Celestial Emperor.

"My mother was attacked, and her attendant killed," I said carefully, even as my voice hitched over the words. "She was from the Southern Sea, so we brought her home."

"I am sorry for your loss." He hesitated, lowering his voice, "I heard news, unconfirmed reports of an attack by—"

"It was unfortunate," I said quickly, my insides clenching. "Intruders to our home. They attacked us without cause." I held his gaze, widening my eyes in a silent warning that I hoped he would heed.

"A difficult time for you and your mother. I hope you will find peace, wherever you are." His words were layered with meaning.

"We intend to seek it, when Her Majesty allows us to depart." A hint of our peril.

Prince Yanxi nodded gravely. "Her Majesty should have no reason to delay you. She will have other things on her mind, the gathering of royals, for one."

I breathed easier at his words. Whatever the Eastern Sea prince knew, he would not expose us.

"Your Highness," Queen Suihe called out. "You seem well acquainted with my guests. Would you share your conversation with the rest of us? It appears most engaging." A note of impatience rang in her voice. Monarchs were unaccustomed to sharing attention in their throne rooms.

The prince shot her a dazzling smile. "We were exchanging

old stories from when the First Archer aided us during Governor Renyu's uprising."

"Your Majesty." I bowed to her, concealing my haste. "We are grateful for your hospitality. Unfortunately, my mother and I must depart, as we have pressing news from home."

"Your home that was attacked?" There was the slightest inflection in her tone.

"The perpetrators have fled," my mother replied, covering my slip. "The moon has been dark without me."

The queen leaned back against her throne, her lips pursing. "Will you not stay for the festivities tonight? My guests from the Eastern Sea will be disappointed if you depart so soon. The monarchs of the Northern and Western Seas will also enjoy meeting you, our elusive Moon Goddess."

"While that is true, matters of home should always take precedence," Prince Yanxi said smoothly.

The queen nodded. "Very well. If you wish, some of our guards could accompany you there."

My mother bowed. "Thank you for the kind offer, Your Majesty. However, we have troubled you enough and my daughter is a fine warrior."

Prince Yanxi smiled. "Indeed, she is."

Someone tugged at my sleeve, a small hand slipping around the curve of my elbow. I glanced down to find Prince Yanming, his face alight with hope. "Can I come with you? I want to see the moon," he whispered. "It's so dull here. Eldest Brother is always in meetings and won't let me go out without him. And he's always ordering me to hold my tongue."

I crouched down to look him in the eyes. "Maybe it's because you say such outrageous things, Your Highness? My mother often advised me to speak with more care if I wanted my words to be given weight." How solemn I sounded when all too often my words trampled courtesy in their wake. Yet something about him sparked in me the desire to keep him safe, to counsel him to be better than me.

"Brother, you are being discourteous to our hostess," Prince Yanxi said pointedly. "Moreover, Xingyin is too busy to entertain you, as she is leaving."

I released Prince Yanming's hand gently. "When things settle down, you must come for a visit. I will show you my home with its silver roof. The osmanthus forest, and the thousand lanterns which you can help us light."

Empty promises to trick children into behaving better, my mind scoffed, even as despair enveloped me. The last I had seen of my home were the flames devouring it. Did any part remain? I did not know . . . and perhaps, I never would.

Prince Yanming's smile stretched across his face. "Promise?"

Liar that I was, I nodded.

Footsteps clicked across the tiles, growing louder. An immortal entered the hall, clad in familiar brocade robes, a black hat upon his head adorned with a piece of flat jade. A Celestial messenger. My fingers inched toward my mother's hand, clutching her in warning.

The messenger knelt before the queen, holding up a scroll between his palms—thick yellow brocade rolled around twin bars of sandalwood—just like the one we had seen before. As an attendant took the scroll and presented it to Queen Suihe, my mouth went dry.

Yet there was still a chance; the messenger did not know us. I forced myself to smile, though I was trembling within. Our only hope lay in a swift exit. "Your Majesty, we thank you again. We will take our leave now." My voice was low, intended to be overlooked, as my mother and I backed away from the throne.

Queen Suihe nodded, her gaze fixed on the scroll, her attention already shifting to matters of greater importance.

As we turned from the throne, Prince Yanxi engaged the queen in polite conversation. I thanked him silently for the distraction, for delaying the inevitable moment when she read the missive from the Celestial Kingdom. I did not know what was written within, though my instincts prickled in warning. We strode briskly past the rows of courtiers, toward the entrance, as I suppressed the urge to run.

"Halt!" Queen Suihe's voice rang out, sharp with command.

The guards before us crossed their spears at once, blocking our way. The pit of my stomach folded inward as I swung to the queen.

Bright-red splotches mottled her skin. "To have my kindness repaid with dishonesty is a grave disappointment," she seethed, crumpling the unraveled scroll in her hands. "Word has been sent across the realm that you and your mother are traitors to the Celestial Kingdom, fugitives from justice. Any who harbor you are threatened with stern reprisal. Do you know all I have done to keep us safe? Only to have it all threatened by a pack of liars who sheltered here under false pretenses."

Prince Yanming pulled free of his brother's grasp. "Xingyin is not a liar! The Celestial Emperor is a—"

"I apologize for my brother's rudeness, Your Majesty," Prince Yanxi interjected, casting a stern glare at his brother. "Perhaps you might listen to what the Moon Goddess and her daughter have to say?" His tones were carefully modulated to show no partiality.

The slightest dip of Queen Suihe's head was the only indication that I should speak. From the hard set of her face, she was not inclined to listen, yet I would try.

"We did not lie, but we did not tell you the whole truth—

that it was the Celestial Kingdom who attacked us, unprovoked, and drove us from our home. For that, I am sorry. We did not intend for any harm to come to your people and were about to leave to avoid trouble." Despite her hostile expression, I plowed on. "Strange things are happening in the Celestial Kingdom: unexpected shifts in power, loyal and trusted advisors being sidelined. Change is on the horizon, and not for the better."

Queen Suihe's eyes blazed, an enigmatic smile upon her lips. "You are right about one thing—change *is* on the horizon, and I intend to be on the right side of it." She turned to the Celestial messenger. "Inform His Celestial Majesty that I have apprehended the Moon Goddess and her daughter upon his request. They will be imprisoned here to await his justice. In return, I ask that he remembers the value of our friendship."

The messenger bowed, yet he did not leave as I expected. His hand shimmered with a greenish light as he touched the jade on his hat. A soft chime rolled through the silence, the stone glowing brighter, before dulling once more. "His Celestial Majesty commanded us to inform him the moment we had news. He will arrive shortly," he intoned.

"We will prepare a suitable welcome for His Celestial Majesty," Queen Suihe said.

A chill sank through my veins. The Celestial Emperor was coming here? Was it because of Liwei? All knew my part in his escape. As the messenger left the hall, I addressed the queen. "Your Majesty, would you reconsider? If you let us leave, you will have a loyal friend in us forever." A paltry offer, but I had little else.

A shrill laugh broke from her, scraping like nails over my nerves. "Leave? That you will, except under my terms. I far prefer the friendship of the one who possesses the might of the Celestial

Army to yours." Her hand flew up in a curt wave to the guard. "Take them to the cells. Find their friend and lock her up too."

Relief flooded me that I had told Shuxiao and the others to leave the palace. I hoped they would flee for there was no sense in us all getting captured. They could return for us later, and I had no doubt they would.

Turquoise armor clinked, golden blades flashing as two guards moved toward me. Wenzhi's warning of their impenetrable prisons flashed through my mind. I could not let them take us. As a soldier reached for my mother, my leg lashed out, kicking him aside with brute force. At once, I snatched up my bow, stripping its bindings free, a beam of light forming between my fingers.

Panicked cries erupted, guests stumbling over themselves as they rushed from the hall. As Prince Yanxi's anxious gaze met mine, I jerked my head toward the doorway, mouthing for him to leave. As an ally of the Celestial Kingdom, his loyalties were bound. He had already tried to distract Queen Suihe on my behalf, to persuade her to listen, which was more than I could have hoped for. Prince Yanxi lifted his brother in his arms and dashed through the entrance, away from the tumult.

My grip tightened around the bowstring as I trained my arrow upon the queen, the only one who could ensure our safe passage. "Order your soldiers to stand back. Let us leave and do not follow." My voice was low with threat.

Queen Suihe's lip curled as her magic surged, jagged shards of ice plunging toward my mother and me. I shielded us at once, dropping my arrow tip to her shoulder, aiming to wound rather than kill. As I let it fly, it streaked through the air, just as a luminous barrier encircled the queen. Her face twisted with contempt as she threw her other hand out, a gleaming wave of power knocking my arrow to the ground. Sky-fire scorched the carpets, blackening the intricate embroidery, gouging a crude hole in the floor. As a tremor shuddered through the ground, the crystal vases tipped over, the scattered shells trampled beneath the feet of the fleeing courtiers.

Several of the queen's soldiers broke away to surround my mother and me. I aimed another arrow at them, hardening myself to strike Ping'er's kinsmen—but something whistled through the air, a translucent arrow hurtling into the guard closest to us.

"Chang'e! Xingyin!"

My father's voice. My heart swelled as he raced into the throne room, his silver bow already drawn. Liwei, Wenzhi, and Shuxiao followed close behind. Shouts erupted, the queen's guards rushing toward them. Swiftly, I summoned a burst of wind to sweep aside those nearest to us.

Magic coursed through the air, the clash of metal reverberating through the hall. My father sheltered my mother, releasing arrow after arrow, his hands moving at a dizzying pace. As a soldier crept up behind him, her sword swung high—I shot her down, my arrow spearing her chest, her body jerking as light crackled across her armor.

Wenzhi and Liwei were encircled by Southern Sea soldiers, their swords flashing in a blur of silver and gold as they made swift work of their opponents. Shuxiao was locked in a ferocious tussle with another guard, his spear clanging against her sword.

Queen Suihe pointed a trembling hand at Liwei. "The Celestial Crown Prince! The emperor will reward us well for this. Call for reinforcements!"

Three guards detached themselves, running toward the entrance. I did not let myself think, an arrow springing from my fingers to strike one, then the next. As I drew another arrow, the last soldier dashed through the doors, shouting for aid.

I cursed myself. In a moment, more guards would swarm the room, barring the only entrance. Already, they might be barreling through the corridors. I frantically searched for an escape route—not the walls, for the throne room was deeply ensconced within and we would have to fight our way through the sole pathway. An impossible feat when we were vastly outnumbered. My eyes flew to the domed ceiling, recalling its decorative spires and low structure from the outside—just a single layer of stone separating us from freedom.

I signaled to the others to raise their shields, even as I strengthened the ones around my parents. Only then did I draw my bow, raising it high, releasing a bolt of Sky-fire at the arched ceiling. It struck in a blinding flash, a web of fissures tearing across the stone with ominous grinding sounds. Another arrow of ice—my father's—plunged after mine. The ceiling shuddered, the cracks splitting wider as clouds of dust showered down. I choked, coughing to clear my lungs as stone fragments fell away, cascading like hail—one crashing through my shield, knocking a gasp from me as it struck my shoulder. More shields arced around me, pulsing with Liwei's warmth, gleaming with Wenzhi's cool energy—just as a spire crashed by my feet, disintegrating into shards. Above us, through the jagged hole torn in the roof, midnight waters embraced the barriers arcing over the city. They had never seemed so inviting before, nor had the air in this place ever pressed on me more.

Shouts rang through the chamber, the remaining courtiers scrambling for shelter. The guards no longer attacked us, channeling their energy to form protective shields around the vulnerable. I spun to the dais to find Queen Suihe's gaze locked on mine, burning with loathing. She would neither forget nor forgive this destruction, a shiver running through me at the thought.

I turned from her, rushing toward my parents. Wind spun

from my fingers, weaving coils of air which swept us high—Shuxiao, Liwei, and Wenzhi doing the same. Together, we soared through the tear in the roof, landing upon the outskirts of the palace. My breathing came labored, for it was a great strain to fly without a cloud.

Fortunately, all seemed calm outside. The alarm had not been raised, perhaps because we had left the throne room in such chaos. Yet at any moment, the queen's soldiers might be rushing forth to apprehend us, or the emperor's troops might arrive.

"We must be careful," I warned the others as we approached the passageway. "If the guards suspect anything, they will seal the tunnel—the only way out from here. We would be trapped like fireflies in a jar."

Four soldiers guarded the entrance, none of whom I had met before. "Who are you? What business do you have here?" one of them demanded brusquely.

"We are Queen Suihe's guests," I replied as calmly as I could.

Another studied us, her eyes narrowing. "Her Majesty commanded that the passage be kept clear for the royal guests from the Four Seas. You must wait your turn, until their arrival."

"Queen Suihe gave us permission to leave today," Shuxiao said with a smile.

As the guard shook her head, light flared from Wenzhi's hand, hurtling into the point between her eyes. The other soldiers aimed their spears at us, yet Wenzhi's power arced wide, striking them swiftly. The soldiers' eyelids sank shut as they collapsed upon the ground like limp pieces of string.

"Why did you do that?" As I pressed Ping'er's pearl into the carved creature's eye socket, the door swung open.

Wenzhi shrugged. "They were rude and suspicious. Better to catch them by surprise."

I stared at the unconscious guards. "Are they—"

"They are asleep. I know your preferences in such things, Xingyin," Wenzhi replied.

"You know nothing of her," Liwei said coldly as we slipped into the tunnel.

"Is that right?" The mocking lilt in Wenzhi's tone was intended to infuriate. "Xingyin and I spent years together, battling creatures beyond your nightmares, seeing places you have only dreamed of. We have camped beneath the skies, at the foothills of the Mortal Realm, in palaces and in tents. I know more of her than you ever will, sitting in a classroom surrounded by teachers."

I burned hot and cold at his words, anger rising at his presumption. "None of what we had was real; none of it meant anything."

"It was real," Wenzhi said quietly. "Lie to me all you want, just don't lie to yourself."

An ache pulsed in my chest. When he spoke to me in this earnest manner, it chipped away at the barrier I had built against him. But I would never relent, I would guard myself better this time—my heart could not withstand more hurt.

Rushing sounds ruptured the silence, growing louder, the streaming wall of water looming before us—a sliver of the ocean's crushing force. As I raised Ping'er's pearl before me, the waters parted. We dashed through the corridor, our magic flowing forth to summon clouds to bear us to the surface, the ring of blue sky above a welcome sight.

The sun blazed down, warm and bright, beginning its descent across the heavens. As we soared through the waters, a breeze surged into my face, infused with the salt of the sea. I closed my eyes, inhaling deeply—but then an unseen force coiled fast around us, yanking us toward the shore so swiftly we tumbled upon the sands.

I rolled up, springing to my feet—the dazzling brightness

of sunlight striking the white sands almost blinding me. Ice plunged down the base of my neck. No . . . it was not the beach that glittered so but the white-gold armor of Celestial soldiers, led by an immortal twirling a bamboo flute between his scarred fingers.

22

"KNEEL BEFORE YOUR EMPEROR, AND I might be inclined to mercy," Wugang commanded.

My eyes flared in disbelief, taking in his pearl-encrusted headpiece, the gold dragon-shaped hairpin pinning it into place. The way the soldiers behind him bent their heads in complete subservience.

"*Emperor?*" Liwei repeated wrathfully. "You dare much, you fraud."

Wugang's smile was riddled with malice. His slender fingers lifted a yellow jade ornament by his waist, so brilliant it appeared gilded over, carved with a pair of dragons encircling the sun. Only one person carried that seal; it was death for another to take it.

"How did you get my father's seal?" Liwei's tone sank with dread. "What did you do to him?"

A long pause, a measured cruelty. "He's alive, for now. He's still of use to me, as is his court. We must retain some semblance of order. However, the guards and attendants who remained loyal to him, who attempted to fight back, did not fare so well." Wugang shrugged. "Fortunately, their deaths sufficed to convince those more reluctant to concede."

My stomach churned until I thought I would be sick. He

spoke of killing so easily, just as he had taken Ping'er's life with no more hesitation than crumpling a sheet of paper. While I could not honestly claim to bear any respect or affection for the Celestial Emperor, those who hurt Liwei, hurt me too. What of General Jianyun and Teacher Daoming? I assured myself they would be safe; they were high-ranking members of the court, valuable hostages. While Minyi would be safe in the kitchens. I dared not ask after them, I dared not show I cared, for he would use that against me.

How had this happened? My mind spun, the pieces falling into place: Queen Suihe's strange words earlier, Wugang's efforts to malign Liwei, to isolate the Celestial Emperor from his other advisors, assuming control over the Celestial Army. I had thought he was maneuvering himself to become the emperor's sole confidant, his chosen heir—not to usurp the throne from the Celestial Emperor whose position had always seemed unassailable. Wugang's carefully cultivated loyalty had blinded all to his true intent. He had orchestrated everything, not on the emperor's behalf, but for himself—to seize my home and the laurel . . . along with the power it could bestow.

Wugang had never forgiven the Celestial Emperor and the immortals for the humiliation wreaked upon him. He had waited all this time to exact his vengeance, just as he had done with his wife and her lover. And while I could understand his pain, while I cared little for the Celestial Court—Wugang had drawn those closest to me into the vicious web of his schemes, destroying our lives with the same callousness as the immortals had ruined his.

"You are nothing but a fraud, a vile traitor, and coward." Liwei was almost shaking from anger. "My father trusted you, he gave you everything, and *this* is how you repay him?"

"He trusted me because I did his bidding without complaint. His loyal *servant*. He gave me all I have here because he had taken everything else, forcing me from the Mortal Realm to this accursed place. I will never forget how he tormented me when I was at his mercy, and I have long awaited the day to repay him in full."

"He honored you beyond any mortal," Liwei said.

"By making me immortal?" A laugh erupted from Wugang's throat. "Such arrogance among your kind. Not everyone wants to live forever. I was content with my lot: my wife, family, and work—insignificant though it may seem to you. I had everything, until it was snatched away by one of your kind. Ruining our lives upon a whim, a moment's lust. My wife was just a diversion to him, but the damage wrought was eternal—turning my loving spouse into a despicable cheat, all my dreams into nightmares."

His breathing came shallow and uneven. "I lost interest in everything. Consumed by despair, I even thought of ending my life. Except why should I suffer for *their* crimes? If I no longer cared whether I lived or died, what did it matter if I challenged the gods themselves? I could avenge myself for this dishonor, make them pay. That would make life worth living. It was the finest moment of my life to sever his immortal head from his neck. Me, an unworthy mortal." His fingers clenched around his flute as though he was reliving the past. "You think immortality is a gift? When you care for nothing, it's a *curse*."

I hardened myself against the anguish in his words. "What of those who've suffered at your hands? Ping'er never harmed you, and still you killed her. You are no better than those you condemn."

Almost trembling, I whipped my bow free, drawing its string, an arrow blazing in my grasp. Soldiers surged forth to encircle Wugang—dozens of them, over a hundred or more. Despite their pallor, their steady bearing betrayed neither fear nor doubt. I squinted to get a clearer look at them, trying to make out their faces beneath their helmets—yet the light glittered too bright against their armor, it seemed to dance upon their very skin. If I released my arrow, if they attacked us, could we flee?

"I would not." Wugang spoke in the knowing tone of a teacher instructing a pupil, a powerful shield gleaming across his body.

Two soldiers dragged an immortal forward. Her headdress sat crooked on her head, her robe ripped on one side and streaked with dark stains. The Celestial Empress. Shock jolted me, as Liwei drew a ragged breath. As she struggled, her gold nail sheaths raked her captors—but they neither flinched nor cried out, despite the poison in those talons.

"Mother!" Liwei bolted forward, but I moved in front of him, my arrow still drawn.

"No," I cautioned. "It's a trap."

"If it's a hostage you want, I will take her place," Liwei called out.

I swallowed my protest, keeping my arrow trained upon the soldiers. Their eyes did not follow it; not a flicker of apprehension did they show.

"A noble son." Wugang laughed. "I am tempted by your offer. It would ensure that *she* behaves herself too." The look he shot at me was steeped in malevolence.

"Liwei, stay where you are," the empress commanded sharply. "I am unhurt."

"Why is my mother here?" Liwei demanded.

"She was caught trying to flee to the Phoenix Kingdom. We couldn't have her whispering into Queen Fengjin's ear, mustering their army in her support." Wugang's eyes shone like cold bronze. "It was a great favor you did me, when you refused the suit of their princess. It opened a rift I was able to exploit—between the kingdoms, within your family itself."

I fought back a flash of guilt. Liwei did not love Princess

Fengmei, and nothing I did would change that. Wugang wanted to divide us further, to sow discord, to make us vulnerable to his manipulation. It was his greatest skill. I stared at the Celestial Empress, trapped among the soldiers. While I had little desire to rescue her, Liwei would not leave her and I would not leave him.

"My messenger informed me that you were Queen Suihe's guests. She will learn to choose her company with greater care." Menace crawled in Wugang's tone, his shift in mood sudden and unsettling. "The queen is fortunate if we do not punish her for harboring you."

"Queen Suihe was ignorant of our situation." I bore her little gratitude, but it was the truth.

"Her Majesty is not easily duped. You've grown more adept than when you were a loudmouthed girl, making crude demands of the emperor before his court."

"As I recall you to be a devious, pandering snake." Bold words, despite the fear that slashed me.

The tightening of his jaw yielded a burst of satisfaction, even as I knew I would pay for my insults. He was not one to forget a slight.

His gaze slid around us. "I thank you for escaping. It saved me the tedious effort of retrieving you."

"How did you know we would be on the beach and not below?" Shuxiao asked.

"You must be careful in whom you place your trust." Wugang's mouth curled as he called out, "My thanks, Your Highness, for your counsel. You have proven yourself of use."

The soldiers parted to reveal Prince Yanxi, clasping Prince Yanming's hand tightly. *Treachery*, my mind whispered, the walls of my stomach clenching. Yet Prince Yanxi need not have aided me before. And the expression on his brother's face, the terror glazed in his wide eyes—I had seen it once in the Eastern Sea, when we had fled from the invading merfolk. Reaching out, Wu-gang yanked Prince Yanming from his brother's grasp, clamping his palms upon his small shoulders. Prince Yanxi's face twisted, frantic with fear.

They were hostages, not allies.

With a wrench, I lowered my bow. I dared not do anything that might endanger them. Ping'er's death had taught me the meaning of loss.

A cloud drifted before the sun, granting a moment's respite from its glare. I examined the soldiers—the gilded scales of their armor so familiar to me, except for the helmets which obscured their faces. And yet . . . Celestial soldiers they were not. Their skin was not just pale but a translucent mottled white, like patches of ice half-thawed. Their features were indistinct, shifting shadows—faint imprints that quivered like reflections on the water. Luminous veins streaked from their necks, across their cheeks and temples, disappearing into their helmets. Two hollows were dug below their brows, from which gleamed pale orbs ringed by an intense glow. Eyes, I had thought them, yet they bore no sign of sight or thought—vacant, unblinking, terrifying. Most disconcerting was the energy that emanated from them, which I only grew aware of now, overlooked in the earlier turmoil. While each immortal's aura was as different as the waves in the sea, those of the soldiers were identical, like bricks cast from the same mold.

My gaze fell upon a jade disc set into the scales of their armor, right where their hearts should be—if such a thing beat in their chests. A single character was carved upon it: 永. Eternity. One of the first words my mother had taught me to write. The greatest mortal dream, though a nightmare for Wugang.

He tucked the flute into his sash. It had been a monstrous axe the last time I saw it, and it gave me little comfort that he no longer deemed a weapon necessary. Gone were those gloves he used to wear to cover his scars. Maybe he no longer feared the scorn of others.

He gestured at his soldiers. "Are they not beautiful? The perfect army: Strong. Loyal. Obedient."

"*What* are they?" The answer darted at the edge of my mind.

"Look closer. Don't you recognize any?" His tone lifted in invitation, his triumph barely contained.

I searched their faces—strangers, all of them. What did Wugang mean? Just then my gaze fell upon one in the crowd, a faint recognition grazing my awareness—of a soldier who had accompanied Liwei and me to the Eternal Spring Forest. Ten had gone, none returned. No . . . this could not be him, despite that elusive prickle of familiarity. There was not the faintest glimmer of consciousness in his face, caught somewhere between the living and the dead.

"How dare you." Liwei's voice cracked with revulsion. "Fallen Celestials are laid to rest in the Divine Harmony Sky, a place of peace for their immortal spirits to rest. Only then can they achieve true tranquility, to become one with our realm."

"It is believed to be a curse to disturb the slumber of the dead, to desecrate the sanctity of this place." Wenzhi's eyes narrowed in disgust.

"Those already cursed have no fear of such things," I said slowly. Wugang's heart was barren. Because he cared for nothing, he feared nothing—and such a thing made him more dangerous by far.

The light emanating from the soldiers' eyes stirred something in me, their pale glow akin to that of—"The laurel seeds," I said aloud, recoiling in horror. "Its power was of regeneration and healing, and yet somehow you've bent it into this."

"Is not the destiny of immortals to live forever instead of

languishing in a grave?" Wugang taunted. "Resurrection is the greatest healing power of all. Truly, the gift of eternity."

I studied their blank faces, my insides writhing like a nest of snakes. "You're a monster. This is no life you've given them."

He slanted his head to one side. "Oh, I didn't do this alone."

"What do you mean?" I demanded.

He fell silent, weighing his reply; he rarely spoke without calculation. "In the Mortal Realm, there once lived a king," he said at last. "A great conqueror, a shrewd politician, a brave warrior—who was afraid of nothing in the world but his death. After he had vanquished all his enemies, he spent the rest of his days seeking the Elixir of Immortality."

He spoke with the rhythmic cadences of a storyteller, drawing me in against my will. "This king, so courageous, was so terrified of death that he built an army to protect him in the afterlife. For decades, countless workers toiled to craft thousands of clay soldiers. Each was molded and shaped from yellow clay, carved with their own distinct features, fired in the kilns, then painted and glazed. The perfect army, who would awaken to defend their monarch against all enemies, even in the afterlife."

"What use is an army of clay against death?" A shudder ran through me as I imagined all that suffering to satisfy one man's boundless arrogance and futile fear.

Wugang tucked his chin between his fingers. "Ah, you speak as a lofty immortal who never had to dread such things."

"I have faced death." Our eyes locked, an itch crawling across the scars on my chest. After all, it was *he* who had incited the emperor to attack me.

"Not the same way. All mortals—peasant, warrior, or king— are born knowing a single, inexorable truth. That no matter how glorious or pathetic their existence, they will die. Whether through illness, war, or accident is of no consequence, for the end is the same."

He continued in that condescending manner as though this were a lesson, one I had not asked for. I let him speak. Wugang was so closemouthed; this was a rare opportunity to unpick the twisted workings of his mind, to uncover any weakness we might exploit.

"For your kind, death is not inevitable. It's a choice, a gamble, the path you set on. I thank the mortal king for his vision. For inspiring . . . this." His arms spread wide to encompass the soldiers. "There were darker rumors, too, that the emperor's own soldiers were entombed alive within those shells of clay. Who would ever know? The tomb is long lost. I am no monster. I sought not the living to build my army, but the spirits of the deceased." An avid light shone in his eyes. "A pity you did not yield the dragons' pearls to the former Celestial Emperor. They would have made a remarkable addition to my army, after they met their end in his service."

I went cold inside. My hand involuntarily strayed to my pouch, to the Long Dragon's scale, but I pulled it back. I would not expose the dragons to Wugang's sinister schemes.

Liwei's hands were clenched, his mouth set into a hard line. "You have violated every principle of honor. The dead should be left in peace, a rule as old as our realm itself."

"Honor?" The word burst from Wugang's lips. "What of my wife making a mockery of our union? The craven immortal bedding her behind my back? When I finally avenged *my honor*—was it fair of your father to play that cruel trick upon me, turning me into the laughingstock of his court?" He held up his scarred palms. "I have long learned that honor is not worth the having. Nor is love, for that matter."

Despite his seeming indifference, his voice broke—was it with grief? I would feel no pity for him. Whatever had befallen him, he alone had made the choices that came after. He had killed Ping'er, destroyed my home, enslaved immortal spirits to create an army of the dead. His suffering was no excuse for the evil he had spawned.

"Why do this?" I asked as steadily as I could. "You have had your vengeance; your wife and her lover are dead. Why not build a new life instead of destroying everything?"

"They are not dead," he muttered, as though speaking to himself. "Their cries ring through my mind. They will not leave me in peace. How shameful, that I loved someone so unworthy. Who thought me so great a fool, so worthless, that I would accept the crumbs of her affection as she stamped my pride into the ground."

I was no stranger to the agonies of heartache, the bitterness that lurked, eager to flourish. "Love is a privilege, not a possession. We can't control our own feelings, much less those of others. Sometimes love means letting go—for yourself, if not for them."

"The answer of a fool." Wugang's laugh rang hollow. "I am the Celestial Emperor now. *All* will kneel to me, and none will dare scorn me again."

I shuddered from the ferocity in his expression. He was mad, I thought. And if not, he was on the cusp of it. There was nothing left to anchor him, to sway him from ruin. Even when the lines across his face smoothed away, calm coating him like glaze over porcelain—it was a thin veneer, liable to crack under the slightest pressure.

Wugang's gaze shifted to someone behind me. "Houyi, the Slayer of the Suns. It gladdens me to see you."

My father glanced at the soldiers surrounding us. "I cannot say the same for you."

Wugang's lips twitched into the semblance of a smile. "A

chance to alter the course of the future lies before us. Don't you want vengeance on those who schemed against you? Acknowledge me as emperor, swear to me your fealty and that of your family—and I will grant you dominion over the Four Seas." His voice softened, growing intimate. "Us of the realm below must cleave together. Who else might we trust? Certainly not those who treated us as playthings for their entertainment, blessing or cursing us upon a whim."

When my father said nothing, Wugang continued, "Are you not grateful that I reunited you with your wife?"

Beside me, my mother stiffened. "*You* sent the note?"

Wugang nodded somberly. "It gave me much satisfaction to play a part in your reunion."

"You did it to further your own ends, to cast my mother into disfavor so you could seize our home," I seethed, half-fearing that Wugang's words might resonate with my father—mortal until yesterday, decades of resentment roiling in his gut for being played false by the Celestial Emperor. But even if my father were inclined to form an alliance with Wugang . . . the woodcutter would remain my eternal enemy.

"I will not join you. I do not care for your methods," my father said bluntly. "Attacking my wife and daughter. Murdering their beloved friend. Desecrating the resting place of the deceased. Some boundaries should never be crossed."

"You disappoint me." Venom slicked Wugang's tone. "I believed you a great man from the legends—ambitious, ruthless, sharp. A true blade, honed to perfection. And now, I find you blunted and dulled. As pitiful as those mortals you lived among, burdened by false morality and useless emotion. Once you wielded the power of the dragons—you could have crushed your enemies, challenged the Celestial Emperor, seized the reins of the realm. Except you chose a life in isolation, leaving yourself vulnerable. No wonder greatness eluded you then. No wonder it eludes you still. Your name might be known, but do you wield any real power? Love has made you *weak*."

Anger seared my veins. I would have lunged forward, but my father's touch on my arm halted me.

"I fight my own battles." He faced Wugang, his back pulled straight. "We each choose the path we walk. For myself, I choose my family instead of those mindless troops you surround yourself with. No honest soldier will follow you, for you have the heart of a coward—striking in the dark, afraid of dissent, craving obedience when you did nothing to earn it. You created this army because you cannot win the allegiance of the living. While they will never betray you, neither will they ever respect, honor, or love you."

Wugang's lip curled. "Spoken like a mortal in the winter of his life, a retired soldier ready to hang up his sword. Your wife and child are your burden to bear. Fortunately, I have none to weaken me. If you will not join me, you must surrender. If you are not my ally, you are my enemy."

I glanced at my father, his stony resolve mirroring my own. Behind him, Liwei and Shuxiao shook their heads, as did Wenzhi. No, we would not surrender. Yet as I studied the horde of soldiers before us, fear slunk into my heart for myself and those I loved, all who stood upon these shores today. Because if we did not surrender, we would fight—and I did not know if we could win.

A slight movement caught my eye—Prince Yanxi tilting his head toward Wugang. He was desperate to free his brother, as was I. While Prince Yanming was in Wugang's grasp, we could not attack.

"Stop lying to yourself, Wugang." I spoke with deliberate rudeness, using the name he disdained. Something flickered in his eyes before it was abruptly doused. I had thought he hated his name for reminding him of his mortal roots, but perhaps it reminded him of what he had lost: his parents, his family, his murdered wife.

"You say you're glad to be free of love, except you *envy* those who have it," I said slowly. "You killed the one you most loved, your family and friends are deceased. And now, you will be alone for eternity."

My words were merciless, intended to edge Wugang into rashness—yet they were shameful nonetheless. As his fingers dug deeper into Prince Yanming's shoulders, a soft gasp slipped from the boy before he bit down on his lip.

Rage flared, dangerously high. "Strike me if you dare. Or do you prefer to hide behind a child, even when you're surrounded by your own troops?"

A snarl erupted from Wugang's throat. With a rough shove, he sent Prince Yanming sprawling to the ground. Waves of azure light erupted from Prince Yanxi's palms, knocking aside the soldiers guarding him, as he snatched up his brother, racing toward us.

I swept up my bow, yet my father's arrow was already streaking toward Wugang. He spun aside, the bolt of ice plunging into the soldier behind—only to shatter into fragments like it had struck stone. The soldier did not flinch, not a single cry did it utter.

Wenzhi's pupils gleamed silver bright. As a glittering wave of his power coursed toward the soldiers, a look of revulsion crossed his face. "They have no minds to confound, no hearts to strike fear into. Nothing to confuse or put to sleep. Nor can I infiltrate Wugang's thoughts. He is shielded; he came prepared."

More soldiers closed around Wugang, the rest stalking

toward us. Their guandao flashed—curved silver blades with a jagged edge, welded to long poles of polished jade. They moved like the wind, as swift as a sandstorm. An army of death.

My fingers were stiff with terror, but I forced them to bend, releasing an arrow that hurtled into the shoulder of the nearest soldier. Sky-fire blazed down its arm, a crack forming all around as the arm fell off with a clunk. No blood spilled, though the soldier's flesh glistened with a translucent wetness. The creature did not pause, seemingly indifferent to its missing limb, impervious to pain or fear.

The Celestial Empress wrenched free of her captors, crimson flames surging from her palms. Those scorched, halted in their stride—the empress running toward us. As a soldier gave chase, I let fly an arrow that plunged into its thigh. The creature shuddered as it fell down, twitching as light crackled around it.

Liwei raced to his mother, flames rippling along the length of his blade. As a soldier leapt before him, raising its guandao, my arrow struck the carved disc on its armor. The jade fractured as Liwei's sword plunged through it, flames coursing into the creature's body, its pale skin melting like wax. Dazzling light erupted from the soldier's chest, the luminous glow of a laurel seed nestled where a heart should beat. Had Wugang planted it there? Was that the source of the creatures' power? The soldier lurched upright then, the first sign of distress I had seen. The mottled patches upon its body thickened—like ice hardening on a lake—as the soldier collapsed into a quivering pile, the glow in its eye sockets waning. Spirals of gold dust slipped from the cavern of its throat, coiling into the air, soon lost amid the streaming sunlight. How I wished the Celestial spirit wrenched from its peace might find it again . . . even as relief surged through my veins.

These soldiers were not invulnerable; they could be destroyed.

"Break the jade discs to get at the laurel seeds within," I called out to the others. "They are vulnerable to heat, to fire and lightning—use what you can."

I tossed the Jade Dragon Bow to my father—his weapon was of no use here, for the laurel's nature was cold. He caught it deftly, his fingers closing around it with practiced ease. The bow settled in his grip as I had only ever seen it do for me. As my father drew back the cord, Sky-fire flashed between his fingers, already hurtling toward the enemy. I grasped my magic to shield my parents and myself, as the rest did the same. Drawing my sword, I ran a finger along its blade, my power gliding across it until it blazed with vermilion fire.

We formed a tight circle—Liwei and Prince Yanxi on my right, Wenzhi on my left. My father took up the other side, with Shuxiao and the Celestial Empress beside him. My mother was tucked in the center, along with Prince Yanming, while the soldiers wound around us like a monstrous serpent, trapping us in its coils. The air rippled with the force of their energy slamming against our shields—holding fast—yet it felt like being kicked in the gut.

It was a clumsy, hacking, brutal battle. Streams of fire shot from Liwei and me, lightning from my father, while Wenzhi and Prince Yanxi deflected the blows that rained upon us. Each wound we inflicted was hard-won, like wood scraping at stone. Still, the soldiers advanced, missing limbs, skin smoking—until my gut cramped with horror.

"Watch out!"

I spun around just as Wenzhi's blade plunged into the soldier before me, striking the disc on its armor. Its tip scraped the jade as Wenzhi's knuckles whitened around the hilt. I gripped his hand, channeling my power into his weapon, flames surging along the metal into the soldier's chest. Cracks streaked across the jade disc, breaking apart with a clink, as Wenzhi's sword drove clean through its body.

We did not relent, arrows of lightning and waves of fire surging forth. Slowly, more soldiers fell back, the light winking from their eyes, their bodies shattering like glass—until the beach was strewn with those glittering shards, the air shimmering with gold dust.

Yet how long could we keep this up? Our movements were growing sluggish, a numbness sinking into my limbs. Our formation had long fallen apart—we were scattered into a thin line, wedged between the sea and Wugang's soldiers. There was no concerted strategy, no planned attack. We were a brawling, graceless mess—a hasty stab here, a quick strike there. General Jianyun would have thrown a book at us had he witnessed our haphazard assault. But all we could do in this moment was to fight to draw another breath.

My mother gasped. I whirled to find her standing alone, unprotected, as two soldiers bore down upon my father. A glint caught my attention, a guandao thrust toward her with unerring accuracy. I lunged forward, a scream forming in my throat—but then, the blade stilled. The soldier's eyes glowed brighter, cocking its head as though listening to something only it could hear.

Abruptly, it turned away, slashing at Wenzhi instead. Wenzhi's sword swung up to deflect the blow, his face taut with strain. As more soldiers rushed forward, our shields wavered against the relentless horde. Fear reared high, yet I forced it back down. Each soldier struck down was one less to fight.

Wenzhi staggered back a step, his breathing roughened. "They've broken the shield," he warned. As his energy gathered, forming it anew—a guandao plunged through to sink into Shuxiao's shoulder. White light crackled along the blade as I dove at her, gripping the pole to tear it away. It slid from her flesh with a wet sound, the metal dripping with blood, a gaping slit left in its wake. Spinning around, I drove my sword through the soldier's chest, bearing down until the jade disc shattered, rivulets of fire pouring into the wound. The creature quivered before going limp, falling to the ground.

Shuxiao's body jerked as she sucked in a gust of air. I pressed her hand, flinching from the chill. "Are you all right?"

She nodded, though her forehead was wrinkled with discomfort. Liwei crouched beside her, his hand gliding over the wound. The blood flow staunched, though she remained ashen.

"Be careful," Liwei cautioned. "Their weapons possess a strange magic, weakening us. It's fortunate you got it out when you did. It spreads like a contagion, a mortal illness—except it affects our powers instead of our bodies. If unhealed, it will drain her energy, consuming her lifeforce."

"Can you cure her?" My voice trembled.

He frowned. "I can't do it here. I've contained it for now, but it won't hold for long."

Shuxiao's eyes were glassy, her breathing labored. My grip tightened around her hand. "Don't tire yourself. Rest. I won't let anything happen to you."

Despite my words, despair seeped through me. This was a battle we could not win. We had to escape, but how? *The dragons*, my mind whispered. They could not fight these creatures, but they could help us flee. While I was reluctant to expose them to Wugang, I would not let Shuxiao die. Fumbling in my pouch, my fingers brushed the paper dragon Prince Yanming had given me before closing around something flat and cool. The scale from the Long Dragon.

Immerse this in liquid to call us, it had told me.

My fingers curled around it, pressing against its fine edge—stinging—as it sliced my skin. Blood trickled forth, slippery and warm, as I rubbed it against the scale.

A thin shout rang out a distance away. Prince Yanming? I glanced up to find him and his brother encircled by soldiers. In the tumult, I had not realized they had been separated from us. Terror clawed me at the sight of a soldier moving silently behind Prince Yanxi. Flames arced from my hand, the creature dipping back to evade them. With a smooth twist of its arm, the soldier swung its guandao toward Prince Yanxi—my cry of warning morphing into a howl, my insides shriveling like burnt paper as someone hurled himself in front of the blade, small arms clutched tight around Prince Yanxi's waist. How warm and soft they had felt around my own. Weapons crashed all around, shouts erupting—yet I heard nothing except that sick, wet squelch as the guandao slid through Prince Yanming's chest, scattering his blood like rain upon the sand.

23

LIGHT CRACKLED FROM THE BLADE into Prince Yan-ming's body, the stench of scorched flesh springing into the air. Just hours earlier, I had remarked he was taller, and now . . . how frail he looked, with that massive guandao jutting cruelly from his chest. Blood pooled, his palm groping at the wound, coming away a glistening red. His small body convulsed, eyes so wide there was a ring of pure white around his irises.

A guttural scream tore from Prince Yanxi's throat as he lunged at the soldier, thrusting his sword through its gut in a single ferocious strike. The creature stiffened, its hands clenching harder around the guandao, holding it fast.

"The blade! Get it out!" I raced toward them, nauseated by the sight of the ominous lights still flowing into Prince Yan-ming's body.

Prince Yanxi clawed the soldier away, grabbing the guandao and ripping it from his brother's chest. The boy's gasp, trapped between a breath and a scream, stabbed like nails driven through my skull.

As the Celestial soldiers started toward me, my mind hollowed of thought, consumed by rage. My power surged, a storm erupting from my fingers, knocking aside those in my path. A reckless use of my energy, a waste I could ill afford—but I no longer cared, my only thought to reach Prince Yanming.

A thunderous rush swirled through the air, the churn of water and wind. My hair flew across my face, cold droplets spraying all around as the Four Dragons sprang from the ocean depths, covering the sky itself. Crimson and yellow, pearl and black, undulating through the heavens with majestic grace, the monstrous press of their auras closing in as they descended to the beach. Arched gold claws sank into the white sands, billowing like mist in their wake.

Shouts broke out from behind me. A scuffle, the clang of blades, before the soldiers abruptly stilled as though turned to stone. I swung around to find Wugang bound by glowing bands of ice, Wenzhi pressing his sword to the back of his neck. Ever quick to grasp an opportunity, he must have seized Wugang amid the earlier chaos. The soldiers stared blankly at Wenzhi and their master, whom they obeyed like puppets whose strings he tugged.

I reached Prince Yanming, falling to my knees beside him, clutching his hand. Stiff and so cold, a shiver coursed through me. His youthful glow was fading fast, like the dying embers of a flame.

My heart clenched so tight I thought it might fracture. "Why? How?" I did not know to whom I spoke, or what answer I sought . . . just that this was so brutally unfair, so very wrong. That I would give anything to set it right again.

"The soldiers separated us." Prince Yanxi's face crumpled as he spoke. "I should not have fought them; we should have run. Yanming should have been the only one that mattered."

I could find no words of solace, my own guilt driving deep. Wugang had come for *us*—Prince Yanming was innocent, simply caught in the fray. They had only fled here because of the turmoil we caused in the Southern Sea. They had even tried to help us . . . and a part of me wished they had not. Nothing was worth this price.

Bodies crowded around, yet I could no longer distinguish friend from foe. All I saw was a small face as pale as the moon, blue eyes darkening to night. A mouth that trembled as he tried to speak.

I bent my ear lower, catching the wisp of warmth in his frail breath.

"We . . . did not betray you. They found us. Don't be angry."

His words wracked me to my core. "I know." I tried to smile but my lips were trembling. "I'm not angry. I'll never be angry at you."

My fingers wrapped tight around his as I grasped my energy, unsure of what I intended. A cut, a burn—such injuries I could tackle. Not this deathlike frost that bloomed from within, sapping the life from his veins.

Someone touched my shoulder, the warmth startling in the cold that shrouded me. Liwei knelt down, folding Prince Yanming's hand in his.

Hope flared. Liwei's Life magic was strong, far stronger than mine. "Help him," I pleaded, though he had already gathered his power.

"Be careful, Liwei." The Celestial Empress's voice sounded like it came from far away. "Don't exhaust yourself."

I wanted to silence her, as much as I wanted to repeat her warning. I did not want to trade one life for another—I just wanted to save Prince Yanming.

The dragons prowled toward me, the evening sun setting the Long Dragon's crimson scales afire, its golden claws alight.

Their amber eyes lingered upon the gleaming remnants of the soldiers piled around us like shards of hewn marble.

What were these creatures? The Long Dragon's tone was equal parts gentle and fierce, flowing with the crystalline purity of a mountain spring.

"Resurrected Celestial spirits, stolen from the Divine Harmony Sky," I replied listlessly.

The dragons reared back, their manes rippling in the wind. *A monstrous act. How is this possible?*

"The laurel on the moon," Wenzhi said.

Ahh. A sigh thrumming with sorrow.

Silence fell over us. The Long Dragon's gaze shifted to my father, shining with recognition. The other dragons stilled, their jaws curving wide. As one, they lowered their heads to him, a sight that stirred me, even mired in despair. They had not known my father as a mortal; all they had heard of the great archer Houyi were the stories told during their imprisonment.

My father bowed, returning the dragons' respectful greeting. "Yes," he said quietly, answering a question for him alone. "I have returned."

The Black Dragon's voice rang in my mind then: *I am glad to be mistaken. I am glad your father is alive.*

"Your pledge to me is honored, your debt repaid in full," my father told the dragons. "You were never meant to have been bound by the pearls. If my powers had not been weakened, I would have freed you the moment you recovered. I'm ashamed that I grew complacent, and content with how things were."

"A tender scene," Wugang sneered. "The reunion of old friends, or rather, old servants with their master."

My eyes narrowed in loathing, thoughts of vengeance a momentary salve to my grief. One thrust of Wenzhi's sword through

Wugang's skull would end his accursed existence. We did not need him alive; the dragons could help us flee his soldiers.

My gaze flicked up to meet Wenzhi's. Our minds rode the same dark tide as his grip tightened around the hilt of his sword. We had killed lesser monsters before in the service of the Celestial Army.

"Release me." Wugang's tone pulsed with sudden urgency. Perhaps he finally realized that we would show him no mercy. "If you hurt me, my soldiers will destroy all of you here, today."

"They are no match for the dragons," I lied, knowing that the dragons could not kill.

Fortunately, the dragons did not betray me, the Black Dragon parting its jaws to display two rows of wickedly sharp fangs.

"My soldiers are more than a match," Wugang said. "The dragons are creatures of water. Their magic cannot harm my army."

"They can tear your soldiers into a dozen pieces," I flung back.

"Kill me, and my army will be unleashed upon the Immortal Realm." Wugang spoke with utter solemnity. "They will spare no one: none of you here, not the former Celestial Emperor, nor any living creature in the Jade Palace, the Celestial Kingdom, or beyond."

"How can they do this if you're dead?" my father demanded.

Wugang glanced at the sun, embarking on its fiery descent. "I am not so careless as to come here without assurance of my safe return. My soldiers have not attacked yet because their sole purpose is to safeguard my well-being. But if you *hurt* me, if you continue to threaten and hold me prisoner—they will descend on you like jackals upon a fresh kill. If I do not return to the Jade Palace by nightfall, the first to die will be the former emperor.

Thousands of my soldiers will rampage throughout the kingdom, leaving no one alive."

"You would murder everyone *after* your death?" My mother's tone was wracked with horror, echoing my own.

"What do I care if the Immortal Realm burns? Don't forget, their lives are not in my hands, but all of yours."

My insides hollowed, but I stifled my fear. "Thousands of soldiers? You don't have enough laurel seeds."

"Oh, I do." His lips stretched into a wide smile as he tilted his head toward Prince Yanming with deliberate malice. "And sometimes, just one will suffice to wreak the most harm."

I breathed deeply, struggling against the urge to strike him. My mind sifted through my memories—the night we fled our home, the laurel seeds cascading onto the ground . . .

He speaks the truth of his army, the Long Dragon intoned. *We have sensed a disturbance in the Celestial Kingdom, the presence of a large force, its power unlike anything we had known—until we encountered it here today.*

My stomach roiled at the devastation Wugang threatened—yet how could we let him go? I glanced at Liwei, still intent upon Prince Yanming, his forehead creased in concentration as his power flowed from him.

"Empty threats," Wenzhi said coldly to Wugang. "Even if you have the soldiers, what proof is there of your other wild claims?"

"Test me," Wugang challenged him with slick assurance. "Would you dare to risk being wrong? Do you think I am not capable of such a thing?"

Wenzhi's sword flashed as the edge bit into Wugang's skin, blood staining the metal. The soldiers lurched upright as one, heads swiveling toward Wenzhi, their eyes shining with that eerie light as their guandao swung our way. Wenzhi's expression was grim as he eased his pressure on the blade. At once, the soldiers lowered their weapons, though their vacant gazes remained fixed on him.

"Care to try that again, *Captain?*" Wugang taunted.

"What do you want?" the Celestial Empress demanded.

"Let me leave with my soldiers. No one will be harmed." As Wugang flicked an uncaring look at Prince Yanming, my hands curled into fists. "No one else, at least. Consider this carefully, for my offer is generous, and it expires at dusk."

He addressed the Celestial Empress. "You don't have much time left, unless you wish your husband to meet an untimely end and the kingdom to fall into ruin. Or do you secretly wish for his downfall for the hurt he has caused you?"

The empress drew herself up tall. "Not all of us believe death to be a fitting sentence for infidelity."

A gurgling rasp snared my attention. My eyes snapped back to Prince Yanming, my heart splintering with dread.

"I'm sorry, Xingyin," Liwei said in a low voice, "His lifeforce is extinguished. Nothing can restore it."

"He's still alive. Do something. *Anything.*" I was hateful in my despair.

"What's left of his energy sustains him for now, but it will fade soon." He left unspoken the words: *he will die.*

An unbearable thought, a vicious reality. Prince Yanming had barely scraped the surface of a mortal's lifespan. Such anguish sank over me, that wracking futility I had felt when Ping'er died.

Prince Yanxi cupped his brother's cheek. "Hold on, Little Brother. I will bring you home. You will be well soon." He smiled warmly, though I heard the lie in the crack of his voice.

Prince Yanming's lips curved. "Home. To Mother." He drew a shuddering breath. "Don't let her be too sad."

I folded over, feeling like a fist had been driven into my gut. He *knew* he was dying; there was no comfort we could offer—neither hollow lies nor promises. Closing my eyes, I reached out tentatively with my power. I trusted Liwei, yet I had to try. I plunged my consciousness into Prince Yanming's body, searching the dullness of his blood, now devoid of an immortal's radiance. His lifeforce, tucked deep in his mind, was no longer dazzling bright but murky and dim. I threw my energy at it, willing it to catch fire as a spark to tinder. Again and again, but nothing took root, my power sliding from him as waves crashing over a rock. My breaths came heavier, my nerves strained from fatigue. My mother's soft cries drifted into my ears—how long had she wept?

I could not save him. No one could.

I fell back, wanting to sink into the sand. To close my eyes and let the numbness take me, a respite from this relentless agony. And I . . . let go. I had failed Ping'er. I had failed Prince Yanming. I was no hero.

As Prince Yanxi embraced his brother, muttering soft words I could not hear, my father gestured to me. "We must decide what to do with Wugang."

I yanked my mind from the grasp of sorrow, for we were still in the gravest of danger. Grief was an indulgence I could not afford. My heart cried out for Wugang's death in retribution for those he had taken, but I could not form the words, the better part of me seeking restraint, to save those we could.

"Is there any question? Let him go!" the Celestial Empress snarled. "He will kill—"

"Your Celestial Majesty," Wenzhi drawled from where he

stood. "I doubt many of us here would mourn the loss of your husband. He has not made many friends of late." He prodded Wugang with his sword. "Offer us something else, something of real value—start by disbanding your army."

Liwei's hands clenched as he rose, but I tugged his sleeve in warning. Wenzhi was skilled at piercing an opponent without a weapon, honing a scrap of truth into a blade, unearthing an enemy's weakness to force them to relent.

Wugang laughed. "Do not take me for a fool. The Celestial Prince certainly cares about his father's fate, and because he does, so would the daughter of the Moon Goddess." His mouth curled into a smirk. "While *you* will not move against her wishes."

Heat flushed my face at his insinuation, while Wenzhi's expression remained inscrutable. "You forget what I'm capable of; I do not lose my head for my heart. What does it matter to me if the emperor dies? I care less for him than I do for his son."

His cold words pricked me. But it was nothing I had not known, and I would be a gullible fool to ever believe anything else of him.

"I know what you *were* capable of," Wugang said cryptically. "Be warned that the army will heed no one but me. Nor will they stop at the Celestial Kingdom, they will engulf the entire Immortal Realm, even your lands, and that of the mortals."

Wenzhi's jaw clenched. "End your vile ambitions, return the spirits you have stolen, and we will let you go. We will not seek retribution. You will be free to build a new life, to earn a second chance to make it worthwhile—even though you do not deserve it."

"I will *not*." Wugang's eyes were chips of muddied ice. "I

would rather die knowing my ambition is fulfilled, my vengeance complete, than to start over with nothing. Let the realms wither to dust if I cannot rule them. You can't frighten me. I have lived through my worst nightmares and come out on the other side."

His gaze lifted toward the darkening sky. "Sundown is almost upon us. Will you let me go or risk everyone? Some of you might survive. Certainly, not all. Not to mention the innocents dwelling in the realms above and below, whose blood will stain your hands."

I smothered my instinctive protest, the violent urge to make Wugang suffer. I had never felt any true satisfaction in killing before, but I could have slain him now without hesitation, relishing the Sky-fire crackling over his face, twisting with the bone-deep torment I knew so well. Yet it would yield just a futile relief, a bandage to a festering wound without its cure.

My eyes searched for Shuxiao where she lay on the ground, alert though quiet, her eyes ringed in purple like they were bruised. There was no real choice here; the stakes were too high. We were outnumbered, weakened, vulnerable. Even if we escaped with the dragons' aid . . . I could not bear the burden of the lives lost in the Celestial Kingdom and beyond. Even that of the emperor, even if it were not for Liwei.

I had lost. *No,* I reminded myself. It was not over. And if winning meant countless innocents would perish—that was no victory.

"Call off your soldiers and leave this place. You will let us go safely and not give chase," I said slowly.

"For now," Wugang agreed. "A day's respite."

"Forever," I demanded. "We want nothing more to do with you."

"I will never agree to that," he said with resolute finality.

"Why not?" I ground out. "What more do you want of us?"

He said nothing, merely looking at me with those pale eyes. He would not relent, nor would he tell us more.

"A week," I countered. Another idea dawned, small recompense though it was. "You will also leave the Eastern Sea in peace. You will not hold this encounter against them."

"Very well. Their offense has been repaid in blood. I will not demand more unless they move against me." Wugang's head tipped toward the sun. "Are we in accord?"

"How do I know you will keep your word?" A lesson I had learned from the Celestial Empress.

"I swear this upon the honor of my parents. The ones who gave me life, whom I cherish though they are long gone." He pressed a fist to his chest. "If I break this oath, may their spirits never find peace, may they haunt me for eternity."

I believed him. How I hated this, but Wugang's death would not bring back those lost, and at least we had salvaged a temporary reprieve. As Wenzhi's sword lifted from his neck and his binds vanished, Wugang strode to the safety of his soldiers. They surrounded him at once, their heads cocked for his command, their guandao clutched tight. For a moment, I feared treachery— except there was still a sliver of honor in him despite his mockery of the virtue. As clouds swooped down to the beach, he leapt upon one, his army taking flight after him.

Prince Yanming coughed, a gurgling sound. I fell to my knees beside him. Words tumbled from my lips, terror seizing me that time was running out. "I'm sorry, I promised to keep you safe."

"You did." His tongue darted over his lips, so cracked and pale. His breathing came hoarser than before, each labored rattle a stab to my chest. "The dragons. I never asked you what they were like."

Could he not see them? Had death begun to glaze his vision, sheathing it in night? We could not save him . . . yet perhaps we might bring him one last glimmer of joy.

I turned to the dragons and bowed low. "Please. The boy needs you."

The dragons prowled closer, their great bodies blocking the red curve of the sun. Sand scattered over us as their tails lashed the air. Prince Yanming tugged his hand from mine with a sudden eagerness, stretching it out to them. His mouth opened, no words emerging—yet such yearning shone from his eyes as they lingered upon the magnificent creatures. The Pearl Dragon with its luminous scales of moonlight, the Long Dragon ablaze like flame, the dragon of deepest night, and the one as golden as the summer sun.

"Can you save him?" Despair choked Prince Yanxi's voice as he fell to his knees in reverence.

This is beyond our power. Infinite sorrow thrummed in those words.

The Long Dragon bent its head to Prince Yanming's brow gently, crimson scales against ashen skin. A shiver rippled through the boy's body—of delight—I sensed. He pulled his other hand from his brother's grip, wrapping his arms around the dragon's neck without a trace of fear.

"You are real," Prince Yanming whispered, pressing his cheek against the dragon's jaw as the others drew closer, forming a circle around us. A tear slid from the corner of his eye, vanishing into the sand.

Do not be afraid, child, the Long Dragon said to him, yet in its mercy, allowed us to hear. *We will watch over your spirit. You will have a place with us for as long as you wish, or become one with the sea whenever you choose to.*

The dragons leaned toward the boy, their amber eyes aglow,

their jaws parted in a gentle smile. An answering one spread across Prince Yanming's face, so warm and beautiful that a wild hope bloomed in me. But then his eyelids sank shut, his arms falling limp by his sides. A wisp of breath slid from his lips, his aura winking out like a candle flame at the end of its wick. And there was nothing left but the stillness and this devouring pain in my heart.

24

H E WAS GONE. SKIN COLD, limbs slack. His radiance extinguished like a lantern snuffed out. Prince Yanxi folded over his brother's body, his shoulders heaving with grief.

"I'm sorry." These words were a thin echo of the sorrow which engulfed me. There was so much more I wanted to say, yet nothing would come, each inane phrase crumbling like sand beneath my feet. How could I ease his pain when I was drowning in it myself? I had loved Prince Yanming for the little time I knew him, while his brother had loved him all his life.

"We must go. Wugang might change his mind and return. We cannot trust so fully in his honor," Wenzhi warned.

"I will bring him home." Prince Yanxi slid his arms beneath his brother's shoulders and knees, cradling him tight, as he rose slowly to his feet. His eyes were dull as they fixed upon Prince Yanming's face, locked in unnatural stillness, this mask of death he would wear forever.

The urge beat in my chest to follow him, to see Prince Yanming laid to rest in the Eastern Sea. A selfish whim, as I should not impose myself on their hospitality, to add to their troubles when they were a kingdom in mourning.

I drew an unsteady breath, my teeth cutting into my lip. My

farewells had been said; I could not ask for more. My fingers instinctively closed around the paper dragon Prince Yanming had crafted for me, its edges still crisp. *A keepsake*, my mind pleaded. *Something to remember him by.* Yet I did not need anything to keep him alive in my heart. With trembling fingers, I tucked the paper dragon into Prince Yanming's limp hand. Bending down, I pressed my lips to his cold forehead . . . and I wept. Tears surged into my eyes, running down my cheeks. My breaths came ragged and hoarse. For never again, would he fling his arms around me, never again would I hear his bright laughter.

"Thank you," Prince Yanxi said quietly. "Yanming would have liked that. He talked about the dragons all the time. He loved their stories best."

The Pearl Dragon glided toward him, its scales shimmering like silvered snow. *He was a rare spirit. I would bear him on this final journey. I would bear you both.*

Prince Yanxi hesitated before bowing low. "It would be our honor."

The Pearl Dragon shook its mane, a mist forming around the Eastern Sea princes that lifted them onto its back. With painstaking gentleness, Prince Yanxi laid his brother's head against his chest. How peaceful he looked; lashes curled like half-moons grazing his rounded cheeks. If only I could delude myself that he was asleep, though even in slumber he could never have kept so still. With a graceful bound, the Pearl Dragon soared into the sky toward the Eastern Sea. I stared after them until they were swallowed by the dark. Had the sun set? I did not notice, the stars shining upon us now.

The Celestial Empress was staring at the other dragons, her lips pursed into a knot. "Come, Liwei. We must go to the Phoenix Kingdom. These creatures are not to be trusted. They bear a grudge against your father."

"They are *not* like you," I said with feeling. "Even though they have every right to resent their imprisonment, they are neither vengeful nor vindictive. They will not harm you or your kin."

Her eyes flashed with anger, even as she turned from me like I had not spoken.

"Venerable Dragons," my father said. "We must stop Wugang's heinous ambitions. Can you tell us what you know of these creatures and the power of the moon laurel?"

The Long Dragon's eyes blazed as they swept over the broken bodies strewn along the beach, like some glistening monstrosity the tide had washed up.

We never imagined the moon laurel could be harnessed to such ends. Its power is of regeneration and renewal. This is a vile corruption—using it to enslave immortal spirits, stealing life itself. Wugang must be stopped.

I dragged myself from despair. "Heat weakens these soldiers, yet it's no easy matter to bring them down. If Wugang's army is as large as he claims, imagine the destruction they would wreak across the realms."

"His army is constrained by the laurel seeds in his possession," Wenzhi remarked. "How many can there be?"

An image of the glittering tree slid into my mind. "As many as there are stars in the sky."

Remember, too, the seeds plucked will regenerate, the Long Dragon cautioned. *There will be no end to this horror.*

"Wugang can't grow his army that quickly." I tried to assure myself as well. "He had to strike the tree with all his might before it yielded a single seed. It was a fortunate coincidence that he managed to harvest so many the last time—"

Coincidence? The Long Dragon tilted its head contemplatively.

My insides curled like a withered leaf. I had not wanted to

remember anything of the night Ping'er died—reluctant to dwell upon it, to relive the horror, regret, and sorrow. But now, I forced the memories into my mind: my mother's blood splattering the laurel, its seeds raining upon the ground . . . the light in Wugang's eyes when he had ordered the soldiers to seize her. And what of his strange words earlier when he had claimed not to be the soldiers' sole creator? My fingers dug into my temple, more recollections surfacing of Wugang chopping at the laurel, the scars on his palms reopening with each strike. My mother weeping in the forest. The two images converging as their blood and tears spilled upon the luminous tree, seeping into its roots, its bark . . . its seeds.

Panic rose, cresting high. "Mother, that soldier did not attack you."

"I was fortunate," she said slowly. "It stopped, almost like it recognized me."

"Mother, Wugang meant *you*."

Her eyes went as wide as those of a frightened deer. "What do you mean?"

I softened my tone, taking her hand. "General Jianyun said the laurel seeds did not exist before. The tears of some immortals are said to contain part of their power. All those nights you wept in the forest . . . it was from *your* tears that the seeds sprouted."

She shook her head violently. "No. Impossible."

I did not want to be right, yet I could not ignore the facts. "The laurel is a part of you both. Wugang's blood can harm the tree, yours can harvest its seeds."

My voice shook over the words and their searing implication: for Wugang had not come at us out of pique, vengeance, or pride—but because my mother, the Moon Goddess, was at the heart of his plots, and he would stop at nothing to seize her.

"I have no magic. How could such a thing come from me?" She was so pale, like she was about to be sick.

"All immortals have magic which manifests in different ways," Liwei explained. "This does not mean your power is evil, nothing starts out inherently so. You might not even be aware that it exists in you. Somehow, what power you inadvertently yielded the laurel has been tainted, likely through Wugang's efforts."

Wugang had not wanted to alert us to his true ambition. This was why he had taken our home, hunted us down, and tried to secure my father's allegiance. He would never let us go . . . which was why I must end him.

My father slid an arm around my mother's shoulders. "If Wugang captures you, he will be able to harvest all the seeds he wants. His army will be unstoppable, he will reign supreme over the earth and skies for eternity." He turned to the dragons. "Will you stand with us, my friends?"

The Long Dragon did not reply at once. Was it conferring with its siblings? Its voice resonated in my mind, startling me— all of us—from the transfixed faces around.

We will aid you as far as we can, though we are constrained in what we can do. This power is far greater than ours. The Moon Goddess must be protected at all costs. The dragon fell silent as its amber eyes swung to me.

Evil must be struck at its roots. Cutting its branches will not suffice.

Did it speak to me alone? How clearly the Long Dragon had seen into my weak heart—my selfish plans of staying clear of trouble, of running away with my family, hoping to never be found. What did I owe the Immortal Realm? We could make a new home for ourselves in the world below. Yet if Wugang prevailed, no place would be safe for us. He was a danger like no other because he believed in nothing, whether tradition, history, or honor. He lacked even the innate care for his people that Queen Suihe possessed. Any compassion or love that might have existed in him once had been long extinguished, for his heart was consumed by hate. Death and misery fed him; he seemed to crave it. He did not care if he brought the realms crashing down with him. There would be no peace when such as him reigned.

Why did he want power? I did not know. Perhaps because he had nothing else.

A heaviness descended over me, a profound gravity. No longer could I hover on the fringes, hoping evil and misfortune would leave us unscathed. I had done this before and now . . . Ping'er and Prince Yanming were gone. Their lives would not be in vain. If left unchecked, this evil would engulf the realm, devouring all in its path until there was nothing left but the cries of the tormented, and the silence of the dead.

This was no honor; I did not want this burden. Yet if I did nothing, I would lose everything—all whom I loved. As I caught the resolute glint in my father's eyes, I was glad to not be alone. Together, we would keep my mother safe.

"We must destroy the laurel." I spoke clearly, giving no sign of the fear unfolding within me, the sadness that thrummed like a plucked string. The laurel had been a part of my childhood, and how I had loved it. Through no fault of its own, it had been fed a lifetime of suffering through Wugang's hatred and my mother's sorrow.

"Is that possible?" Shuxiao asked. Her movements were sluggish, her face drained of color—an urgency rising in me to get her to safety.

The Long Dragon's eyes rolled up like it was searching its

thoughts. *The laurel's nature is cold, as are those who draw their strength from the moon. To destroy such a thing, you would need the most potent flame in the realm.*

"Where can we find this?" Wenzhi asked.

"What of the Phoenix Kingdom?" I ventured. "Those strong in Fire come from there."

The Long Dragon said nothing, slanting its great head toward the empress.

"Mother, could you help us?" Liwei asked.

I thought it more probable that she would claw me to shreds—but surely, she would understand the threat of Wugang should take precedence over all else. When she remained silent, I let a note of disdain slide into my voice. "Perhaps you do not know. Perhaps only the great Queen Fengjin has the answer."

"I know far more than an ignorant girl like you does," she hissed. "You are wrong; what you seek is not in the Phoenix Kingdom. The Sacred Flame Feather grows from the sunbird's crown."

Sunbird. As the word resonated through the silence, my father's face contorted with pain. I did not think he regretted saving the Mortal Realm, yet it did not mean he relished his victory.

"The sunbird resides in the Fragrant Mulberry Grove. The domain of Lady Xihe." Wenzhi's gaze was sharp and assessing. "I doubt Your Celestial Majesty will grieve should the goddess attack us."

She would have just cause. Lady Xihe was the Goddess of the Sun. Mother to the sunbirds, nine of whom my father had slain.

The empress's lips curled. "Don't you dare look at me that way. I am no liar—not like you, you treacherous spy." She swung to my father. "Murderer of my kin, surely you remember the day you slew them. You have felt the potency of their heat. You have seen the feathers I speak of."

She laughed, a brittle sound. "Thanks to you, there is only

one left in the world, when once there were ten. A fitting penance to have you grovel for Xihe's mercy, to witness the suffering you wrought upon her family."

I took an involuntary step back. "Lady Xihe will never aid us, not even if the Immortal Realm burned to ash."

"Yet we must try," my father said gravely.

"How can we find the grove?" Liwei asked his mother. "I have heard it's no easy place to enter."

"Follow the trail of the sun's descent, the path the sun chariot traverses as it returns home. You must be quick and not fall behind its shadow. If you do, the way will be shut to you, and you must wait another day." The empress spoke slowly, as though unearthing memories long past.

She had been close to Lady Xihe once—as intimate as sisters—until the sunbirds were killed while under her protection.

What of the key, Your Celestial Majesty? the Long Dragon pressed.

"Key?" Liwei repeated.

Three were crafted, for the three who were the closest of companions. One in Lady Xihe's keeping, one given to Queen Fengjin. And one to Her Celestial Majesty. To enter the Fragrant Mulberry Grove without key or invitation, is to perish.

"I was going to tell you." Red bloomed in the empress's cheeks, but I had dealt with far better pretenders. Perhaps her loathing of me was too great—that she was unable to mask it, unable to discern between wanting me dead and aiding her own cause.

"Why don't you help us?" I asked her without rancor. "You despise me, think me beneath you. But Wugang took my home, and now he's taken yours. He threatens all we love, the entire realm itself. Nothing should matter except stopping him."

"I don't need your help to do that," she snarled.

Liwei stepped between us. "We need all the help we can get."

The Long Dragon's gaze was intent upon me, its words for me alone. *The nine slain sunbirds were arrogant, selfish, and capricious. However, they did not deserve their fate. While your father saved the mortals from certain calamity, you should not forget that the sunbirds, too, were unfortunate participants in this farce—they on one end, your father on the other. One tricked with false coin, the other forced to pay an impossible price.*

Before, I had felt little grief for the sunbirds, blaming them for tormenting the world. To be reminded that they had been young and foolish, and they had family who grieved for them still . . . it hurt, for I had tasted the bitterness of loss. And yet, that was incomparable to a mother's sorrow.

Lady Xihe's grief is vast, her rage unquenched, the dragon continued. *It simmers each morning as the sun illuminates the skies, roiling as she bears her lone child in the chariot, reminded anew of those she lost. It pulses in the vicious lash of her whip as she strikes her mount. She was not cruel before, though her heart is now hardened by misery. The most dangerous hate is that which festers unsated.*

Why are you telling me this? I asked in the silence of my mind, not wanting to draw the attention of the others.

Only you can ease Lady Xihe's pain. Only you can make amends. The grove is the home of the sun, and yet, all these decades—the darkness is all they have known.

How can I do this? I wondered, almost beseechingly. *What would satisfy Lady Xihe except my father's death or mine?*

Death need not be repaid in kind, but the chain of vengeance must be snapped, and the hatred spawned extinguished—else they will flame into an untethered blaze. Catastrophic, in times as these, when our world hovers on the brink of destruction.

The dragon stretched its neck out to the skies. *Who could have imagined that the fate of the realm now rests upon a single feather? Ease the Sun Goddess's torment. Don't let the wood-cutter turn her to his side, or devastation will surely follow.*

My father's voice rang out. "What is the matter, Xingyin?"

"Father, you must not go," I said quickly, evading his question. "Lady Xihe would show you no mercy. You won't be safe there."

"She will show you no mercy either," he reminded me.

"She does not know me, but she would recognize you and Mother at once," I reasoned. "Your presence will only enrage her further. You don't have your powers; you can't defend yourself against her. You should go someplace safe, along with Shuxiao."

Come with us, the Long Dragon offered. *We will tend to your wounded.*

"Can you heal her?" I asked the Long Dragon.

Yes, though it will take some time to remove the taint from her blood.

I lowered my head. "I am grateful."

I crouched down beside Shuxiao, placing my hand over hers. "I will see you soon, my friend."

She smiled weakly. "Count on it."

The Long Dragon cocked its head toward my father. *Will you return to your home?*

My father nodded as he handed the Jade Dragon Bow to me, and after a brief hesitation, I accepted it. Relief flooded me that they would be safe with the dragons, out of harm's way.

The Long Dragon straightened, its tail lashing the air. A luminous mist flowed forth, surrounding my parents and Shuxiao, and lifting them upon its back. As it took flight, my mother and Shuxiao sat stiffly with their hands clenched, while my father showed no trepidation—he must have ridden upon the dragons countless times before.

Clouds were summoned to bear us away. As I started toward

Liwei's cloud, Wenzhi caught my arm in a light hold. Before I could snatch it away, Wenzhi cast a meaningful glance at the Celestial Empress. "Would you prefer to ride with her?"

My gut recoiled at the thought. As I strode to Wenzhi's cloud, Liwei's guarded expression pricked me. The moment we were out of sight, I pulled free of Wenzhi's hold, though his touch—anyone's touch—was a thread of comfort amid this sea of sorrow.

The wind blew incessantly against us, and I was glad for its howling to drown my thoughts. Wenzhi was silent at first, perhaps sensing I was not in the mood for conversation.

"Don't blame yourself, Xingyin," he said at last. "Prince Yanming's death was an accident, a great misfortune. No one could have foreseen it. Perhaps this is fate, as the mortals would say."

"No," I said fiercely, a fire roused in me. "I don't believe in fate, destiny, or letting things take their course. If so, I would still be serving an unworthy mistress in the Celestial Kingdom, my mother would be a prisoner on the moon, my father would have died in the Mortal Realm and . . . Ping'er and Prince Yanming would be alive."

The tightness in my chest squeezed harder. "If only we had not fled, if only I had killed Wugang earlier. If only I had not gone to the Southern Sea—"

"Stop this." Wenzhi gripped my shoulders, his tone urgent. "Were you wrong for wanting to protect your family, for wanting to take back what was yours? Should we have surrendered on the beach and let Wugang take us prisoner? He would have killed us all—if not then, eventually."

"Not Prince Yanming." My voice was hollow. "He would have been safe."

"Would you have traded him for your mother? Your father?

Shuxiao? Your . . . beloved?" Brutal questions, impossible to answer—yet it yanked me from the pit of my misery, yielding a moment's respite to the pitiless anguish.

His tone gentled. "Do not take on the burdens that are not yours to bear. Wugang's actions are not your doing; he would have come for the laurel and your mother regardless. Prince Yanming died protecting his brother. If he had not, Prince Yanxi would have been killed instead—both terrible consequences. Never forget, this was his choice, just as it had been Ping'er's decision to save your mother. Do not belittle their sacrifices when they should be honored. Do not let them have died in vain. Do not let this break you."

"I have made so many mistakes." My voice was choked with suppressed emotion.

"Xingyin, no one is infallible. Use the past to guide the present, but do not let it trap you. Grow from your mistakes, don't let them become a weakness." He lowered his head to mine, his voice throbbing with intensity. "There is good in what you have done. You saved the Celestial Army. You freed the dragons— though I will admit, I was furious then." His lips pulled into a wry smile, before drawing straight once more. "You reunited your parents. You fought for what you believed was right, when so many others would have given up."

I bit down on the inside of my cheek, his unexpected gentleness tearing down the last of my barriers.

"Cry," Wenzhi said quietly. "Let your pain go."

I was ripped raw inside, just as the night I had fallen to the Celestial Kingdom, alone and afraid—when my heart was broken by Liwei's betrothal, and yes, even by Wenzhi's treachery. Somehow his ruthless logic and empathy stemmed the flood of despair I had been drowning in. The tears came then, streaming down in a silent current—for those I had lost, all that was forever beyond my reach. Gasps wrung from my throat in a broken rhythm. And I allowed myself this weakness, because I could no longer hold it in.

For I could not dispel the sinking dread that no matter what I did, death and suffering trailed in my wake as surely as the night follows the dusk.

PART
III

25

THE SUN HAD DWINDLED TO a crimson ember. We
waited upon our clouds, hidden from sight, our auras
masked. It was no easy matter to gain passage to the
Fragrant Mulberry Grove—we had been too slow before, the
pathway darkening before us, an impenetrable barrier forming
that we could not breach. Since our grace period from Wugang
had lapsed, we were on constant guard for fear of discovery. A
hard task, when my mind kept drifting to the sight of Prince
Yanming in his brother's arms. And when I closed my eyes to
block out these searing images, his frail gasp echoed in my ears.

"Xingyin. Be ready," Liwei warned.

As a rush of power stirred the air, a gleaming chariot of
white jade streaked past. We shot after it, our clouds speckling
the skies as we chased the simmering trail of heat, keeping out
of sight yet careful not to fall behind. The phoenix soared with
breathtaking speed, each feather a curl of writhing flame, sparks
scattering in its wake like a cloak of stars. A stately immortal
rode upon it, her black hair coiled into a gold and topaz headdress, her vermilion robes billowing in the wind. A shining harness was fastened around the phoenix's neck, its strap wound
around her hand. As she flung her other arm forward, blazing

ropes of flame uncoiled, lashing the phoenix. It let out a piercing shriek as it raced onward, dragging the chariot after it.

This burst of speed had caught us unaware before, but we were ready this time, our clouds surging ahead to keep pace. Already, the curtain of dusk was descending, the glare from the chariot waning. For the first time, I caught a clear glimpse of the creature sheltered within—a being of incandescent light.

The sunbird, the last of its kind. Sorrow gripped me as I imagined the sunbird's existence, as solitary as my childhood had been—but with the added pain, the yawning ache of knowing all it had lost. Did it relive the horror of seeing its siblings struck down, their wings stilling as they fell from the sky, their light fading to dark? I had felt the agony of losing a loved one, but dared not fathom the loss of nine at once. My father had saved the world, yet he had also taken these beloved children from their family. An act of greatness did not lessen the sorrow inflicted, for love could not be tallied and weighed.

Every hero was a villain to the other side . . . and to them, my father must be the greatest monster of all.

Just ahead, towered a luminous wall of yellow marble that surrounded the Fragrant Mulberry Grove. Gold spikes ringed the top like the teeth of a comb, a powerful magic winding between the points in gleaming rivulets, seeping into the stone itself. The chariot dashed through the arched entrance, the doors sealing shut after it. Its circular panel was split into two, carved into phoenix wings on each side, the tips of their gilded feathers weaving together in a seamless embrace. Twin bodies arched along the frames, their necks grazing in the middle from where they curved into opposing directions.

As we landed, my flesh prickled with foreboding. A foolish thing to enter the dwelling of my father's enemy uninvited. Unwelcome.

The Celestial Empress remained on her cloud. "Liwei, let them go on. Come with me to the Phoenix Kingdom. We must convince Queen Fengjin of the threat Wugang poses to the realm. Only with the armies of the Phoenix Kingdom can we reclaim what is ours." She spoke clearly, intending to be heard. "Queen Fengjin is still keen to renew the betrothal. Our alliance is more crucial than ever. A marriage would bind them to us and we will have a place there, even if we lose the Celestial Kingdom."

I looked away, trying to calm the erratic beat of my pulse. The empress was shrewd, striking while Liwei was ignorant of the bargain she had forced upon me. He believed I did not want to marry him, that I had given him up of my own will . . . that another lay in my heart, one whom he despised above all. The empress's offer would be undeniably tempting: Why should Liwei not marry the princess? Why should he not do what was best for himself, his family and kingdom—as he had done before? I could not be selfish; I had no right to be. What was another loss today?

"No, Mother. I will not barter myself for a crown." Liwei spoke with such resolve, the tautness in my chest loosened.

"Don't be a fool," the empress cried. "You can have it all back—your position, your power. Now that you know what it's like to be without."

He drew away from her, his expression hardening. "Don't ask this of me again."

"Unfilial child! What about your family? You must do this for your father and me."

Her desperation shook me. How would Liwei feel hearing it, when she had always been so haughty and unyielding before?

"Mother, I will honor and protect you. I will fight to reclaim our position. I will ask for Queen Fengjin's aid as our ally, but no more," he said. "What I will *not* do is marry someone I do not love."

She cursed then, spewing hateful words. Liwei turned from her, his eyes opaque, my chest caving at the sight. The empress raised a hand after him, then let it fall—her face twisted not with rage or cunning, just a wild fear that she might have driven away the one who was most precious to her.

But she was never one for self-recrimination. As she spun to me, I flinched from the blazing hatred in her gaze. "This is all your doing. *You* cleared the way to Wugang's rise."

"This is not Xingyin's fault," Liwei said at once.

It is, my mind whispered. While Wenzhi had spoken the truth before that I had not guided the choices of others, neither had anyone forced my hand. I had wanted to free my mother, to save my father, to help the dragons. Wugang's actions were his own to bear, but mine had enabled his ascent nonetheless.

"My dear son." The empress's tone was iron. "You discarded the engagement that would have secured your position. As the heir to the Celestial Kingdom and son-in-law to Queen Fengjin, you would have been unassailable. Your feelings for this insignificant girl have brought you as low as she is. Daughter to the villainous Houyi and that grasping mortal Chang'e—she is unworthy of you."

Rage surged through me as I stalked to the empress's cloud. My days of being scorned by her were over. I was not afraid of her, for what else could she do to me that she had not tried? "I know my own worth and that of my family. My father saved the Mortal Realm. My mother saved me. And while I may not have the gilded lineage you so admire, I *am* worthy—" I stopped before I spoke Liwei's name; my vow to her had stripped that right from me.

"It is *you* who is unworthy to speak my parents' names," I said instead.

Heat sparked in the air. Spurred by instinct, I darted aside—

just as tongues of vermilion fire sprang from the empress's palms. Magic rippled from my own hands, arcing over her flames, glazing them like frost. Her mouth clamped tighter, eyes pinched as she bore down with greater force. My teeth ground together—a struggle to keep steady under her assault—yet I held my ground, my energy pouring forth in waves to engulf her flames, throttling them into thick spirals of smoke.

My hand fell, the last glimmers of magic fading to dark. The empress and I stood facing each other, her expression pitted with fury. A part of me had always known it would come to this one day—that she would try to kill me, or I her. I could have shielded myself instead of smothering her attack, but I had *wanted* to challenge her, to prove that I was more than what she believed me to be. That my power rivaled hers in the way that mattered more than any meaningless title and crown—both of which she had taken such pride in, both of which she had lost.

Wenzhi released the hilt of his sword as though he had been about to strike, while Liwei rounded on the empress. "Mother, how could you?" His tone pulsed with rage.

The empress lifted a shaking finger at me. "You tricked me. You plotted this all along."

I stared at the empress blankly, until her meaning sank in and a weight fell from my chest. She had attacked me, though I had given her no cause. She had broken the terms of our pact in the mortal teahouse . . . which meant my vow to her was void. With one stroke, I could sever the misunderstanding between Liwei and me, setting us free of his mother's malice. We could be together again. The words hovered on my tongue: my promise to his mother, my coldness in pushing him away, the lie of Wenzhi.

Yet as I stared at the empress's pale face, taut with distress, I found I was not so cruel as to savor a moment that brought such pain to another—even one I despised as much as her. I did not want to widen the rift between Liwei and his mother. This was not the time to divide us further when the threat of Wugang loomed over us all.

But in truth, that was not the sole reason. I was not so noble to keep my silence for the empress alone. There was another reason folded deep in my heart, one I was afraid to examine too closely, ashamed of what I might uncover . . . that the lies I had told Liwei to set him free—I was no longer sure what they were. Try as I might, I could not forget how I had wept in Wenzhi's arms, how he had comforted me in my times of greatest need, how his words had eased the anguish that almost broke me then. It meant nothing, just a momentary weakness, I assured myself—yet still I would hold my tongue. The empress's spiteful accusations were ringed with truth. I *was* unworthy of Liwei, not because of my lineage but because he deserved better than my divided heart. And I would not offer it again until it was whole, until I was certain, and until we were safe.

I fixed the empress with a hard stare. "I plotted nothing; it was you all along. But no matter the hatred and wrongs between us, you are Liwei's mother. That means something to me, even if it's nothing to you."

As some of the color returned to the empress's face, Liwei's gaze searched me. "What do you mean, Xingyin?"

"Just that we should stop turning on each other, for it only aids our enemy." I looked away from him, so he would not discern the lie.

Wenzhi glared at the empress. "While this has been undoubtedly fascinating, we still need the key to enter the grove. Will you give it to us?" His voice hardened as though expecting objection or trickery.

The empress spun to Liwei. "I will give you the key, my son. All I want is a small favor in return."

"You would bargain with me?" he bit out.

"Only because you will not see sense." Her tone was almost cajoling. "Come with me to the Phoenix Kingdom to meet Queen Fengjin. *You* cannot enter the Fragrant Mulberry Grove."

"I must, Mother," he said. "I cannot let—"

"You will *not* go," the empress repeated vehemently. "I would rather destroy the key than leave you at Xihe's mercy. Xihe hates me. Vengeance runs thick in her blood. She will spend her rage upon you, my son, in repayment for what she believes are my offenses. In her mind, I failed to protect her children. She blames me for their deaths."

"I am not afraid of her," Liwei said. "If you won't give us the key, we will find our own way in."

"You would not survive three steps into the grove without it," the empress warned. "Only those who possess the key may enter. Only one of you."

"We need the key," Wenzhi said to Liwei, his arms folded across his chest. "Will you do as she asks, or should we *take* it from your mother?"

When Liwei did not reply, the empress added shrewdly, "You promised to protect me. Wugang's soldiers caught me at the border to the Phoenix Kingdom the last time. They will be keeping a close eye there, and it is safer if you accompany me."

Liwei's jaw tightened as he nodded. "I will return here after we've spoken to Queen Fengjin, no later." He extended his palm to his mother. "Where is the key?"

She looked at Wenzhi and me. "Which of you will enter?"

"Why does it matter?" I countered.

An impatient sigh slid from her mouth. "I must relinquish the key to the one who will enter. No other."

"I will go," Wenzhi said at once.

"No," I told him. "It should be me."

"Why?" he challenged calmly, his gaze boring into mine. "That would be an unnecessary risk. Lady Xihe bears me no ill will; she has no reason to harm me. I have the best chance of persuading her."

"It is true, Xingyin." Liwei added acidly, "His skills are uniquely suited to deception."

Wenzhi's eyes narrowed. "At least they are of *some* use."

His offer tempted me. More than the sense behind his suggestion—I did not want to see the goddess and her sole child, to witness the misery my father's deeds had wrought. But I could not be a coward now.

As I stepped forward, Wenzhi moved swiftly in front of me, extending his hand to the empress. She seized Wenzhi's wrist, pressing their palms together. As a flash of scarlet light sparked between them, he recoiled.

"What was that?" His voice thickened with suspicion.

"The key is in my hands. It was why Xihe could not retrieve it." A trace of sadness clung to the empress's tone, her shoulders drooping before she straightened. "I cannot give it to you. The key cannot be yielded to any who intend to harm the goddess."

"I don't want to harm Lady Xihe. All I want is the feather," Wenzhi said tersely.

The empress laughed as she threw a sly look my way. "You were ever single-minded and ruthless in your purpose, Captain. Regardless, you cannot enter the grove." As she swung to me, the empress's smile widened. "Daughter of the Sun Slayer. Will you enter the home of your greatest enemy?"

In response, I raised my hand. Swiftly, the empress pressed our palms together, heat rushing from her skin into mine, a soft white glow suffusing us unlike the harsh light that had jolted Wenzhi before. When she dropped her hand, I examined mine, discerning no visible difference.

"It is done," she said flatly.

Striding to the entrance doors, I pressed my palms against the carved feathers to push them apart. They tingled, flushed with sudden warmth, amber light rippling across the golden wings of the phoenixes. Slowly, as though awakening from a dream, the phoenix heads twitched, twin beaks parting as their eyelids snapped open. Rubies glittered from their pupils, tiny flames dancing in their depths as their wings lifted away, leaving the path clear to the domain of the Goddess of the Sun.

Liwei caught my sleeve. "Don't tell Lady Xihe who you are. If there is even a hint of danger, leave at once. We will find another way." He added quietly, "I cannot lose you."

"You must be careful too." I wished that I could say more, that I could promise him what he wanted to hear.

"Come, Liwei," the empress urged. "We must go."

He strode stiffly toward the empress's cloud, stepping upon it. As it soared into the night, he turned around once to look at me.

"He is right," Wenzhi said, after they had vanished from sight. "Under no circumstances must you reveal your identity to Lady Xihe. Wait till she is asleep, then take the feather and flee."

It would be the safest way. If I stole the Sacred Flame Feather from the slumbering sunbird, I could escape unscathed in both mind and body. It would be a kindness for us all . . . except it would be rooted in cowardice. Such an act would only feed Lady Xihe's wrath, thicken our enmity, and we would end the worse for it.

What if the goddess did not survive? an insidious voice within me whispered. Was this not a worthwhile cause, to save the realms above and below? Was this not the choice my father had faced? Yet a sharp ache pierced my chest at the remembrance of the goddess's grief, the sight of the lone sunbird in the chariot when once there had been ten. I could not wrong them

further. I could not do this craven thing; I would be as contemptible as Wugang if I did.

I did not believe Wugang had been born evil. Perhaps the
seed of it lay in us all. But while Wugang had been betrayed,
most cruelly—he had chosen this path. So much in life was left
to chance. Some had to curve and twist to get ahead, forced to
bend with the wind to remain standing, suffering storms that left
others unscathed. Yet we could not blame fate for the choices we
made—the rewards were ours to reap, as were the consequences
ours to bear. And it was moments as these that formed who we
were . . . what we would become.

"I can't," I told Wenzhi. "Not after all we've taken from her
and her family. I will ask it of her."

Wenzhi stiffened. "Xingyin, consider this carefully. Lady Xihe
is no benevolent immortal who will stroke your hair and praise
you for your honesty as she sends you on your way, feather in
hand. She has nursed her pain for as many years as you have lived.
If she learns who you are, she will *kill* you." His voice roughened
with emotion. "And if she does, rest assured that *I* will kill her."

A tremor ran through me at the vehemence in his tone. Was
this why the key could not be given to him? "I won't tell her who
I am. I will convince her of our need."

"You would lie to her but not steal?" Wenzhi's eyes blazed.
"Xingyin, what is honor to your life?"

"What is life without honor? Untethered, we are no better
than Wugang."

"No better than I was," he said bitterly.

"That is not what I meant." Once I had believed it of him.
And now, I was no longer sure. "Lady Xihe will see reason; Wugang is a threat to us all. If she tries to attack me, I will defend
myself."

Wenzhi sighed as his hand came down on mine. Before I

could pull away, his power enveloped me like a dense mist, tingling and cool—a powerful shield gleaming from my skin. "This will help protect you. If she attacks you, run. I will wait for you here. She cannot fight us both together."

I nodded, concealing my trepidation. If Lady Xihe discovered who I was, she would never yield the feather, she would seek vengeance—and I dared not imagine what she would take from me in recompense.

26

SHINING GLOBES OF LIGHT FLOATED in the air like a hundred tiny moons had descended, casting their luminous glow all around. Mulberry trees rose from the grass, as golden as the summer harvest in the Mortal Realm. Their lush fruit clustered upon the branches like strands of garnets twined between the leaves. A rich sweetness pervaded the air, that of ripened berries, their juices spilling from fragile skins. The trees were beautiful, yet there was something eerie about their gnarled forms, a wretchedness in the twist of the branches, the sharpness of the roots jutting from the ground. Towering above them was a building of fiery carnelian, flanked by agate pillars and a tiered roof of gilded tiles. Panels of silk fluttered from the walls, delicate and light as they danced in the breeze.

There were no guards, no one to announce my presence as I approached the entrance. I was glad for it; fewer to combat should the need arise, should I need to flee. Something clinked above, a wind chime hanging from the ceiling. As a breeze drifted past, copper tubes and jade discs collided in a soothing melody. My heart thudded to a frantic rhythm as I lifted my hand to knock, my knuckles grazing the door. An ancient power pulsed from within, the same one woven through the walls encircling the grove. Light flared from the foot of the entrance, crawling over me as the door swung open to reveal Lady Xihe, the Goddess of the Sun.

Though we were of a similar height, Lady Xihe seemed to loom above me, even without her headdress of shining stones. Her black hair was coiled upon her head, held in place by a circle of ruby pins, the tips as sharp as daggers. Her black eyes were ringed with gold like a hawk's and her cheeks were flushed with the radiance of dawn. Delicate lines traced her skin in intricate imprints of feathers as the rounded curves of her face flared from her pointed chin. Talons arched from her fingertips, a glossy red like they were dipped in blood. The light from the chamber beyond cast shadows across her, lending her a forbidding air. Or was it the way her lips pulled into a thin slash, the power that emanated from her like heat from a flame? She looked as different from my mother as ink from water, the sun from the moon—and utterly striking in her own way.

"Who are you?" She neither inclined her head nor invited me in—prudent, as that might be an unnecessary complication. After all, it would violate the rules of hospitality to kill a guest.

The lies I had practiced stuck in my throat. In the silence, the goddess's eyes narrowed to slits. "Tell me who you are," she repeated, this time in a tone of command.

Caution warred with my heart, honor battling self-preservation. Prince Yanming's face flashed through my mind, my chest squeezing with agony. Such lies might have fallen glibly from my tongue before, but they stuck in my throat now, and I knew they would ring false. Something in me was forever changed since death had shadowed my life. I hurt for all the goddess had lost, for what she suffered. Had I become weaker? Perhaps, but I preferred to believe this was a different type of strength. Oh, I did not intend to sacrifice myself to her vengeance, yet this was a chance to do what the dragons had wished of me, to say what should have been said a long time ago—to try to ease the goddess's anguish.

Cupping my hands together, I stretched them out and bowed low. I was not begging for mercy, nor was I deluded enough to think this adequate recompense. "Lady Xihe, I am Xingyin, the daughter of Chang'e and Houyi."

"*I know.*" Her words rang with indisputable certainty, seething with fury. "Whoever gave you the key did you no favor. It reveals your identity, for I tolerate no pretenders in my grove."

Inwardly, I cursed the Celestial Empress, and myself for not suspecting the trap. She had yielded it too eagerly—purposefully, I had no doubt. She would be glad for my death, or was I intended as her peace offering to the Sun Goddess?

The light in the globes wavered, the air rolling into wild gusts that tore through the mulberry trees. Above, the wind chime clanked in jarring bursts, swinging so forcefully I thought it might snap. Dread sank through my flesh—the same gray chill as when I had entered Xiangliu's cave, when Governor Renyu's venom had frozen my limbs, when I awoke in the Demon Realm and discovered my love had become my worst enemy

I shielded myself instinctively—just as Lady Xihe flicked her palm forward, waves of crimson flame surging toward me. They engulfed me whole, searing even through the barrier, the scalding heat more potent than the Celestial Empress's attack.

The gold in the goddess's pupils had spread across her entire eyes, light radiating from her skin. "How *dare* you come here? Did you wish to gloat over my misery, to tempt my wrath?" Each word pounded like the beat of a drum.

"No, Lady Xihe. On behalf of my family, I ask your forgiveness—"

"Forgiveness?" She spat the word like a foul thing. "Never."

"I do not presume to understand your loss, but I grieve for it nonetheless." I spoke through gritted teeth, struggling beneath the force of her might. I did not attempt to extinguish her fire, I did not want to challenge her—I was her enemy, but she was not mine.

She stilled. "Why aren't you fighting? Do you think to trick me into mercy? You will find none."

"I ask your forgiveness," I repeated hoarsely, channeling more of my energy into my shield as her flames raged across it, unabated. "And I am here to beseech your aid."

A laugh rang out, arched in bitterness. "How convenient that your conscience affects you now. That you only came here when you needed something."

I stiffened at her derision, though it was well-deserved. "Only recently did I learn more about the circumstances behind this tragedy. While the threat to our realm drove me here, I mean what I say, nor did I attempt to lie to you when I could have."

"If you had, you would already be dead," she snarled. "How can you imagine I would *ever* aid the kin of the Sun Slayer, the one who murdered my children?"

Even as shame flushed me, I made myself say, "This is not for me alone. The Immortal Realm is in grave peril, for the Celestial throne has been usurped. A terrible evil threatens the realms above and below, and the only way we can vanquish it is with the Sacred Flame Feather."

"I do not care." Despite the heat of her fire, her voice was like ice. "The Celestial Kingdom failed me, their empress most of all. Regardless of who sits on the Celestial throne, the sun will rise and set as it did when I had ten children, as it does when one remains."

Her aura undulated like storm-ridden waves, her hunger for

violence stamped on her face, glowing as bright as a sword from the forge. "You are an arrogant fool to come here. Today, I will avenge my dead children. Today, your father and mother shall weep over your body. Today, they will taste unimaginable loss and live the greatest nightmare of any parent."

Terror spiked through me, yet I forced myself to meet her gaze. "No, Lady Xihe. You have not earned my death. It would be dishonorable to strike me when I came to you in good faith."

"A simple formality, one easily rectified. Run. I will hunt you down, and then my vengeance will be complete." A carved silver handle appeared in her hand, from which coils of flame sprang forth—the same weapon that had wrenched such agonized cries from the phoenix.

My throat constricted, my mouth going dry. "The Mortal Realm was in danger. My father—"

"*Murdered my children!*" she cried wrathfully. "Reasons have no place or meaning here." Light rippled in her eyes like molten metal. "I have just one daughter left. Now I will take one life—yours—for the nine who were slain. A pitiful exchange, yet it will suffice." As she raised her hand, the ropes of flame writhed like snakes.

Sweat broke out over my skin, cold and damp. Her power was immense; I could not fight her alone. I might make it beyond the grove to where Wenzhi waited, we could challenge her together . . . although that would not earn us the feather. I fought to preserve a veil of calm, for revealing my fear might feed her rage, inflame her bloodlust—and set us on a path from which there would be no return.

"Will it ease your pain to kill me? Will it bring your children back?" I spoke quickly to hide the quiver in my voice. "I did you no wrong. If you hurt me, I will fight back, and I am no weakling. Even should you take my life, it will not end there. My family and friends will seek vengeance. You have one daughter left, would you risk her too? What if she was to grow up motherless, after losing her siblings?"

Her gaze shifted to the stairway behind her, perhaps where her child slept. A low blow, to strike at a mother's terror. How I despised these vile threats, but I hoped they would give her pause, stem her vengeance, steer her from the exquisite temptation of killing me. Far too much blood had already been shed.

"I did not come to anger or hurt you," I said quietly. "A common enemy threatens us all, and the feather is our only hope. Will you give it to us?"

"I will *never* give anything to you. I do not care what happens to the world." Yet her tone hitched with a note of uncertainty.

"If the immortal and mortal realms are destroyed, who will care if the sun rises or falls? You *do* care for the mortals' worship, that you are needed, that they love you and your child. You cherish it, the only time of day when you can lose yourself in your task rather than dwell on your sorrow."

It was a guess, and yet it was not. For as long as I could remember, I had seen my mother toil over the lighting of the lanterns each night, a reprieve from the torment of her mind. And when she had stood on the balcony, gazing at the world below, hearing the songs sung and seeing the offerings laid out in her honor . . . she had found solace in the mortals' adoration. It brought new meaning to her life, all the more precious after what she had lost—to know she was wanted, needed, and loved.

When Lady Xihe did not speak, I continued, "Killing me will only yield a fleeting satisfaction, for vengeance is no cure. My father did what he had to. Your children were destroying the world; you would have stopped them yourself if you could have, because you care for the mortals—because they give these infinite years meaning."

The gold receded from her eyes, though her aura still churned ominously. As she drew her arm back and lashed the air with her whip, sparks showered down like rain. I braced myself—but then a shriek broke the stillness, a blazing creature rising in the horizon and soaring toward us, magnificent and utterly terrifying. The phoenix that had borne the sun chariot glided down to land beside the goddess. Its crest was the golden brown of a pheasant, while its body was shaped like the snug barrel of a mandarin duck attached to long, graceful legs. Beyond its ink-tipped wings, its plumage was a breathtaking riot of color, a peacock-like tail sweeping across the grass in feathers of crimson and yellow, blue and green—each one blazing like it was afire. Dark, liquid eyes swept over us, its pupils flecked with light, its curved claws spanning the breadth of my palm. As its beak parted, the tips glinted sharper than spears.

The phoenix bent its neck in subservience to the goddess, even as an untamed wildness flared in its eyes. A strong yet frenetic energy pulsed from it like a hundred dragonflies beating their wings. It spread its tail wide, its feathers fluttering like a rainbow, though their swish was that of arrows whistling through the air.

The goddess pointed at me with her whip. "If you are sincere in your desire to seek forgiveness, you must face my champion—the fire phoenix. While its heat is not as potent as my beloved sunbird's, it is a far more skilled fighter. Defeat it, and you will earn your life, along with the feather you seek." She raised her head high as though daring me to object. "Blood must be repaid in blood. Perhaps then, my children's restless spirits will be appeased, their eternal cries silenced."

I nodded, my fear braided with relief. Lady Xihe would never have been satisfied by words; I would not have accepted them as recompense for Ping'er and Prince Yanming. Pain and suffering, these were the currency in which such debts were repaid. But I hoped this might be the end of it . . . or at least, a new beginning.

Her eyes pinched in speculation as she stared at my bow. "A few rules. You cannot draw a weapon or use your magic."

I shook my head. "A weapon must be allowed."

"Do you think I don't know what you carry?" As she spoke, an unseen force ripped my bow from my back, hurling it across the ground. Another, crafted of bamboo, appeared before me, alongside a quiver of wooden arrows.

Little wonder that she had been so close to the Celestial Empress. Their natures were hard and unyielding, and they both drove an unfair bargain.

"Is this the justice of the great Sun Goddess?" I challenged. "A mortal weapon is of no use against the phoenix."

Lady Xihe stiffened as she raised her hand. Light streaked across the bow and arrows, their tips gleaming brighter. I would have preferred the Jade Dragon Bow, but this was the atonement the goddess demanded—and a part of me whispered that she could have asked for more.

"I must be allowed to shield myself." I did not ask, speaking it as a fact.

"Very well," she agreed icily, already raising her whip once more.

I bent to snatch up the bow. It was light in my hands, an inadequate weapon. "What happens if I lose?"

"You die." A mirthless smile spread across her lips. "There is a reason *I* am not fighting you, why I needed your consent. No court in the Immortal Realm will find fault with me, and your kin will have no cause to seek vengeance upon your death."

The assured way she spoke stung. "If I win, this ends here. You will not seek further vengeance against my family."

A mirthless smile curled on her lips. "*If* you win."

I grasped my magic, weaving it over Wenzhi's shield, glad for his foresight and that he could not interfere. He would not have stood idly by in this battle, a thought that both eased and tightened the tension coiled within me.

The goddess's whip lashed the air, flames crackling forth. The phoenix reared up obediently, stretching its wings wide as it dove toward me. Scarlet tongues of fire erupted from its beak, searing through my shield. I darted back, evading the phoenix's attack, as my fingers instinctively plucked the bowstring—unfamiliar and stiff. An arrow hurtled toward the phoenix, which shrieked as it flew aside. Swiftly, I released another, hurtling into its side, but the creature tore the shaft away as though it were a splinter. The phoenix plunged forward once more, pecking wildly at my barrier. Its power crashed against mine, pummeling my shield, its claws puncturing through to rake my arm. As a deep gash split my flesh, a gasp burst from my throat. I shoved the creature aside, the needle-like barbs on its feathers slicing my palm.

The phoenix flew at me again, the tip of its beak sinking into my shoulder, burying silk into flesh. Such fiery agony engulfed me as I stumbled back, shooting an arrow into its wing. The creature barely flinched as it soared toward me again, its claws curved like sickles. A slender tongue slithered from its beak, stained with the same dark shade as the mulberries, the sweetness of its breath smoked with char. As it ruffled its feathers, flames streaked toward me, my body still stinging from the violence of its attack—

I ran, my feet pounding over the grass. My weapon was of no use, I needed time to form a plan. Gnarled branches loomed before me as I ducked, weaving my way between the trees. As my shoe caught over a raised root, I stumbled, catching my balance. The heat from the phoenix suffused the air as the creature soared above. Was it toying with me? I was an easy target, barreling through the forest, my steps thudding against the ground. Diving deeper into a thicket of trees, I stretched my arms wide to slap the branches, intentionally rustling their leaves. As the phoenix swung around, drawing nearer—I crawled away stealthily in the other direction. Out of the creature's sight, I scrambled up a mulberry tree, scraping my palms against the rough bark. My heart raced as I crouched within the shelter of the twisted branches.

Above, the phoenix shrieked as it circled the grove, searching for me. My sleeve was torn where the phoenix had clawed it. The cords around my wrist had come undone, hanging loose. I ripped them free, tucking them into my sash. Climbing upon a thick branch, I flattened myself against the trunk to keep out of sight. Another cry rent the air, the phoenix, impatient for blood. How I wished I could summon a gale to sweep the creature away, but I was bound by Lady Xihe's terms—onerous though they were.

I breathed deeply, catching the sweetness threaded through the air. Something surfaced in my mind—that of the phoenix's breath, the stains on its tongue . . . the mulberries, did it like their taste? Slinging my bow upon my back, I bent down to grasp handfuls from the tree, ripe and sticky, as I piled them onto the branch in stacks of ruby, rich currant, and black. As I crushed a handful along the branch, rubbing their syrupy juice into the wood, the fragrance thickened, cloyingly sweet and heady. The phoenix's cry grew louder, wind coursing through the air as its wings flapped closer. Did it smell the mulberries? I moved back into the thicket of branches, an arrow nocked to my bowstring—my body stiff with terror, my fingers like ice.

The phoenix approached my tree, its eyes fixed upon the berries, it's beak parted eagerly. My arrows had little chance of penetrating its body, but what of its tender mouth? The softness of its throat, the gateway to its skull? Bile crowded the back of my throat, but I swallowed hard. Oh, I did not want to do this, but I did not want to die.

I sprang forward, my arrow aimed at the dark hollow where the creature's beak parted, at the scarlet throat beyond. A perfect shot. My fingers clenched harder, emotions roiling within—fear mingled with revulsion and anger, that we had been forced into this confrontation that neither of us wanted. The phoenix had done no wrong. It was a victim of Lady Xihe's misery, merely obeying her command. And fool that I might be, I lowered the bow. An enraged screech erupted from the phoenix, its eyes glinting with murderous intent as it lunged at me.

I dropped down to evade its attack, clasping the branch tightly as I sprang off to dangle below. The phoenix burst through where I had stood a moment before, then circled around to soar toward me once more. My nails dug into the rough bark as I swung myself along the branch, bracing for the phoenix's inevitable return. I was shaking, my arms burning from the strain of my weight. As the phoenix shot forward, now just beneath my feet, I let go—

Falling through the emptiness, the air rushed against my body as I slammed against the phoenix's back. Pain tore through me, of scorching heat—the creature's feathers piercing my flesh like a nest of pins. Grasping my magic, I wove a stronger shield, forcing my mind to clear as the phoenix bucked wildly beneath. I clung harder, its barbs scraping my skin, searing even through my barrier. Swiftly, I snatched the cords from my sash, looping them around the phoenix's neck, knotting them to form a crude harness. I yanked it, just as I had seen Lady Xihe do when we followed her, the creature shrieking as it dove through the air at a blinding pace. The wind surged against my face—trees and clouds blurring as they melded together, the phoenix spiraling in tighter circles, frantic with rage. I clung fast, clenching my thighs around its body, gripping the reins as I uttered soothing words and entreaties until at last its pace gentled, the heat subsiding from its body.

Only then did I loosen my hold. The phoenix circled once around the grove before obediently flying back to where Lady Xihe waited, the wind chime stirred into a haunting melody.

"It lives. You did not win," she snarled.

As though sensing her displeasure, the phoenix's head drooped, its wings trailing on the ground.

"You did not say I had to kill it," I countered, sliding down from its back. "It would be a needless waste of life when it was merely obeying your command."

The goddess's knuckles whitened around the hilt of her whip, the flames surging brighter as though channeling her wrath. "How dare you pretend to care for another's life? *You*, the daughter of that butcher Houyi."

"Do not insult my father." My voice came low and furious. "I kept my word; I defeated your champion. It is you, trying to break yours." In truth the terms had not been fully laid out, each of us interpreting them to suit our ends.

As Lady Xihe raised her arm, her whip blazing—I summoned the Jade Dragon Bow, flying up from the ground into my grasp. Yet I did not draw it. I did not want to hurt her, I never had.

But I would defend myself.

Her whip descended upon my head, crackling ropes of flame unfurling. My energy surged forth, crafting a barrier of wind that slammed between us. Fire thrashed against the translucent surface, the goddess baring her teeth as she channeled more of her power, the heat intensifying. Cracks rippled through my shield like cobwebs, flickers of flame bursting through, the pain almost blinding. I staggered back, digging my heels in as I sealed the shield's cracks, panting from the strain. As Lady Xihe snarled, her palms aglow with crimson light—I tensed for another blow—but then she stilled, slanting her head back as though listening for something.

A radiance shimmered behind her, the dark vanishing with its approach. As the goddess spun around, the hilt of her whip fell from her hand.

"My daughter," she whispered, crouching down to sweep her into her arms.

The sunbird was the size of a gourd, with great solemn eyes. Where the phoenix was a rainbow of color, the sunbird was fire incarnate. Three legs were tucked beneath her body, the rich vermilion of a sunset, while her yellow plumage emanated a radiant glow. At her crest, a single feather curled—of deepest crimson edged with gold, as dazzling as the heart of a flame.

Lady Xihe hugged the sunbird tightly, murmuring to her in a language I did not know. Tears streamed down her face, visible only when she looked up. Muffled sobs fell from her in an aching rhythm—even after all these decades, her pain was still raw. The sunbird craned her neck, nuzzling her mother as though used to such violent outbursts.

The lone child in her arms, the vulnerability of the great goddess in her misery . . . how I ached at the sight. Blood oozed from my wounds, my torn flesh afire—yet it was nothing to their suffering that no magic in the world could heal. Only time might ease it, and even then, immortal memories were eternal.

Without knowing what I was doing, I dropped to my knees on the ground. Straightening my back, I stretched my arms out before me, folding over to press my brow to the floor. Not in some contrived plea for mercy, but because from the bottom of my heart, I regretted her pain—that we were inexorably linked by the death of her children. I did not speak, for no words could capture the enormity of their loss, the grief I felt for them.

A stillness fell over us. Something rustled, the sunbird gliding toward me, sheathing me in its luminous warmth. As her somber gaze met mine, part of me recoiled, fearing an attack— yet the sunbird's eyes were gentle and knowing, brimming with untold sorrow. Spreading her wings wide, she bowed her head. The crimson feather fell from her crown, its shaft pulsing like liquid flame, an incandescent white. My spirits leapt, though I dared not presume the sunbird's intent—until her curved claw pushed the feather toward me.

"I . . . thank you." Such simple words for this priceless gift, and yet there was nothing more apt. The sunbird's generosity moved me deeply, and I resolved to be worthy of her gift.

"Its true power lies in its shaft. Plant it at the source of your target's might. Now, take it. Leave," Lady Xihe said in a hollow voice. "I will not harm you further, nor will I give you aid. Do not test my mercy again; it died the day I lost my children."

She gathered the sunbird tenderly in her arms, striding away without a backward glance. The doors closed after her, the wind chime quivering in a mournful melody. Though they had gone, along with their light, darkness was kept at bay by the blaze of the feather before me. I reached out to take it, halting, as the heat surged forth in shimmering waves, as though its full might had been unleashed only after it had been plucked. I wove a shell of hardened air around it, then slipped it into my pouch. The enchantment would not hold, the heat already thawing the barrier—a strain to keep it intact, yet preferable to being burnt to cinders.

Sinking onto my heels, I trembled from the emotions colliding within me—relief layered with remorse, sunken by a bone-deep weariness. I was not so presumptuous as to think Lady Xihe had forgiven us; these wounds went too deep. But perhaps we had come to an understanding of sorts, and I hoped with all my heart that mother and child might find their happiness again.

27

I HEALED MY WOUNDS AS WELL as I could, though my body still ached from the ordeal. Only then did I leave the grove, the wings of the entrance closing after me, the carved feathers weaving together into a tight embrace. Wenzhi was pacing outside, alone—the tautness in his expression easing at the sight of me.

"Has Liwei not returned?" I asked.

As Wenzhi shook his head, light flared from my pouch, a sudden heat scorching me. The enchantment around the feather was weakening. I thrust my hand into my pouch, my thumb brushing the scalding surface of the sphere, my energy flowing to seal the fractures. Despite the warmth which permeated this place, a shiver ran through my flesh. I sank onto the ground, almost trembling from exhaustion.

Wenzhi shrugged off his outer robe, draping it over my shoulders. My eyes darted up to meet his, my face flushing against my will. I looked away, at his robe instead, a dark gray silk embroidered with clouds. A memory drifted into my mind of the last time he had done this—on the rooftop of the Jade Palace when we had pledged ourselves to each other . . . before his treachery tore us apart.

Never again, I swore to myself, discarding his robe. We were

311

allies now, friends, perhaps—but no matter these uncertain mur-murings of my heart, I would never allow myself to be his pawn again. Trust, once broken, was impossible to restore; the cracks remained even when glazed anew.

Wenzhi's eyes were a forbidding gray. "Did Lady Xihe hurt you?"

As another wave of heat slipped free from the orb, I winced. "No, it's the feather. It burns."

"Let me help."

As I dug it from my pouch, he plucked the sphere from my grasp. A relief to yield it to another, even as I resisted the urge to snatch it back. The sight of the feather in Wenzhi's hand re-minded me uncomfortably of the pearls he had once taken. The feather seethed with fire, its barbs quivering like they were alive. As Wenzhi lifted it up to examine it, a streak of flame surged from within, piercing the barrier to strike his shoulder. He did not flinch, his grip tightening around the sphere, light flowing from his fingers to wrap the orb in frost.

My eyes followed the feather in his hand as he sat down be-side me. Before I could demand its return, he held it out to me. The orb was cool to my touch as I slipped it back into my pouch, knotting the cords.

"Thank you," I said stiffly. "For shielding me earlier. For . . . this."

"It was the least I could do when you bore the brunt of fac-ing Lady Xihe." His voice dropped dangerously low. "What did she do to you?"

I did not reply, glancing at his wound from the feather, the skin a mottled red. "Does it hurt?"

A small smile played across his lips. "Are you concerned for me?"

I shrugged, feigning indifference. "No. It would be an inconvenience if you died."

"An inconvenience," he repeated slowly. "Such unfeeling words."

I would not be baited into a reply, turning to stare at the grove. An unearthly radiance emanated from the trees, the mulberries blazing like they were afire. Their light rippled through the night, brushing the sky with crimson and rose. Soon, Lady Xihe and her daughter would be mounting their chariot.

Wenzhi leaned back against a tree, his eyelids drooping shut. He rarely showed signs of discomfort. Had the feather's power caused some internal injury? The marks across his shoulder were as glossy as melted wax. I frowned, unable to stop myself from reaching out to inspect them. As I halted, wary of causing discomfort—Wenzhi's palm swept up, pressing my hand to his chest.

Heat flared across my neck. As I snatched my hand away, his gaze searched mine. "What are you afraid of?" he asked.

"Not you." I lifted my head higher. "Liwei will be back soon. He will heal your wound."

"I would rather suffer your inept ministrations than those of the most accomplished healer in the realm."

"I did not offer to tend to you," I told him tightly.

"Nor will the Celestial Prince, for that matter. He would be glad to prolong my suffering, no doubt. As it would give me great satisfaction to do for him." A wry smile spread across his lips.

"Liwei would not do that."

"Of course not." An edge slid into his tone. "He is the perfect one. The noble one. The one who would never hurt you."

My silence was a reproach. Wenzhi knew how hurt I had been when Liwei betrothed himself to another—a different kind of pain from his own calculated betrayal.

"That was thoughtless of me." He inclined his head as he rested an arm upon his knee. "I used to believe we would spend the rest of our lives together—when you were mine as I am yours. These days, I barely have a moment alone with you."

"The way we are now . . . it is far more than I ever thought we would be again," I told him.

"Yes. To hear you say my name without hate or wariness, is a desire that has haunted me for the past year. Some days I thought you would despise me forever—as I deserved." A drawn breath slid from him. "I should be grateful, but I can't help wanting more."

"Never." The barest crack in my voice. "You destroyed what we had. By right, I should hate you forever."

"Hate me then, for I would rather have your hatred than indifference." His eyes were the shade of wintry rivers, glints of light traveling in their depths. "The past can't be undone, but my hope lies in our future. Trust me with your heart again and you will find the truth of mine. For you are the reason I rise each day, for you I live and breathe."

His declaration, spoken with such unflinching passion, struck all thought from my mind—an unexpected warmth flaring through me. I swallowed hard, fighting to conceal how shaken I was, hiding behind a mask of indifference. "Words are easily spoken."

His gaze pinned mine. "Then let me express them through deeds."

My pulse was racing, my breaths shallow. I did not know what emotions churned within me, nor did I want to examine them too carefully. He leaned forward, drawing closer—slowly— like I might startle. I should have moved, yet I did not. His breath grazed my lips, his scent filling my senses with pine, with the night breeze, with too many things I wanted to forget. Could he hear the thud of my heart? The evidence of desire I tried so hard to suppress?

My eyelids lowered, a tantalizing warmth coursing through my blood. But then he stopped, raising his hand to cradle my cheek.

"Do you want this?" His low voice curled at the edge of my hearing.

I should have moved away. Stumbled to my feet, and fled. Yet my head tilted toward him instead, as though tugged by an invisible thread. Something shifted in his expression, darkening with desire. His throat worked, a moment before his hand slid down the curve of my neck. His touch was firm yet tender, drawing me to him with a restrained passion that broke the last of my defenses. His mouth pressed against mine, seeking and fierce. My lips parted as he deepened the kiss, clasping me to him with a hunger that stole my breath. As his arm tightened around my waist like a band of iron, I arched closer, the press of his body firm and cool. Heat jolted down my spine, light flashing before me like the stars afire. Perhaps this spark had been there all along, muted, not extinguished. Perhaps it was my longing to feel something other than fear or despair—even if it was these confounding emotions he roused in me. Or it might have been his heartfelt words, the hurt I sensed deep within him.

Excuses. Lies, to shroud myself from the shameful truth that a part of me wanted him still, even after all he had done. A weakness that I wished I could undo. Almost shaking from the effort, I pushed against Wenzhi. He released me at once, breaking the embrace—his grave expression devoid of the triumph I expected.

"I had wondered all this time if it was him, alone, in your heart. How I longed to know if I was there too." A fierce light shone from his eyes. "You still feel something for me, even though you're too stubborn to admit it. Or are you afraid to?"

"Desire is not love." I was eager to dismiss what had passed between us, to cheapen it and cast it from my mind. Why was it that I advanced readily into battle yet remained a coward in such matters?

"It is not," he agreed. "But you, Xingyin, would not desire someone you care nothing for."

My blood simmered at the assurance in his tone, yet I could not find the words to deny it. As his gaze flicked behind me, I swung around to find Liwei standing there, as still as stone— staring at me as though I were a stranger.

28

I SCRAMBLED TO MY FEET, FUMBLING for words that would not come. What could I say?

This is not what it looks like.

I can explain.

It meant nothing.

Except it *was* what it looked like, nor could I explain what had just happened, not even to myself. As for the last . . . I could not utter that lie. Whatever it was, it meant something, no matter how I wished it did not.

"Is this what you want? Have you decided?" Liwei asked steadily, his eyes devoid of light.

"No." An ache stabbed my chest at the hurt in his expression.

"Decided, what?" Wenzhi demanded. I had not told him how I ended things with Liwei, the false things I had said of us.

"He is unworthy of you," Liwei said forcefully.

"I could say the same of you." Wenzhi uncoiled his legs and rose to his feet. "*You,* who gave her up to wed another. A fool's choice, something I will never do."

"You just wanted her on your own terms." Liwei stalked closer, his movements stiff with anger. "Are you even capable of love, or is it just possession you are after?"

"What exists between Xingyin and me is none of your concern. Look to your own faults before you imagine mine." Wenzhi's face hardened. "What kind of life did you intend to offer her? Did you think she would be happy in the Jade Palace with the Celestial Court? Would you have fastened a leash on her, turning her into an ornament for your life when you would never have deigned to become part of hers? You are not strong enough to do—to surrender—what it will take for her happiness."

I laughed in disbelief as I rounded on Wenzhi. "*You* locked me up. *You* took away my power. *You* tried to impose your will upon me, and you dare speak of my happiness?"

"Yes, I did all that, and I was *wrong*," Wenzhi answered fiercely. "A part of me knew it then, but I was selfish and afraid. I did not want to lose you. I wanted us to have a chance together, away from all else. From him." He turned his back to Liwei, closing the distance between us, speaking to me alone. "But I have looked into the mirror since, and not liked what I saw. I have changed, if you would only see that. If you can believe he will not hurt you again—why not me?"

"Because what you did was unforgivable," I said bitterly. "It does not matter whether you've changed or not, *nothing* can change what you were, what you did, and what you destroyed."

He flinched like I had struck him, but his gaze remained steel bright. "Then let's build something new together."

"Enough with these lies." Liwei's tone was harsh with scorn. As his long fingers clamped over Wenzhi's shoulder, Wenzhi seized his wrist and flung it off, swinging around to face Liwei. "Try it again if you dare, Your Highness. I fought my first battle while you were studying calligraphy and painting."

"Your lessons were sorely lacking in *many* regards," Liwei flung back as his hand went around the hilt of his sword.

I moved swiftly between them. "Enough. We are not the enemy."

They glared at each other, finally stepping apart. Liwei looked at me, his unspoken question hanging between us—how could he not wonder after what he had seen? I could have claimed confusion or remorse. He would have accepted them without question, yet we all deserved better, for such lies would yield just a temporary salve . . . even though lies were all I had to offer now, even to myself.

But this could not go on; far greater matters were at stake. These knots could be untangled later, once we had the leisure to do so. For if we failed . . . none of this would matter.

I faced them both. "Nothing is more important than stopping Wugang, an impossible task in itself. For what lies ahead, we must be strong, and we are stronger together than apart." As I rubbed the back of my neck unthinkingly, I flinched from the discomfort of my wounds.

They did not speak at first, finally inclining their heads. "You are hurt. What happened with Lady Xihe?" Liwei asked.

"Old debts repaid. She was merciful."

"Merciful?" Liwei's tone twisted in disbelief. "Your wounds run deep."

"I had to fight the phoenix. It was Lady Xihe's challenge for the feather." My chest cramped with the remembrance of her sorrow. "She knew who I was; she could have asked for more. Nine of her children are dead."

"*You* did not kill them," Wenzhi reminded me.

"Nor did she kill me," I countered.

"How did Lady Xihe find out who you were?" Liwei asked gravely.

My fingers curled at the reminder of his mother's trickery, but this was not the time to cast blame. Once we had dealt with Wugang, I would not let this pass. "The Sun Goddess knows all within her domain."

"You were lucky to make it out alive," Wenzhi said.

"Yes, along with this." I pulled out the feather, curled in the orb like a fragment of the sun. Flames simmered along its shaft, its tendrils clawing against the barrier. I felt no triumph—rather, an almost unbearable burden to have taken more from those who had lost so much.

"We must get the feather to the laurel. How do we get past Wugang's soldiers on the moon?" I asked.

"The moon is closely guarded against intrusion," Liwei warned. "I heard the soldiers speak of this while I was imprisoned—they wondered at the troops sent to secure the place when fewer efforts were taken to protect the Jade Palace."

My home, in Wugang's possession. Bitterness gnawed at me as I imagined the Pure Light Palace, so tranquil and peaceful—now at the center of these devastating plots. Another thought struck, one even less welcome. "My lifeforce regenerated so swiftly because of the laurel's power. What if Wugang's soldiers are stronger there too? How can we attack them at the heart of their might?"

"We can't," Wenzhi said decisively. "Even if we mustered an army to aid us, Wugang would sense the moment our forces approached, and he would crush it with everything at his disposal. It would be carnage."

"It would also alert Wugang," Liwei cautioned. "If he knows we intend to destroy the laurel, he will stop at nothing to keep it safe. We would never be able to reach it."

"Then we must endeavor to keep him in the dark," Wenzhi agreed.

My spirits lifted to hear them speaking this way, without resentment or hostility. "In the Eastern Sea, we had to entice Governor Renyu to come to us," I said to Wenzhi. "What if we could trick Wugang into bringing us to the laurel?"

His lips pressed taut as he pondered my words. "There is only one person Wugang will let near the laurel," Wenzhi said finally, a trace of reluctance weighing his tone.

I stilled, catching his meaning. There *was* only one person Wugang would allow near the laurel . . . not because he trusted her but because it would mean the fulfillment of his schemes.

My mother.

"No." The air seemed to close around me as I searched for the flaws in his suggestion.

"We will protect her. She will come to no harm."

Wenzhi was not one to shy from hard decisions. A part of me wanted to lash out at him, even as my mind whispered that he was right. This was our best chance . . . perhaps our only one.

"Wugang's soldiers do his bidding, but they will not hurt her," Wenzhi said. "You saw how they acted on the beach."

"Perhaps, but Wugang will have no qualms in doing so," I argued. "He will draw my mother's blood to harvest the seeds. We cannot let him take her—not just because I won't let anyone harm her, but because once she is in Wugang's power, *he wins*."

I continued, plunging onward. "Mother has no magic, nothing to either conceal or release the feather's power. Wugang would sense it on her at once, if it doesn't destroy her first, and if we lose the feather—we will have failed."

I was shaking, I only realized it then. Liwei touched my arm. "You are right. We will find another way."

"What if we disguised someone as your mother?" Wenzhi proposed.

I had done it before; pretended to be Lady Anmei in the Eastern Sea. Except such a ruse would never work here. "Wugang is far more astute than Governor Renyu; a mere change in clothing would not suffice. He knows my mother from his stay with us—her voice, mannerisms, and aura—and he will not forget."

"What about an enchantment?" Liwei suggested. "Though the few I am aware of are merely surface deep, an illusion of the face and form."

I recalled Tao's enchantment when we had broken into the Imperial Treasury, and what he had told me of another. "I heard there is a rare magic that can replicate not just one's appearance, but their aura and voice too." I added slowly, "If so, I could disguise myself as my mother."

Liwei frowned. "Auras are as unique to us as the whorls on our fingers. This must be an ancient magic, for no one speaks of such a thing these days."

"Ancient and forbidden," Wenzhi said gravely. "The Divine Mirror Scroll is one of the most powerful Mind enchantments. For as long as it holds, it would be almost impossible for someone to detect the difference."

"A *forbidden* scroll?" Liwei's tone was one of revulsion.

"One of many your father destroyed," Wenzhi replied coldly. "Fortunately for us, they were restored."

"Where is it?" I asked Wenzhi. Perhaps Liwei thought me a hypocrite, willing to use whatever means necessary to win. With such stakes, he might be right.

"The scroll is with my father. It is one of his most treasured possessions."

"Will he give it to us?" I asked, doubt flashing through me.

"I will ask, but he will be wary of my request. My father doesn't trust anyone. Neither his courtiers nor his consorts, and least of all his children. The greatest threat of betrayal is when there is the most to gain or lose," Wenzhi said grimly.

Something flickered in his expression. Did he recall how he had betrayed me for the dragons' pearls? Greed, ambition, and fear were powerful forces that could cloud one's heart and mind.

A bird trilled, a vigilant herald of dawn. Wenzhi glanced at the lightening skies, of crimson and rose. "I will return to speak to him before he heads to court."

"We will wait for you near the border of the Eastern Sea. I dare not linger here, as Lady Xihe will be emerging soon."

Wenzhi nodded, raising a hand to summon a cloud. Tension gripped his body, his expression somber. Did he dread the confrontation with his father? What a strange relationship these royals had between parent and child. Was it power that muddied the bond? Those onerous expectations of duty? The Celestial Emperor had disparaged Liwei for his lack of ruthlessness and blunted ambition, while Wenzhi's father feared his son had too much of it.

NEITHER LIWEI NOR I spoke as we flew toward the Eastern Sea. It struck me that this was the first time we were alone since our flight from the Jade Palace—just days earlier, yet it felt like decades. I was no longer the girl who had entered the Courtyard of Eternal Tranquility; I was not even the same one who had helped him escape. Some years swept by, leaving little mark on our lives, while a single moment sufficed to upend them.

Death had ravaged an intrinsic part of me. With this constant weight bearing down, happiness seemed an elusive prospect. Liwei stood a palm's width away, though it might as well have been ten, with a wall between us. Strands of his long black hair fell across his face as he stared into the sky.

"Do your wounds still hurt?" he asked.

"No." The discomfort was a welcome distraction to my other pains, those unseen.

He leaned forward, taking my hand. The warmth of his energy surged into my body, healing the last of my injuries and replenishing the well of my power that had sunk dangerously low. I breathed easier as the strength returned to my limbs.

"What happened in the grove?" he asked, drawing away. "Lady Xihe and her phoenix are powerful. How did you withstand their attacks?"

"Wenzhi helped. He shielded me."

His face shuttered. "You are right that this is not the time for such matters, but I must say this—if you are confused, that is his doing. He is a master of manipulation."

"No," I said slowly. "My feelings are my own."

His dark eyes held mine, unfathomable, when once I had read them so clearly. "Did you want to kiss him?"

I looked away then. "I wish I had not." Not a full answer, and not what he wanted to hear.

"What you feel now . . . I believe it will pass. Do not let him cloud your feelings."

The intensity in Liwei's tone startled me. As I searched his face, I found new lines across his brow, the corners of his mouth. These days had taken their toll on him too. "Liwei, are you well? You must be worried for your parents."

"Mother hides her worries, though she is afraid. As for Father—" His voice trailed off. "I must return to the Jade Palace. I must help him—"

"You would just be walking into a trap. Few things are more precious to usurpers of thrones than displaced heirs," I said bluntly.

"He will kill my father."

"No, Wugang is prudent. He will keep your father alive until his own position is secure. He is vulnerable as long as he doesn't have you." I added solemnly, "If Wugang wanted to kill your father, he would already be dead." The unvarnished truth sometimes offered the greatest comfort.

How strange that a few weeks ago, it had been the Celestial

Emperor who struck terror into me, whom I loathed. Yet compared to the senseless cruelty of Wugang, the Celestial Emperor was the preferred choice for the realm . . . although I could not help thinking Liwei would make a far better ruler.

"Will Queen Fengjin stand with your family?" I asked.

"With the situation so uncertain, the Phoenix Queen is hesitant to move against Wugang. It is no longer a question of defending our position but of wresting it back—a far harder exercise, requiring far greater conviction."

A bond stronger than an alliance.

"You should marry Princess Fengmei." These words almost choked me, but the princess could give him more than I ever could: A kingdom, a crown, a future. While all Liwei had ever asked me for was my heart, and I could not even yield that.

"Do you want me to, Xingyin?" A note of sadness threaded his tone.

I stifled my instinctive protest, forcing myself to say, "You must do what is best for you and your family."

He clasped my hand tightly, and for a moment I was lost in the remembered warmth of his touch. "You have always fought against what life threw at you, whether you had a hope of winning or not. You dreamed of the impossible, making your own way when there was none. Don't give up on us now."

"I'm not who you think I am." My voice was low. "I have made so many mistakes. I have hurt those I cared for, failed those I would have given anything to save." These confessions were torn from the deepest part of me.

"No, Xingyin—for you have been tested more than most. Those forged through fire form the strongest blades." He smiled at me, an echo of the companion of my past, then his expression turned somber once more. "I will not give up as long as you don't, and I will stay by your side for as long as you let me."

My emotions wound tighter, on the brink of snapping. I craved his strength, his comfort and kindness—all of which I had fallen in love with, that I loved still. "I don't know what I want. And right now, it does not matter."

"Just tell me, am I in your heart?"

"Yes." I did not hesitate, for it was the truth.

"As you are in mine." He tilted his head toward me. "Not knowing is not the same as not wanting. While there is hope, I will wait."

Before I could reply, something pulsed through the air. My head darted up as I searched our surroundings. "The wind has shifted direction. Swifter. Colder."

"Clouds, heading our way," he confirmed grimly.

"We must flee. They must be Wugang's soldiers."

"They could be Wenzhi's. Another trap." His voice was edged with suspicion.

I shook my head. The feather would have been a great temptation, yet when I had emerged from the grove, weakened and hurt, Wenzhi could have seized it with ease. I did not know what lay in his heart, but it was not treachery—at least, not anymore.

As our cloud swept higher, a force struck from behind, yanking us to an abrupt halt. I staggered, catching my balance as our cloud was reeled back like a fish caught on a hook. We were harnessed. Trapped. I spun to find Wugang's undead soldiers upon our trail, six of them—vacant-eyed, yet set with deadly purpose. Ominously silent, their lips sealed shut. Their armor gleamed gold and white, their translucent skin almost silver, the luminous web of veins on their faces aglow in the awakening dawn.

Had Wugang learned of the feather? No, else he would have sent his entire army to retrieve it. Not even the dragons had been aware of its existence, just the empress—for she, alone, had been close to the Sun Goddess. This must be one of the patrols sent to comb the skies for us, as Wugang would be searching for my mother.

The soldiers soared toward us, pale hollows shining in their eye sockets like twin lanterns. As they raised their hands in unison, their guandao thrust in our direction—light crackled from their blades, leaping across the sky to strike our cloud.

As it shuddered violently, fire erupted from Liwei's palms, coiling around one of the soldiers. Yet the creature did not scorch and break as on the beach. A white glow pulsed through its skin, healing its injuries—as the remaining soldiers slashed through Liwei's flames like ribbons. Drawing my bow, I released an arrow at a soldier, a bolt of Sky-fire plunging into the disc on its chest. The soldier stumbled back from the force, yet the jade did not fracture. Had it been reinforced? I shot another arrow after it, but a shield sprang up around the soldiers, holding fast against my blow.

"They've learned to defend themselves. They've learned to help each other," Liwei said, his voice strained.

My gaze fixed upon the nearing soldiers, my skin crawling at the sight of the guandao in their hands, agleam with malevolent power. In a moment, they would be upon us. "Then we must strike hard, all at once," I said.

Fire blazed from Liwei's palms, arcing toward the soldiers, churning above like a flaming cloud. The soldiers' heads swung up in unison, their faces blank with a chilling detachment. A shiver rippled across my skin, but I forced my hands to steady, releasing an arrow at Liwei's flames. Sky-fire stuck, splintering the seething mass, cascading over the soldiers in a fiery torrent. The air reeked with an acrid bitterness, of scorched flesh and skin—if they were made of such things. Yet the soldiers did not utter a sound as pale wounds bloomed upon their bodies like mold upon rotted fruit.

Liwei drew his sword, slashing at the unseen tethers that bound our cloud. As their hold snapped, our cloud shot into the skies. Magic coursed from our fingers, channeling a wind to spur us onward. Our robes fluttered wildly, my hair whipped free from its coils. I glanced behind to find the soldiers standing just where we had left them, an eerie light suffusing their bodies— already regenerating.

My gut twisted. They were the perfect weapon: tireless and fearless, swift and strong. An army of them would cut through the realms like a scythe through barley. We had escaped this time, but what of the next? What if there was nowhere left to run?

We soared swiftly southward, above the lush forests of the Phoenix Kingdom, staying far from the borders of the Celestial Kingdom. Finally, the sands of the Golden Desert glittered on the horizon. A tall figure was flying toward us upon a violet-gray cloud.

"I sensed your presence," Wenzhi said as he drew nearer. "Why are you here?"

"Wugang's soldiers found us. They've grown stronger; we barely escaped," I told him.

"They won't be able to enter the Cloud Wall," he assured me. "We have ways of keeping out unwanted guests."

"Whatever they are, they might not work on Wugang's soldiers," Liwei warned.

"Perhaps," Wenzhi agreed, his forehead furrowed. "Let's hope Wugang has no desire to test us for now. He has enemies aplenty throughout the rest of the Immortal Realm."

"Did you speak to your father? Will he help us?" I asked him.

His eyes were the shade of a storm-tossed sea. "There is a price to his aid."

I should not have been surprised. It seemed to be the way of kings and queens—those who possessed the most, unwilling to relinquish anything without advantage.

"What does he want?" I asked warily.

Wenzhi's gaze pinned mine, his voice deepening with intensity. "Xingyin, I tried everything I could to get my father to change his mind."

Dread gaped within me. "What do you mean?"

"My father will give us the scroll . . . as a wedding gift."

29

THE SCENT OF SANDALWOOD CLUNG to the air, wafting from the bronze incense burners scattered around the room. Rows of silk lanterns, strung from the ceilings, cast their fiery glow upon the obsidian walls. All around, the guests lounged on brocade cushions as they sipped from gilded porcelain cups. Small plates of food were laid before them on low mahogany tables: steamed dumplings topped with glistening crab roe, thin slices of roast pork drizzled with a ginger and scallion sauce, delicate spring rolls fried to a golden crisp.

The Cloud Wall immortals seemed to favor vivid colors, clad in jewel tones of amethyst and emerald, ruby and aquamarine. I must have appeared a drab flower among them, though the palace attendants had offered me a dazzling array of garments. In no mood for gaiety, I had chosen the most somber outfit I could find—a green silk so pale, it bordered on gray. Yellow chrysanthemums were embroidered on the skirt, nodding their heads as though tossed by the wind that swirled through in silver curls of thread. My neck and wrists were unadorned, my hair pulled through a plain band of silk, the long ends brushing my back.

"We are a matched pair," Wenzhi remarked from beside me, a small smile on his lips.

"We are *not*." I was in no mood to be agreeable. My insides knotted from being here, a place I never imagined I would return to. The incense fragrance clogged my nostrils, the dark walls seeming to close in tighter—unsettling memories surfacing that I clung to, reminding myself to never lower my guard.

"I meant our clothes are matched," Wenzhi said, his smile widening.

He had changed, too, into a high-collared moss-green robe, a pattern of leaves embroidered along the hem in gold thread. The color highlighted the angular planes of his face, the darker hue of his skin. As my heart quickened, I crushed the treacherous impulse.

I was not here upon a whim. We needed King Wenming's aid, and I hoped to sway him from his outrageous condition. I had not come to play the role of a docile daughter-in-law. I would be a thorn, a viper, the falcon Wenzhi had likened me to once.

King Wenming sat on an ebony throne upon the dais, his back straight, his gaze alert and assessing. An ornate gold crown rested on his head, fringed with amethyst beads that fell over his brow. His robes were a muted ash, in startling contrast to the brilliant garments of the three women who stood behind him, their exquisite robes of vermilion, coral, and lapis studded with pearls.

Wenzhi led me to a low table in the front. As we sat upon the flat brocade cushions, my eyes darted around the room yet always returned to the dais. According to rumor, King Wenming had no queen but numerous wives, and I assumed the three present were the most favored.

"My mother is the Noble Consort of the third rank, the one dressed in coral. While the Virtuous Consort of the first rank is Wenshuang's mother," Wenzhi explained as he lifted the porcelain jug and filled our cups with wine. "Having multiple consorts is as common here as in the Celestial Kingdom."

"Why settle for one when there are so many?" My question

332 ~ SUE LYNN TAN

emerged in a more biting tone than intended. It did not seem fair; so many attending to just one, whether queen or king—unless it was by choice. For if not, this jostle for affection and position was an unenviable situation.

Wenzhi's fingers toyed with the rim of his cup. "There might be a field of flowers, yet all I need is one."

"Some flowers have thorns," I said coldly. "If you pluck them, you will get pricked."

His gaze flicked to mine. "Those are the most precious of all."

I ignored the leap in my pulse, shifting my attention back to the dais. As a shadow fell over us, I looked up into a pair of yellow eyes, as bright as a serpent's. Prince Wenshuang. Something hot and bitter crowded the back of my throat, my stomach churning violently. The memory of how he had pressed his body against mine rushed over me, of his foul breath against my neck. My hands reached instinctively for a weapon I did not have, before clenching helplessly in my lap.

Prince Wenshuang's brocade robe glittered with amethysts, his hair tucked into a gold headpiece. Ornate rings encircled his fingers, the same ones he had slammed against my cheek and ground into my flesh. Panic crested, but I forced it back. I would not cower from him; *he* should run. He had hurt me when I was weak and vulnerable, and I had beaten him nonetheless.

"Our sparrow has returned," he sneered. "Did you miss my company?"

My hand itched to strike his face. Instead, I raked him with a look of scorn. "The carcass of a rat would be better company than you."

Prince Wenshuang's skin mottled with rage. "I could have you flayed for that."

"Try it. Just remember what I did to you *without* my powers."

My tone was hard, showing neither the revulsion nor fear he roused in me.

"Get lost, brother." Wenzhi uncoiled to his full height, his voice thick with menace. "Do not forget what I did to you the last time—you're only standing because of Father's intervention. I warned you then and I'm warning you now, stay away if you value your life."

Prince Wenshuang flinched as he stepped back. A fierce satisfaction coursed through me as he stalked away without another word.

"I should have protected you from him," Wenzhi said.

"*After* I drugged you and left you for dead? How noble you are." I spoke flippantly, trying to steady myself from the repulsive encounter.

He sighed as he extended his hand to me. "Only with you, Xingyin. I wish you did not evoke such inconvenient sentiments in me." When I did not move, he added, "For the sake of appearances, if nothing else. My father believes we are to be wed."

I nodded, placing my hand in his lightly, his fingers closing around mine. My breathing quickened as we approached the dais, the guards shifting to allow us to pass, though their watchful stares never left us. Following Wenzhi's lead, I bowed to the king from my waist. This close, his aura swept over us, as slippery and opaque as a frozen pond. As I lifted my head, my eyes collided with his—almost white, with a shimmering iridescence like that of opals. The lines of his face were sharp, while his body was lean and long. Thin reddish streaks formed his lips, which curved into a humorless smile.

"You are welcome here, daughter of Chang'e and Houyi."

His greeting was cordial and his voice silken, though my insides flinched at the sound. "Thank you, Your Majesty."

One of the women stepped forward—the Noble Consort, Wenzhi's mother. Jade hairpins were tucked into the coils of her dark hair, strung with chains of coral that cascaded to her shoulders, the same vivid shade as her robe. Her round eyes were the rich brown of chestnuts, set in the oval of her face. Despite the delicacy of her features, a quiet strength emanated from her.

Wenzhi bowed to her, his voice warmer than when he had addressed his father. "Mother, you look well tonight."

She beamed at him, radiant in her joy. "Thank you, my son. I am glad you are here. The Virtuous Consort said you would not come." Wenzhi's mother glanced at the vermilion-clad lady behind her whose mouth was curled into a sneer.

I kept my expression calm as Wenzhi gestured toward me. "This is Xingyin."

"I have heard much of you." A laugh thrummed in her voice, one of humor not scorn. She pulled off a jade bangle from her wrist and held it out to me, the stone a vivid translucent red. "A gift for you."

"Thank you, Noble Consort. I must decline." My refusal came out stiffly, discordant to the generosity of the gesture.

A frown puckered her brow as she slipped the bracelet back over her hand. Perhaps she thought me shy, or more likely, believed me ill-mannered. Except I really did not want it. I was never at ease accepting gifts from strangers, particularly when I did not know their true price.

"Did my son tell you of my terms?" The king's words hurtled like darts, his keen gaze upon me.

"Yes, Your Majesty, but I do not understand the need for this union," I said carefully. "Wugang is a grave threat to us all. We should unite to defeat him."

King Wenming's fingers tapped the armrest of his throne in a ceaseless, unhurried rhythm. "My son has shared this and more. According to him, Wugang's army is almost invincible, capable of destroying an immortal with a single strike of their blades. They might even be impervious to our magic, though that has yet to be fully tested."

I took heart from his words. Perhaps we might be able to convince him of our urgency. "Wugang does not seek to rule just the Celestial Kingdom but the entire Immortal Realm. He will cast his eyes toward the Cloud Wall too, it is only a matter of time."

"Indeed," the king agreed smoothly. "Yet the fact remains, you have a favor to ask of me."

I swallowed, pushing through the thickness in my throat. "We need the Divine Mirror Scroll to stop him."

"You make it sound like a simple request. Many have sought this to further their own ends. What do you intend to do with the scroll?" His tone hardened, his fingers stilling against his armrest.

Did he think me a liar? Plotting with his son to usurp his power? "If Your Majesty performs the enchantment on me, I can get close enough to Wugang to end this." I did not reveal the rest of my plan; I did not trust him with it.

"Father, I would have no part in this," Wenzhi emphasized. "*You* would perform the enchantment on her alone. Moreover, Xingyin has no talent in our magic; she is no threat to you."

"I will be the judge of that," the king said, raising his hand.

Before I could decipher his meaning, violet light streaked from the king's palm toward me. I reached for a shield, too late, as it struck—jarring, like dust blown into my eyes. I writhed as the discomfort sharpened, stinging like splinters pressed into my scalp. My pulse stuttered, my fingers clawing at my head, trying to wrench myself free of this enemy that had crept in unbidden, unheard, unseen. I grasped my powers, scrambling to erect a barrier—a task as hopeless as plastering sand onto porcelain. The force slammed harder against my consciousness, the pain stabbing deeper, a scream forming in my throat—

"Father, enough!"

The fury and terror in Wenzhi's voice pierced my daze. His magic surged forth in a dense mist that swept over me, prying loose the malevolent hold on my mind. As he grasped my hand, holding me steady, his power rushed through my veins with a reviving force. My breathing eased yet I could barely move, my senses still scattered from this vicious intrusion.

"Treachery!" the Virtuous Consort snarled, pointing at Wenzhi. "How dare you attack your father, our king?"

"I did not attack." Wenzhi spoke with stony calm, his eyes glittering dangerously. "No one is allowed to hurt her, not even you, Father."

His words stirred a warmth in me, underscored by the urge to disdain his protection. But I kept silent from caution, for this place was no less perilous than the Celestial Court.

"The Virtuous Consort makes a wild accusation. She must be drunk on wine," Wenzhi's mother said with a bright smile, as she bowed to the king. "Your Majesty, my son did not attack you. He was merely protecting the girl, his intended."

The king's face was taut with displeasure as he faced Wenzhi. "I will forgive you this once, but *never* raise your hand to me again. Guard your feelings better if you intend to rule."

As the last of the agony subsided, I was shaking, hunched over from the ordeal. Nauseated, feeling violated from within. But I raised my head to meet the king's gaze. "Never do that to me again," I warned him, despite the remnants of fear that scraped me.

The king smiled as though savoring my discomfort. "She is strong," he mused aloud. "However, no talent in our magic, as you said."

"Next time, Father, accept my word instead of resorting to this." Wenzhi's hands were still clenched by his sides.

"I trust only my own eyes and ears. You should learn to do the same, once you ascend the throne."

Anger flared, that the king had dared to do this contemptible thing to me, as carelessly as flicking a speck of dirt from his robe. I bit down on my tongue, tempering my rage, relieved to not have yielded my thoughts to him during our brief struggle.

He would not have liked what he saw.

A shudder ran through me to think of Wenzhi's early years—a brother who would have gladly murdered him, a father who scented treachery everywhere. It was little wonder he had grown into such a ruthless strategist; he had been practicing since he was a child, against his own family, no less.

"Father, have I not proven my loyalty?" Wenzhi demanded. "I wish to rid our kingdom of this threat—a far greater danger than the Celestial Kingdom ever was."

Silence hung in the air. The king leaned back against the throne, a cunning gleam in his eyes. "This is a great favor you ask. How can I be sure you are no Celestial spy? Did you not serve them before?" The accusation slid out, sudden and swift.

Such winding thoughts from the king . . . I almost missed the blunt fury of the Celestial Emperor. "Your Majesty, this is no trick. If I lied, would you not have sensed it?" A challenge tossed down so lightly, I hoped he would take the bait.

He shook his head as though to say: *Not good enough.* Balancing an elbow on the armrest of his throne, he rested his chin upon his fist. The Virtuous Consort offered him a cup of wine, which he refused with an impatient flick of his wrist.

"The Divine Mirror Scroll is a precious treasure of our realm. It can only be used once. A difficult enchantment to perform, one which comes at great cost to the caster. Are you worthy of it?

Can I trust you, an outsider, unbound to us by blood or name?"
He spoke slowly, with deliberate measure. "If you were family,
that would be a different matter. You know my condition for the
scroll."

"Why do you want this, Your Majesty?" Part of me dreaded
his answer.

The king's laugh was like rocks ground together. "You have
no kingdom nor title, though your lineage is strong—as is the
power that flows in your veins. I have heard of your accomplishments from my own informants: your standing in the Celestial Army, the dragons, and yes, even your flight from our
hospitality."

As muted laughter rippled through the room, Wenzhi swung
around. His glare quelled them as effectively as a drawn blade,
yet his face gave no indication of his thoughts.

The king leaned forward, his gaze fixed on mine. "Marry
my heir, and the scroll is yours."

"No." The refusal sprang to my lips before I could stop it. To
hear his demand spoken in such an implacable manner jarred me.
But I bit back my harsher words, for I could not risk offending
the king. To him, this was not so unreasonable a request. Royal
children often married to suit their parents' preferences—whether
to secure an alliance, strengthen ties, or settle old rivalries.

Except I was no royal and I was never one for obeying commands, particularly those issued by overbearing monarchs.

The king's mouth slanted in a cunning smile as he gestured at
Wenzhi. "Come, now. My request is no hardship. My son is not
displeasing to look at. Moreover, he is no stranger to you; you
liked him well enough in the past."

I gritted my teeth as Wenzhi shot me a warning look. I did
not need his reminder; I would not lash out like some petulant
child. "Your Majesty, you honor me." The words crumbled like

stale bread in my mouth. "However, I am promised to another."
I had no compunction about lying to him. Beside me, Wenzhi
tensed, his face impassive.

The king shrugged. "Such things change as quickly as kingdoms are lost."

"Spouses are not as easily traded as heirs." My furious reply
rolled off my tongue.

"Ah, you are wrong, my dear." The king shifted, resting his
palms upon his knees. "The heads of both can be just as easily
dispatched."

The threat plunged into the silence like a brick tossed into a
pond. Relief flooded me that Liwei was waiting in the Golden
Desert, safe from the king's ruthless machinations.

"Your Majesty must be mistaken," I tried again. "I am no
matrimonial prize. I can bring you neither power, a kingdom,
nor allies."

"That is not quite true." The king lowered his tone to a con-
spiratorial whisper. "I know who your father is—the dragons he
used to command, the heavenly creatures he slew. His blood and
strength flow in your veins."

"The dragons are freed of their bond. They no longer answer
to him." I was guarded, unsure of his intent.

"Such ancient ties are not easily broken. If he calls, they will
come. Besides, the Cloud Wall needs such strength as you can
bring to our line, the children you will bear."

Red flashed through my vision at his words. I would not dwell
on his meaning; rage would engulf me if I did. "The urgency is to
defeat Wugang. Now, before he becomes unstoppable."

"Perhaps he is already unstoppable." The king spread his
hands wide. "Wugang has offered us an alliance. It would be
prudent for us to accept. At least for now."

I glanced at Wenzhi, who shook his head.

"My son knows nothing of this. I will accept the newly crowned Celestial Emperor's offer if you refuse mine. I have no love for the Celestial Kingdom; it gladdens me to see them brought low. Yet Wugang's rise threatens us too. Not now, when there are greater prizes to seize, the jewel of the Celestial Kingdom for the taking. But new horizons will beckon to him soon, his thirst for conquest unquenched. Such as he will not be satisfied with one kingdom when there are eight."

"Then we must stop him—"

"Among all the kingdoms in the Immortal Realm, the Cloud Wall alone has the choice to bide our time," the king interjected. "To study our enemy, to fortify ourselves when others are weakened, to eliminate enemies of the past—and to strike when it is least expected."

"Wugang will only grow stronger," Wenzhi cautioned. "His army will multiply with none to stop him, and once the other kingdoms fall, their armies will be his to command."

"Whatever is left of their armies." The king spoke with a brutal callousness. "Nor will we be idle; we will prepare ourselves for any eventuality. This new order might be to our favor, for we are weary of being the outcasts of the realm."

"Father, surely you do not believe that—" Wenzhi protested.

The king's hand flew up. "Enough. My patience is wearing thin."

Perhaps the king had been isolated in his domain for too long, not comprehending the danger to the realm. Or perhaps it was a cunning tactic to force our hand. *My hand*, I thought wrathfully.

"If we are to risk defying Wugang, we must be well positioned to share in the spoils of victory after," the king declared. "Not to be discarded after our usefulness is gone. The Dragon

Lord was revered throughout the kingdoms. Now he has returned, a union with your family would benefit us greatly."

"Father, I've told you I do not want this," Wenzhi said adamantly. "Not this way."

The intensity of his tone caught at me. Despite his assurances, a part of me had wondered if this had been his plan. He always played to win, bending the rules in his favor . . . however, this was no act.

"Don't deny that you want her." The king's words slithered around us like the coils of a snake. "*This* is how you hold a throne; *this* is how you seize what you want. I thought you understood, which is why I named you heir. I forgave you for losing the dragons' pearls, but do not disappoint me again." Menace coated his tone as he added, "Don't forget, I have another son."

"Never," I spat, my stomach lurching at the thought.

The king leaned back against his throne, his eyes glinting like shards of ice. "There are ways to secure your cooperation."

I recoiled at the reminder of what he had done to me a moment earlier. Wenzhi had promised to never use such magic on me, but his father possessed no such scruples.

Wenzhi's eyes widened with a silent plea for my trust before he bowed to the throne. "Father, thank you for your wisdom. We accept your decision."

I did not wholly trust him, yet there was no choice. If I refused, the king would either cast his lot in with Wugang or force me into marriage with Prince Wenshuang—a fate worse than death.

Victory in his grasp, King Wenming accepted a cup of wine from the Virtuous Consort, lifting it in a toast. "The wedding will be in three days."

"No." I grasped wildly for a way out. "We must move on Wugang now. The wedding can be held after."

"*You* do not get to decide this. Learn your place if you wish my favor. Be careful," the king added, "lest three days become one."

I held my tongue, inclining my head in seeming acquiescence—even as despair flooded me like I had been swept into waters too deep, and could no longer feel the ground with my feet.

30

I WILL NOT DO IT," I told Wenzhi, the moment we entered my room. Fortunately, it was not the same chamber I had been locked in before, this one furnished in mahogany and rose brocade, with ink washed paintings of mountains hanging from the walls.

Wenzhi shut the door behind him. "Xingyin, I know you do not want to marry me. Despite my feelings, I have enough pride that I won't force you into a union." A wry smile broke across his lips. "I'm certain you would make my life an unpleasant hell if I did."

I breathed out, a little of my tension easing—though something picked at me still. Was it resentment, to have been forced into this predicament? Anxiety for what lay ahead? Pulling out a stool, I sank onto it, my head beginning to pound. The king demanded that we wed, but I had no intention of obeying him. Yet if I refused, he would not aid us. Meanwhile, Wugang was hunting my mother, and soon, his gaze would turn toward the Eastern Sea. The Immortal Realm teetered on the brink of destruction, and our paths were closing rapidly.

"Do you think your father will ally with Wugang, or is it an empty threat?" I asked.

"My father is no fool. The pretense of an alliance will suffice to keep us safe, for now." He paused. "Father is playing a double game, the type he plays best. Keeping Wugang at bay with hollow promises while working to advance his own ends."

"Why won't Wugang attack you?"

"Because he would rather have an ally than another enemy," Wenzhi said. "The Celestial Kingdom knows better than to underestimate our abilities again; they do not understand our magic. Moreover, our wards protect this place. While Wugang's soldiers might not possess a consciousness of their own, something exists that enables them to accept his commands—which we might be able to harness, should the need arise."

I searched his face. "Why is your father set upon this marriage? Surely there are more suitable candidates out there?"

"Few kingdoms in the Immortal Realm would consider a betrothal with us, a circumstance I am glad for," he said with feeling. "Like it or not, Xingyin, this would be a powerful alliance for us—one which would be mutually beneficial." He added quietly, "One which could be happy."

His words reached deeper than I wished—a temptation to accept the aid offered, the easier path. Yet beyond our fractured past, I would hate being bartered in marriage; I would never give such an accursed union a chance. I now understood the strain Liwei had been under when he agreed to the betrothal with Princess Fengmei, and why he was adamant on refusing it this time. I would not marry Wenzhi; I would not be a pawn for the king's twisted machinations. This was my life—and it was love, or even the promise of it, that gave it meaning.

"Can we delay the wedding, or try to reason with your father again?" My imagination soared. "Disguise someone else to complete the ceremony?"

Wenzhi's expression shuttered as he leaned against the door.

"Once my father's mind is made up, he will not relent. And I will not bind myself to some stranger, not even for you."

"That was thoughtless of me," I admitted, even as my mind still sought a way out. "Could you perform the enchantment instead of your father?"

"Yes, if I study it," he replied. "But the greater problem is how we might obtain the scroll. I must tread carefully. If I jeopardize my position, my mother will be left to the mercy of the other consorts. The Virtuous Consort has grown spiteful with the displacement of her son as heir. She would seek any opportunity to harm us."

In a family as venomous as his, the safest place was on top. It was why Wenzhi had gone to such lengths to secure his position. Why should he pit himself against his father, risking it all? I, myself, was reluctant to sacrifice anything so precious on my part—whether my mother, my freedom, or my love.

Yet what if there was no choice? Could I let my mother face Wugang alone and defenseless? Could I do nothing as Wugang unleashed his soldiers? No. Never. I was not so heartless, nor reckless enough to risk the fate of the realm. As my resolve wavered, I rebuked myself. There must be another way. If I kept thinking there was none, I would stop searching—and then failure would surely follow.

"What if *I* steal it?" I offered, as desperate as a fisherman down to his last bait.

"You can't. My father keeps the Divine Mirror Scroll on him at all times. In here." Wenzhi tapped his temple.

I stared at him. "How is that possible?"

"It's not easy," he conceded. "It consumes a vast amount of energy. Only the most powerful among us are capable of such a thing, and only certain artifacts can be hidden so. But it is the most secure place, as the items can't be stolen or taken by force, not without killing the vessel and destroying the artifact."

"Why didn't you hide the dragons' pearls that way?" I asked.

"Oh, I considered it. I'm glad I did not. I might be dead, and not by my brother's hand."

I lifted my chin. "Do you think I would have killed you?"

"Yes, maybe without even knowing it. The item is tethered within the core of one's lifeforce, and opening its pathway weakens one immensely." He paused, before adding, "As you did once."

I had done it to sever the dragons' bond with their pearls, to set them free. The agony, the wrenching loss, were not things I was eager to relive.

He continued, "It is a drain on one's power to keep the artifact intact, shielded from our internal energy. I could not have risked it then, not with the looming confrontation with the Celestials. The slightest slip in my concentration and the pearls would have been destroyed, and me along with them. This is why my father does not venture from our borders, why he is always surrounded by guards."

"You could have given your father the pearls for safekeeping," I remarked.

"Trust is something which goes both ways. I had always plotted for and taken what I wanted before. It was the only way to survive here—to thrive." He held my gaze. "I learned too late there was another way, that trust need not be a weakness. If only I had been honest with you from the start."

"It would not have mattered; I would never have agreed to what you did." Such righteous words I spoke, though the anger that should have accompanied them had faded.

"Perhaps," Wenzhi said slowly. "But I would like to think we might have found our way together. That you might have understood, and that we could have helped one another without hurting each other."

I hardened myself. "A fairy tale."

"My mother always said that I never believed in fairy tales. It was because I had known monsters since the day I knew my name." His lips curved into a small smile. "Indulge me. Let me tell you how it played out in my mind on the days I allowed myself to dream."

My emotions warred within; one part of me curious, the wiser part afraid.

"You have no love for the Celestial Kingdom," he began. "Perhaps I could have offered my father something else in place of the pearls. Perhaps I could have renounced my claim to the throne once I secured my mother's position. We could have left this world behind us and made our own way, whether in the realm above or below."

"You would have given up your crown? After all you did to secure it?" My voice lifted in disbelief.

The light in his eyes rivaled that of the moon. "I would give it all up for you, if you would only ask."

My mind went blank, an ache writhing in my chest. Yet he was cunning enough to say what he thought I wanted to hear. "I will not ask." Somehow, I managed to speak steadily. "For it would change nothing between us."

A shadow fell over his face. "What you told my father just now . . . are you really promised to the Celestial prince?"

"No." I could not lie.

He pushed away from the door, coming to sit beside me. "I must ask, would you give this a chance? We could wed to please my father, to obtain the scroll. Once we defeat Wugang, we would have eternity before us. I would release you from your vows anytime you wished—whether a month, a year, or a decade after. We could live as you choose, doing nothing you did not want to. I will do everything in my power to make you happy, even letting you go whenever you wish because . . . I love you."

He spoke plainly, haltingly, his voice catching a little over the words—and *this* moved me more than any practiced declaration. I could not feign ignorance of his intentions; he had implied them a hundred different ways. I had tried to avoid this, cravenly preferring to tread the surface of what we were, rather than risk drowning in its depths again.

Something else pierced me, something unexpected—a sliver of joy that he loved me still. Amid the rubble of our ruined dreams flickered the embers of something that could not be extinguished, no matter how I had tried. I had loved him, and then despised him—I believed I would hate him forever. Yet how could I truly hate someone who had saved me, whose life I had saved in turn, whom I had loved once? As I stared at his face, so grave and solemn, heat flashed through me at the recollection of our kiss—beyond desire, there was something else that frightened me, that could destroy all I had fought for if it was unleashed again.

My pulse quickened, an erratic pace. I almost despised myself for these thoughts, a betrayal of Liwei and myself. But I could not deny these feelings, nor should I be ashamed of them—for they were a part of who I was. The heart was an unfathomable thing that could not be tamed to one's will. Some might think I was toying with them. That I was selfish, or a fool? In truth, I hurt too, for with my heart cleaved I would lose either way. Breathing deeply, I reined in my emotions. I could not allow such distractions to cloud my mind or weaken my resolve . . . to make me want things I could not afford.

"I will not." I ignored the pang in my chest. "We have no future together."

He stiffened. "Because of Liwei?"

I shook my head. "Because regardless of my feelings—I could never trust you again, not in the way that matters."

"You are unforgiving, Xingyin." A trace of sadness threaded his tone.

I lifted my head. "There are worse things to be."

The light in his gaze dwindled, like the fading of stars come dawn. "Thank you for your honesty."

"I thank you too." A sudden tightness pressed around me, a hollow gaping within. A door shut, a path untrodden. A future unlived.

"What do we do now?" I asked. "How do we persuade your father to give us the scroll?"

"My father expects a wedding, so we will have to give him one." His smile did not reach his eyes. "Try not to look so distraught at the prospect of marrying me, Xingyin. A wedding need not mean a marriage."

THIS TIME, THERE WAS no barrier upon my window, no guards outside my door. After Wenzhi had gone, I left to meet Liwei in the Golden Desert. The sky glittered with sparks of white flame, starlight casting their radiance upon the sands—yet even they could not dispel the void left by the moon's absence. As we stood there, a warm breeze wound between the dunes, tinged with a rich sweetness.

"A wedding?" Liwei repeated stonily, his pupils darker than the night. His expression had grown thunderous after hearing the Cloud Wall king's demand.

"He will not relent. This is the only way to get King Wenming's help," I explained.

He searched my face. "Is this what you want, Xingyin?"

"How can you think that?" I countered. "The last thing I need is some devious monarch dictating my future. This is only a means to an end."

"Or is it a convenient excuse? You do not seem particularly unhappy, when you broke our own union with such ease."

His anger stung. "I tried to refuse. King Wenming was adamant. He threatened to form an alliance with Wugang, and worse."

"Don't go through with this," he said. "What if something goes wrong?"

"Wenzhi promised not to hold me to anything."

Liwei's expression hardened. "You must not believe him."

"I trust my own instincts, not him. He does not want to be forcibly wed to me either," I assured him. "Nothing will go wrong, though I will need your help."

"Anything." A faint smile formed on his lips. "It would give me great pleasure to incapacitate the groom."

"If he plays me false, I will help you." Despite my answering smile, there was little humor in my tone.

With a step, he closed the distance between us, clasping me into his arms. My eyelids drifted shut as I leaned against him, the warmth of his skin sliding through the layers of silk. Part of me wanted this moment to last forever—just the two of us, as we had been in the Courtyard of Eternal Tranquility, the fragrance of peach blossoms drifting in the air, the lightness in my heart when I awoke each day. A pure and uncomplicated joy, an undivided heart. If only I could shut out our past, our doubts and regrets. The troubles that bore down upon me, the searing heat from the Sacred Flame Feather even now burning its way through the enchantments woven around it. A constant struggle to keep it whole, to keep it from destroying me.

"Let him go," Liwei whispered into my hair. "He's not good enough for you; he never will be."

I fought the urge to wind my arms around him, to ease his hurt and mine. To let us find some joy in the little time we had. The dream of happiness was at once a strength and a terrible weakness, and I dared not succumb while the future was so bleak. I would make no promises I could not keep.

As I drew away from him, his eyes shadowed with pain. Hurt wrenched me within, twisting and sharp—yet I forced myself to walk away, even as I sensed his gaze upon my back. I did not turn, no matter how much I yearned to.

The wind howled mercilessly against my face as I closed my eyes, letting the tears slide down my cheeks. I did not need to conceal them anymore, for no one could see them. Despite the heat of the Golden Desert, a shiver coursed through my flesh. For a life without love was a night without stars, and only the darkness awaited me now.

31

THREE DAYS SLIPPED BY LIKE three hours, consumed by elaborate plans and preparations. I played little part in them—nodding when I was asked about the embroidery on my gown, the jewels on my headdress, or the food that would be served at the banquet. A most agreeable bride, a most indifferent one. All the while my mind churned incessantly with thoughts of what lay ahead, of the devastation that awaited us should we fail.

The day of the wedding dawned pale and gray. There was no joy in me, just a sinking foreboding like the moment before the dark clouds break, when you stumble and know you will fall. I stared at my reflection in the golden surface of the mirror. The heavy brocade gown was a vivid red, the color of joy and luck—*and blood*, my vigilant mind whispered. Magnificent phoenixes in gold and turquoise, and peonies with jade-green leaves were embroidered upon the cloth. An exquisite headdress crafted with coral flowers was fitted onto my hair, strands of pearls falling to my shoulders. Crescent-shaped brows arched over my eyes, plucked by a diligent attendant who cared little for my grimaces, while my lips and nails were painted a glossy scarlet. A part of me wanted to laugh at the futility of these efforts, but I merely clenched my jaws with frustration. None of this would help us stop Wugang. What use was soaking in a rose-petal bath or combing my hair with camellia oil until it gleamed like a river of ink? This was my wedding, but I was no bride.

An attendant arranged a red square of satin over my head-dress, draping it over my face. For a moment I could not breathe, stifled by the veil, the weight of the ceremonial robes hanging from my shoulders and the gold upon my head. All I glimpsed was a crack of the ground through where the cloth gaped—as an attendant took my arm, guiding me from the room.

Four bearers carried my palanquin, its latticed windows covered by thick cloth. Lifting the veil, I peeked through the curtain to find a grand pavilion with malachite pillars rising from the violet clouds. Sunlight struck its arched roof, glittering across its tiles. As my gaze shifted to the crowd of guests within, my insides twisted into knots. I fell back against the cushioned seat, my hands clasped in my lap as I sifted carefully through the mingled auras. Finally, I sensed his warmth—Liwei, in the skies above, out of sight. Some of the tautness within me eased, even as my mind wandered to all the things that might go wrong: What if we failed in our pretense? What if Wenzhi and I wound up truly wed? Would he honor his vow to release me? If this was a trick, another of his schemes, I might really kill him this time.

The palanquin lurched to a halt, the back of my head knocking the wooden panel behind. I hastily rearranged the cloth over my face, sensing the forceful approach of Wenzhi's aura. The curtain rustled, then parted, as Wenzhi reached in to help me out. Gold dragons were embroidered over his crimson brocade sleeve, the accompaniment to the phoenixes on mine. A tremor ran through me, my heart pounding so hard I thought it might burst. Drawing a deep breath, I placed my hand into his and stepped from the palanquin.

We walked toward the pavilion at a measured pace, the cloying fragrance of incense and flowers almost stifling me. My beaded slippers crushed the petals strewn thickly across the walkway—a lush carpet of azaleas, camellias, peonies. As a breeze teased at my veil, I suppressed the urge to rip it away. Why did brides have to be covered in this manner? Was it so they would not flee at the sight of their grooms?

Before the altar, Wenzhi halted, lowering himself to his knees. I sank down beside him upon the flat brocade cushion, my pulse racing. Three unlit sticks of incense were pushed into my palm. Three bows were all it would take to seal us into an eternal union. A hiss pierced the silence, heat grazing my hand as the incense caught fire—wisps of fragrant smoke drifting in the air. Together, Wenzhi and I pressed the incense sticks into the brass brazier.

"The ceremony will begin," a voice intoned formally, likely a high-ranking official or respected elder in the Cloud Wall. Whoever he was, I hoped Wenzhi had bribed him well.

"The first bow to Heaven and Earth," the marriage official cried out.

As I folded over, the weight of my headdress dipped precariously forward. As I quickly raised myself, the official continued, "The second bow to the parents and ancestors."

As we turned to King Wenming, I was glad for the veil to hide my strained expression as we bowed. I had made excuses for my own parents' absence, for I would give the king no more weapons against me.

The official cleared his throat. "The final bow to each other," he called out, with the barest quiver in his voice.

This was the act that would bind us together for eternity. I should have positioned myself to face Wenzhi, but something in me refused to move as though I had been transformed to stone.

As the guests began to murmur at the delay, Wenzhi placed his hand over mine, his thumb brushing my palm.

"Trust me," he whispered from under his breath.

I did not. At least, not wholly. Yet something in the intensity of his tone jolted me into movement, giving me the strength to turn toward him. This was not the time to waver. Through the veil, I made out the hem of his scarlet robe, the gleaming embroidery sewn on the cloth. His aura, so close to me, flared fierce and cool, steady and strong. As sweat slicked my hands, I fought the urge to wipe them on the priceless brocade of my skirt. I was trembling as befitted the image of a docile bride, as I bent my neck—

A gale burst through the pavilion, rustling silk and satin, the scents of azaleas and camellias springing into the air as the carpet of petals was swept high. Gasps broke out from the guests—some delighted, others surprised and irate. As my veil flared up, I caught a glimpse of the petals that rained down like a fragrant storm, brushing my bared skin with a feathery softness. One of the king's consorts swept a fan before his face to shield him, which he pushed aside with an impatient wave. And then Wenzhi was already lifting his head as he rose with deliberate emphasis—while I let my veil fall back into place and straightened as though I was rising from a bow that I had not made.

The rite was unfinished, the ritual meaningless. We were not wed.

I steeled myself for cries of outrage, for a sharp command to complete the ceremony. Yet there was none. Somehow, it had worked, Liwei's enchantment having bought us a precious moment of deception.

"The three bows are performed, the ceremony is complete.

May the couple find everlasting happiness together," the official called out eagerly. "Raise the veil."

The satin covering was pulled gently from my face. I blinked against the sudden brightness, my eyes meeting Wenzhi's, the pale hue of sunlight in winter.

An exuberant cheer broke out from the guests. The smile that lit my face was unfeigned, my fingers threaded through Wenzhi's in a hollow pretense of a harmonious couple. Wenzhi led me toward the king, for once not surrounded by his guards, his consorts seated alongside him. Prince Wenshuang was absent, I was relieved to find—perhaps in a pique from our last confrontation.

The king's gaze speared me. For a moment I feared he had seen through our ruse, but then he nodded to an attendant, who hurried to us holding out a tray with a gilded porcelain tea set emblazoned with the symbol 囍, representing the twin joys of newlyweds embarking on their life together. In our situation, it could not have been less apt.

Kneeling on the ground, I picked up the cup and offered it to the king with both hands as tradition dictated. He accepted it, bringing it to his lips though he did not drink. I waited for him to reach for the bridal gift as was customary—typically a piece of jewelry or something precious, except the only thing I wanted was what had been promised. Yet the scroll did not appear, nor did he speak, merely staring at me over the rim of his cup.

"Father." I faltered over the word. "The ceremony is complete. May I have the scroll?"

The surrounding guests exchanged pointed looks of disapproval. They thought me ill bred. Mercenary. Unheard-of, for a bride to demand her gift, except what did I care for such courtesies when I had been coerced into this farce?

A deep chuckle rolled from the king's throat. His eyes gleamed like he had gotten the better of me. "Why the rush, my dear daughter-in-law? There is still the banquet and then, the consummation. After that, I will perform the Divine Mirror Scroll on you whenever you wish."

I lurched upright, a protest rising to my lips. Before I could speak, a sharp whistling sliced the air, hurtling past me to plunge into King Wenming. His body jerked violently, his eyes rounding in horror at the sight of the spear thrust clear through his chest, its pointed tip wet with blood.

32

SHOCK RIPPED THROUGH ME, JAGGED and sharp. My gaze flew to Wenzhi, his face twisted with horror. Calling for the guards, he leapt to his feet, grabbing a sword from a nearby soldier as he raced in the direction of where the spear had been flung.

King Wenming's hands flew up to clutch his wound, groping at the wooden shaft and tearing it from his body. It slid out with a sucking sound, the spear tip falling away, dissolving into a grayish, frothing liquid that seeped into his blood. The shaft fell from his hand, his fingers splayed limp. Around him, his consorts fluttered like frantic butterflies. Only the Noble Consort—Wenzhi's mother—had the presence of mind to try to seal his wound, her magic pouring from her palms into his body. Yet his blood continued to spill from the gash, tinted with a dark sheen as though an ink-laden brush had been run through his veins.

King Wenming snarled, a bestial sound, his aura thickening with murderous intent. "Treachery," he panted, between stuttering breaths. "You . . . and your accomplices." As he pointed a trembling finger at me, a flash of violet light streaked from it, striking my temple.

Pain shot through me like a hundred needles stabbing my head in a merciless rhythm. I fell to my knees, ripping off my headdress, tearing at my hair—every nerve in my body afire, broken gasps tumbling from my mouth. Grasping wildly at my power, I flung up a shield to protect myself, wrenching away his tethers on my mind—just as I had seen Wenzhi do before. The king collapsed onto the ground, convulsing, his consorts weeping openly as they clustered around him.

The agony dispersed into merciful nothingness, though I could not stop shaking, the echoes of its torment reverberating through me. I drew a ragged breath and then another, until my muscles loosened, my strength flowing back to my limbs. A thought jarred me, that I should not have been able to throw off the king's attack so easily. I had been clasped in its throes before, suffered his unyielding power . . . which meant the king was gravely weakened.

As someone shouted for the healers, a chilling laugh rose above the chaos. Prince Wenshuang. When had he arrived?

"It's too late. The spear is charmed to drain his energy." Prince Wenshuang spoke in a bored tone as he stared at his father, spasming in agony.

"You don't have that kind of power." Wenzhi stalked back into the pavilion, his body taut with rage.

A feral smile stretched across Prince Wenshuang's face. "I am capable of far more than you can imagine."

"Why Wenshuang?" the king gasped as he struggled to raise himself onto an elbow.

"Father," he spat, each syllable throttled with rage—all semblance of indifference gone. "If I should even call you that after you shamed me before all. Stripping me of my position, replacing me with my half-brother. He is of common stock, while my mother is the Virtuous Consort of the first rank!"

A high-pitched wail raked the silence. The Virtuous Consort did not seem to approve of her son's actions.

"This is contemptible, even for you. How dare you do such a thing?" Wenzhi's knuckles were white around his sword.

Prince Wenshuang threw his head back and laughed. "Oh, I would dare much more, Brother. Across the generations, many a long-lived king has been hastened to his death by an impatient heir. The one who sits on the throne dictates the past and shapes the future, and I will no longer stand on the sidelines."

"You forget one thing. *You* are no longer the heir." Wenzhi's tone was calmer, though his eyes were shards of ice.

Prince Wenshuang flicked his hand in a dismissive gesture. "A small matter, which will be swiftly remedied."

"Challenge me if you dare, fight me without hiding behind your soldiers. Show them who is fit to rule. Otherwise, who will support you? Who will respect you? A son without honor, who murdered his father. Who cannot even wield his own blade."

Wenzhi's words were carefully chosen to stir his brother to rashness. For the days were long past that Prince Wenshuang could have bested him, and outnumbered as we were, single combat was our best chance of remaining alive.

The guests murmured, the braver ones nodding in agreement. Still, Prince Wenshuang displayed not a glimmer of concern. "Don't play your tricks on me; I've seen them all before. I don't need to prove myself to you or anyone. Those who do not obey do so at their own peril. Since Father rejected the Celestial Emperor's offer, he was pleased to accept mine." His mouth curled into a smirk. "My throne for the Moon Goddess. More than a fair exchange. The emperor even gave me this." He kicked the bloodied spear shaft to the side.

"You have grossly miscalculated," I told him with a smile. "My mother is not here."

"*You* are here, her beloved daughter. She will come. I just have to wait."

Guards encircled us, my spirits sinking to find their weapons pointed our way. Grasping my power, I held it at the ready, magic flickering at my fingertips.

"My parents have returned to the Mortal Realm. They will not come here again. What do you think Wugang will do to you for failing to honor your promise?" Never had a lie brought me more satisfaction as rage mottled Prince Wenshuang's face.

"If that is true," he ground out, "there is no reason to keep you alive after all."

Prince Wenshuang lunged at me, his sword thrust forward, scarlet flames rippling across its surface. Cursing my heavy garments, I darted aside, casting a shield over myself. He was indeed a coward, attacking one who was weaponless. Wenzhi called to me as he grabbed a sword from a nearby soldier, tossing it to me from across the pavilion. Catching it deftly, I tore its scabbard away, swinging around to catch Prince Wenshuang's blow.

His strikes rained down with brute force, though he lacked the innate grace of the finest swordsmen. I caught each hit, flinging it back—his attacks growing more vicious. A struggle to match him on physical strength alone as I was driven back, out of the pavilion, upon the bed of violet clouds. As his next blow crashed down, I swerved out of reach, summoning a burst of wind that slammed him back into a pillar.

He sprang up, his expression murderous as he flung his hand out, a fistful of fiery daggers hurtling toward me. I dropped low just as a furious shout rang out from the pavilion. Wenzhi, fighting his way to me through Prince Wenshuang's guards. With a kick he sent one sprawling, thrusting his sword through another. Yet more soldiers swarmed around him until I could no longer see him in their midst. My heart plummeted. As I started forward, a searing heat lashed my back. I swallowed a cry as I spun to face Prince Wenshuang, my magic rippling forth to quench his flames.

As his energy sparked again from his fingers, coils of air sprang from my palm, flinging him onto his back. A moment's reprieve before he rolled to his feet, stalking toward me once more. His sword swung down, narrowly missing my face as I dipped back. As he stumbled, I leapt forward, my foot connecting with his gut. A furious gasp choked from his throat as my glittering energy wound around his sword, yanking it from his grip.

Six of his soldiers rushed toward me, bolts of ice and flame plunging my way. As I grasped my powers, a translucent arrow hurtled past me, sinking into one of my pursuers with a squelch. I glanced at the soldier rolling on the ground, clutching at the icy shaft speckled with blood. My father's arrow.

More shouts rang out as Liwei and my father descended from the skies, their cloud soaring toward me. My father's arm moved so swiftly it was a blur, each arrow striking its mark with unerring accuracy, while bolts of fire streaked from Liwei's palms, scorching the soldiers. Several scrambled to flee, the braver ones erecting shields and holding their ground.

As their cloud swooped down before me, my father stretched out his hand. "Come, Xingyin! We must go!"

I hesitated. One step, and we would be free of this wretched place—my father, mother, Liwei, and me. Yet I could not move; I did not want to. If we left . . . Wenzhi would die. "I can't leave him here surrounded by enemies."

Liwei's face was expressionless as he sprang from the cloud, coming to stand beside me. "Then I will fight with you."

"Father, you must stay on the cloud, out of reach," I urged him. "It's too dangerous without your magic; we might not be able to protect you." I added the last to force his hand. My father was not one to remain on the sidelines of a battle.

He nodded grimly. "I will cover you from here." Raising his silver bow, another arrow gleamed between his fingers.

Guests had fled the pavilion, running across the clouds. Shouts rang out, confused and afraid. My father's arrows plunged forth in swift succession, our bolts of magic streaking through the air, crashing against the soldier's shields as Liwei and I fought our way back into the pavilion. At last I saw him, the tall figure clad in crimson, his robes a match to mine.

Wenzhi and his brother circled each other. Sweat glistened on their faces, light streaming from their palms into their swords. Prince Wenshuang swung his weapon in a wide arc, slashing at his brother's head—Wenzhi driving his blade up to catch the blow. They struggled, metal scraping, faces taut with strain. Wenzhi's hands whitened around the hilt, ice crystals rippling along the blade as he pressed forward, breaking his brother's hold—Prince Wenshuang staggering back. Catching his balance, Prince Wenshuang hurled streaks of crimson flame toward Wenzhi, who summoned waves of water to engulf it. Their magic arced through the air, dazzling and dangerous, their blades crashing in a frenzied rhythm until my insides recoiled at the sight. While Wenzhi fought with his usual grace and skill, he held back each blow, tempering his strikes . . . unwilling to kill.

As more of Prince Wenshuang's soldiers advanced toward Wenzhi, I channeled my magic to summon a gale, hurling them back. Beside me, Liwei unleashed waves of flame, keeping the rest at bay. This fight would be a fair one, the victory clean.

Fire and ice scattered in a hellish storm. The combatants were tiring, their skin glistening with sweat and blood. Wenzhi raised his sword high, only to drop it low at the last moment, spinning around to drive it through Prince Wenshuang's gut. Blood spurted out in a crimson stream. Prince Wenshuang cried out, his sword falling from his hand—as Wenzhi's arm swung down again, pressing the edge of his blade against his brother's neck.

Triumph soared through my veins, tempered by a churning unease. Victories tainted by blood were not easy ones to relish.

"Finish it," Prince Wenshuang snarled, his eyes squeezed with loathing.

I willed Wenzhi to lift the blade, to slice the tender veins of his brother's throat, to stab the core of his lifeforce. His half-brother had poisoned his father, tormented Wenzhi, plotted against him at every turn, even tried to slay him in cold blood. Prince Wenshuang had earned his death ten times over. Still, Wenzhi said nothing, even as his hand remained steady and his gaze, hard.

"I will not kill you. In our father's name, I exile you for eternity. You will take nothing with you, you will say no farewells. Leave now, and never return."

I did not think he would show mercy to his brother. I had thought, hoped—he would kill him as just vengeance. After today none would fault him. It was what Wenzhi had taught me himself, long ago: *To show mercy in a battle was to leave your back unguarded.* A lesson I wished he had remembered today. Yet even as my heart sank, a part of me already fearing this mercy might be his undoing—an undeniable warmth suffused me.

As a shattered gasp broke from the king, Wenzhi's face creased with worry. He turned, starting toward his father—a mistake, my instincts screamed—as Prince Wenshuang sprang at him, swift as a striking serpent, a drawn dagger glinting in his grasp. The metal gleamed with an unnatural brightness, coated in a shining liquid—some malevolent magic or venom. My mind went blank, my arm drawing back as I hurled my sword at him. It sliced through the air, plunging into the base of Prince Wenshuang's skull. His eyes went wide, a wet gasp sucked into his mouth, his body jerking violently before crumpling onto the floor. As his blood pooled, the metallic scent of salt and earth entwined with the lingering sweetness of flower petals crushed beneath our feet.

Adornments for a wedding, now gracing death.

A scream rang out, racked with anguish. The Virtuous Consort ran to Prince Wenshuang, falling down to cradle him in her arms, raw sobs choked from her throat. His gaze slid to me, glazed with disbelief, the thrum of his aura fading away. His mother's desperate cries stabbed me. I was trembling, cut by remorse—yet Prince Wenshuang had been a monster. I would waste no tears on him.

A stunned silence settled over the pavilion. Most of the guests had fled, leaving the remaining soldiers and the weeping consorts amid the bodies of the fallen.

King Wenming coughed, a withered, hacking sound. Wenzhi fell to his knees on the ground beside him, his lips moving in a question I could not hear, though the healers' sorrowful shakes of their heads were an answer itself.

The king clutched Wenzhi's hand, pressing it to his chest. His arms trembled, though his words rang clear. "My true and faithful son," he rasped. "My heir and . . . the king."

He released Wenzhi then as he cupped his hands, engulfed by a sudden glow. An imperial seal of purple jade appeared within his palms. Then an onyx ring, a bottle carved of jasper, and finally— the scrolls, slender pieces of golden bamboo rolled together. The treasures the king had guarded with his body, his very life.

Wenzhi's eyes were bright with unshed tears as he grasped his father's shoulders, leaning closer to him. Their relationship was neither tender nor loving, but the bond of parent and child was eternal—even when buried beneath mistrust and resentment. The king's eyes were wet as his gaze flicked toward Prince Wenshuang's body, and I sensed it was with grief rather than rage.

What whispered words Wenzhi and his father exchanged, I did not hear—still, I ached for him. A father and brother lost in a day. No matter how they had treated him in life, sorrow was inevitable. There would be no chance to repair that which had been broken, of speaking the words that might have healed the hurt. Death was the final parting.

As a shadow fell over me, I looked up to find Liwei. His hand pressed my shoulder in silent comfort, a welcome relief. As agonized shrieks erupted from the king's consorts, Wenzhi lifted his head, meeting my gaze across the pavilion, a storm swirling in his expression. Grief warring with gratitude, shock entwined with knowing.

He knew this had been no accident, that my aim had been true. Prince Wenshuang's death was on my conscience. *This* I had done for myself, and for Wenzhi. Prince Wenshuang was a true demon; he would never have stopped until one of them lay dead. He would have threatened me, too, for his hate went deep. And so I had taken from Wenzhi the burden of slaying his own kin.

He had not lied to me that day, so many years ago, in Xiangliu's cavern. Killing did get easier.

33

I STOOD BY THE MALACHITE PAVILION, surrounded by violet clouds. How different it appeared, devoid of the crowds—the petals swept away, the bloodstains scrubbed from the stone floor. My hair swung across my back in a loose tail when just a few days ago it had been coiled into a headdress of coral and gold. I had knelt before the altar to be married, and since then, the Cloud Wall had buried a king and crowned a new one. Wenzhi had moved with ruthless swiftness, elevating those loyal to him and removing those he mistrusted. His mother, the Noble Consort, was raised to the rank of Dowager Queen—an unassailable position of authority, second only to his. While Captain Mengqi, whom I had escaped from in the past, was now the general who led the army. I had not attended either funeral or coronation. My existence was best forgotten, for I was an ill omen; a bride drenched in blood.

How they must have sighed with relief that I was not their queen. Our farce of a marriage had been officially annulled before the court. No questions had been asked, for the deference accorded to a king was different from that to an heir. A prince could be questioned, plotted against, supplanted—while a king was to be obeyed.

There was no time to observe the customary mourning period.

News had reached us that Wugang's forces were advancing upon the Cloud Wall, gathering along the border. How strange the turns life could take—when I was last in this place, the Celestials had been my savior and now . . . they were our promised doom.

Had Wugang heard of the recent shift in power here? Unlikely, as Wenzhi had sealed the palace to prevent news from slipping out. Or was Wugang eager to claim the prize Prince Wenshuang had promised him? The keys to infinite power would be an irresistible temptation. The only thing certain was that the kingdoms teetered on the brink of war as precariously as a coin rolling on its edge.

Sensing the presence of other immortals, I turned to find Liwei coming toward me, along with my parents. My mother and Shuxiao had arrived just before Wugang's forces closed in on the Cloud Wall. A relief to be reunited, yet I might have been more at ease with them away—for this had become the most dangerous place in the Immortal Realm.

"Wenzhi has studied the Divine Mirror Scroll. He will cast it when I am ready," I told them without preamble. "With Wugang so near, we must move quickly." A chill glazed my skin, yet there was nothing to be gained from dreading the inevitable—the best I could do was ready myself for it.

I recalled Wenzhi's frown when he had inspected the scroll, holding the slender bamboo strips up to the light. He did not like this plan any more than I did, but if there was another way, none of us had thought of it. "You must be careful," he had reminded me. "While the scroll will confer your mother's attributes upon you, you must heed your actions and words. You must trick Wugang's mind, as well as his eyes and ears."

My mother cleared her throat, her fingers digging into her

skirt. "I can do this, if you tell me how. Don't risk yourself when it is me he wants."

"No, Mother," I said gently. "Without magic, you can't bear the Sacred Flame Feather, you can't unleash it. Wugang will use your blood to harvest the laurel seeds—an endless cycle, as new ones will sprout. Even if the entire realm was to unite against him then, it would be too late."

"What about you? What if you fail?" my father pressed. "Wugang will show you no mercy."

"Then at least Wugang won't get the laurel seeds." My voice faltered, but I leashed my terror before it devoured my fragile resolve.

My mother placed her hand on mine. "We could leave this place, return to the Mortal Realm. Our real home. We do not have to stay here."

My mind drifted to the indulgence of a dream, a life without the cares of discovery, capture, or danger. Without the unwelcome fate of the world crashing upon my shoulders—not an honor but a burden. There would be no shame in running away, for what did I owe the Immortal Realm?

I shoved aside these dangerous wants. A temptation to leave such weighty matters in the hands of greater people. Yet those were the fantasies of someone with no ties to the world. It was *my* loved ones whom Wugang hunted, whom he had hurt . . . and the Immortal Realm had become our home.

I did not want to do this, yet who else could? It was not arrogance or pride that drove me, but the irrefutable fact that I alone had the best chance of deceiving Wugang, of getting the feather close enough to the laurel, of destroying it. If I did nothing, I would lose everything, and all whom I loved would die.

Was this how my father had felt the day he set out to face the sunbirds? I had always believed greatness ran through his veins, that he was brave and wise, just as a hero should be. He had been lauded for his courage, but surely he must have been a little afraid—of death, of never returning to his family? Yet no one else could have wielded that bow, no other marksman could have brought down the sunbirds. If he had not gone, the Mortal Realm would have been destroyed, along with my mother and me.

Perhaps, at its core, heroism was a less pretty tale. Words like *honor* and *valor*, gilded over necessity and the harsh truth—that there was no choice.

"I must do this." I searched my father's face, hoping for a nod, any sign of assurance. Perhaps it was what most children sought, regardless of their age, this precious validation only their parents could bestow.

My father's forehead creased as it did when he was deep in thought. How I relished learning his moods and gestures, gathering these threads and weaving them into a pattern that took shape until he was more than a name in a book, a silhouette in my dreams. And how I resented having this chance snatched from me after we were finally reunited.

"Daughter," my father said, "I will do it. The Divine Mirror Scroll would work on me too."

I shook my head. "It will take more than physical resemblance to convince Wugang. You know Mother as your wife, the mortal. I know her as the Moon Goddess. Wugang won't be easily fooled, but I can convince him. Is that not what matters in times as these? Do you not assign soldiers to the tasks they are best equipped for?"

"Wugang will kill you," my mother cried out.

"Not if I kill him first." I lifted my head. "I am not going to die; I am going to *end* this."

"How will you keep Wugang from sensing the Sacred Flame Feather?" Liwei asked.

My smile was bright, my voice infused with false confidence. "The same enchantment that allows me to bear it."

"It won't work," Liwei said flatly. "I sense the feather on you now."

He was right. Even bound by these enchantments, heat radiated from the feather in waves, thrashing against its shield. "I will keep it in here." I tapped my temple lightly as though it were a simple matter.

"*Within* your lifeforce? Just like how King Wenming kept his artifacts?" Liwei's tone was incredulous. "One slip, and the feather will incinerate you."

"There will be no slip." I had become a fine actress; my gaze unwavering, my tone calm. For if I quailed, if I showed the slightest flicker of unease, they would redouble their efforts to stop me. And I did not know if I had the will to withstand it.

Finally, he relented. "I will be close by. If you are in danger, I will come to you." His fingers strayed toward the Sky Drop Tassel by his waist, brushing the clear stone.

My mother tugged at my father's sleeve. "Houyi, come. Let's go."

"I have more to say—"

"It can wait." Her voice was laden with meaning as she turned away, my father following her.

Liwei stared after them. "After all these years, they finally found their way back to each other. A great love story, as the mortals might say."

"Yes," I agreed. "Though my parents would have preferred the joy without the suffering."

"No love is perfect."

"Only in fairy tales," I conceded. "And if it were so for my parents, no one would know their names."

"Is that a fair price?" he asked.

"Not to me," I said pensively. "Fame is how the world sees you, what they imagine of your life. A fleeting thing, as capricious as smoke, and as easily reshaped through malice."

Liwei's face darkened—did he recall how swiftly he had been maligned and abandoned by his court? Nor could I forget how readily others had believed the rumors of me.

"True happiness springs from within, a contentment with oneself. And while it may be humbler and quieter, there is nothing more precious and lasting," I added.

"We could have that," he said gently. "We could be happy again, if you would let us."

I drank in the sight of him: the sculpted planes of his face, the way the light fell upon his eyes, glittering over their dark surface. As he moved toward me, his blue robe swirled in the breeze, the glossy tail of his hair swinging behind him. He looked just as he did when we first met by the river. So much had changed since then, and yet he was still the young man brimming with compassion, as I was the girl with fire in her heart. Although this time, the blaze might consume me.

I dropped my gaze, folding away these wistful recollections. "Let us get through today before we think of tomorrow. We must keep our minds on what lies ahead."

His hand touched my chin, lifting my face to his. "I wish I could tell you not to do this."

"I am glad that you do not."

Wordlessly, I rested my head upon his chest, sliding my arms around him, stealing his warmth for a moment of comfort. As he clasped me tighter, my fingers glided lower to his waist, brushing the smooth orb of the Sky Drop Tassel. A faint flicker of my power, almost imperceptible, and my energy was leeched from the stone—our link severed. As I pulled away, breaking the embrace, regret yanked at my heart until I thought it would break.

"I don't want to lose you," he confessed in a low voice. "I am sick with fear."

There was so much more I wanted to say to him—tender assurances, words of promise, yet they stuck in my throat. For in truth . . . I was sick with fear too.

SLEEP ELUDED ME THAT night. From the deep stillness it was far from midnight, closer to the edge of dawn. Rising, I crossed the room to throw the windows open. As the cool air rushed in, the rustling of unfamiliar trees teased my ears, my skin prickling with unease. I felt like a child again, afraid of the monsters lurking in the shadows. Even then, I had wanted to drag them out into the open, to look them full in the face—as nothing could have been more terrifying than the nightmares in my mind.

Not this time.

Someone knocked softly upon my door, unexpected at this hour. Light streaked from my palm, illuminating a lantern, as I hastily pulled on a yellow robe and tied a sash around my waist. My hair, unbound, fell over my shoulders.

"Come in." I grabbed my bow from the table, more a force of habit than from expecting any real danger.

The doors slid open, Wenzhi standing in the entrance. I lowered the bow at once.

"Are you sure, Xingyin?" He asked gravely. "Not too long ago, you wanted to shoot me."

"Not too long ago, you deserved it and worse."

"What about now?"

That inflection in his tone, the light in his gaze stirred something in me. "Why are you here, Wenzhi? Don't you have other things to do this late at night—petitions to read, court officials to terrify? Sleep, perhaps?"

Concubines to bed. The unwelcome thought seared, and I discarded it at once.

"Undoubtedly," he agreed, leaning against the doorframe. "There are many other places I *should* be, which would be far more welcoming than your cold reception."

"Perhaps you should seek them out," I said icily, closing the door, but his hand shot out to grip the wooden panel.

Only now did I notice his attire, unused to seeing him in such finery. His moss-green brocade robe was embroidered with dragons that reared up amid swirls of silken mist, a belt of silver links fastened around his waist. A crown rested on his head—different from his father's—a carved gold headpiece set with an emerald.

"I could not sleep either," he confessed. "Would you come with me?"

I hesitated. "It's late."

"It's not far," he assured me.

As I nodded, moving away from the entrance, he strode into my room toward the windows. A cloud was already hovering there, as though he had known I would agree.

"Why not through the door?" I asked.

His nose wrinkled. "I'm not my father. I do not want or need a guard tailing me at all times."

And there were few threats he could not handle on his own.

He climbed through the window, dropping onto the cloud. I did not take the hand he offered, grasping the wooden frame as I slipped out. The cloud soared high, circling the palace, the wind gliding through my hair. When we came to a halt, I turned to him, my eyebrows arched. "The roof?"

"I know your fondness for them," he said lightly.

Something tightened in my chest. He meant the times I had found solace upon my rooftop in the Jade Palace, as I stared into the sky longing for home. And yet it was also where we had pledged ourselves to each other, and where I had almost shot him to make my escape. I shrugged aside the past, both the good and the bad—for with tomorrow so uncertain, I would yield them no place tonight.

The tiles here were carved of iridescent stone that gleamed like they had been dipped into a rainbow. Yet the true beauty of this place lay in the endless horizon encircling it. Glowing lanterns floated through the air, borne on some enchanted breeze. The arched roofs of the buildings below shone like jewels. And beyond the bank of violet-gray clouds curved the Golden Desert, aglitter as stardust.

The wind teased at Wenzhi's hair, draping long strands across his face. "Thank you for coming with me. This is where I came whenever I wanted to be alone. I've wanted to bring you here for a long time, even before I knew what it meant."

He lowered himself upon the tiles, resting an arm upon a raised knee. While his expression had always been aloof and unreadable, there was a new gravity set into his features.

"What is troubling you?" I asked.

"I have wanted to be king ever since my brother began tormenting me and those I cared for. Each insult, every injury drove me to seek my father's favor, through any means necessary."

He spoke so rarely of his past—once before, when I had first learned of his treachery. I had not wanted to hear him then; nothing could have excused his actions. This time, I listened without acrimony or anger—for the first time in a long while, without seeking lies in each word.

"My father was neither doting nor kind, but he was more ambitious than cruel—always pushing us to better ourselves. Partly because he remembered what it was like when we were weak and downtrodden, the outcasts of the Immortal Realm." Shadows darkened his eyes. "And now, he is dead and I wear the crown. There is no triumph in this. Even though it might have been inevitable, I never wanted to wade through my family's blood for the throne."

"Nothing can change that," I said quietly. "You will be a good king." These were no empty words of solace. The Celestial soldiers had revered, respected, and loved him. A rare combination that few rulers could attain.

He paused. "There is another reason I came. Somehow, news got out about my brother's and father's deaths. Wugang has demanded that we surrender your mother. If we comply, he will leave us in peace. If not—he has threatened swift retaliation."

"What will you do?" What *could* he do? A monarch's responsibility was to their kingdom. Wenzhi had always made clear where his priorities lay, and what was I to him? Not even a false bride anymore.

"My advisors want to concede. Before, Wugang's eyes were turned elsewhere. He would not have attacked us while more attractive prospects lay before him for the taking, while he believed we might ally with him. But that has changed."

"Will you surrender us?" I did not think he meant to betray us—but that he could not harbor us, that we could no longer count on his aid.

"It is what my father would have done. We are unprepared. An attack now would be catastrophic. We should buy time so we can stand against him another day."

A hollow gaped in my chest, though I should not have expected more. But I would try to reason with him as I would have done with another. "You were never one for a quick victory at the expense of the greater scheme. Yielding to Wugang is not the answer."

"You mistake my meaning," he said at once. "It was what I was advised to do, what my father would have done—but not what I will do. Surrendering your mother would merely offer a temporary reprieve, for it would make Wugang invincible. He will sweep through the Immortal Realm like a pestilent plague, and when it is barren, he will devour us then. He might be an ally at present, but he is undoubtedly our future foe. My father realized this too—which is why he preferred to aid us, though he would also have dealt with Wugang to further his own ends."

His gaze held mine. "Yet that is not the only reason. I confess, *you* are a strong inducement to think of another plan."

I steeled myself against letting my heart soften. "This can be an opportunity. We might be able to use this to our advantage."

He nodded reluctantly, for he had thought of this too. "I do not want this. It will be dangerous."

"Yes," I agreed. "But less so than letting Wugang rampage unhindered." Still, it was too soon. I was not ready . . . if I would ever be.

"It's the best way. I can't appear in some inexplicable coincidence; Wugang would suspect a ruse at once." I spoke quickly before terror stifled my words. "Do what they expect of you, what any cautious ruler would when faced with this threat. Surrender my mother. Except it will be me in her stead. Let Wugang think he has us where he wants us, that victory is in his grasp. It will lull him into a false sense of security and—"

"You will make him pay," Wenzhi finished my sentence for me, his expression grim. "Except Wugang will not accept our acquiescence easily. He believes that I—unlike my father or brother—would be loath to accept an alliance with him. He knows that I would never surrender the Moon Goddess willingly, for no other reason than the fact she is your mother."

I remembered what Wugang had said to us before, the knowing looks he had cast at Wenzhi and me. "This will not work if Wugang has a flicker of suspicion, if he tests my disguise. What if you refuse his terms? Have one of your courtiers offer the information to Wugang in exchange for a reward. I could allow myself to be captured, let him bring me to the laurel."

"An illusion, mirroring what he expects." He nodded. "That could work. Either way, we must prepare our forces to stand against him—in part to fit our ploy, in part for defense. I believe he is set on attacking us. Too many of his soldiers have gathered along the border for this to be a simple excursion."

He spoke the truth, yet the thought of battle turned my stomach. "That would be prudent. It would also distract Wugang and divide his forces, to keep his mind occupied so he doesn't question or examine anything too closely. He will be impatient to harvest the seeds to seal his victory, and therein lies his weakness." I frowned as another worry struck me. "How will you withstand his army? You will need allies."

"We will send word to the other kingdoms. However, we have been isolated for so long, I doubt any will heed our call."

"A common enemy turns adversaries into allies." Just as I was protecting the same soldiers I had fought against before.

Who else might we count on? The dragons were no tools of war yet could be invaluable for defense. Their support might swing the Eastern Sea to our side, though their court was deep in mourning. The Southern Sea had declared their allegiance when they attempted to capture us to win Wugang's favor. We had no contact with the Western and Northern Sea, and there was no time to cultivate relations with them. The Phoenix Kingdom had always been a firm ally of the Celestial Kingdom—yet it remained to be seen if their loyalty lay with the ruling family or the kingdom itself. If they joined Wugang, it would be a grave blow.

"I will send word to Prince Yanxi, and Liwei to his mother. Perhaps she can sway Queen Fengjin," I said.

He rose to his feet and inclined his head. "Thank you. I apologize for disturbing your rest. Let me bring you back." As his gaze met mine, a sigh slid from him. "I promised myself I would say nothing; you have made your choice. But I will never be free of you. Perhaps that is my penance."

"I do not wish that." I pushed myself up to stand beside him, ignoring the pulse of hurt within me. "We are friends, after all. Those who want the best for each other."

"Friends?" he repeated, after a moment's pause. "Yes, I would welcome your friendship. I would welcome any part of yourself that you choose to give me."

Before I could respond, he drew me into his arms—his skin, usually so cool, burning me. I did not protest, closing my eyes, inhaling the crisp scent that rolled off his skin. And when his arms loosened, there was a prickling in my eyes which I blinked away, a part of me mourning the end of something precious . . . that never truly had a chance to begin.

34

CLOUDS HUNG LOW IN THE skies from the immortals riding through the heavens. A storm beckoned on the horizon, not of wind or rain but brewed with bloodshed and betrayal, thick with ancient grudges. The Celestial Kingdom had been overthrown by one of mortal heritage, and the Cloud Wall was defending those who had cast it from its borders. The Four Seas were divided once more; old alliances broken, and new ones forged in the span of days. It was like the world had been turned over and shaken for good measure. The Immortal Realm might never go back to what it once was, and I did not realize how much I regretted this until faced with its loss.

Liwei and I soared over the Cerulean Mountains, a jagged ridge of peaks that lay to the north of the Cloud Wall and west of the desert. Sunlight gleamed across Liwei's gold armor, while I wore just a dark blue robe, with my bow slung across my back. Behind us flew Shuxiao, along with my mother and father.

Wenzhi was already here with his soldiers, working to reinforce the wards ahead of the impending confrontation. As he flew toward us, the light danced off his black armor in glints of bronze. His great sword was strapped to his side, a green cloak swirling from his shoulders.

As his cloud drew alongside ours, he inclined his head in

greeting. "We expect Wugang's forces to strike soon. Tomorrow, or the day after."

"Is there any news from the other kingdoms?" Liwei asked.

"No. Perhaps they will not come," Wenzhi replied, the corners of his mouth tightening.

In the distance, the soldiers of the Cloud Wall had gathered, casting a shadow over the pale sands beneath. Such terror they had struck in me before, and now I wished there were more of them. *Not enough*, my mind whispered. Not enough to stand against Wugang's deadly soldiers, the vast white-and-gold army that curled like a monstrous serpent along the edge of desert and cloud.

The wind strengthened, whipping my hair across my cheek. As I brushed it aside, I caught a brightness on the horizon. Soldiers in blue and silver armor, soaring toward us, led by Prince Yanxi. My chest caved at the memory of the last time I had seen him, bearing his brother's body in his arms. While Prince Yanxi's expression was somber, he greeted Liwei and me with warmth. However, he stiffened at the sight of Wenzhi.

"Your Majesty." He spoke with cool formality, and it startled me to hear Wenzhi addressed so. "The Eastern Sea does not march on behalf of the Demon Realm. I am here to avenge my brother."

Wenzhi inclined his head. "Nevertheless, we welcome your aid. We need not be friends to be allies."

Shrill cries rang out, accompanied by the swish of air. Soldiers in bronze armor flew across the skies, mounted upon magnificent phoenixes. Crimson sparks trailed in their wake, their plumage so bright as though coated in flame, with rainbows fluttering from their tails. In their midst soared the Celestial Empress—she would always be that to me, whether she had a throne or not. I almost did not recognize her, the purpose shining upon her face, devoid of her habitual malice or tension. Was this a glimpse of who she was before? Had her bitterness been born from the disillusionment of her marriage, of having her wings clipped by life in the Celestial Kingdom? I did not like her any better, but perhaps I understood her a little more.

The empress halted by our cloud, sliding off her mount with ease. "Queen Fengjin will join our fight against the villain Wugang," she announced with pride.

"We are grateful for her aid," Liwei said, adding, "as we are for yours, Mother. You must have changed her mind, for the queen did not seem inclined to support us before."

"Wugang must be stopped." She cast a scathing look at Wenzhi. "I did not do this for *you*; they do not fight for the Demons. I could not care less what happens to your wretched kingdom."

Wenzhi's eyes flashed. "Neither do I care what happens to the Celestial Kingdom, for it has already fallen."

As the empress's red lips twisted into a snarl, Liwei cleared his throat. "There is nothing to be gained by insulting each other. We are glad for reinforcements."

"Indeed." A mocking smile tugged at Wenzhi's lips. "How fortunate that while we are loathed by most of the Immortal Realm—they hate Wugang *more*."

"As they should, for Wugang is the greatest threat we have ever faced," my father said, alighting from Shuxiao's cloud to ours. His bow lay across his back like a crescent of silver. My mother followed him, her face pale and drawn.

"Are you well enough to be here?" I asked Shuxiao anxiously.

"Well enough and bored enough. Anything would be better than another week of lying down and being fed vile herbal concoctions." She shuddered, crossing her arms. "The dragons are wise and powerful, yet their medicines are foul."

"Bitter medicines are preferable to fatal wounds." I examined the armies, relieved at the sight—and yet my spirits had never been lower. How many would still stand after a battle? How many would return to their families? There would be no mercy from Wugang or his soldiers; I did not think they were capable of it.

My gaze shifted to the swath of clouds on the other side of the mountain range, those I had avoided examining too closely before. Wugang's soldiers, a forest of them, glittering like sunlight upon snow. Alongside them were the turquoise-armored troops of the Southern Sea. Queen Suihe was said to have a talent for picking the winning side, and I hoped this time her assessment was flawed. There were other soldiers too, whom I did not recognize, clad in armor of copper and of green.

"The Northern and Western Sea will fight against us," Liwei observed tersely. "They were not our allies, but this is a blow. I had hoped they would steer clear of the confrontation."

"Queen Suihe must have won their support for Wugang during the gathering of the Four Seas," I said.

"Before the battle commences, we must do one thing," Liwei said. "We need someone familiar with the Jade Palace to rescue my father, General Jianyun, and the other courtiers imprisoned by Wugang. Otherwise, they will be in grave danger; they will be used as hostages."

Shuxiao bowed. "I will go. General Jianyun has been kind to me, to all of us under his command."

"A few of our soldiers can accompany you." Wenzhi gestured to the immortal behind him, who stepped forward and bowed. As General Mengqi straightened, she cast a baleful look my way, no doubt recalling how I had duped her before.

"General Mengqi, assemble a group to head to the Jade Palace," he instructed her. "Shuxiao, previously a lieutenant of the Celestial Army, will lead them."

The general's lips tightened as she studied Shuxiao. "Your

Majesty, is she competent? I will not risk our soldiers' safety recklessly."

"She is as competent as you are," I replied with an edge in my voice. "And not so easily fooled." A petty taunt, but I would not stand by while my friends were insulted.

Shuxiao's eyes narrowed. "After this is over, you may test my competence with any weapon of your choice."

For her sake, I hoped General Mengqi would not select the bow.

"Such childishness. Do not indulge such rash impulses when the lives of my soldiers are at stake." General Mengqi's stare was forbidding, yet bright with speculation.

Shuxiao deliberately turned her back to the general. "Xing-yin, take care." Her words were laden with meaning as she glanced at my mother.

I clasped her hand. "As should you. I will see you when we return."

"Till then," she agreed. "We will share our stories over a jug of wine."

"Are you ready or do you have more farewells to make?" General Mengqi asked brusquely.

Shuxiao's lips parted in more of a grimace than a smile. "I'm beginning to regret this. Battling undead Celestials would be preferable." Shaking her head, she followed General Mengqi. They stood apart as they mounted a cloud, soaring toward the Cloud Wall soldiers.

The sun descended, a lull falling over us, riddled with gloom and a shred of relief. There would be no confrontation this evening. Battles were for mornings, which offered the shining promise of glory, the dawn of hope. The nights were for slinking back into the shadows to lick one's wounds, for stifled cries and fears, unbound . . . and those dark acts of deceit.

Wugang would come for my mother soon. With the impending battle, he would need a fresh harvest of laurel seeds to replenish his depleted forces. Dread warred with anticipation, not because I hungered for danger but because my nerves were strung taut. The heat from the Sacred Flame Feather seared through my pouch, surging against the barriers woven around it. I did not know how much longer I could sustain this drain on my power—a struggle to maintain this farce.

"Mother, we must get you someplace safe," I called out for the benefit of Wugang's spies, to whet his appetite. The Cloud Wall courtier had been dispatched to betray my mother's location to Wugang in exchange for a favored position. A lie concealed within a lie.

My mother and I flew back to the Cloud Wall palace, making our way to her room. It was elegantly furnished with mahogany furniture, the dark wood inlaid with iridescent mother-of-pearl. Bronze incense burners flanked the entrance, and I had grown accustomed to the rich scent.

She helped me into a set of her garments, draping the white silk robe over my shoulders, tying the vermilion sash around my waist, then fastening upon it a few of her jade ornaments. Finally, she coiled my hair up, securing it with gold hairpins before sliding a red peony just above my ear.

The weight in my chest sunk lower. Was it the familiarity of her gestures that caught at me? It was like I was a child again, being dressed by her. How effortless life had seemed then, akin to gliding through a lake rather than wrestling with these turbulent waters.

"Ping'er would not have wanted this." My mother's eyes were bright with unshed tears. "She would not have wanted you to risk yourself this way, not even to avenge her. She only ever wanted you to be happy and safe."

My throat closed tight. "This isn't just about vengeance; this is greater than us all. I want Wugang to pay for what he's done, but more than that—I *must* do this. He is a tyrant, a ruthless madman, who thinks nothing of sending his armies on an endless rampage of death. He has killed so many, and he will murder countless more if not stopped. What future will await us under his reign?"

I turned to look her full in the face. "I used to think the outside world did not matter, as long as they left us untouched. I prided myself on not being unduly burdened by the inconveniences of honor or ambition, caring only about my home, my family and loved ones. I was wrong." My voice broke then. "Trouble reached us, no matter how we tried to keep clear of it. Our home was taken. We were hunted. We lost those we loved."

Evil must be struck at its roots. The Long Dragon's words echoed through my mind.

My mother pressed her palm to my cheek and I leaned against it. She did not speak, the love shining in her face thawing a little of the ice in my heart.

A knock on the door broke the tender moment. As my father, Liwei, and Wenzhi entered, I rose to my feet and grasped the Jade Dragon Bow. It tingled with a frenetic energy, as though sensing my intent. Had it hoped for this all along? Had I merely been its custodian? It did not matter. This was something I should have yielded before, except I had been too selfish—relieved even, when my father had refused it the first time. It hurt to give it up, but I did not need it where I was going, and I was glad to have finally found its true owner.

"Father, this is yours." I bowed, raising my hands to offer him the bow.

He pushed it aside. "Keep it, Xingyin. I do not need it."

"The Jade Dragon Bow belongs to you," I repeated. "You

must take it. Sky-fire can bring down Wugang's soldiers. Use it to keep Mother and you safe. Be careful not to exhaust yourself." I stopped then, feeling a little foolish like I was trying to teach a fish how to swim. This weapon was an extension of his arm.

He made no move to take it, but perseverance was a trait we both shared. Taking his hand, I pried his fingers apart to press the bow into his grip. The jade glittered, light rippling through the frame across our joined hands—just as when I had first touched it—my skin flushing cold, then hot. The carved dragon writhed and shuddered, before stilling once more.

And then, it was gone—that pull I had always sensed from the bow. I let go, leaving it in my father's grasp. An ache pierced me, as though I had bid a dear friend farewell; I did not think I would miss it so. Wielding the bow had made me feel special. Powerful. Strong. Yet I did not need it to *be* those things.

"Wugang's soldiers are on their way. We must make haste," Wenzhi said.

As I nodded, Wenzhi drew out the scroll from his sleeve, unrolling the yellowed strips of bamboo, crammed with tiny characters. As he passed his palm over it—agleam with power—the characters leapt off the scroll, hovering in the air like dark moths.

"This enchantment can only be performed once," he cautioned, taking my hands firmly in his.

"What should I do?" I asked.

"Look upon your mother. Keep her face firmly in your mind," he instructed.

I studied her slender eyes beneath delicately arched brows. Skin of moonlight, hair of night. When I was young, I had wished to look like her, and now it might be the death of me.

Wenzhi's power pulsed from his fingers, his energy coursing through me with the force of a storm. The black brushstrokes of the characters broke apart, encircling me like a chain, swirling across my body, gliding over my limbs and face before stilling—a heartbeat before seeping into my skin like spilled ink. Pain seared, jagged and raw, like the words were being carved into my flesh. A hoarse gasp broke from me, sweat beading on my brow.

Wenzhi's grip tightened around my hands. "Shall I stop?"

I shook my head, gritting my teeth. "Continue."

The hurt swelled until each breath was a struggle. It erupted through every pore on my body, my skin, bones, and teeth—pressed, squeezed, and scorched like I was being made anew, shaped from clay and fired in a forge . . . like those soldiers Wugang had spoken of, who guarded the mortal emperor's tomb. Just when I could bear it no more, a scream rising from my throat—the agony subsided, leaving a dull throb throughout my body and an unfamiliar tautness like the thinnest of threads stretched between Wenzhi and me.

As he released my hands, I staggered back, clutching the table. My vision blurred then sharpened once more. I lifted my fingers to my face, running them over my chin, the slender arch of my nose and cheekbones.

My eyes collided with my mother's, hers widening with disbelief. "Your face," she stammered.

"Did it work?" I started to hear her bell-like tones emerging from my throat.

"Yes. For as long as the enchantment holds," Wenzhi said.

"How long do I have?" I asked.

"As long as you need." He tilted his head toward me. "You must be careful not to unleash the feather's power while it's within you. Keep yourself shielded from it at all times."

"I will," I assured him.

"Will Wugang sense your magic?" Liwei asked anxiously.

As I glanced at Wenzhi, he shook his head. "It will be masked, along with your aura."

A powerful spell. Little wonder that his father had kept this scroll with his most treasured possessions. "Is it a strain on you?" I asked.

He smiled. "I can bear it as long as you can."

"How will you fight?" I wanted to know.

"General Mengqi will lead the army in my stead. You and I are linked through this spell; I can't be too far from you. I will follow at a safe distance." His brow creased, unease flashing across his face. He did not like leaving his army in the care of others, yet some battles were not won on the field.

"What if Wugang's soldiers sense you?" I asked him.

"I will go with him," Liwei said.

Wenzhi stiffened. "I'll take my chances with Wugang's soldiers."

"I would be glad to let you," Liwei countered. "But I will risk no disruption to the spell. For tonight, I will guard your safety as I would Xingyin's."

Wenzhi hesitated, before inclining his head in acceptance. Warmth suffused my heart at this exchange; a deep sense of peace. There were far too many reasons for them to be at odds— the Celestial Heir and the Demon King—and I was glad to no longer be one of them.

"I will be there too," my father said. I would be glad for his presence, that they would keep each other safe.

"How will you unleash the feather?" Liwei asked me.

"Once I'm close enough to the laurel, I will undo the enchantment which binds it. Wugang will be too distracted trying to save the laurel to prevent my escape," I said smoothly. Only someone assured of success would speak so . . . or a practiced liar.

Wenzhi's gaze narrowed. "Have you decided where to plant the feather?"

"By its roots." For that was how the laurel had drunk of Wugang's blood and my mother's tears—and that was how I would end it.

Despite my glib answers, this was no simple matter. There were far too many things that could go wrong, countless terrifying scenarios I had replayed through my mind to better prepare myself. My greatest fear was Wugang might sense a trap, that he would see through my disguise and destroy the feather before I had a chance to unleash it. There was just one Sacred Flame Feather left in the realm; I could not waste it. Which meant, I had to maintain my pretense until the last possible moment . . . and that I would have the barest sliver of time to escape.

I glanced up to find Liwei staring at me. Perhaps he sensed the dread that thickened my blood, the anxiety tangling my insides. "Be careful, Xingyin. Once you unleash the feather, hide. Don't take on Wugang alone. We will come the moment you need us."

"If Wugang detects your disguise, if the link between us is severed—I will sense it at once. You won't be alone, even if you don't see us there," Wenzhi assured me.

"It is almost time," my father said. Now that our path was set, he would show no doubt. Half the battle was won in the mind.

I glanced out the window, concealing my face. Dusk had fallen, a veil of violet splendor—elusive and fragrant, with mystery and promise. Yet a hollow numbness sheathed me as I clasped my hands together to hide their shaking. One breath, and then another—until finally my heart calmed. Only then did I dare to look at them, pressing each of their beloved faces into my mind. Precious remembrances to sustain me through the hell ahead.

"You should go, before Wugang's soldiers arrive." I did not know how much longer I could sustain this mask of calm.

My mother embraced me, her arms tight around my neck

and shoulders. I swallowed hard, inhaling the faint sweetness of her scent, trying to ignore the tears which fell from her eyes onto my robe. She released me, hurrying from the room. Liwei and Wenzhi bowed to me then, their faces solemn as they straightened. I bent my head to them in turn, my throat crammed with unsaid words, my heart heavy with suppressed emotion as they left. In a moment, my father would be gone too.

"Father, wait." An involuntary cry I could not prevent. I had faced dire situations before, been dragged to the brink of death— yet there was a difference to this one. The burden was almost crushing, for the stakes were greater by far: not just my life and those of my loved ones, but of every mortal and immortal in the realms above and below. I could not fail; I dared not. And yet . . . could I prevail?

My father came toward me. "Daughter, what is it?"

"How did you feel when you faced the sunbirds?" A halting question.

"Afraid," he said bluntly.

His answer comforted me, soothing my fraught nerves. "Why did you do it?"

Grief shadowed his face. He looked older in that moment, an echo of the mortal I had first met, stooped with the cares of time. "I did not want to. I knew I would pay a heavy price, for they were beloved by the gods. Yet if I did not, all whom I loved would perish."

"I don't want to do this." My words fell out in a low cry. "I am not courageous; I am afraid. I am no hero." I did not shy from sharing these thoughts with him. More than anyone, he knew the price that must be paid, the hard choices that had to be made.

"You are," he said with feeling. "For the fools do not fear the odds, the reckless do not care—and only the truly brave proceed regardless." He placed a hand on my shoulder, steady and warm.

"It was either the sunbirds or the world. And along with the world, my wife, you—my unborn child—my friends, and every other living creature. There is nothing more worth fighting for."

He reached out and hugged me, his palm stroking the back of my head. "I am proud of you, my daughter, whether you do this or not. If you cannot, there is no shame. Say it now, and we will find another way."

There was no other way.

"Houyi, is Xingyin all right?" My mother appeared at the entrance, looking anxiously at me.

"Thank you, Father." It was a relief to have said all this aloud, to confront the inner demons that plagued me. And even though the impossible task lay before me still, I did not feel so alone anymore.

He released me. "Remember, my child, if you believe in yourself, in what you're doing—no one can take that from you."

He left then. All of them gone, each carrying away a piece of me. As the doors slid shut, their footsteps faded, the silence deepening with foreboding.

I stared at the mirror, my mother's face looking back at me. Reaching into my pouch, I pulled out the translucent orb containing the feather. It shivered like a living creature, each barb ablaze, shining golden bright. It warmed to my touch, straining against the restraints that bound it. Drawing a ragged breath, I released my magic inward, plunging it into the core of my lifeforce as I had done once before, the day I released the dragons. I clawed it apart, the glittering pool spilling free, incandescent with the light of the heavens. I did not hesitate, not allowing myself to think as I pressed the orb against my forehead, shut my eyes, and let my magic sweep over it. The feather seared as it sank through my skin and flesh, like a pebble pressed into damp sand—giving way as it slid into the core of my lifeforce.

The heat scorched, startling in its intensity—and at once I wove a shield around it, tightening the barriers until not a pinprick slipped through.

It was done. My head throbbed like a hammer was pounding it from within. How had King Wenming borne this? It would suffice to drive anyone to madness. A shudder rippled through my body as I sank upon the bed, a sob wrenched from my chest before I buried it—for at the very moment my life was illuminated by love, it had never seemed so dark.

35

THEY CAME SWIFTLY, THEIR AURAS creeping closer—mirrored reflections with the stillness of ice. Throttled gasps swelled from the corridor beyond, something heavy striking the ground with a thud. I flinched at the thought of the guards, but then the door burst open, my fears turning inward.

Eight of Wugang's soldiers stood in the entrance, their skin mottled with frostlike patches, their eyes alight with that eerie glow. I tried to muster a spark of hatred for them for so callously snuffing out Prince Yanming's life, but it was like trying to hate an arrow that had hit its mark. These creatures were no more than weapons themselves, though far deadlier than any I had ever encountered.

As two of them seized my arms, I cried out and struggled, tempering the urge to fight back in earnest. They dragged me effortlessly into the silent corridor, past the crumpled bodies of the guards. Their fingers bit into my arms as they hauled me outside the palace. My slippers scraped a jagged stone, the silken threads rupturing, the beads from the embroidery scattering upon the ground.

A large cloud hovered just beyond the entrance. One of them pushed my back, and I stumbled upon it. As it took flight, soaring high—I almost knocked into a soldier. I blinked, studying its face. This one appeared younger than the rest, a strange thought when these creatures seemed at once ageless and yet not quite alive. The same light emanated from its hollowed eyes, however something more grazed my consciousness—a shadow of remembrance, an echo of who he used to be . . . a stark dread of what he was now.

It could not be him. Prince Yanming was a Sea Immortal; his spirit did not lie in the Divine Harmony Sky. His brother had brought him back to the Eastern Sea. A rush of emotions crashed upon me, a terrifying thought sliding into my mind: What if those killed by Wugang's soldiers were somehow bound to his will, even in death?

"Prince Yanming?" I whispered, even as my heart clenched, rejecting the thought. When he showed not a flicker of recognition, I tried again, choosing my words carefully. "Do you remember your parents? Your brother? The Eastern Sea?"

The soldier's head lifted ever so slightly—if I were not watching him, I would have missed it. I followed his unseeing gaze, catching a glint of sapphire and pearl on the horizon—the sea, awash with midnight stars. His lips parted, his eyes fixed ahead like he was seeking something . . . even though he might not know it. Hope unfurled in me that perhaps a part of him remained untarnished by this vile power, that the dragons were watching over him after all.

"Go far from here," I told him quietly, unsure if he could hear or understand. "Return to the Eastern Sea. Find the dragons; they will keep you safe."

His head seemed to dip into a nod. So slight, it might have been a trick of my mind seeing what it wanted to, but I clung to this wild hope. I was shaking, fighting the urge to retch at the thought of what lay ahead—what success might cost me and the unspeakable price of failure. Breathing deeply, I fought for calm. A clear mind was the greatest weapon when one had relinquished all else.

Our cloud climbed north, toward the Golden Desert. I dared not probe for a trace of my father, Liwei, or Wenzhi. All my energy in this moment was centered on the feather borne within my body, keeping it whole—and me, alive. As screams and cries rang out from below, I glanced down, my insides turning to ice.

Chaos reigned. Wugang's army had struck earlier than anticipated. The colliding forces were caught in the throes of battle, weapons gleaming as they clashed, currents of magic illuminating the night. I leaned over the edge of the cloud, my veins hardening to stone at the sight of the snarling monsters that prowled alongside Wugang's army. An enormous boar with a mortal's face charged into a troop of Cloud Wall warriors, skewering them upon its curved tusks. Blood sprayed into the air—a fine mist—amid the desperate screams and pleas. An eerie light shone from the boar's eyes, its tusks glowing just as the soldiers' guandao did, with the same malevolent power.

A shadow fell over me as a monstrous winged tiger swept down to sink its claws into an Eastern Sea soldier, flinging her high into the air. Her scream was swallowed by an ominous thud, yet the creature did not pause, already pouncing on another victim.

Taowu. Qiongqi. Legendary beasts, renowned for their vicious cruelty, having devoured countless mortals and immortals until they had been slain by the Celestial Army. And now, they were resurrected by Wugang to serve him, to reap devastation across the realms.

My nails cut into my palms. If only I could fight alongside our soldiers, if only I could have helped them. Yet it would not be enough. I could stop one monster, perhaps—a handful of soldiers . . . but thousands?

A flash of brightness streaked across the sky, gleaming with the gold of summer. The Yellow Dragon soared forth, its spiked tail lashing the air, churning it into a gale. Its force slammed into Qiongqi, the winged tiger's claws unclenching—its victim plummeting through the skies with a scream—but the Black Dragon shot forward, catching the soldier upon its back. Further below, the crimson scales of the Long Dragon blazed as it cleared a path for the soldiers fleeing Taowu's charge. As the dragon opened its great jaws, torrents of water crashed upon the boar, sending it rolling across the sands.

Though leaden with terror, a lightness crept into my heart. Sharp cries rang out then, the phoenixes sweeping into the fray in a flurry of shining feathers and talons. As they circled in graceful flight, their tails rippled behind them like rainbows arched across the night. The Celestial Empress flew among them upon her mount, a spear in her hand. A fierce radiance suffused her, as though she were a bird whose cage had sprung open, who could finally spread her wings and soar. Flanking the Phoenix Army were Prince Yanxi's forces, bearing down upon the armies of the Northern Sea.

The sun had not yet risen, and already the clouds were drenched with blood. The glittering sands of the Golden Desert— so dazzling from the palace rooftop—now glistened with a dark wetness. How many lives would be lost? Death would feast well tonight, gorging itself over the immortal table it had once been cast from.

Despair shrouded me, dank and cold. I wanted to shut my eyes to the unfolding nightmare, but forced myself to watch, biting down on the inside of my cheek till it was raw. *This* was the horror that awaited us if Wugang prevailed—an eternity of chaos, destruction, and death. And I dared not dwell on what might happen to the spirits of those slain by his creatures. This was not just a battle for the realm, it was one for its soul. I would not falter, I could not fail.

The cloud swerved sharply away, climbing higher. I tore my mind from the devastation below, for my own battle lay before me. Long moments ticked away, sheathed in silence. All the while, the feather strained against its binds, pounding against my skull. My energy flowed in a constant trickle to hold the shields fast, my tension coiling tighter until I thought I might snap.

At last, the silver roof of my home gleamed ahead. Tiles were cracked and charred, several missing, part of the lower tier fallen away. A far different homecoming from before, when joy had brimmed over with anticipation—for all I felt now was a withering dread, coupled with the relentless stab of fear.

It was cooler than I remembered, the tranquil stillness edged with desolation. Never had the night felt so oppressively thick, with the lanterns unlit, the once-luminous earth as dull as ash. A trace of cinnamon wound through the air, a musty tang clinging to it, a remnant of stale smoke. My gaze darted over the blackened walls, the cracked stone path, the stump by the entrance where a mother-of-pearl pillar had once towered. It had been a nightmare of my youth, to return home and find it in ruins—achingly silent, without the voices of my mother and Ping'er.

The cloud glided to the ground. Before I could descend, a soldier shoved me forward. I stumbled, tripping over my skirt, as another grabbed my arm, pulling at me. Anger flared in me to be treated like some beast, yet there was no malice in their rough handling, rather the detachment of performing an appointed task. I was glad when the young one remained on the cloud, unmoving, though his gaze kept flicking to the skies. Did he intend to take flight? How I prayed he would.

The soldiers hauled me along a familiar path, winding between the osmanthus trees—I could have walked blindfolded and found my way. Something rustled, the gentle clink of leaves from the laurel towering above. Its silvery bark seemed darker than before, cast in shadow—or perhaps because it was no longer bathed in the light of the moon.

Wugang stood there, a glint in his hawkish eyes. The gold scales of his armor rippled across his chest and down his arms, tapering to his wrists. His great axe was strapped to his back, its green tassel swinging from its bamboo handle. A powerful shield gleamed around him, my spirits sinking at the sight. Gone was my faint hope of catching him off guard. Even surrounded by his soldiers, his guard was still up.

He clasped his hands in seeming delight. "Chang'e, it warms me to see you again. I have long awaited this moment."

I seethed at his false geniality. As his eyes narrowed with speculation, I dropped my challenging stare, trembling from the strain of not striking him, which I hoped he would take for fright.

"Release her." His hand lifted in a careless wave.

The soldiers loosened their grip at once, their heads cocked toward him.

"I hope they haven't made you too uncomfortable," he said. "My soldiers can be overzealous when obeying my orders."

How polite he sounded, like I was an honored guest. As though he were asking after my well-being, without the slightest intent of drawing my blood.

"Why did you bring me here?" My mother's voice slid from my lips.

"Goddess of the Moon, I think you know." His arm swept toward the laurel.

How many times had I climbed its pale branches and tugged at its seeds, admiring its exquisite beauty? All I saw now was that same ethereal light curving from the eyes of Wugang's soldiers and monsters—resurrected, not to life, but to eternal slavery in death.

"Bind her to the tree," Wugang commanded.

A gray chill sank through my flesh. I did not imagine he would *tie* me to the laurel. How would I escape? Panic surged, my struggles in earnest as I kicked at the guards.

This is what you need, the better part of me whispered—the part that was brave and wise. There was only one way to get the Sacred Flame Feather into the laurel, and that was if Wugang allowed it. Being bound to the tree was an undeniable advantage, though there was no relief when it would also trap me. Magic tingled at my fingertips, yearning to be released—to cast the soldiers aside, to flee. The same urge that had driven me to claw victory from despair, life from death—was now a hindrance, chipping at my resolve.

I forced myself to go limp, dropping my head to hide my churning thoughts. As Wugang's soldiers wrenched my arms around the tree, cords of light slithered around my wrists, spiraling across my chest, waist, and knees, locking me in this forced embrace. The bark stung against my body like I was pressed to a column of ice.

There was no need to feign terror; I shook with it—that Wugang might discover our trick, that I might fail . . . or die. I had weighed the danger, steeled myself for what lay ahead. I had imagined being held at sword point, restrained, threatened, and hurt—yet, I had also dreamed of a swift escape. I was quick; my magic was strong. All I had to do was lose myself in this forest I had known all my life. I had not expected to be trussed up like some cruel sacrifice—though, that was what I was. Yet as fear froze my blood, a rush of relief spilled through me that it was *not* my mother here.

I shoved aside my terror, probing my bonds cautiously. It was a strange magic I was tempted to test, but was wary of arousing Wugang's suspicions. A sudden pain pierced me from within, the feather's power lashing free. At once I channeled my energy to strengthen my shield, unable to afford a moment's distraction. As my chest cramped with despair, I closed my eyes, fighting for calm. Images of my parents slid into my mind, along with Liwei and Wenzhi, of Shuxiao, Prince Yanming, and Ping'er. Something hardened along my spine, a warmth spreading over me.

Those truly powerful have no need for love.

It was what Wugang had said to me before, when we stood in this very place.

You are wrong, I told him in the silence of my mind. *Love is what gives me the strength to do this. To stop you.*

Never had I so much to lose, yet so much to fight for. My eyes rolled up to meet Wugang's. When had he drawn so close? I fought down the bile that crowded my throat, the dread that stiffened my limbs. My head seared like it was crammed with hot coals, tendrils of heat from the Sacred Flame Feather already surging free from its binds. *Now* was the time, before Wugang sensed it, before he struck—for what if he rendered me unconsciousness?

With a wrench, I loosened the enchantments around the feather, channeling my energy to pierce its shaft, crushing it into glittering shards. My magic coursed over each fragment, forming a thin shield to protect me from the feather's power—and it was this alone that kept me alive. Even through the barrier, the brutal heat seeped into my veins until my blood blazed like liquid flame. Sweat dripped down my brow and neck, my silk robe sticking to my back. I gasped, sucking in a breath of cool air that yielded a pinprick of relief as I fought the urge to crumple. A little longer, I urged myself, struggling to hold steady. Time was running out. I needed Wugang to strike soon, to release the power dammed within me, before it consumed me whole. Still, he waited, a triumphant smile on his face as though savoring the moment . . . even as I burned within.

I would not wait for him; I would move the pieces on the board instead of waiting to be played. "It's not too late to reconsider," I told Wugang, my eyes wide and innocent. "If you return the emperor's throne, if you beg for mercy, he might forgive you." My voice was gentle, my words needle-sharp.

Wugang's lips peeled into a feral snarl. A swish through the air and his axe descended, carving a clean slash along my arm, one after the next. Pain seared, silken smooth. Blood spilled from my torn flesh, speckled with the gold of the feather's power—seething hot, with the tang of iron and char. Thin trails ran down my arms, falling between the undulating roots, sinking into the darkening earth. With each drop of my blood, another fleck of the feather's power slid from my body—such relief, short lived though it was. For the heat seeped into the very thing I was tied to, the laurel's bark already warming against my body.

A hoarse gasp broke from me as my scorched blood coursed through my veins. Heat radiated from my pores, glazing my skin as the cords that bound me dissolved. Freedom—yet I barely sensed it, consumed by unfathomable agony. The acrid tang of smoke choked my lungs, a sizzling and crackling crowding my ears. Just the thinnest of threads held me whole, the enchantment that tethered me to Wenzhi. I grasped at it like a drowning person, clinging to my sole solace from this nightmare as my blood continued to flow into the laurel's roots. Any moment now, it would catch fire.

As would I.

Wugang's head was tilted up to the branches, his face creased into a frown. When my mother's blood had scattered over the laurel before, its seeds had fallen like ripe plums shaken down. Perhaps he thought it a delay or a miscalculation on his part that the blood of the Moon Goddess had not yielded the desired harvest.

The laurel shuddered, its bark smoked and charred. Yet its glowing sap was already spreading across, healing itself. Despair raged. Why had it not been destroyed? Why was it not enough? And it struck me then—the power that shielded me from the feather's devastation, shielded the laurel too. I would fail because I was still trying to protect myself, because I was afraid.

Yet this was not the way. If I failed, Wugang would kill me along with everyone I loved. There was no real choice, just as when my father had faced the sunbirds—though it was one that had to be made nonetheless.

I pressed my arms tighter around the laurel, squeezing my eyes shut. Not giving myself a moment to ponder as I reached inward, ripping away the barriers that guarded me, undoing the shields over the feather fragments—all that kept me whole. As the last one broke, heat erupted throughout my body—a scorching summer, a raging blaze. I was . . . undone. The thread tethering me to Wenzhi snapped, his enchantment unraveling as my skin stung and stretched, pain shuddering through my limbs. My blood gushed forth, spilling through the cuts on my arms, and bearing with it the last of the Sacred Flame Feather's raw power—seeping into the roots of the laurel. Would it be enough?

The blazing heat in my body subsided, leaving nothing but a bone-deep weariness. I could not move. My skin was drenched with sweat, and yet I shivered. Smoke clung to my breath, a powdery bitterness coating my tongue as though I had chewed ash. A miracle that I breathed at all, that this wisp of life remained . . . frail and fleeting though it was.

My eyes flew open, blinking against the glare. All was curved where it should be straight, shuddering when it should be still, until everything appeared slick with flame. Deep cracks fractured the laurel's silvery bark, from which smoke and sap gurgled forth—no longer bright gold but a coppery-red, as though churned with my blood. With a whoosh, its pale branches caught fire like a flaming crown.

"No!" Wugang's roar was a far cry from his usual calm.

Nothing but silence greeted his outburst. His soldiers faced him, awaiting his command. Obedient. Alert. Unfeeling. Fear did not clutch their hearts—nor did loyalty, love, or honor. Such things Wugang had scoffed at, derided and scorned. Such things that might work wonders in times of desperate need.

A grinding wrenched the air as the cracks swelled across the laurel's trunk, gaping wider, deeper—a moment before it broke apart. The glittering seeds above morphed into lumps of blackened coal, shriveling to ash that drifted with the wind like clouds of soot.

Wugang's soldiers stilled. The light faded from their eyes, winking out until just the hollows remained. Clear liquid ran down in rivulets from their faces, across their necks, like ice thawing beneath the sun. Chunks of their limbs broke off with a clink, coming apart like ill-made works of clay. As they crumbled to the ground, gold dust coiled from their wracked forms, spiraling into the air. A rustling sprang up like a great sigh. Was there regret in it? Relief? How I prayed these spirits would regain their stolen peace. The shimmering specks vanished then, leaving nothing but an unearthly silence and a charred stump where the laurel had once towered, surrounded by dark swaths of damp earth.

It was over . . . Wugang's army destroyed. This terrible devastation, this grave threat to our existence had ended. I inhaled a shaking breath, closing my eyes. Such terror had reigned over my mind and sunken my heart during these endless days—it was hard to believe it was no more. A sweet lightness swept through me, a moment's respite from the pain. The realms would be safe, along with my loved ones. The battle by the Cloud Wall would have ended abruptly, with Wugang's soldiers and monsters gone. Not dead, for they had never truly been alive.

Come dawn, the sun would rise unhindered over the Immortal Realm.

I would not see it.

Wugang loomed above me, his face crimson with rage, his aura thick with murderous fury. My fingers lifted to my face, brushing the cleft in my chin, the rounded curve of my cheek. I was myself again.

"How is this possible? Her aura, her voice—" Wugang's grip tightened around the hilt of his axe. He would waste little time uttering pointless words of rage. Death was the only atonement for my offenses.

I met his gaze without fear; I was already hollowed through, what else could he do to me? The Sacred Flame Feather had burned me up, devoured every bit of my strength. It was a mercy I was not already dead, though eternal darkness was beckoning. What was left was just skin stretched over bones, and wilted breath in my lungs. Was this how Ping'er and Prince Yanming had felt? It was not as terrible as I had dreaded, this numbing fatigue that stole over me, the weight pressing over my limbs like a shroud of stone—yet a lightness fluttering within like I was almost free . . .

"Xingyin."

My mother's voice yanked me from my fevered daze. When

had they arrived? I glanced up, my eyes colliding with hers. Such pain in them, such terror—as black as the abyss that yawned before me. Beside her was my father, Wenzhi and Liwei, their cloud soaring faster than the wind and yet . . . too late.

I struggled to raise myself up, leaning upon an elbow. My breaths came quick and shallow, the shadow of Wugang's axe dark on my face. There was nothing left in me to evade or block the blow that would surely fall. Drawing a deep breath, the crisp air filled my lungs, laced with the sweetness of osmanthus. *Home at last*, my mind whispered.

Wugang's axe arced high. No matter what he had lost, vengeance would be his. He was a master at exacting it in full. I closed my eyes, unable to bear the terror flashing across the faces of my loved ones. If they called my name again, I did not hear it. A shiver rippled through my flesh. How strange to be cold when moments before I had burned. Something whistled, hurtling toward me. I braced for pain—yet it plunged past my head, rending a stunned gasp from above. My eyes flew open to find an arrow of Sky-fire embedded into Wugang's chest. His mouth hung open, gaping like a fish torn from the waters—as another arrow hurtled into the center of his forehead, light streaking across his face, down his neck, trailing along the very scars on his palms. He staggered back a step, and then another. A gust of air slipped from his lips, carrying a woman's name in a tortured breath. His wife? Did he love her still? My heart flinched at the thought. He had been cruel, yet most cruel to himself.

Wugang slumped to his knees, falling upon the grass. His body shuddered violently, his eyes blinking at a frantic pace, before widening and going still, the color draining from his flesh until he was as pale as the petals beneath him. Death had claimed him at last—the mortal who had clawed his way to immortality, overthrown the Celestial Emperor, and reshaped the Immortal Realm.

There was no pity in my heart for him, nor did triumph sing through my veins that Ping'er and Prince Yanming were avenged. There was nothing left except this void within me, this hollow of winter. My legs gave way as I collapsed into the soft embrace of the earth. Footsteps pounded toward me—my parents, Liwei, and Wenzhi racing my way. A torment and a joy to have them close.

My greatest loves, my deepest regrets.

Wenzhi's face was ashen, the silver in his eyes dulled to slate. Even in my weakened state, the sight jarred me. Something was wrong; his powerful aura diminished. As he fell to his knees beside me, a guttural sigh wrenched from his chest. I reached out just as he did, our fingers grazing, entwining—by instinct, almost. How cold his skin . . . or was it mine?

His hand lifted to cradle my cheek. "I did not break the enchantment. I hope it was enough."

"How long do I have?" I had asked him before.

"As long as you need," he had replied.

It was *I* who had severed the connection, not him. And in a flash, I understood. He had not let go, not even when the enchantment had drained the last of his powers. To keep me safe, he had sacrificed his very life. Why? For his kingdom, or the realm? Deep down, I knew the answer; it was one he had told me himself.

Because he loved me.

Not with the selfish love of the past, where I was but a means to an end. He had wanted me then, yet had been unwilling to yield anything that might make his love worth having. Never did I think he would do such a thing, placing me above all else. I had smothered my emotions, clung to principles and pride, deceived myself at every turn. I had refused to believe he could change, until he had shown me—irrefutably—just how much he loved me. More than the crown and kingdom he had once betrayed me for.

More than his life.

I would have wept except there were no tears left, the flames had burned them away. Silent screams of agony clogged my throat. The white-hot pain that stabbed me was like something vital had been ripped from my core.

"I'm sorry." My words were a shattered whisper.

"I am sorry too." His chest heaved as a faint smile stretched across his lips. "Live. Be happy." As he glanced at Liwei, they exchanged a long look—without hostility or rancor. Liwei inclined his head in a respectful salute. Wenzhi fell back, a sharp breath dragged through his clenched teeth.

This was agony, not the fire in my veins or the axe slashing my skin. I gripped his hand as hard as I could. His skin had always been cool, yet never this immutable ice.

"I love you," I said to Wenzhi. Only now did I know it was the truth, despite everything I had done to destroy it.

This was no time for pride or resentment, for anything except honesty. It was not a betrayal of Liwei. The simple truth was that I loved them both. Perhaps it made me a bad person, yet it was not something I had sought. This fracture in my heart . . . I only knew it was there after it had formed. And strange though it may sound, it was what made me whole—for they each were a part of me.

A smile spread across Wenzhi's face, radiant and fierce. My friend, my enemy—whose love and treachery had clawed the deepest grooves in my heart. One did not cancel out the other, yet the truth was that the Wenzhi who had betrayed me would never have sacrificed himself so. The fantasy of what might have been flashed across my mind—if he had been born of a different family, as had I. One untainted by power, suffering, and secrets. We would have been happy, as he had promised. Perhaps it was as he'd said: we never had a chance to begin, because there was already another in my heart. And then, he had lost my trust—forever, I'd believed. Only in this moment did it dawn on me that I *had* forgiven him long before. That I loved him, still . . . and it was too late.

His eyes pinned mine, a tremor coursing through him. I clutched him tighter, more afraid than I had ever been before, as though this simple act would suffice to bind him to me. But then his smile wavered as his eyelids sank down, closing over the turbulent gray. A breath left his body, his pulse slowing. His aura dwindling away until all that made him precious—was gone.

Grief ravaged me like a devouring beast. I could neither breathe nor move from the wracking agony, each moment an eternity of night. Scant consolation that I would follow him soon after. Perhaps then, I might find the peace that had long eluded me.

Someone lifted me away from Wenzhi, from the aching stillness of his body—once so powerful and strong. With the last of my strength, I turned to Liwei, to my mother and father. It was almost more than I could bear. Their eyes were ringed red and wet with sorrow. Liwei clasped his hands around mine, his touch bringing an echo of warmth to the chill that engulfed me. His energy poured into me with a rush of heat, a shallow comfort like the sun without warmth, the moon without light. My lifeforce was gone; I could not channel his magic. I wanted to tell him to stop. That I was sick and tired of partings and sorrow, that I was already dead inside.

He would not listen even if I could have spoken in that moment, his magic sweeping over me like rainfall, gliding off my skin as I continued to fade. Lights flashed across my vision like a thousand stars spinning across the heavens. My head fell to the earth, my gaze falling upon Wenzhi's body. How calm he looked, how young and peaceful, the cares wiped from his face. The grass beneath me was wet with morning dew. It was still dark, the lanterns unlit. If only I could have seen their glow one last time.

"I love you," I whispered. To Liwei. To my mother and father. To my home, where I would lay forever.

And then, I was free. Severed from the husk of my body, floating above. Such lightness, such calm. Love without pain, joy with sorrow, and the promise of the infinite. I stared down at the carnage before me. Wenzhi. Wugang. The broken remnants of those soldiers.

A cry erupted from Liwei that would have torn the heart from my chest if it beat still. My father's head bowed with grief as he wrapped an arm around my mother—her weeping resonating through the air, her tears streaming into the soil. A shudder rippled through the ground, the lanterns around us flaring to sudden life—luminous and bright. The moon eagerly awakening to greet its mistress after so long an absence.

My mother pulled free of my father's hold, kneeling by my side to grasp my hand. Tears slid down her face, falling upon the withered roots of the laurel. "Xingyin," she wept, again and again, in the sorrowful rhythm of loss.

Something gleamed, a rivulet of bright gold sap trickling forth from the laurel's stump. It streaked across the wood, between the charred crevices, spilling upon the ground. The earth shimmered with light, warmth erupting in the air like a burst of summer—a force yanking me back into my body, even as pain and grief latched onto my consciousness once more with excruciating clarity.

I sucked in a heaving breath, bolting upright. My eyes met my mother's, wide with shock and disbelief, a moment before she threw her arms around me, clutching me tight. A tingling warmth surged through my flesh, coursing through my veins. Over her shoulder, I saw the last of the laurel stump crumble away, its once-glittering sap fading to brown, scattering like sand over Wenzhi's body. No breath rattled in his lungs; he was as lifeless as stone.

"Is he—?" I could not speak the word.

"He is gone," Liwei said hoarsely.

"Why? Why him and not me?" I burst out, unreasonable in my grief.

Already, my mind was piecing the fragments together. That somehow, my mother's tears had revived the laurel. It had just enough power left to save one of us and it had chosen me. Was it obeying the Moon Goddess's command? Or was this the laurel's final gift to me? For all those years I had played beneath its shade, perhaps it knew me too.

Yet even as life pulsed through me once more, as I gazed at Wenzhi—a part of me remained dead, and no magic in the world could bring it back again.

36

WUGANG WAS DEAD. HIS ARMY gone. Yet the scars of his brief reign remained, some reaching so deep, they might never heal. Would it have pleased him to know this? I believe it would. He had achieved immortality in a way he would treasure more than the infinite years bestowed upon him, that he had squandered in vengeance and hate. He did not deserve this; he deserved to be forgotten, his name trampled to dust along with his body. As for me, I would cast him from my mind, for he was unworthy of a place there alongside those I had lost, whom I still cherished with every breath I drew.

I glanced around the Hall of Eastern Light, my gaze falling on the Celestial Empress's body in the coffin of clear crystal upon the dais. She had died in battle—a hero's death, with songs already composed in her honor. When I knelt before her body today, it was the first time I had ever meant the respect the gesture conveyed.

Her magnificent silver brocade garments were embroidered with gold phoenixes and their rainbow-hued tails—a splash of color in the sea of white mourners, like winter had descended upon the Hall of Eastern Light. A crown of pearls and gold feathers glittered from her hair—was it the one that had captured my childish imagination before? Her hands were clasped across her stomach, her nail sheaths glinting against her pale skin. A skilled artist had painted her face until her cheeks were radiant, her closed eyelids swept with gleaming powder. She looked beautiful, for eternal slumber had eased the perpetual tension from her features. Or perhaps, I saw her now through new eyes: who she had been, what she might have become had life taken a different turn.

How strange it was to be stirred by her, this unfamiliar pity unfurling in my chest. The Celestial Empress had threatened my mother, forced my flight from home, scorned and schemed against me at every opportunity. She had driven Liwei and me apart. She would have sent me to my death without a second's hesitation. I had feared her, resented and despised her, even. And yet, she was Liwei's mother and she had loved him too. Now that she was dead, all that had been wrong between us seemed of less consequence, like chasing shadows through the night. I could never have loved her, but neither could I find it in me to hate her still, no matter what she had done.

Beside me, Liwei shifted. He sat straight with his shoulders thrown back, his head held high before the endless stream of mourners who came to pay their final respects to the empress. His mother would have been proud of him, not a flicker of weakness did he show.

I reached out, wanting to comfort him—but with the weight of all the eyes upon us, I drew back. It was not my vow to his mother that restrained me, for it had been voided the day she attacked me. There was something else . . . this ceaseless pain in my chest, since that day of loss on the moon.

The Celestial Emperor was present, for once without his crown. A pure white band of mourning was tied around his brow, the same one Liwei wore, the long ends grazing his back.

It was the first time I had seen the emperor since his ill-fated birthday celebration. Before, I had marveled at the agelessness of his face, and now it was lined in sorrow, his body stooped like something vital had been lost. Strange that his wife's death should affect him so, when he never seemed to have much affection for her before. Perhaps we only valued something once it had gone. I buried the thought, a pang striking me deep.

The emperor and Liwei rose to their feet, approaching the dais with measured steps. Behind them, followed Zhiyi, Liwei's half-sister. Funerals were a family matter, bringing together even those estranged. They knelt before the coffin, pressing their palms and forehead to the ground—once, twice, and thrice. A final obeisance to the empress. When Liwei rose, he raised his hands, his power sheathing the coffin in light. It floated into the sky, toward where the spirits of deceased Celestials lay, in the restored Divine Harmony Sky. As my gaze followed the coffin, a stream of glittering sparks burst forth, forming the shape of a fiery phoenix that soared alongside it into the heavens.

Once the ceremony concluded, the mourners surrounded Liwei, a few nodding to me in acknowledgment. My presence confused them, that I sat with the royal family despite having no official position. Their attention troubled me less these days, my mind already drifting to matters of greater import—lingering on precious memories, past regrets, and the faces of the fallen. They would haunt me for the rest of my days.

THE WEEKS THAT FOLLOWED passed in a blur. Liwei had offered me quarters of my own, but I chose to stay in my old room in the Courtyard of Eternal Tranquility, across from his. Perhaps a part of me hoped to find the peace I had known before, to regain some of what had been lost. This place had been my haven once—yet now its walls pressed closer around me with each passing day, the fragrance of flowers clogging the air. Nightmares tore me from slumber as I jerked upright—trembling, cold with sweat—trying to block the recollection of the feather's heat searing my veins, the chill glazing Ping'er's skin, of Prince Yanming's lifeless body . . . and the light fading from Wenzhi's eyes.

The Celestial Emperor did not return to court. He stayed in his courtyard and admitted few visitors. Was he still in mourning or recovering from his imprisonment at Wugang's hands? I doubted he had been treated well. I doubted his pride would ever recover from being held hostage by one he had disdained as a mere mortal. The burden of the realm fell on Liwei more, to drag his kingdom from the claws of terror it had been clutched in. To repair frayed alliances and rebuild all that had been destroyed.

His cares were great, his responsibilities onerous. It was no easy thing to be a monarch, or at least a good one. Fortunately, he had sound advisors by his side like General Jianyun and Teacher Daoming. At Liwei's urging, I accompanied him to court as we listened to endless petitions and briefings. I stayed by his side, offering what support I could—though inwardly I recoiled from the hard stares of the courtiers, the constant jostling for favor, the tedium of matters I had little interest in. Some days I could not bear it, wanting nothing more than to flee to the quiet of my room. Though even there I found little peace, trapped in the bleak solitude of my mind.

The nights were the hardest, for the shadows that enveloped me stretched longer, thickening until the darkness was all I saw. I tossed in bed, inhaling great gulps of air laced with the fragrance of spring, though there was nothing but winter in my heart. A longing consumed me whenever I thought of my home. My mother and father did not come to the Celestial Kingdom,

perhaps because they wanted to be alone after all they had endured. Perhaps they had too many unsettling recollections of
this place, of the gossip and spite, the secrets and lies. I understood how my parents felt, because I loathed it too.

The favor Liwei showed me fanned the boundless speculation that a betrothal was imminent. He did not speak of it to
me, nor did I ask. Whenever I tried to imagine my future, my
chest would cramp, wrenched with unspeakable longing. The
threat of Wugang had clouded my future once, yet it was nothing to these torments I now faced—for this was a battle I could
not win, an enemy I could not fight. For these demons . . . came
from within. My only solace was when Shuxiao was with me,
although she was leaving soon to return to her family. Everyone
was moving on to seek their own happiness. Everyone except—

I shoved the ungrateful thought aside. It was a miracle that
I was alive, to be surrounded by those I cared for. Yet why did I
feel so empty inside?

On Shuxiao's last evening, we shared a meal together. It was
just like we used to, except for the pair of attendants standing
behind me. They lurched to attention whenever I so much as
cleared my throat, their eyes constantly darting up to check that
our cups and plates were filled. When I gently suggested that they
leave, they exchanged such aggrieved looks, I could not insist.

I sighed, my head beginning to ache from the weight of gold
and jade ornaments in my hair, the ones I let my attendant adorn
me with. I went through my days in a state of apathy, not caring
what I wore or did—with no desire for anything that had once
brought me pleasure, whether music, food, or wine. I found myself thinking of the Celestial Empress more, and if she could live
her life over, whether she would have chosen differently. I would
never know these answers . . . and perhaps neither did she.

Shuxiao frowned as she placed a piece of braised beef on my

plate. A pile of stir-fried beans and shrimp followed, along with a plump wedge of fish steamed in ginger and wine.

"Why aren't you eating?" she asked. "Are you disappointed that a wedding date hasn't been set? Or worried the emperor might not give his permission?"

I lifted my cup, draining it in one gulp, the wine burning a path down my throat. "Maybe I should be alone," I said listlessly.

With love came pain, and I had drunk my fill of it.

Shuxiao glanced at the attendants, lowering her voice. "Don't you want to marry Prince Liwei?" she asked with her usual bluntness. "Just imagine those arrogant courtiers who'll have to bow to you then."

"A pleasant thought." A thin smile stretched over my lips as I imagined striding into the Hall of Eastern Light, the entire court falling to their knees like a rippling tide. An alluring temptation, to elevate those who had stood by my side and humble those who had scorned me before. Yet such satisfaction would be short-lived. This was not the life I wanted, not even with its trappings of power.

Shuxiao searched my face. "Why have you been so unhappy? Not just today, but since we returned here."

I had not told Shuxiao of my feelings for Wenzhi. I had only learned them myself, still grappling with what he meant to me, what I had lost. Turning around, I gestured for one of the attendants, suddenly glad for their presence as a shield against these probing questions. She hurried forward, bowing low to me, her cupped hands stretched out. Such reverence unnerved me more than it pleased, but I had learned to feign indifference.

"Could you bring us some glutinous rice balls? The ones dusted in crushed peanuts and sugar."

Minyi, who headed the kitchens, had sent some over with the afternoon meal. I had eaten them alone at this very table, stabbing one pillowy sphere after another with a jade pick, as though I could drown my misery in sweets. It had not worked, my stomach churning at the memory—even as a weak part of me craved the distraction, the fleeting pleasure on my tongue.

"Shuxiao, must you leave?" I asked. "General Jianyun leads the army again. Wugang's sycophants have been dismissed. Things will go back to how they were."

"I did not like it much, even then." She laughed, resting her elbows on the table. "Even if I did, *I* am changed."

As am I. Once, I had wanted nothing more than my family reunited, my home restored, a life with Liwei. And now, all those things were within my grasp, yet happiness eluded me still. Victory was not as sweet as I had imagined, or perhaps it had cost me too dear.

"Where will you go?" I asked.

Shuxiao's eyes glazed over, a faraway look in them. "Home. I have been gone far too long. My brother will take my place here. He is of age, and this is what he wants. For me it was always a matter of duty."

I basked in the warmth of her joy, though I would miss her dearly. "What will you do then?"

"Nothing." She drew the word out, savoring it. "It would be good to spend a few decades doing just that."

My chest clenched with envy, that I might never be so free. Shameful, for she deserved better. "Nothing?" I repeated with a smile instead. "What does your new friend, the formidable General Mengqi, think of this plan?"

It had been nothing more than a teasing guess. Together, they had orchestrated the rescue of the Celestial Emperor and the prisoners from the Jade Palace. Somehow, the animosity that had sparked between them had morphed into a grudging respect. Shuxiao spoke of the general several times after, in friendship I had thought, if not for this deep flush spreading across the back of her neck. I had never seen her so affected before, and I was both thrilled and afraid for her. Shaking my head, I cast my trepidation aside. Love did not wound all who reached for it.

An answering smile lit Shuxiao's face. "She will join me, now that . . . things have changed in the Cloud Wall."

I flinched. *Now that Wenzhi is dead*, was what she would have said, had she not suspected I grieved for him still.

"I am happy for you," I told her as she rose to leave.

She leaned over and hugged me. "Let yourself be happy."

It was what Wenzhi had told me with his final breath. A wish for my happiness, alone, knowing he could not be with me. Tears pricked my eyes, which I blinked away, the pain in my chest piercing so deep I could not breathe.

Someone knocked on my door, an attendant rushing to slide it open. Zhiyi stepped into the room, the hem of her brilliant green robe almost brushing the floor. Lilac orchids were embroidered on the skirt, along with azure birds that stretched their wings as they chirped.

She inclined her head in greeting. "I am leaving tomorrow and wanted to bid you farewell."

I concealed my surprise. "That is most thoughtful of you."

An immortal peach gleamed in her hand. Ripe, with a luminous blush from its stem to tip, a radiance emanating from its skin. "Liwei gave me this for my husband. If a mortal is not suffering any internal illness, this will extend their life. We will have time to wait for the elixir. Liwei has promised it to me, though it will be years before it is ready."

"I am glad you will have it," I told her with feeling. It still weighed on me that she had given up the elixir, that my parents' happiness had come at the cost of hers. I had not forgotten my vow to her—it was one I would keep even though she had not demanded it of me, even though the urgency had passed. The most binding vows were those from the heart.

"I must go," Shuxiao said, rising to her feet.

"Safe travels." As I extended my hands to her, she clasped them tight. I did not want to let go, but then she released me and left.

Zhiyi's gaze slid across the attendants hovering behind me. "Leave us." She did not raise her voice, yet it was laced with unmistakable authority. Without a protest, they hurried out, closing the doors after them.

"Are all royal children born with that skill?" I asked.

She sat down, arranging her skirts as they pooled on the floor. "When I lived here, I preferred to be alone. There were too many who spied on me, on my stepmother's behalf."

"I am sorry they did." Not for the first time, I was grateful for my own childhood, simple and solitary though it had been.

"When your wedding date is set, I will return." Her smile dazzled, an echo of Liwei flashing in her black eyes. "We will soon be sisters."

Wedding? I reeled from her words, spoken with such sincerity and certainty, unlike the whispers of the court. "Liwei and I are not betrothed."

Her smile vanished. "Why do you look so frightened? I thought you wanted this, that you cared for my brother. It is certainly what everyone else believes."

I met her stare without flinching, tired of strangers prying into my affairs. "That is between Liwei and me."

Her face hardened as she stood. "A warning then. Do not

toy with my brother's heart. I will not forgive you if you do." Without another word, she strode toward the door.

"Wait!" A question sprang to my lips, one I had not known I wanted to ask. "Do you regret it? All you gave up to live in the Mortal Realm?" The crown had been her heritage, but it would be my shackle.

She did not speak at first, toying with the jade bangles on her wrist. "No, because what I gained was far more. It's not a sacrifice when there is love enough." Her eyes fixed on me. "A question in exchange for yours. Do you love Liwei?"

"Yes." The barest pause, but it was the truth. I would always love him—yet doubt tugged at me still.

For while I had loved Liwei first, I had loved another after. One who had given his life for mine, whom I could not forget. I was learning that death had the kindness of diminishing one's sins, allowing one to remember the good in them. When Wenzhi had been alive, all I recalled were his treachery and wrongs. But now I could finally think of him without the taint of bitterness, and it gave new clarity to all he had said and done since I let him back into my life.

"I am glad." She hesitated, before adding, "If not, it would be a greater kindness to end things now."

I did not reply, irked by her presumption—my temper had grown shorter of late. And yet there was also a trickle of relief that there was another path. I had a choice, difficult though it would be.

IT WAS A CLOUDLESS morning, the sky a brilliant azure. Liwei and I sat inside the pavilion in the Courtyard of Eternal Tranquility. The waterfall rumbled into the pond, peach blossom petals drifting from the trees. Liwei waved away the attendant, lifting the teapot to refill my cup—just as he used to when we studied together, when it was just the two of us. The attendant's gaze lingered on him with reverent admiration as he bowed, leaving us alone.

"It is the autumn season in the Mortal Realm," Liwei said.

I nodded, returning his smile. As he set my cup before me, his sleeve brushed my hand, the embroidered silver herons soaring through the blue brocade. His hair was pulled into a gold and sapphire headpiece, just like the one he used to wear. I could almost imagine we were heading to the Chamber of Reflection after this, instead of the Hall of Eastern Light where Liwei governed the realm. Emperor in all but name.

He handed me a wooden box, painted with a woman in green robes, a crimson sash around her waist and gold ornaments in her hair. Clouds swirled around her feet, a silver orb gleaming above.

I traced my fingers over it. My mother, the Moon Goddess, as depicted by the mortals. As I pried the lid open, a rich, honeyed scent slipped out. Four golden-brown mooncakes were nestled within, their tops molded into a pattern of dragons and phoenixes. Liwei lifted one out and with a small knife sliced it into eight plump wedges. He offered one to me, a vermilion crescent of egg yolk glistening from the dark-brown filling. The lotus-seed paste was dense and sweet, the crust crumbling against my tongue. The yolk added a salty grittiness that cut through the sweetness, balancing the flavors perfectly. I closed my eyes as I chewed, imagining the mortals eating this as they listened to the tale of Houyi and the ten suns, and of Chang'e flying to the moon. A tightness clutched me; a longing to see my parents.

"Liwei, I want to go home. I cannot stay here." As I spoke, an urgency rushed through me. *This* was the way out from the nightmares that haunted me—to get away from the Jade Palace with its endless ceremonies and rules, the courtiers and attendants, the burdens of the kingdom.

His face paled, his fingers curling on the table. "Xingyin, I was going to ask you to marry me. My father is retiring to a life of isolation. He asked me to ascend the throne, to become the emperor."

I stared at him blankly, something tightening around my chest like I was being suffocated. This had always been his heritage, but even when I had dreamed of a future with him, I thought we had centuries more until his father relinquished the throne. It had been my one hope and consolation.

"I know this is a lot sooner than we imagined. That this is not what you want."

"I must go." The words came slowly, the decision crystallizing as I spoke—and I knew it was the right one, even as the ache in my heart sharpened.

His eyes blazed as he grasped my hand. "Why must you leave?"

"I want to go home," I repeated, pulling free of his hold, not from petulance, but because I could not allow anything to sway me.

A heavy silence settled over us as we stared at each other. "I know you are not happy here. I wish I could go with you," he said at last. "But I can't abandon my father and my kingdom. There is no one else who can rule in my stead."

"I understand." This was no hollow sentiment, for it was his choice as much as mine. We had to do what was right for ourselves, yet how it hurt that our paths had diverged. "Your place is here. There is no one better than you to rule. I would not have asked this of you."

"You have every right to ask anything of me," he said fiercely.

"I do not want to add to your cares." Yet if I had not done this, I would not have known what I truly wanted—what I needed that he could no longer give me.

I swallowed hard, pushing myself to my feet. "Perhaps it is too late for us, Liwei; we can never go back to what we were." There was no resentment in these words, only sorrow, for they hurt me too.

Liwei stood up, clasping me into his arms. I let myself lean against him—one last time, delaying the inevitable moment of pain. Yet though his warmth seeped through my robe and skin, it could no longer reach my heart.

"I'm sorry if I failed you," he whispered into my hair. "You don't have to decide this now. You could return home and come back whenever you are ready. I will wait for you."

"You did not fail me; I failed us." My voice cracked then. "Once I had accepted this as our life. And now I cannot bear it. I am weaker than I thought. I am tired of trying to be strong. And I . . . I cannot forget him. I do not want to."

"You don't have to face this alone." He spoke with such fire, a little of the coldness within me thawed. "I will help you forget him. We will be happy, just as we were before. You would be a fine empress."

I would not.

The life he offered would be a fairy tale to many, but a nightmare to me. A shudder rippled down my spine as I imagined eternity yoked to the cares of the Celestial Kingdom, the weight of the crown growing heavier with each year. The endless struggle for favor and power, the restless and judgmental stares trained upon me—impatient for the timely emergence of an heir.

Would I grow shrewish, trapped in such a life? How long would it take for our love to be tarnished? How long before it turned to resentment, and then . . . hate?

I pulled away to gaze into his handsome face, those dark eyes so dear to me. Was my heart strong enough to be shattered again? Somehow, I managed to speak through the agony that tore me apart. "I can't marry you. I can't live here. I would not be happy, and I would make you unhappy too."

He was silent for a while. "I tell myself that the past no longer matters, that I should not envy the dead. However, seeing you both in Lady Xihe's grove, seeing how you grieve for him . . . I cannot help but wonder, would you have chosen him, had he lived?"

I would have thought it impossible before, yet my despair was a rude awakening. I could not deny that my feelings for Wenzhi had gone far deeper than I'd known. I could not deny this pain in my chest when I thought of him, the sharp ache of loss.

"He should not have died, least of all for me," I said dully.

"I don't think he would have done it for anyone else." He studied my face, speaking gently. "Do not blame yourself for his death. Do not cling to misery, pushing everything aside, thinking you don't deserve happiness. He wanted you to be happy."

Then he should have lived.

I silenced the impossible, ungrateful thought. As I looked up into Liwei's face, the ache in my chest swelled. It would have been so easy to ease our suffering with a single word, a touch, a promise. But it would not be right; it would not heal what was broken inside me—if anything ever could. There was no room in my heart for love while it overflowed with grief. Tears clogged my throat, so tight, like it was being squeezed. Spinning around, I strode from the courtyard, not daring to turn—even as my limbs shook, and a chill glazed my skin.

A frightening thing to surrender a future, to plunge alone into the unknown. But this was my life, and I would claim it . . . the darkness, hurt, and all. Once you had looked death in the face, every moment after was a victory—a new hope, a new beginning. And I was no longer afraid.

37

A SMALL RABBIT BOUNDED BETWEEN MY feet, its fur gleaming like the purest white jade. Crouching down, I gathered it into my arms. As I stroked its head gently, the rabbit nestled closer, its long ears lying against its body.

I carried it as I walked toward my home, restored from the devastation wreaked upon it. The roof shone silver bright, the cracked tiles replaced. Gone were the scorch marks on the stone walls, and the broken mother-of-pearl columns were whole once more, rising proudly from the earth. If only the other wounds inflicted then were as easily mended.

The doors swung open, my parents appearing. My mother had discarded her habitual white robes for one in a brilliant rose, tied around her waist with a lilac sash. A red peony was tucked into the coils of her hair, just as she always wore it. As they came toward me, their warm smiles chipped away at the lump in my chest.

My father nodded at the rabbit in my arms, burrowing its nose in the crook of my elbow. "I thought your mother needed some company after you left."

"I was replaced by a *rabbit*?" I was affronted, and yet an urge to laugh gripped me. A precious lightness, a thawing of the cold that clung to my core.

My mother smiled. "The rabbit is more peaceful."

I could not disagree. "What is her name?"

"We call her Yutu." My mother traced the characters in the air: 玉兔.

"Jade Rabbit. It suits her well." The rabbit's ruby-red eyes fixed upon me as I stroked her head again. When I set her down, she bounded once around my mother, before leaping into the forest.

As I entered the Pure Light Palace, I discovered new touches—a wooden side table in the corridor, silk carpets in vivid hues to replace those charred by flame. Scroll paintings of horses and soldiers hung from the walls, alongside porcelain vases crammed with stalks of fresh osmanthus. Had my father cut those for my mother?

My father strode beside me, the Jade Dragon Bow slung across his back with a soldier's caution. Its power brushed my consciousness, more a gentle greeting than the eager tug of old. It did not fly into my grasp, content where it lay. And despite the pang in my chest, I had no regrets.

"Father, have your powers returned?" I asked.

His fingers flexed wide, then closed again. "A little. I can draw the bow easier, but it's like climbing a steep hill." A crooked smile spread across his lips. "While there's not much need to use it here, it's a comfort to have it again."

If the laurel still thrived, it might have hastened my father's recovery, as it had mine. But it was gone, disintegrating to nothingness after it had expended the last of its powers to restore me. I glanced through a window that overlooked the osmanthus forest, a void of sky where the laurel had once towered.

"Where is Liwei?" My mother had exercised great restraint to not ask before.

"In his home, as I am in mine." I did not say more, my emotions raw.

"Was this your decision?" A dangerous note slid into my father's voice.

"Yes," I said hastily. "I wanted to come home. He is not at fault."

"You are always welcome here." My mother hesitated before adding, "Do you intend to go back? I thought you and Liwei—" Her voice trailed off as she exchanged an anxious look with my father.

"No, Liwei will ascend the throne. And I . . . will not," I said flatly.

My mother said no more, wrapping her arms around me. I closed my eyes, feeling a little of the heaviness within me lessen. Oh, I was lucky to be here, fortunate beyond measure to have my parents, and our home restored. But I was hurting inside; I needed to heal. I had no idea how, but it was not by becoming the Celestial Empress, living a life that was not mine.

Settling back into my home came as easily to me as a fish darting through the water. It was just as I remembered . . . and yet not. Some nights I awoke in bed, fogged with slumber, sweat pouring down my face, a half-formed cry curled in my throat. I almost expected to hear Ping'er's firm footsteps padding along the corridor. When a door creaked, I turned, my heart leaping at the impossible hope that it would be her—before plunging at the reality that she was gone. Yet there was comfort in knowing a part of her would always be here, interwoven with our memories.

There were good changes too. At last, I fulfilled my cherished dreams of walking beside my father in the osmanthus forest, the three of us having our meals together. We talked of mundane things: what we would cook next, the improvements to our house, what flowers we might plant—and it was music to my ears. I began training archery with my father. We set up targets in the forest, and he would correct my posture, the way I held my bow as I released my arrows. And if there were things I felt *he* could have done better, I kept them to myself as any dutiful daughter might—at least for now. Such moments were precious indeed, and though they did not quite fill the existing hole in my heart, it replenished it in other ways, yielding me a different kind of happiness to what had been lost.

Some evenings I took over my mother's task, lighting each lantern by hand, glad for the work to divert me—for the opportunity to indulge in my thoughts. As each lantern flared to life, I imagined the light of the moon shining brighter upon the world below, the mortals turning their heads up to the skies.

Those nights, I did not dread being alone with my memories—falling asleep, mercifully spent. For the light in my father's eyes whenever they fell on my mother, the answering smile that spread across her lips—these things suffused me with joy and a nameless pain. For despite what I told myself, I could not help longing for the love they shared. The love I had disdained, discarded, and destroyed.

A YEAR FLEW BY and then another, sweeping like rainfall until I lost count of them altogether. Those were good years, when we grew as a family, in a way that we never had the chance to do before. The healing of the mind was slower than of the body, for these wounds cut deeper and it was harder to mend what was unseen. I did not know when it began, that these fractured pieces of me slowly began to come together again—healing, if not perfectly, at least enough so I felt almost myself. I no longer woke, gasping the names of those lost, reliving the fire searing my veins or the terror freezing my flesh when Wugang's axe had descended upon me.

My memories were kinder, cruel remembrances blunted, interwoven with fragments of remembered joy: Ping'er, telling me the stories of the Immortal Realm as I sat rapt before her. Prince Yanming, his face alight as he swung his wooden sword.

And Wenzhi . . .

All the parts of him that had touched me not once but twice, even through the barriers I had built against him. His intelligence and indomitable will, his ruthlessness and tenderness, the softening of his expression when he looked at me. And most of all, how he had loved me and then died for me.

As the pain dulled, its edge worn off, something else stirred in its place. A restlessness—just as I had felt as a child, craving the horizons beyond. A relief, that this spark in my soul was rekindled, that the hollowness in me had begun to fill with a yearning . . . for more.

A simple truth, a cruel one, that this was no longer my home.

I left to visit Shuxiao. She lived with Mengqi by the southern curve of the Celestial Kingdom, in a quiet place ringed by bamboo, shadowed by blue-gray mountains. The sight of the stone house with its arched roof of red tiles warmed me—the home my friend had always dreamed of, along with the companion of her heart. It soothed my spirit to sit with her and talk as we used to, beneath the shade of the trees in her courtyard. I was glad for the love she had found, even as it made me long for my own.

Impossible, my mind scoffed. There had been two great loves in my life, and there was no room in my heart for more.

I steeled myself for my next destination, the Eastern Sea. It was something I had to do, to quell the merciless voices within, to satisfy the grief that tore at me still. I did not know if that young soldier had been Prince Yanming—I never would—and wherever his spirit lay, I hoped he had found the peace he deserved. The dragons' promise was a great comfort, and on the days when I was kind to myself, I imagined that he found some joy with the creatures he most loved, and that they loved him too.

The sight of the Fragrant Coral Palace sparked in me the same wonder as before, with its luminous rose quartz walls rising from the sapphire waters. Yet a weight bore down upon me, my feet dragging along the crystal archway which led to the entrance. The guards did not allow me in, an attendant dispatched in search of Prince Yanxi, yet I did not have long to wait. Prince Yanxi greeted me warmly, though his smile was somber. The sight of me would have brought back unwelcome recollections, those that hurt. When I shut my eyes and breathed in the salt-laced air, I could almost hear his brother's bright gurgle of laughter, the patter of his footsteps as he ran toward me. My head lifted, my pulse quickening in anticipation, but then other memories crashed upon me—of his pale face a heartbeat before the guandao plunged through his chest. Ah, the pain cut deep. It was as Ping'er had once told me: *Some scars are carved into our bones.* And I thought to myself, *some might even break them.*

"May I see him?" My voice was tentative, part of me expecting a refusal. What right did I have to come here? I was neither kin nor close relation. But I had loved his brother and mourned him, and was that not a right in itself?

To my relief, he nodded. "Yanming would like that. Seeing you always made him happy."

I followed him through the palace, my insides tightening with trepidation at what I might find. A cold stone altar tucked away in a lonely room? I need not have worried. They had built him a beautiful remembrance in a garden of coral, warmed by the rays of the sun. A lacquered altar of ebony and mother-of-pearl stood in the center, and upon it lay a single sandalwood plaque inscribed with Prince Yanming's name, flanked by twin candles, their light unwavering even in the breeze.

Prince Yanxi and I stood unspeaking, our heads bowed, our hands clasped before us. There was no need for the incense the mortals lit, hoping it would bear their words to the heavens. Nevertheless, I whispered a prayer for him, imagining that the wind might carry it to wherever his tender spirit lay—whether one with the ocean he had loved, with the dragons, or here, in his beloved home. Tears trailed down my cheeks. Even after all this time, I had not wept myself dry.

A hoarse sob tore from my throat. "I promised to protect him. I failed."

Prince Yanxi's voice was gentle and grave. "I blame myself too. If only I could relive those moments, I would not have brought Yanming to the Southern Sea. I would have gotten him to safety earlier. But this was not our fault. We must end this cycle of remorse, which leads only to despair. Yanming would not have wanted that. He was a joyous spirit, filled with love and laughter, and that is how I want to remember him. Not how he died, but how he lived."

These words of his were a balm to my pain, a reminder that while there was death in life, there was life in death too. That all need not be lost. Prince Yanxi fell silent, perhaps giving me time to gather my battered composure. Like him, I had tormented myself in the solitude of my mind, wondering whether I could have saved Prince Yanming had I been quicker, if I had killed Wugang the first chance I got. A hundred ifs, unknowns, and possible endings haunted me, as fleeting and intangible as the mist at dawn. All the regrets in the world would not change the past.

We remained there for hours, until the moonlight caressed the place in shades of silver and white. At last, I rose to my feet and bowed. "Thank you," I told Prince Yanxi. "I will take my leave now."

"Where will you go?" he asked.

There was no invitation to stay. And even if there had been, I would not be so callous as to accept. I would spare his parents the sight of me. I had not killed their son. I would have laid my life down for him—and yet, his blood stained my hands.

I left the Eastern Sea with a violent hunger gnawing at me for someplace new, untainted by the past. Gripped by a desire to wander and roam, to drown my senses with unfamiliar sights across emerald forests, silver mountains, and untouched oceans. There was one place that called to me stronger than the rest, one place I had stayed away from, afraid of reopening old wounds that had never quite closed.

Finally, I yielded, traveling to the Golden Desert, trekking across the glittering dunes as the sunrays beat down upon my head. If the Celestial Kingdom was spring, the desert was a pitiless summer. I slept in the afternoons and walked in the evenings when it was cooler, beneath the light of the moon. Some nights I fell asleep upon the rough sands, only awakened by the fierce glare of day . . . and those were the times I slept best of all.

At the border of the Cloud Wall, I froze—jolted by the sight of those shifting violet clouds, emotions crashing through me. Through snatches of news that trickled my way, I heard there had been a great power struggle after Wenzhi's death. His mother, the Dowager Queen, had emerged victorious, ascending the throne and proving she was a capable and wise ruler. Just as her son would have been, had he not the misfortune of loving me.

The Cloud Wall prospered, no longer the outcast of the realm. Immortals ventured freely to this place they had feared for so long, and the name "Demon" was uttered less. A sudden urge seized me to journey there—where I had known both anguish and hope. But Wenzhi's mother would rightfully cast me from her presence, the one who had cost her son so dear. No, I could not impose myself upon her, stirring up grief anew. She was no friend of mine; I had no claim to her patience, even as I longed to grieve with her for what we had both lost. The greatest service I could do for her was to disappear.

There was fragile solace in knowing that after an immortal's passing, their spirit lived on in our realm, whether in the skies or the Four Seas. Even though their consciousness was gone, at least they were not wholly lost. Death was a strange thing for an immortal to ponder, yet how could I not when it had claimed those I loved?

I lifted my head, inhaling deeply. Something in me—the part which still hurt—craved the very air here, the trace of him I sensed among these clouds. A hard thing to grasp, impossible to define. Was I attuned to it because of our closeness, because we had been tethered by the enchantment that killed him? Or perhaps, it was merely the kindness of my mind, conjuring illusions to ease the hurt.

I dropped to my knees as I gazed upon his land, indulging in my memories. There was a time I wanted to forget everything to do with him, and now I pressed each remembrance close to my heart, even those that wounded me—because they were all I had left. I had thought I hated him, eager to tear him from my life, unaware that the roots of my feelings went deeper than I knew. Each time he had fought to recover what he'd so recklessly destroyed, I had shoved him away, too afraid to examine the feelings he roused in me.

"I am sorry," I said aloud. I was forever apologizing these days. "I was too proud and stubborn to realize what I felt, to understand what you tried to tell me before. I loved you then . . . and I miss you still."

Clasping my hands before me, I pressed my forehead to the prickling sands. A crisp breeze blew over me, laced with the faintest scent of pine, so familiar and dear—the ache in my chest tightened until I could not breathe. Closing my eyes, I lifted my face to the wind, breathing it in until the clawing pain subsided, whispering of broken dreams and hopes, those that would never come to pass—and I imagined wherever he was, he heard me.

Such fairy tales, I told myself then.

38

I NO LONGER COUNTED THE TIMES I returned to the Cloud Wall border; it had become a ritual without which I felt lost. This place I had once despised was now the only balm to my grief, though not without pain of its own—to sense a wisp of Wenzhi's spirit, forever beyond my reach. Perhaps I was being cruel to myself; it would be a kindness to forget . . . but I would not let his memory fade.

The wind rolled in fierce gusts today, roiling with unrest. Magic flowed from my fingertips to steady the cloud I rode upon. Strange weather in our realm, unease churning in my stomach since I had left the moon this morning. Ahead, the Golden Desert appeared leeched of color, tinted with ash beneath the darkening skies. It would have been prudent to turn back, yet impatience spurred me onward. No enemy could be worse than those I had faced, nor those that lurked in my mind.

Leaping down, I strode toward the clouds ahead. My insides clenched as I lifted my chin, bracing for the rush of memories, the braided comfort and torment that had drawn me back each time like an invisible cord wrapped around my heart.

There was nothing.

I picked up my skirt and ran onward until it was no longer

the crunch of sand beneath my feet but the soft embrace of the clouds. Reckless, to venture into the Cloud Wall, yet I did not care. I closed my eyes, searching frantically for the echo of Wenzhi's presence, that gentle graze against my consciousness—only finding a hollow stillness. Had I lost my mind or finally regained it? Perhaps there had been nothing all this time, just the false manifestation of my desires. If this was healing, I did not want it.

No, whatever it was it had been real; I was not one to be satisfied with delusions and dreams. Fear and resentment rose bitter and thick, that even *this* had been taken from me. I did not know what had happened, but I would find out. And there was just one person who might have the answers I sought, or the power to demand them.

I summoned my cloud, soaring northward through the skies. The carved dragons upon the Jade Palace rooftop glittered like they were afire as I made my way up the white marble stairs, between the great amber pillars that bore the three-tiered jade roof. Pale tendrils of incense coiled from the jewel-studded burners, the scent of jasmine springing in the air. The guards at the entrance did not halt me, allowing me through without a word.

It had been years since I was here, yet my feet still knew the way. I strode through the Outer Court and Inner Court, toward the Hall of Eastern Light. At this hour the court would be in attendance upon the Celestial Emperor. By the doorway, I hesitated. This would be no easy confrontation. More than the avid scrutiny of the court, this would be the first time I would see Liwei since I had left. While it had been my choice to leave, it hurt me too. Wherever I had journeyed, there was news of him—the young Celestial Emperor of whom dreams were made. Benevolent and wise beyond his years, and though no betrothal was yet announced it was only a matter of time. Emperors must have heirs.

The thought pricked me—an old habit that faded as abruptly as it began. As I stepped into the hall, a hush fell over it. Courtiers swung my way, some stiffening in recognition, while those more recently appointed scowled at the disruption of my presence.

"Petitioners must wait outside until they are summoned," a courtier warned me, his nostrils flaring wide.

Another cupped his hands and bowed to Liwei. "Your Celestial Majesty, shall I summon the guards?"

"No." Liwei's voice rang with irrefutable command. "She is always welcome here."

Thinly veiled envy shone in the eyes of the courtiers, while some smiled with sinuous ease. As I passed Teacher Daoming and General Jianyun, I bent my head low in greeting. It gladdened me to find them here, high in favor. Wise advisors with the courage to speak their minds were rare indeed.

As I approached the dais, Liwei's aura swept over me: warm, bright, and achingly familiar. Lifting my eyes to the jade throne, a tenderness suffused me, threaded with remorse—yet devoid of regret. I would not have been content by his side here, nor could I have made him happy when I was yearning for something that no longer existed.

Liwei's features were arranged into a regal mask, betraying none of his thoughts. His yellow brocade robe was embroidered with azure dragons, a heavy gold and sapphire crown upon his hair. The pearl strands of his father's crown were gone, and I would be glad to never hear their ominous clicking again. How magnificent he looked, like the emperor he was, granting an audience to a commoner.

I clasped my hands and lowered myself to the ground, stretching my cupped hands before me. He had not demanded it, yet it was expected by all, and I would not diminish his dignity here. As I lifted my head, I caught the slight narrowing of his eyes as he gestured for me to rise. He did not like this any more than I did, his fingers curled in his lap. If he were still the prince, he might have sent them all away—the attendants, courtiers, and guards. But an emperor was at once elevated to greater power, yet bound tighter to ceremony, decorum, and the weight of infinite expectations—at least for a ruler who strove to be worthy of their position.

"Why are you here, Xingyin?"

"I have something to ask of Your Celestial Majesty." I spoke formally, my tone guarded. Every word uttered here would be weighed and turned over. How I missed the ease of the past when it was just the two of us in the Courtyard of Eternal Tranquility, but those days were gone as irrevocably as water slipping into the soil.

Liwei inclined his head. "Ask anything you wish."

Restraint was prudent, but I was too anxious for news. "Your Celestial Majesty, what does it mean when an immortal spirit leaves our realm?" A pause, before I added, "I can no longer sense him."

He straightened, his shoulders seeming to clench beneath his robe. "Whom do you mean?"

"Wenzhi." His name fell out like a broken chord. While I had dreamed it, whispered it in my mind—I never thought I would speak it aloud again, and certainly not in this hall of Celestials.

"Have you been searching for him all this time?" A note of sadness weighed his tone.

"Yes."

"What did you find?" he asked.

"The shadow of his presence, like a dream without a face." My voice shook as I remembered Wenzhi's eyes closing, his chest hollowing with his last breath. "I know he is dead. But I thought . . . I believed part of his spirit remained in the Cloud

Wall—until now." I fell silent, realizing the foolishness of my words, already regretting the impatience that had led me here, clinging to nothing but a mirage.

It was so quiet in the hall, surely all could hear the rustle of my sleeve, the breath which slipped from my mouth. Liwei leaned forward, his eyes dark and opaque. "He is in the world below, but not as you know him. Not yet."

I could not move, staring at him, wide-eyed and numb. And then his meaning sank in—a blazing lightness sweeping me up, even as a hundred questions slammed through my mind. Disbelief warred with a wild hope that refused to be tamed, for it had been caged far too long. I was trembling, my heart still piecing together what my mind was beginning to grasp. My father had spoken of the few times when immortals had been sent to the Mortal Realm at the Celestial Emperor's behest, just as he had been sent to slay the sunbirds. A rare exception, requiring the emperor's permission, and the promise of restoration.

Liwei was the Celestial Emperor now.

"Wenzhi is mortal? How is that possible? He died," I said haltingly.

"He was fortunate. His consciousness was preserved along with his immortal spirit, something we had never seen before."

"The laurel." A lump formed in my throat as I recalled the fading remnants of its sap scattering over Wenzhi's body. "It brought me back. It saved a part of him too."

"Why did his spirit only leave now? Why not before?" My voice shook, the enormity of the revelation still unfolding in my mind.

The Keeper of Mortal Fates stepped forward, approaching the dais. "We could not do it at first. His spirit was greatly weakened; we were unsure if it was strong enough to sustain a mortal existence, the only way he could return without losing his immortal self." He stroked his long beard contemplatively. "Yet over the years his spirit gradually strengthened, as though something was helping him heal—a most unusual circumstance. Only then, could he be sent to the Mortal Realm."

"But that was after the laurel was destroyed, its power is no more." Even now, I dared not wholly believe it, afraid it was not real, that this happiness would be snatched from me again.

"Not the laurel. You," Liwei said gently.

All the times I had returned to the Cloud Wall . . . had Wenzhi sensed me too? Had he found comfort in my presence as I had in his? Had he been fighting to return to me? I should have known that he would haunt me if he could. Tears surged into my eyes, falling to the stone floor—when had they gathered? How I hated crying in front of the court, but nothing could have tempered my emotions—the elation cresting through me, this incandescent joy.

Liwei raised his hand and motioned for me to ascend the dais. As I stepped forward, an attendant rushed to set a chair beside the jade throne. A relief to be able to speak to him away from the ears of his court, though their eyes remained on us still.

"Why did you not tell me?" There was no resentment in my question, just wonder.

"We dared not raise your hopes. Nor could I send him to the Mortal Realm until after I had assumed the throne, until I was sure it was safe," Liwei explained.

"Thank you, I am grateful." How inadequate these paltry words. "I will repay you," I added fervently.

"You don't owe me anything, not even your thanks." His mouth stretched into a faint smile. "For if we were to keep count, my debt to you is greater. What matters is your happiness—you deserve it more than anyone."

"You did this for me?" An aching gratitude swelled within.

"What other reason could there be? It was certainly not for *him*. I saw how you grieved; you were a shadow of yourself. You must have . . . you must love him greatly." A breath slipped from him, drawn and soft. "Any hardship he endured in the world below was essential to strengthen his immortal spirit, to hasten his return. It is no trivial matter to overcome the adversities of the Mortal Realm, whether illness, loss, or heartbreak."

My insides twisted at the mention of the last. *I would bring him back.* "I have a boon to ask of the Celestial Emperor," I said slowly.

He did not hesitate. "Ask it from your friend, instead. We are friends, are we not?"

"Always." A promise and a farewell.

Something wrenched from my chest, a weight I had been carrying all this time. Such lightness bloomed in its place, relief that this rift in me would finally heal—even as a pang struck my chest, a part of me still reluctant to surrender the dream of us that I had cherished for so long. Liwei had been so deeply entwined in my life, it was like tearing away a part of myself. Yet he would not be lost to me. I would always love him, even though my heart no longer beat to his.

As Liwei raised his hand, the entire court bowed before him. He wanted them to hear what he said next, to extinguish all doubt. "Xingyin, daughter of the Moon Goddess and of the Sun Warrior, for your service to the realm in destroying the everlasting laurel and the traitor Wugang, ask your heart's desire and it shall be granted."

I rose and made my way to the front of the throne. Cupping my hands together, I bowed low before him. I would play my role; I would honor him this way so none could fault him. I had earned the right to ask this and I would do it with pride. "Your Celestial Majesty, the only thing I wish for is the Elixir of Immortality."

Liwei nodded. "It shall be yours. One is almost ready—" His words cut off, unease flashing across his face.

A memory surfaced, penetrating my haze of emotion: Zhiyi showing me the peach, the joy in her face when she spoke of the elixir for her husband, the one Liwei had promised her. And what of my own pledge to her? But there was no urgency, she had an Immortal Peach, my mind whispered—for I did not want to wait.

I turned to the Keeper of Mortal Fates. "Is Wenzhi safe?" Honor dictated my action, but if it came at the cost of his life, I did not think I could do it. If there was just this one chance, I would not relinquish it, though it would stain my soul.

The Keeper nodded. "He is in good health, living in a place called Silver Cloud City. Even should he encounter danger in the realm below, even should he die—it will not affect his true self. Once he is restored to the skies, he will regain his immortal form, his memories and power."

His words were intended as assurance, yet my hands clenched at the thought of someone hurting him. Mortal or not, they would pay. Yet I forced myself to calm, to think. Wenzhi was alive, he would be restored to all he had lost, he would return to me.

I searched Liwei's face, catching the wavering light in his eyes. If I asked for the elixir, he would not refuse. His sister need never know of this; she lived in the world below. Silence ensued, my desires battling the better part of me, a voice within screaming at me to not be a fool, to grasp the happiness that lay within my reach—I had waited long enough. And yet, could I dishonor my promise when I owed her my father's life? Could I burden Liwei with this decision? For it would grieve him to break his word. He had done so much for me, I could not take more.

As long as you are mine as I am yours, we have all the time in the world.

It was what Wenzhi had said to me when I had asked him to wait, when he first learned of my identity. The beginning of our unraveling, and yet buried beneath the deceit—the emotions had been true. We would have time; I would make sure of it. It would be far more meaningful, far more precious, if our joy was untarnished by shame and guilt. For it would haunt me that I had twice taken what another had claim to, that I had broken this promise. I would not be giving Wenzhi up, I could never do that—rather, I would be delaying our reunion.

We had done so many things wrong, *this* we would do right. We would start anew, upon a stronger foundation, to give us the chance we never had. The one we deserved.

I lowered myself into another bow. "Your Celestial Majesty, I wish for two elixirs. The first for your sister, and the second for myself." The words were bitter on my tongue, my heart sinking when a moment ago it had soared. I was not so noble that I could yield this easily, my insides curling with resentment and longing.

Liwei nodded, the tension easing from his bearing. "Are you sure? It will be years. Decades, perhaps."

"I repay my debts," I said. "As long as there is another elixir, I will wait." Perhaps I had finally learned the art of patience, after all.

"You will have it, I promise." A solemn vow before his court, though I did not need it from him.

My gaze met Liwei's, a warmth spreading through me at the understanding I found there. A single thought consumed my mind: Wenzhi was alive, and it was Liwei who would restore him to me. My world had been turned inside out, and yet it had never been more perfect.

Liwei rose and strode toward me, his power coiling around us to form a shield of privacy. No one could hear what he spoke next. "There is something else I want to say. I wish I had not let you go the first time, for even when you came back to me your heart was no longer mine alone. Later, when you left, I should have gone with you. I should have helped you heal."

"I did not expect you to come. You have your obligations," I said.

He shook his head. "You should have come first, above all else. You should not have needed to ask. I knew you were hurting, that life here would not make you happy. I believed— selfishly—that if we were together, that would be enough."

"It would have been enough, more than enough—but I have changed, as have you. Life has shaped us in different ways." My voice was thick with emotion. "I will always be grateful that you took pity on a girl who had nothing and shared your life with her."

He inclined his head. "As I am forever grateful for you, Xing-yin."

My fingers reached into my sleeve, closing around something I carried with me always. The lacquered hairpin, his promise of a future that was no longer ours. I handed it to him, feeling like a knife was sliding between my ribs—or was it being pulled out?

"I don't deserve this." I did not mean to be cruel, but it was the truth. I did not deserve his love because I could not offer him mine.

His eyes were ink and shadow. "Keep it, as a gift of friendship. It belongs to no one else. Go to him. Be happy." His hand reached out to graze mine, his remembered touch sending a sliver of pain through me.

Except it was the good type, where healing lay on the other side.

39

DAWN BROKE ACROSS THE SKY in streaks of gilded rose. I glided to the Mortal Realm upon a cloud, landing by the outskirts of the city. A high stone wall encircled it, a black lacquered plaque hanging above the arched entrance, carved with the words:

银云城

SILVER CLOUD CITY

It was autumn here, when leaves shed their green to russet red, a crisp coolness threaded through the air. Despite the early hour, the streets were lined with stalls, bustling with mortals. Some carried straw baskets, others gripping their children's hands as they wound through the crowd. Chickens squawked from rattan cages, porcelain jars of wine were crammed onto a table, small wooden toys heaped on another. The savory aroma of crisp sesame pancakes and pork dumplings wafted from a vendor's stall, mingling with the remnants of food strewn on the ground, tinged with the sourish edge of spoil. Sugared figurines artfully shaped into birds and flowers caught my eye, but I hurried past the merchants hawking their wares.

Perhaps I should have waited until I had the elixir, perhaps

I should have left Wenzhi to the peace of his mortal existence—
but I could not stay away. My feet quickened along the stone
path, though I did not know where I was going. Strands of my
hair fell from its coils, curling across my forehead and down
my neck. My heart was racing even as I reminded myself that
Wenzhi would not even know my name. Not yet, but he would.

Memories flashed across my mind: the battles we had
fought, the times we had saved each other. Our friendship and
love, betrayal and enmity, transforming into something new
altogether—stronger and more precious by far. I had not believed he could change, I had not wanted to. Only in the terrible
moment of his death did it dawn upon me that he was the one
who could make me whole, even as he had been the one to tear
me apart. For when he had broken me with his treachery, he had
broken himself too. Despite my coldness in pushing him away,
my indifference and resentment, he had fought relentlessly for
us, trying to prove the depth of his emotions, his sincerity and
love . . . a selfless love that I never imagined he was capable of.

A large manor rose ahead, white walls holding up an arched
roof of moss-green tiles, aglitter in the rays of the sun. Pine trees
swayed as they towered over the walls, strings of white lanterns
dangling beside the lacquered door, swaying in the gentle breeze.
A horse pranced outside, its reins gripped by a young man as its
hooves pawed the ground impatiently.

He was here; I could sense him, just as I had in his kingdom.
Mortal or immortal, I would know him anywhere. Stumbling
to a halt, I brushed down my lilac robe, adjusting the crimson
sash around my waist. Chrysanthemums were embroidered in
soft pinks upon the silk, the flowers of the season. Despite my
impatience, vanity had roused me to change. I had missed the
pleasure of a fine gown, this desire to flatter my appearance. An
urge gripped me, to stride to the door and knock—but I would

be a stranger to him. A discourteous one, arriving at this hour, without invitation or good cause.

The door swung open as a tall man stepped out, his black hair pulled into a smooth topknot. His robes were of fine indigo brocade, fastened around his waist with a silk sash. Rooted to the spot, I drank in the sight of him: his sculpted cheekbones, thin lips, his clear eyes ringed with gray. A rare shade for the mortals to possess, one that had haunted my dreams during those long restless nights. There were slight differences in his features and form. One less used to battle though still strong; taller, with a more scholarly air. Yet his keen intelligence shone in his gaze, and he moved with that same effortless grace.

It was him, as surely as I knew my own name. Such aching joy swept through me, surging through my veins, ablaze with the light of the heavens. A smile broke over my face. I wanted to laugh from the exhilaration crashing over me that this was no dream. He was alive.

Wenzhi strode past me, then stopped. As he swung around, our eyes collided—a tingling rush coursing through me like my skin was brushed with morning dew, a breath of autumn, the fall of new snow. Caught staring, heat flushed the back of my neck. He blinked, taken aback by the intensity of my gaze. No smile stretched across his face; no recognition dawned. He looked just as he did the first time we met: Cold. Unapproachable. Disinterested.

The young man clutching the horse's reins, bowed to him deferentially. "Minister Zhao."

As Wenzhi nodded in acknowledgment, I searched for something to say to capture his interest, to stop him from leaving, but then he came toward me, his steps halting as though fighting the impulse.

"I do not mean to offend you, but have we met before?" His manner was guarded.

My mind went blank. "Yes. Long ago. You would not remember."

His eyes narrowed. "I apologize that I cannot place you. I would not have forgotten."

Were those hollow words of courtesy? Or was there something more in the dip of his voice, the way his eyes lingered on my face?

A lady appeared through the doorway, moving toward him. Her face was shaped like a teardrop, a sprinkling of freckles across the slender bridge of her nose, her lustrous hair coiled elegantly upon her head. In the crook of her elbow nestled the handle of a three-tiered lacquered basket that she held out to Wenzhi. "Your breakfast. Don't forget to eat this time."

His wife, who else might she be? Something pierced my chest, searing deeper when Wenzhi thanked her, his lips forming a familiar smile. I had no right to feel this way. He had forgotten me, built a new life for himself where he had fallen in love, married, perhaps even fathered children. My joy should have been complete that he lived, that he had found happiness here. It should have been enough, more than enough . . . *if* I were a better person. But I was a jealous and selfish creature, fighting to quell this burst of irrational emotion. Wenzhi had loved me, he had died for me— except I had not wanted his love then and he did not remember me now. I wanted to laugh and weep at the way fate had twisted us around until I was torn between wanting to embrace him and the urge to kick him in the shin. How could I have hoped for him to remain mine when he had forgotten my name? When I had faded to an elusive shadow in his mind, the echo of a song he would never recall. At least, not in his mortal lifetime.

Perhaps sensing my avid interest, the lady glanced at me curiously before turning back to Wenzhi. After exchanging a few more hushed words with him, she returned to the house.

"Your wife is thoughtful." I had always been eager to pick at the scab before it healed, to yank despair into the open.

"Wife?" he repeated, tilting his head to one side. "She is my sister."

"Sister!" Relief flooded me. This sister was preferable by far to his wretch of an immortal brother. "She is thoughtful to think of your well-being. Most kind and gracious and—" I bit down on my tongue, conscious of my rambling.

"Minister." The attendant bowed again, adding urgently, "The council is expecting you."

"I must go," he told me.

I nodded, though I did not want him to leave. This brief interlude was a drop of water to a parched throat, a star in a solitary night.

"May I see you again?" His words came out tinged with disbelief, as though he could not believe he was asking such a thing.

My smile was both inviting and warm. "If you want to."

He shook his head as though trying to clear it, and how I wished I could read his thoughts. "I do. Yet I do not want to impose upon you." He tensed, before adding, "You are welcome to refuse. I would take no offense though I would be disappointed."

"Do you make a habit of inviting strangers out?" I asked lightly, even as a thrill coursed through my veins.

"This is my first time. Yet you do not feel like a stranger." He spoke slowly as though trying to unpick his own thoughts. "If it would put you at ease, I could invite my sister to join us, though she will interrogate you mercilessly." Even now he was quick to sense an opening, to secure victory.

"There is no need," I told him. "Just you will be enough."

"Thank you for your trust." His expression was grave as he glanced around the quiet neighborhood. "You might be new here, but much danger lurks in this city. Be careful whom you accept an invitation from. If there is any trouble, just—"

"I can look after myself," I assured him.

A warmth spread through me that even now, he still watched out for me. Of course, he did not know who I was, what he had been—that no mortal danger could threaten me. Yet the perils of this realm were great for *him* and if he let me, I would stay by his side and watch over him, until we were together again in the skies above.

A slow smile broke across his face. "I am certain you can." He was silent for a while, before saying, "If you wish, my attendant can accompany you back."

I shook my head to decline. "I live far from here, up north. Though I come here often." I hoped Liwei would not mind the transgression.

"I am glad to hear that." He swung himself effortlessly onto the saddle, gripping the reins with one hand as he ran the other over the horse's neck. "Do you like osmanthus wine?"

"Yes." My heart leapt at the mention of my favorite drink. Perhaps—deep down—a part of him remembered me still.

"There is a place by the lake, Sun Moon Teahouse. The view is beautiful at sunset, and it serves the finest wine in the region. Shall we meet there, tomorrow before dusk?" His lips curved into that slow smile which set my pulse racing.

"I will be there." A promise for today, for all the days after.

I stared after him as he galloped away upon the horse, until he turned the corner at the end of the road. Only then did I lift my head, staring at the sun above. Its golden rays streaked across the cloudless skies, dispelling the lingering shade of night. My path stretched before me, unhindered, ablaze with light. Never had it been so clear before, never had it felt so bright.

I had believed all my hopes buried so deep, they could never be unearthed again. But I found my mind drifting once more to the realm of tomorrow, and the infinite possibilities that awaited there. My dreams were neither grand nor noble—not of defeating monsters, of peace in the realm, not even of my mother or father . . . but smaller and humbler, for myself alone.

Tomorrow, when the sun began its descent, when day converges into night, I would make my way to the teahouse by the lake. Wenzhi would be waiting for me in the garden, his dark green robe fluttering in the wind as he gazed upon the scenery—as wondrous as he had promised with the scarlet rays of the sun fragmenting upon the silvery waters. As I drew closer, he would turn, his lips stretching into a smile. If a twinge of recognition plucked his heart, he would not know what it meant—and one day, I would tell him. Beneath the darkening violet sky, we would sip osmanthus wine from porcelain cups, speaking as we used to—openly, without hesitation or recrimination. Perhaps I might even laugh again, for I had almost forgotten its sound. In the days and weeks to come, he would show me this city he lived in: its cypress-lined pathways, the arched bridges, the elegant buildings of stone and wood. Perhaps he would open his home to me and introduce me to his sister. In his courtyard, shaded by pine trees, we would read the classics of the realm, of ancient legends and poems of beauty. Some evenings we might even play the qin together, our instruments set side-by-side as our music rippled forth in seamless harmony. And during the festivals when the mortals gathered to light the lanterns they set upon the waters, when they lit incense sticks and prayed to the gods—I would whisper of my own desires, for the day we would be truly reunited whether in this lifetime or his next.

He was not my first love, but he would be my last.

Such were the dreams I wished for. Such were the memories I longed to make with him, the promise of our future brimming with simple yet profound joy. In the past, when I had grappled with Wenzhi's betrayal, I wondered how things might have turned out had we been two ordinary people, our past and present unencumbered. What lay before us now was a rare chance to start anew. Oh, I was still afraid of the years before us, when he would grow to know me all over again. Would his feelings change after regaining his immortality? Perhaps only heartbreak lay ahead, but I was never one for surrendering while the battle remained unfought. Whatever time we had here I would embrace it. I would grasp this chance and hold it close, because I had known what it was like to have it snatched away. I had lost him once, I would not lose him again.

A voice in my mind whispered that I did not deserve such happiness when the faces of the dead haunted me still. I silenced it, for now I knew better. The time I'd spent in seemingly aimless wanderings had not been wasted. I had needed to heal, to learn to live with my pain, and to uncover the secrets of my heart that had long eluded me.

These wounds and scars would not break me again. I would honor those I had lost by keeping them alive in my heart, not by casting joy from my life, not by refusing to live. No longer would I shut love from my life, in all its wondrous yet devastating manifestations—the greatest power in the world, capable of moving the hearts of mortals and gods to both evil and good. For we were complex creatures of shades of gray, capable of wonderful and terrible things . . . of change, because our natures were not fixed like the stars in the sky but flowing as the river toward an unknown horizon.

Everyone knew the tale of how my father had shot the suns, of my mother flying to the moon—yet sometimes in these legends it was not the *how* but the *why*. Some might think us weaker for our love, but it gave us strength we did not know we possessed. No longer would I flee, no longer would I doubt. I would step out from the shadows of my past and turn my face to what lay ahead. To live a life with love, was to live without regret.

At last, I was home.

DRAMATIS PERSONAE

THE MOON

XINGYIN (星银 | Xīngyín)—Daughter of Chang'e and Houyi who was hidden from the Celestial Emperor since birth. Formerly the study companion to Prince Liwei and First Archer of the Celestial Army.

CHANG'E (嫦娥 | Cháng'é)—Moon Goddess and wife to the archer Houyi. When she was mortal, she took her husband's Elixir of Immortality, becoming immortal and ascending to the skies.

PING'ER (平儿 | Píng'er)—Loyal attendant to Chang'e, youngest daughter of the Chief Attendant of the Southern Sea.

CELESTIAL KINGDOM

LIWEI (力伟 | Lìwěi)—Crown Prince of the Celestial Kingdom, son of the Celestial Emperor and Empress.

CELESTIAL EMPEROR—Emperor of the Celestial Kingdom, who also rules over the Mortal Realm.

CELESTIAL EMPRESS—Wife to the Celestial Emperor, empress of the Celestial Kingdom.

SHUXIAO (淑晓 | Shūxiǎo)—A lieutenant of the Celestial Army, and a close friend to Xingyin.

WUGANG (吴刚 | Wúgāng)—The mortal sentenced to chop the laurel tree on the moon. Elevated to immortality by the Celestial Emperor.

JIANYUN (建允 | Jiànyǔn)—General of the Celestial Army who trained Xingyin and Liwei.

ZHIYI (芷怡 | Zhǐyí)—Daughter of the Celestial Emperor, stepdaughter to the Celestial Empress, half sister to Prince Liwei.

KEEPER OF MORTAL FATES—A high-ranking official who oversees the Mortal Realm.

DAOMING (道明 | Dàomíng)—Teacher of magical skills to Xingyin and Liwei.

HUALING (华菱 | Huálíng)—Formerly the Flower Immortal.

FEIMAO (翡懋 | Fěimào)—An archer of the Celestial Army who helped defeat Xiangliu, the nine-headed serpent.

CLOUD WALL–DEMON REALM

WENZHI (文智 | Wénzhì)—Second son of King Wenming and the third-ranked Noble Consort. Crown Prince of the Cloud Wall, formerly Captain of the Celestial Army.

WENSHUANG (文爽 | Wénshuǎng)—Eldest son of King Wenming and the first-ranked Virtuous Consort. Formerly Crown Prince of the Cloud Wall.

WENMING (文铭 | Wénmíng)—King of the Cloud Wall, also known as the Demon Realm after their separation from the Celestial Kingdom.

VIRTUOUS CONSORT—First-ranked consort to King Wenming, mother to Prince Wenshuang.

NOBLE CONSORT—Third-ranked consort to King Wenming, mother to Prince Wenzhi.

MENGQI (梦绮 | Mèngqǐ)—Captain of the Cloud Wall Army.

EASTERN SEA

YANXI (彦熙 | Yànxī)—Eldest prince of the Eastern Sea and the heir to the throne.

YANMING (彦明 | Yànmíng)—Youngest prince of the Eastern Sea, brother to Prince Yanxi.

YANZHENG (彦峥 | Yànzhēng)—King of the Eastern Sea, father to Prince Yanxi and Yanming.

ANMEI (安美 | Ānmĕi)—A high-ranking lady at the Eastern Sea Court, and governess to Prince Yanming.

SOUTHERN SEA

SUIHE (绥河 | Suíhé)—Queen of the Southern Sea.

PING'YI (平一 | Píngyī)—Eldest daughter of the Chief Attendant of the Southern Sea, and sister to Ping'er.

BINGWEN (炳文| Bǐngwén)—A renown shell merchant in the Southern Sea.

PHOENIX KINGDOM

FENGMEI (凤美 | Fèngmĕi)—Princess of the Phoenix Kingdom, daughter to Queen Fengjin. Formerly betrothed to Crown Prince Liwei of the Celestial Kingdom.

FENGJIN (凤金 | Fèngjīn)—Queen of the Phoenix Kingdom.

THE SUN

XIHE (羲和 | Xīhé)—Sun Goddess and mother to the ten sunbirds.

SUNBIRDS—The ten children of Lady Xihe, nine of whom were slain by the mortal archer Houyi. Only one remains to light the realms.

THE FOUR DRAGONS AND RIVERS

LONG DRAGON—The leader of the Four Dragons from the Eastern Sea. Creator of the Changjiang (长江) in the Mortal Realm, also known as the Long River.

BLACK DRAGON—Formed the Heilongjiang (黑龙江), also known as the Black River in the Mortal Realm.

PEARL DRAGON—Formed the Zhujiang (珠江), the Pearl River in the Mortal Realm.

YELLOW DRAGON—Formed the Huanghe (黄河), the Yellow River in the Mortal Realm.

HOUYI (后羿 | Hòuyì)—Husband to Chang'e, the Moon Goddess, father to Xingyin. Dragon Lord and slayer of the sunbirds, shooting down nine of the ten.

ACKNOWLEDGMENTS

My deepest and most heartfelt thanks to the readers of *Daughter of the Moon Goddess*, who followed Xingyin into *Heart of the Sun Warrior*. Hearing from you has helped me through the hard times of which there were many in the writing of this book. To the booksellers and librarians who took a chance on the duology, who read it and placed it into the hands of others—I am so grateful.

To Naomi Davis, my literary agent, whose empathy, insight, and advice have helped me weather many a storm—I am so grateful we're in this together! Much thanks to BookEnds Literary Agency for all its support.

To David Pomerico, my US editor—to put it simply, the duology would not exist in this form without you. I am so glad we shared the same vision from the start. You are a brilliant champion for these books, and your insightful edits have elevated the work immensely. To Francie Crawford and Jori Cook—you are amazing, and I am so thankful for all you've done, and glad to be working with you both! Much thanks to the wonderful Mireya Chiriboga; to Rachel Weinick and Rachelle Mandik for your invaluable help with the manuscript, and your patience with my comments and edits; and to Alison Bloomer for the beautiful interior design. Thank you also to Liate Stehlik and Jen Hart.

It is a joy and privilege to also be a part of the Harper Voyager family in the UK, to work with my fantastic editor, Vicky Leech Mateos—your insight and guidance have really helped me navigate this challenging year. I am also fortunate to work with the incredible Maddy Marshall and Susanna Peden, and I could not have asked for a better team. Special thanks to the wonderful Natasha Bardon, Leah Woods, Sarah Munro, Elizabeth Vaziri, and to Robyn Watts, the dream-maker of books and special editions.

There are so many people in HarperCollins around the world who played a part in bringing these books to the shelves. Thank you to the teams at HarperCollins Canada, the international teams, to everyone who worked on the duology—I am so grateful.

It gives me such joy to look upon the *Heart of the Sun Warrior* covers—the blazing sunlit match to the evocative night of *Daughter of the Moon Goddess*, and they are both perfect in different ways. Words alone cannot express how much I love them, how they have captured the heart of the story. Thank you, Kuri Huang, for your stunning illustration of the US cover—I am in love with each exquisite detail and keep finding new things to marvel about it. Much gratitude to Jason Chuang for illustrating and designing the breathtaking UK cover. I adore everything about it: the stunning flowers and symbolism, the intricate artistry, and striking colors. Thank you also to Jeanne Reina for the art direction in the US, and to Ellie Game, in the UK.

I cannot imagine a more perfect narrator for these books than Natalie Naudus—thank you for bringing the characters to life, just as I imagined them!

It is utterly surreal that the duology will be translated into several languages, and I could not be more excited for the editions to come! Much thanks to Katherine Falkoff for helping to bring these stories to other parts of the world, and to the publishers who have given the duology a home.

I speak of dreams coming true, but there are some that I could never have conceived of when I began my publishing journey. It was such a joy to collaborate with FairyLoot on *Daughter of the Moon Goddess* and *Heart of the Sun Warrior*. Thank you to the amazing Anissa de Gomery and the wonderful FairyLoot team for these exquisite editions, more beautiful than anything I could have imagined. I will treasure them always, and am grateful to you and your readers.

Thank you also to Fox & Wit, the Mysterious Galaxy Book Crate, Satisfaction Box, Emboss and Spines—I have loved seeing the pictures and unboxings! While I love art, I sadly have no talent in it, and am grateful to all the amazing artists who brought the characters to life in different but stunning ways—among them, Grace Zhu, Rosie Thorns, Arz28, Katie, Xena Fay, Yingting, Marcella, Julia, and to Azurose Designs for the stunning pin.

Writing can be both consuming and isolating. There are times when I barely step outside, when I live and breathe the manuscript. I am thankful for my husband, Toby, for his endless understanding, for being my first reader and harshest critic, for helping me talk through tricky plot points (or at least letting me ramble on unhindered), and to my beloved children, Lukas and Philip, for keeping me tethered in the real world. I would be nothing without my family and I am forever grateful to my mother and father, my sister, cousins, aunts, and uncles. And to Julia and Christian for their support and consideration during my deadlines over the busiest period of my life.

Endless thanks to Sonali Singh and Jacquie Tan for your

friendship, for reading my early drafts, for your insightful and unflinching feedback, and putting up with my last-minute panicked messages—you are both my pillars of support! And to my dear friend Eunjean Choi, for being a part of my writing journey from the start, for your kindness and encouragement. To Lisa Deng, for your thoughtful advice on Chinese words and names, for tolerating my many questions. To my friends everywhere, I cannot express how much I appreciate your support of my book, sending me pictures from around the world—and some of you were even kind enough to read it! So much gratitude to the authors I am fortunate to know over the course of this journey, who shared their advice and insight, and who generously read and blurbed the book.

As I am not often on social media, I am grateful to the readers and my team who sent me links that I might not have otherwise come across. My heartfelt thanks to the readers, bookstagrammers, book bloggers, booktubers, and to the BookTok community and its amazing creators. While I was unable to respond to everyone—and am hesitant to intrude where I was not tagged—you have all filled my heart with your words, your beautiful pictures, reels, and videos. Thank you, Melissa & Isabel, Steph, Lauren, Cait, Elle, Luchia, Katie, Cath, Sam, Danica, Giota, Tatiana, Shanayah, Ishtar, Gemma, Lina, Caitlin, Jenn, Jean, Tammie, Pamela, E-Lynn, Kevin, Bella, Amelia, Sonia, and Jenna—I am likely missing many others as I am writing this on deadline and due to the submission timing! Thank you to all the book tour hosts for *Daughter of the Moon Goddess*, and to the amazing contributors. I am so grateful to the booksellers and librarians for the incredible work they do in supporting authors, to Kalie, Kel, Jennifer, Steph, Michelle, Dayla, Gabbie, Dan, Mike, Rayna, Meghan.

A few years ago, when I was writing *Daughter of the Moon*

Goddess on my dining table, during the rare moments when I allowed myself to dream—even then, I never imagined the journey the book would take me on. I say I am grateful a lot, but I feel it with every part of me—for the people around me, for the opportunity to write, for all the readers without whom none of this would be possible, and to you for reading this far.

ABOUT THE AUTHOR

Sue Lynn Tan writes fantasy inspired by the myths and legends she fell in love with as a child. Born in Malaysia, she studied in London and France before moving to Hong Kong with her family.

Her love for stories began with a gift from her father, her first compilation of fairy tales from around the world. After devouring every fable she could find in the library, she discovered fantasy books—spending many of her teenage years lost in magical worlds.

When not writing or reading, she enjoys exploring the hills and lakes around her home, the temples, beaches, and narrow winding streets. She is also grateful to be within reach of bubble tea and spicy food, that she unfortunately cannot cook.

Find her at www.suelynntan.com, or on Instagram @suelynntan.